Dear Reader

How To Keep A Secret is an exciting new direction for me. I've always written about relationships, but previously my main focus has been on the romance between the two central characters.

I wanted to broaden that to include the relationship between sisters, friends, mother and child, grandparent and grandchild. I wanted to create more complex, layered characters and to explore them in more depth.

This book has interwoven story lines, all of them connected, and tracks the shifting nature of relationships within one family. There is still romance, but also an exploration of broader themes and a cast of multi-generational characters.

Unlike my previous books, this story won't be part of a series and I hope readers will enjoy having the whole reading experience in one book.

Being able to write something a little different has been satisfying and exciting for me. I can't wait to hear what readers think.

Thank you for reading.

Sarah
x

Sarah Morgan lives near London with her husband and two sons. An international bestseller, her books have been translated into more than 30 languages and she has sold over 15 million copies. For more about Sarah visit her website www.sarahmorgan.com, and sign up to her newsletter. She loves to connect with readers on Facebook (www.facebook.com/AuthorSarahMorgan), Twitter (@SarahMorgan_) and Instagram (www.instagram.com/sarahmorganwrites)

SARAH MORGAN

How to keep a Secret

ONE PLACE. MANY STORIES

HQ
An imprint of HarperCollins*Publishers* Ltd.
1 London Bridge Street
London SE1 9GF

This paperback edition 2017

2
First published in Great Britain by
HQ, an imprint of HarperCollins*Publishers* Ltd. 2017

Copyright © Sarah Morgan 2018

Sarah Morgan asserts the moral right to be
identified as the authors of this work
A catalogue record for this book is
available from the British Library

ISBN: 978-1-84845-716-4

MIX
Paper from
responsible sources
FSC **FSC™ C007454**
www.fsc.org

Printed bound in Great Britain by CPI Group (UK) Ltd, Croydon CR0 4YY

How to keep a Secret

For my sister (from whom I have no secrets!)
If I could have chosen my sister, I would have chosen you.

For there is no friend like a sister
In calm or stormy weather;
To cheer one on the tedious way,
To fetch one if one goes astray,
To lift one if one totters down,
To strengthen whilst one stands.

Christina Georgina Rossetti

PROLOGUE

Sisters

"WHAT ARE WE *going to do? We shouldn't even be here."* I *tugged at my sister's skirt to pull her away from the window.* "If *we're caught, we're going to be in big trouble."*

I *wasn't about to wait around for that to happen.*

My sister was taking those big gulping breaths that always preceded a fit of crying.

Giving her a final tug, I dropped to my hands and knees and scurried back along the path the way we'd come, grateful for the protective shadow of darkness. I wanted to stand up and run, but if we did that we'd be seen, so I stayed low, crawling like a fugitive. It had been a long, hot summer and the earth was dry and crumbly. It was only when I felt a cooling splash on the backs of my hands that I realized I was crying, too. Small stones bit into my palms and knees, and I clamped my teeth together to stop myself making a sound. I brushed past the jungle of honeysuckle and the sweet cloying smell almost choked me. There was nothing sweet about what we'd seen and I knew that when I was grown up and had a house of my own I'd never have honeysuckle in the garden.

There was a rustling sound behind me. I hoped it was my sister and not some nocturnal creature with sharp teeth and an appetite.

I couldn't see the gate, but I knew it was there. Beyond the gate was the footpath. If we made it that far, we'd be protected by the high hedge. Through the panicked pumping of blood in my ears I could hear the rhythmic crash of the sea. It sounded closer than usual, louder, as if the tide was colluding, helping to drown the sounds of our escape. The salt breeze dried my cheeks and cooled my skin.

Finally I reached the gate and slid through the gap, ignoring the twigs that stabbed my back. There, right in front of me, was the path. Leaning against the hedge were our bikes, right where we'd left them. I wanted to grab mine and pedal hard into the night without looking back, but there was no way I was leaving my sister.

I'd never leave my sister.

There was another rustle and she emerged through the gate, her hair wild from our frantic retreat.

Now that safety was within reach, anger burst through the anxiety.

"It was your idea to come here tonight." I almost choked on the emotion that had built up inside. "Why do you always have to do what you're not supposed to do?"

"Because the things I'm not supposed to do always seem like more fun." The wobble in her voice reminded us both that this hadn't been fun at all.

I felt her hand creep into mine and instantly I forgave her. We stood like that for a moment, clinging for comfort.

My sister moved closer. "If I could have chosen my sister, I would have chosen you."

I would have chosen her, too, although right then I wished there was a way of curbing her adventurous spirit.

"I wish we hadn't looked."

"Me, too." For once my sister sounded subdued. "We can't ever tell anyone. Remember what happened to Meredith?"

Of course I remembered. Meredith was a cautionary tale.

"I hate keeping secrets."

"It's a small secret, that's all. You can keep a small secret."

I swallowed, my throat so dry it hurt. We both knew that this was a lot bigger than the other secrets we kept. This wasn't sneaking out after dark to play on the beach, stealing flowers from Mrs. Hill's garden or raiding Mrs. Maxwell's strawberry patch. This was something different. What we'd seen felt like a weight crushing me. Deep down I knew we should tell, but if we told, everything would change. We'd left our childhood back at that window and there was no going back to get it.

"I won't tell. I'll protect you. We're sisters. Sisters always stick together. I made a promise."

Of course most people who made a promise like that, I thought, didn't have a sister like mine.

PART ONE

PART ONE

CHAPTER ONE

Lauren

*Premonition: a feeling that something is going
to happen, often something unpleasant*

YOU COULDN'T REALLY blame the party for what happened,
although later Lauren wished she hadn't organized such
an elaborate affair. If she hadn't been so wrapped up in
the small details, she might have noticed something was
wrong. Or would she? To notice something was wrong you
had to be looking, and she hadn't been looking. She'd been
focused on the moment and the excitement of the big day.

And the day started early.

Waking before the alarm, she rolled over in the bed and
kissed Ed. "Happy birthday."

Should she say the word *forty*? How did he feel about it?
How did *she* feel about it?

She still had five years to go before she hit that number

which seemed far enough away not to be worth worrying about. And forty wasn't old, was it?

Maybe not, but when she'd taken delivery of the birthday cake the day before and looked at the forty candles waiting to be added, she'd thought, *We're going to need a bigger cake.*

Ed was still dozing so Lauren lay for a moment, cocooned by the peaceful calm of their bedroom. This had been the first room she'd decorated when they'd moved in. She'd designed it as a sanctuary, a peaceful haven of white with accents of gray and silver. In summer the room was flooded with sunlight and she slept with the window open so she could hear the birds. Now, in January and with London in the grip of a cold snap, the windows were firmly closed. Their house, in an exclusive and sought-after crescent in fashionable Notting Hill, backed on to private gardens. Every morning for the past week the trees had been coated with frost. The cold air slapped you in the face the moment you opened the door, as if daring people to leave the comfort of their homes.

Lauren, who had been raised on Martha's Vineyard, a small island off the coast of Massachusetts, wasn't afraid of bad weather.

She peeled back the covers and ran her fingers through his hair. "Not a single gray hair. If it's any consolation, you don't look a day over sixty." There was no reaction and she leaned forward and kissed him again. "I'm kidding. You don't even look forty." Except lately, at certain times of the day and when the sun was bright and harsh. Then he looked every day of forty. Working too hard? Ed had always worked long hours, but recently he'd been coming home later and later and seemed unusually tired. She'd subtly planted the idea that he might visit the doctor, but he'd ignored all hints. It was easier to persuade a toddler to eat broccoli than to get Ed to the doctor.

Her phone told her it was past six o'clock, and he showed no sign of moving.

Lauren gave him a gentle nudge. Her day was planned to the minute, and it all kicked off at precisely six fifteen.

She heard the sound of clomping on the stairs. "Mack's awake. How can one teenager sound like a herd of elephants?"

She wondered if Mack was coming upstairs to the bedroom, but then the sound of footsteps faded and she heard the kitchen door slam.

Why wasn't Mack at least putting her head round the door to wish her father happy birthday?

Anxiety gnawed at the edges of her happiness. It wasn't that long ago that Mack would have come charging into the bedroom proudly carrying the birthday card she'd made herself. She would have leaped into the middle of the bed and the three of them would have snuggled together. Even when she'd hit the teenage years, Mack had been easygoing.

All that had changed a month before. Overnight she'd transformed into a sullen, moody caricature of a teenager and Lauren couldn't put her finger on why.

The Christmas holidays had been stressful. Ed, who rarely took time off, had reacted badly to the tension and Lauren had taken on the role of peacekeeper. As a result, she'd spent most of the festive period with tight knots in her stomach.

"Do you think it's a phase, or is this it?"

Ed stirred. "Is this what?"

The way she's going to be for the rest of her life.

She didn't voice her thoughts.

Today was Ed's birthday, and she had a party to run.

Thinking of everything she had to do to make it perfect made her fidget.

This being Friday, she was meeting her friends Ruth and Helen at ten o'clock in their favorite coffee shop, which happened to be exactly thirty-five steps from the hairdresser where Lauren had an appointment exactly forty-five minutes later. By eleven thirty she'd be at the florist and after a fifteen-minute walk home—ticking the boxes for both steps *and* sunshine—the rest of the day was devoted to making final preparations for the party.

"Ed—" She nudged him again. "Wake up, honey. I need to give you your gift before I head downstairs. I have the whole day planned out to the minute."

Ed finally opened his eyes. "When have you ever not had the whole day planned out to the minute? If I ever invent an organization app, I'm calling it The Lauren."

Was that a criticism?

"It's important to take control, otherwise time drifts."

Lauren had other reasons for keeping control on life, but she and Ed never talked about that. Sometimes she wondered if he remembered. Time had a way of fading events until they were distant and indistinct. It was like hanging a painting in sunlight. Lines blurred and colors lost some of their sharpness.

Occasionally her mind drifted there, but mostly she managed to keep herself in the present.

Hoping to stir him into action, she threw back the covers and stood up. Usually she started with a few yoga stretches, but today she was distracted by the thought of Mack downstairs in the kitchen.

Why was she up so early?

Perhaps she was making a surprise birthday breakfast for Ed.

Or maybe that was wishful thinking.

Lauren walked to the window and glanced into the street.

With luck today would be one of those perfect sunny winter days, but this being London it was unlikely. As long as their guests didn't have to battle snow, she wasn't going to complain. England, she'd discovered years before, didn't cope well with snow. Ten large flakes were all that was required to send the country into a screaming panic.

Ed finally heaved himself out of bed, too.

Lauren turned and studied his hunched form. "Are you okay?"

He turned his head to look at her, distracted. "What?"

"You look tired."

"I am tired. I could lie in bed for a month and not move."

She decided the time for subtlety had passed. "You should see a doctor." Why was it men needed to be told that?

"For being tired? The advice will be 'Go to bed earlier.' I can't afford the time to hear him state the obvious."

"Her."

"Excuse me?"

"Our doctor is a woman," Lauren said. "Eleanor Baxter. If you won't see her, at least slow down a little. Leave the office earlier."

"Slow down? Lauren, do you have any fucking idea what my job is like?" He closed his eyes and ran his hand across his jaw. "I'm sorry, sweetheart. I didn't mean—forgive me. I'm not feeling great."

"It's fine." But it wasn't fine, was it? Ed never swore, at least not in her presence. He was always polite and courteous—to friends, to the teachers at their daughter's school, even to the mailman if they happened to bump into each other. It was his even temper and unshakable calm that had drawn her to him. He was dependable. With Ed she'd never felt swept away or out of control. She'd never had to worry that her heart might fracture or her breathing might stop altogether. If there had ever been a part of her that craved something different, it was now a mere speck in her past, barely visible to the naked eye. "I know you're busy, but it's not like you to be this tense."

Ed was a whiz kid financier who had made a fortune with a big hedge fund in the city before leaving to manage his own portfolio. James, an old college friend who rented office space with him, said Ed was a financial genius. Lauren had no reason to doubt it.

This house, Mackenzie's school, *their perfect life*—all of it was paid for by Ed's brutally long hours in the office.

Once, she'd had ambitions, too, but that had been before she'd had sex on a beach and found herself pregnant. Not that she undervalued her contribution to the family. Being a stay-at-home mom had been her choice and from the moment Mack was born, Lauren had *loved* being a mother. She considered herself Ed's equal in every way and knew her role was every bit as important as Ed's. She was the Yorkshire pudding to his roast beef, to use a British analogy, which she always tried to do in order to ingratiate herself with her fearsome mother-in-law, who, even after sixteen years, remained appalled that her precious only son had married an American.

Ed was still sitting on the bed, staring at the floor, and Lauren reached into the drawer by the bed and pulled out the box she'd wrapped carefully.

"Happy birthday." She handed him the gift and felt a thrill

of anticipation. "I wanted to give it to you now because later on it's going to be crazy here with a houseful of people all wanting a piece of you."

Ed opened the package and stared at the contents. "You bought me a rain forest?"

"Not a *whole* rain forest. A patch of rain forest. I know how committed you are to environmental issues. You cycle everywhere, you're always talking about saving the planet. I thought—"

"It's a scam, Lauren." He sounded tired. "I can't believe you spent money on that. You do realize you've probably financed the cocaine industry?"

"It's not a scam. I'm not stupid." And he knew it. He knew she'd graduated top of her year at school and had a place at an Ivy League college before her world had crashed down. Ed had been the one to encourage her to pick up the threads of her dream once Mack had started senior school. She'd been studying for an interior design qualification and was finally poised to embark on her own career. When she'd passed her exams, they'd celebrated with champagne. "I researched it carefully. We can visit whenever we like."

"Right. Because flying to Brazil is great for the planet." He tossed the box on the bed and she felt her throat thicken.

"I was trying to give you something original and thoughtful."

"It was thoughtful." He rubbed his fingers across his chest. "It's not you, it's me. Ignore me. I need to start the day again."

He heaved himself off the bed, walked into the bathroom and closed the door.

Moments later she heard the hiss of water.

She stood there, flummoxed.

This wasn't about a patch of rain forest. Was he on the verge of a midlife crisis? Was he about to start wearing skinny jeans and have an affair with someone barely older than Mackenzie?

Making an effort not to overthink and overreact, she went in search of her daughter.

She found her in the kitchen, hunched over her phone at the kitchen island. A pair of oversize pink headphones covered her ears.

Mack hated pink. The headphones had been an attempt to fit in with a group at school who teased her for not being girly enough. Mack called them "the princesses," and they'd made her life a misery.

If Mack heard her mother come into the room, she gave no sign of it.

There was no tray laid for breakfast. No sign of any birthday treat.

Nothing except a single overflowing bowl of breakfast cereal that Mack dug in to.

Lauren tried to work out what she could say without causing an explosion. "Hi, honey. You haven't forgotten Dad's birthday?"

Mack looked up from her phone and removed her headphones in an exaggerated gesture.

"What?"

"Dad's birthday. Today."

"Yeah?"

"Aren't you going to wish him happy birthday?"

"Does he want to be reminded? Forty is pretty old. Not quite a senior citizen but that landmark is definitely on the horizon." Mack took another spoonful of cereal. "I figured he might rather ignore it. And it's six fifteen. I'm not a morning person. I guess I could have made him tea, but he hates my tea. He always moans that it's too weak." She put the headphones back on her ears and went back to Snapchat. Dressed in an oversize T-shirt, she looked younger than sixteen. Her hair was the same sunny blond as Lauren's, but Mack allowed hers to flop forward in an attempt to hide the stubborn spots that clustered on her forehead. Her braces had come off a few months earlier but she still smiled with her lips pressed together because she'd forgotten she no longer needed to be self-conscious.

It was only when Mack picked up her empty bowl to put it in the dishwasher that Lauren noticed the two pink streaks in her hair.

"What have you done to your hair?"

"I woke up with it this way. Weird, huh? Fairies or gremlins."

"Mack—"

Her daughter sighed. "I dyed it. And before you flip out, everyone is doing it. All the other mothers were fine about it. Abigail's mom helped her do hers."

This was her cue to be like "all the other mothers." It was a pass or fail test, and Lauren knew she was going to fail. "Why didn't you discuss it with me?"

"Because you're such a control freak you would have said no."

"You have beautiful hair. Is this about trying to fit in?"

"I don't care about fitting in."

They both knew it was a lie.

Lauren picked her words carefully. "Honey, I know it's hard when you're teased, but it happens to a lot of people and—"

"That does *not* help, by the way. It makes no difference

to me how many other people have been through it." Nonchalance barely masked the pain and Lauren felt the pain as if it were her own.

"Your individuality is the thing that makes you special. And you need to remember that most people are thinking about themselves, not anyone else." She decided that this wasn't the time to raise the school issue again. "I know you're upset. Has something else happened?"

"You mean apart from the fact that my mother is always on my case?"

"I'm trying to be supportive. We've always been able to talk about anything and everything."

Mack scooped up her phone. "Yeah, right. Anything and everything. No secrets in *this* house."

Her tone made Lauren feel uneasy.

"Mack—"

"I need to get ready for school. My mother had a place at an Ivy League college, so nothing short of Oxford or Cambridge is going to be good enough for me. Education is everything, right?"

It was too early in the morning to deal with teenage attitude. Lauren opened her mouth to remind her to wish her father a happy birthday, but Mack was gone.

Another slammed door. Her world seemed full of them.

No secrets in this house.

Feeling a burn of stress behind her rib cage, she took herself downstairs to the basement gym they'd installed and tried to run off her anxiety on the treadmill. She flicked on CNN, giving herself a taste of home.

Storms in Alabama. An alligator thirty feet long in Florida. A shooting in Brooklyn.

A wave of homesickness almost knocked her flat. She

yearned for morning runs on South Beach, the smell of the sea, the taste of seafood caught fresh that morning, the sight of the sun setting near her sister's house in Menemsha.

Twenty minutes later Ed appeared. He was dressed in cycling gear and had his phone in his hand.

Lauren breathed a sigh of relief. This was routine. Ed cycled to the office and changed once he got there, and it seemed that today was no different except that he was running later than usual.

"Have a great day, birthday boy." When he didn't answer, she muted CNN and slowed the treadmill until it stopped. "You seem really distracted today. Does it bother you being forty?"

"What?" He glanced up from his emails.

"Forty." Maybe she'd treated the whole thing too lightly. She needed to make sure he knew he was still handsome and desirable. More sex wouldn't hurt. Sometimes the days slipped past and she'd realize it had been a week. Sometimes longer. The truth was sex between them had always been comfortable rather than urgent.

Was that normal? She had no idea because it wasn't a topic she'd dream of discussing with friends.

Maybe he *was* having an affair?

Even though she'd stopped the treadmill, her heart rate continued to accelerate. No. Ed wasn't like that. They didn't lie to each other. That was what they'd agreed that first night they'd met. Lauren trusted Ed implicitly.

And they were happy. Happy couples didn't have affairs.

"Are you worrying about Mack? I know she's been difficult lately."

She decided not to mention the pink hair. Let him notice it for himself later.

"All teenagers are difficult. I remember your mother saying your sister was a nightmare."

Lauren realized she'd forgotten to call her sister the day before. Preparations for Ed's birthday had eclipsed everything.

"All my mother wanted to do was paint, and she was irritated by anything that disturbed that." Still, when Lauren thought back to some of the things she'd done with Jenna, it terrified her.

They were lucky to have come through childhood unscathed. *Or mostly unscathed.*

"She's growing up." Ed was calm. "She doesn't have to tell us every little thing. She's pushing for independence, and we've always encouraged that. And as for being difficult, it's nature's way of making sure teenagers want to leave home and that parents are ready to push them out of the door."

"She's sixteen, Ed. It's years until she leaves home. And you know what the school told us. Mack is skipping homework and failing English. She's always been a straight-A student. English is her best subject."

Ed frowned. "Physics is her best subject. Last year she wanted to do aeronautical engineering."

"That was before those girls started teasing her for being like a boy. Remember that horrible Facebook page they set up? Mack-the-man." She'd been so upset she'd wanted to charge into school and chop off their damn princess hair with rusty scissors. It had taken a lot of maneuvering to have the page taken down and Mack had been left wounded. "She is smart. She could do what she likes, providing she works hard, but that's the point. She isn't. If she carries on like this, she's going to fail her exams." Unless there was an exam in sarcasm. Mack would ace that.

"There's more to life than being a straight-A student, Lauren."

"I know. But I also know how competitive the world is now. If you mess up your exams then you don't get into a good college, and without a good college you don't stand a chance of getting a good internship because there are literally *thousands* of people applying for every position. Sue Miller's eldest graduated last summer and since then she has put in one hundred and fifty applications and hasn't had a single interview. *One hundred and fifty.*"

"Calm down. Mack is going to be fine, Lauren."

She was irritated that he didn't even glance up from his phone.

"But what if she isn't? The school told us she's not speaking up in class." And since when had her daughter not spoken up in class? Mack had been speaking up ever since she'd learned how to put two words together. "And then there was that incident a month ago—"

He glanced up. "That was a one-off."

"She was *drunk*, Ed! Our daughter was drunk and Tanya's mother had to drive her home." And Mack had refused to offer any explanation. She'd shut them out. That had disturbed Lauren more than anything. Was that when Mack had changed?

"Teenagers experiment. Tanya's mother should have kept a closer eye on the vodka bottle."

"It wasn't a one-off. What about the time she took money from my purse? Our child *stole*, Ed." What if Mack was experimenting with drugs? The more she thought about the list of possible horrors, the more surprising it seemed that today's teenagers ever made it to adulthood. "I think she's keeping something from us." She recognized the signs, and it made her uneasy. A secret, she knew, could eat away at you slowly. It created a barrier between you and the people you loved.

"Since when do teenagers tell their parents everything? You need to chill. Mack is doing okay. She's not the problem."

Lauren stared at him, wrong-footed.

"What do you mean?"

"Nothing."

"You said, 'She's not the problem,' which means something else is."

"Forget it." His attention was back on his phone. "I might be late tonight."

"You're kidding. Tonight is the party."

"The—what?" He looked confused and then closed his eyes briefly and muttered something under his breath.

"Your party. Had you forgotten?"

The pause was infinitesimal, but it was there.

"No."

He was lying, and he never lied.

Who forgot their own fortieth birthday party?

What was on his mind?

"We have thirty people coming, Ed. Friends, colleagues, your mother—" She managed not to wince and Ed nodded.

"I'll be there. See you later." He grabbed a bottle of chilled water from the fridge they kept in the gym, and Lauren studied him from the back and wondered if tight Lycra cycling shorts on a man of forty was still a good look.

He slammed the fridge door shut and straightened.

"Thanks for the rain forest. It was a sweet thought and

I'm sorry I overreacted." He kissed her cheek. It was a dry, asexual gesture. "I love you. You're a good woman, Lauren."

A good woman? *What did that mean?*

"Maybe you should take time off. Mackenzie has three weeks at Easter. We could go away."

"Let's talk about it tomorrow."

Lauren watched him leave.

She's not the problem.

By the time she left the house to meet her friends, she'd persuaded herself that Ed was having an off day and she was having a massive attack of overthinking. She felt invigorated after her workout, happy that everything was on track for the party, and reassured by the fact that Mackenzie had spoken at least eight words before leaving for school. Fortunately the school they'd chosen was close by. One of Mack's friends lived a few doors away and they walked together.

Most days Lauren managed to resist the temptation to track Mack's phone to check her daughter was safe.

She buttoned her coat against the cold and walked briskly along tree-lined residential streets.

As someone who had lived her life on an island until the age of eighteen, the prospect of city living had daunted her, but she'd fallen in love with this area of London from the first moment Ed had brought her here. She loved the secret communal gardens, the elegance of the stucco-fronted houses and the candy-colored charm of Portobello Road. She enjoyed browsing in the market for secret treasures and discovering restaurants down hidden side streets. In those early years she'd explored the city with the baby tucked in her stroller, loitered in galleries and strolled through London's many parks. She'd spent hours in the Tate Modern and the Royal Academy, but her favorite place without a doubt was the Victoria and Albert Museum, which had been a source of inspiration for designers and artists for over one hundred and fifty years.

Lauren could happily have moved in there.

She reached the coffee shop at the same time as her friends.

She went to the counter to order while Ruth and Helen grabbed their usual table in the window. They'd started meeting for coffee when their children had moved to the same girls' school and conversations at the school gate had become impossible.

She ordered coffees and a couple of pastries for her friends and pushed her credit card into the machine. It was promptly declined.

With a murmur of apology, Lauren tried again and the card was declined a second time.

"I'll pay cash." She slipped the card back into her purse and scrabbled around for money. Red-cheeked, she carried the tray over to the table and set it down.

"Thanks." Ruth lifted a cappuccino from the tray. "My turn next time. It's freezing out there. They're saying we could still have snow."

Lauren sank into the vacant chair and unwrapped her scarf from her neck.

The British preoccupation with the weather was one of the things that had fascinated Lauren when she'd first arrived in London. Entire conversations were devoted to the weather, which, as far as Lauren could see, was rarely newsworthy. On Martha's Vineyard bad weather frequently meant being cut off from the mainland. She wondered what her British friends would have had to say about a hurricane. It would have kept the conversation going for months.

"Did you want to share this croissant?" Helen broke it in half and Lauren shook her head.

"Just coffee for me." She pulled out her phone and sent a quick text to Ed.

Credit card not working. Problem?

Maybe the bank had seen a transaction that was out of the ordinary and frozen it. She probably ought to call them later.

"I wish I had your willpower." Ruth ate the other half of Helen's croissant. "Don't you ever give in to your impulses?"

Lauren dropped her phone into her bag. "Giving in to impulses can lead to disaster."

Both her friends stared at her in surprise, and she wished she'd kept her mouth shut.

"Disaster?" Ruth blinked. "You mean like not fitting into your jeans?"

"No. I—" She shook her head. "Ignore me. I've had a crazy morning. Busy." It was Ed's fault, for making her think about things she didn't want to think about.

"Ah, yes, the birthday. How was Ed?" Helen picked up her spoon and stirred circles into the foam on her coffee. "When Martin hit forty he bought a sports car. Such a cliché, but I get to drive it so I've stopped complaining."

Lauren sipped her coffee. "Ed seemed fine about it."

She's not the problem.

"I had a crisis when I turned forty," Ruth said. "Having a sixteen-year-old daughter reminds you how old you are. I don't have daughter envy yet, but I can see how it could happen. You don't have that problem—" she glanced at Lauren

"—because you had Mack when you were still in your pram, or whatever you call it across the pond."

Lauren laughed. "I was nineteen. Not *that* young."

But she'd been pregnant at eighteen, which was only two years older than Mack was now.

"And you still look twenty-one, which makes me want to kill you." Ruth waved a hand in disgust. "At least your daughter doesn't think you're too old to understand anything."

Thinking of some of the conversations she'd had with Mack lately, Lauren gave a tight smile. "Oh, she does."

"But you have *energy*. I'm too tired to cope with a teenager. I thought the terrible twos were supposed to be the worst age and now I'm discovering it's sixteen. Peer pressure, puberty, sex—"

Lauren put her cup down. "Abigail is having sex?"

"It wouldn't surprise me. She has a 'boyfriend.'" Ruth stroked the air with her fingers, putting in the quote marks. "The phone pings all the time because he's messaging her."

Was that the problem with Mack? Was it a boy?

"Phoebe is always on her phone, too," Helen said. "Why is it they don't have the energy to tidy their rooms, but manage to hold a phone? Last night when I finally wrenched it from her grabby hand and told her all electronic devices were banned from the bedroom, she told me she hated me. Joy."

Lauren's sympathy was tinged with relief. Even during their most prickly encounters, Mack had never said she hated her. Things could be worse.

"They don't mean it," Ruth said. "It's one of those lines straight out of the teenage phrase book, along with *I hate my life—my life is so crap*."

"And *but all my friends are doing it.*"

"*Nobody does that stuff, Mom.* It's the moods that get me. I know it's hormones, but knowing that doesn't help." Helen finished her coffee. "It makes me feel guilty because I *know* I was the same with my mum, weren't you?"

Ruth nodded. Lauren said nothing.

As long as they weren't doing anything that interrupted her painting, her mother had left her and Jenna alone. It was one of the reasons she and her sister were close.

"The only one with a predictable temperament in our house is the dog." Ruth gave a wicked smile. "Do you ever wonder what your life would have been like if you'd married your first boyfriend?"

"I'd be divorced," Helen said. "My first boyfriend was a total nightmare."

They looked at Lauren and she felt her face heat. "Ed *was* my first real boyfriend."

It wasn't really a lie, she told herself. *Boyfriend* meant someone you had a relationship with. The word conjured up images of exploratory kisses, trips to the movies and awkward fumbling. A boyfriend was a public thing. *I'm going out with my boyfriend tonight.*

Using that definition, Ed had been her first boyfriend.

"You've been with one man your whole adult life? No flings? No crazy, naughty teenage sex?"

Lauren felt her heart pick up speed. *That didn't count*, she told herself. "For me it's always been Ed."

"Well—" Helen spoke first. "I'm going to stop talking before I incriminate myself."

"I auditioned a lot of men before finally awarding the role of my husband to Pete." Ruth finished her croissant. "I'd better go. I left my house in chaos." She reached for her bag. "See you at the party tonight, Lauren. Sure there's nothing we can do?"

"No thanks, I've got it covered."

"Is your sister coming over from the States?"

"No, she can't get away from school right now."

Lauren felt another stab of guilt. When they'd last spoken, Jenna had confessed that her period was late. Lauren had heard the excitement in her voice and felt excited with her. She knew how desperately Jenna wanted a baby and how upset her sister was each month when it didn't happen. She'd intended to call, but party planning had driven it from her head.

"What about your mum? She's not coming either?"

Lauren kept her smile in place. "No."

Of course that had a lot to do with the fact that she hadn't been invited.

Lauren had never had a close relationship with her mother, but things had been particularly strained last time she'd visited home. Her mother had seemed preoccupied and even more distant than usual.

When her father had died five years earlier, Lauren had expected Nancy to be devastated.

She'd flown home for the funeral and been humbled by how strong her mother was. Her father had been a much-loved member of the community and there had been plenty of people sobbing at his funeral. Her mother hadn't been one of them. Nancy Stewart had stood with her back as straight as the mast of a ship, dry-eyed, as if part of her was somewhere else. Lauren assumed she handled grief the way she handled everything else life threw her—by vanishing to her studio and losing herself in her painting.

Lauren stared into her coffee.

Growing up, her father had been the "fun" parent.

"Let's go to the beach, girls," he'd say, and scoop them up without giving a thought to what they were doing. He'd bring them back long past bedtime with sandy feet, burned skin and salty hair. They were hungry and overtired and it was their mother who had dealt with the fallout.

Nancy would be waiting tight-lipped, the supper she'd prepared congealing on cold plates. She'd serve the ruined food in silence and then dunk both girls in the shower, where Jenna would scream and howl as the water stung her burned flesh.

By the end of the summer the sun had bleached their hair almost white and freckles had exploded over Jenna's face. To Lauren they looked like sand sprinkled over her skin, but Jenna thought they looked like dirt. She'd scrub at her skin until it was red and sore and the freckles merged.

"You could at least remember sunscreen," Nancy had said to Tom one night and Lauren had heard him laugh.

"I forgot. Loosen up."

It seemed to Lauren that the more her father told Nancy to loosen up, the tighter she was wound.

She'd long since given up wishing her relationship with her mother were different.

She and Ed returned to Martha's Vineyard for ten days every summer, but Lauren felt edgy the whole time. It was part of a life she'd left behind, and being there made her feel uncomfortable, as if she was dressing in old clothes that no longer fit. Not having her father there with his endless jokes and energy made the visit even more awkward.

The only good part about it was seeing her sister in person.

Lauren saw Helen stand up and realized she'd missed half the conversation.

Her friend reached for her bag. "Have your girls finished this wretched ancestry project? Martin's been wishing we'd picked a different school to send her to. One that doesn't take education so seriously."

Lauren grabbed her coat, too. "What ancestry project?"

Helen and Ruth exchanged looks.

"This is why we envy you," Ruth said. "Your Mack is so smart she does all these things without your help."

"Mack does tend to figure these things out on her own." All the same, she made a mental note to ask Mack about it, just to be sure.

"Everything okay with Mack?" Helen held the door open for them and they swapped warm scented air for frozen winds. "No more trouble with those bitches from the year above?"

Lauren was tempted to mention the pink hair and the fact that something felt "off," but decided not to. She was still hoping it was nothing.

"Everything seems fine."

"Abigail hasn't mentioned anything, and she was the one who found that Facebook page when it happened." Ruth squeezed her arm. "I'm sure it's over and done."

She hoped so. She knew she had a tendency to blow things out of proportion. According to Ed, she catastrophized.

If he was right, then his words earlier should be nothing more than a throwaway comment.

If they had a problem, they would have talked about it.

She checked her phone and saw she was on time for her hair appointment. "I'll see you both later."

Ed was going to be fine and so was Mack. True, she was behaving oddly but the chances were it was nothing more than a phase.

It didn't mean she was keeping secrets.

Lauren tried to ignore the voice in her head reminding her that she and her sister had kept secrets all the time.

CHAPTER TWO

Sisters

> *Loyalty: the quality of staying firm in your friendship or support for someone or something*

"PLEASE DON'T DO IT." I watched her climb onto the railing. Below lay the water, dark and deep.

It was early morning and the beach was deserted. Later in the season the place would be teeming with tourists all lined up waiting to jump off the Jaws Bridge, so called because it featured in the movie, but right now we were the only people.

And we weren't supposed to be here.

Our bikes lay on the edge of the path, abandoned. The beaches on either side of the bridge were deserted. No cars had passed since we'd arrived five minutes earlier.

"If you're afraid, go home." She issued the challenge with a toss of her head and a blaze of her eyes.

My sister, the rebel.

She was right. I could have gone home. But then who would have taken care of her? What if she knocked herself unconscious or was swept out to sea? The current was pretty strong and you had to swim hard away from the bridge once you jumped. I'd positioned myself down on the beach because I figured that was the only way I'd be able to rescue her.

The seaweed was slippery under my shoes and the wind was cold.

I was shivering, although I wasn't sure whether it was through cold or fear. I wanted to be anywhere but here.

Like all families, we had rules.

My sister had broken all of them.

Was I my sister's keeper? Well yes, I was. Self-appointed, admittedly. What choice did I have? I loved her. We told each other everything. She was my best friend. I would have died for her, although I would have preferred that to be a last resort.

I tried one more time. "The sign says No Jumping Off the Bridge."

She looked across at me and shrugged. "Don't look at it."

"Mom will kill us."

"She won't know. She doesn't know about any of the things we do. She only cares about painting."

"If someone tells her, she'll care."

"Then we'd better hope no one tells her."

That was her answer to everything.

I squirmed at mealtimes, terrified Mom might ask what we'd done all day. Guilt stuck to my skin until I was sure she would be able to see it. I felt as if I was glowing like a neon sign.

Fortunately for me, our mother usually had other things on her mind.

"It isn't safe. Come back in the summer when there are more people."

"I hate the crowds." She clambered onto the top of the railing, balancing like a circus performer, arms stretched to the sky. "I'll go on three. One, two—"

Throwing a wicked smile in my direction she pushed off and flew.

She sailed through the air and hit the water with a splash, disappearing under the surface. I felt a moment of raw terror. If she was in trouble, would I be strong enough to save her? The image in my head was so real I almost felt her body slipping from my hands. It was only when her head bobbed up and I let out a relieved sigh that I realized I'd been holding my breath. My toes hurt and I realized I'd curled them tight inside my shoes, ready to push off the rocks into the water.

She swam toward me, working hard against the current that was trying to pull her out to sea.

"You almost gave me a heart attack." I threw her the towel, relief making my legs shaky. Another one of my sister's wild adventures and we were still alive. There were days when I felt like her mother, not her sister. "We need to get home before someone sees you with wet hair."

"No one will see us." She emerged from the water, her clothes dripping and clinging to her skinny arms and legs. "Dad is away and Mom is in the studio."

"What do we say when she asks what we did today?"

"She won't ask." My sister rubbed her head with the towel and tossed her hair back. She looked exhilarated and excited the way she always did when we did something we

weren't supposed to. "But if she does, we'll tell her we went for a scenic bike ride."

This was part of our pact. We always made sure there were no flaws in our story.

Whatever happened, she knew I'd protect her.

She was my sister.

CHAPTER THREE

Jenna

Yearning: an intense or overpowering longing

NOT PREGNANT.

Were there two more depressing words in the English language?

In the small bathroom of their two-bedroom cottage on the island of Martha's Vineyard, Jenna dropped the remains of the pregnancy test onto the bathroom floor and resisted the temptation to grind it under her heel.

She wanted to swear, but she tried never to do that even in the privacy of her own bathroom in case one day it slipped out in front of her class of impressionable six-year-olds. Imagine that.

Mrs. Sullivan said fuck, *Mommy.* FUCK. *It was her word of the day. First we had to spell it, and then we had to use it in a sentence.*

No, swearing was out of the question and she refused to cry. She already had to contend with freckles. She didn't want blotches, too.

"Jenna?" Greg's voice came through the door. "Are you okay, honey?"

"I'm good. I'll be out in a moment."

She stared at herself in the mirror, daring her eyes to spill even a single drop of the tears that gathered there.

She was not okay.

Her body wasn't doing what it was supposed to do. What it was supposed to do was get pregnant on the first attempt, or at least the second, nurture a baby carefully for nine months and then deliver it with no crisis or drama.

All those times she'd peed on the stick in the grip of panic, hoping and praying that it wouldn't be positive. The first time she'd had sex with Greg, both of them fumbling and inept on the beach, she'd been more terrified than turned on. *Please don't let me get pregnant.*

Now she badly wanted it to be positive and it wasn't happening.

They'd been having sex all winter, although to be fair there wasn't much else to do on the Vineyard once the temperature dropped. Sex was a reasonable alternative to burning fossil fuels. Maybe she should teach it in class. *Hey, kids, there is solar energy, geothermal energy, wind energy and sex. Ask your parents about that one.*

She was burning more calories in her bedroom than she ever had on a treadmill.

She was thirty-two.

By thirty-two, her mother already had Lauren.

Jenna's sister, Lauren, had been pregnant at *eighteen*. She'd barely said "I do" to Ed before announcing she was expecting. It seemed to Jenna that her sister had gotten pregnant by simply brushing against him.

And yes, that made her envious. She loved her sister, but she'd discovered that love wasn't enough to keep those uncomfortable feelings at bay.

She'd wanted to be a teacher since her sixth birthday when her mother had bought her a chalkboard, and she'd forced her sister to play school.

Everyone knew it was only a matter of time until she had her own family.

At first she'd been relaxed about it, but as each month passed she was growing more and more desperate.

She'd tried everything to maximize her chances, from taking her temperature every day to making Greg wear loose boxer shorts. They'd had sex in every conceivable position and a few inconceivable positions, which had caused one broken lamp and Greg to mutter that he felt like a circus performer. Nothing had worked.

The injustice made her heart hurt, but worse was the sense of total emptiness. It embarrassed her a little because she knew she was lucky. She had so much. She had *Greg*, for goodness' sake. Greg Sullivan, who was loved by every single person on the island including Jenna. Greg, who had graduated top of his year and had excelled at everything he'd ever tried.

She'd loved him since she was five years old and he'd pulled her out of the ditch where she'd fallen in an ungainly heap. He was her hero. They'd sat next to each other in senior year and run the school newspaper together. People talked about them as if they were one person. They were Jenna-and-Greg.

Until recently, being with Greg was all she'd ever wanted.

Suddenly it didn't seem like enough.

The worst thing was that she couldn't talk about it with anyone, which had led to some almost awkward moments because she didn't find keeping things to herself easy. *Chatty*, her school reports had said, much to her mother's irritation. *You're there to learn, Jenna.*

She might be chatty, but even Jenna drew the line at talking about her sex life while browsing the aisles at the local store.

Hi, Mary, good to see you. By the way, how many times did you and Pete have sex before you got pregnant?

Hi, Kelly, I'd love to stop and chat but I'm ovulating and I need to rush home and get naked with Greg. See you soon!

"Jenna?" He rattled the handle. "I know you're not okay, so open the door and we can talk."

What was there to talk about?

She was desperate for a baby and talking wasn't going to fix that.

She opened the door. She was Jolly Jenna. The girl who always smiled. The girl who had always tried to accept things she couldn't change. She had freckles on her nose, hair that curled no matter what she did to it and a body that refused to make babies.

Greg stood there, wearing what she thought of as his listening face. "Negative?"

She nodded and pressed her face against his chest. He smelled good. Like lemons and fresh air. "Don't say anything." Greg was a therapist. He'd always been good with people, but right now there was nothing he could say that would make her feel better and she was afraid sympathy might tip her over the edge.

She felt his arms come round her.

"How about 'I love you.'"

"That always works." She loved the way he hugged. Tightly, holding her close, as if he meant it. As if nothing was ever going to come between them.

"We're young and we haven't been trying that long, Jenna."

"Seventeen months, one week and two days. Don't you think it's time we talked to a doctor?"

"We don't need to do that." He eased away. "Think of all the great sex we can have while we're making this baby."

But it's not working.

"I'd like to talk to someone."

He sighed. "You're very tense all the time."

She couldn't get pregnant. What did he expect?

"If you're about to tell me to relax, I'll injure you."

He pulled her back into his arms. "You work so hard. You give everything you have to those kids in your class—"

"I love my job."

"Maybe you could go to yoga or something."

"I can't sit still long enough to do yoga."

"Something else then. I don't know—"

This time she was the one who pulled away. "Don't you dare buy me a book on mindfulness."

"Damn, there goes my Christmas gift." He cupped her face in his hands and kissed her gently on the mouth. "Hang in there, honey." The look in his eyes made her want to cry.

"We're going to be late for work."

Twenty hyperactive six-year-olds were waiting for her. Other people's six-year-olds. She adjudicated arguments, mopped tears, educated them and tried not to imagine how it would be if one of those kids was hers.

Every day at school she taught the children a new word.

Definitions had a way of flashing through her head even when she didn't want them to. Like now.

Disappointed: saddened by the failing of an expectation.

Frustrated: having feelings of dissatisfaction or lack of fulfilment.

"It would be easier if people didn't keep asking when we're going to have a baby."

"They do that?"

"All the time." She grabbed her makeup from the bathroom. "It must be a woman thing. Maybe I should stop being evasive. Next time someone asks me I should tell them we're having nonstop sex."

"They already know."

"How?"

He grinned. "A couple of weeks ago you texted me at work."

"Plenty of wives text their husbands at work."

"But generally those texts don't say Hey, hot stuff, I'm naked and ready for sex."

"What's wrong with that?"

"Nothing, except Pamela had my phone."

"No!" She felt a rush of mortification. "Why?"

"She's my receptionist. I was with a client. I left it with her in case someone had an emergency. I wasn't to know you would be having a sex emergency."

"I don't know whether to laugh or hide." Jenna covered her mouth with her hand. "Pamela was my babysitter. She still treats me as if I'm six years old."

"We can rest assured she now knows you're all grown up."

"What did she say?"

"Nothing. She handed me my phone back, but I have

no doubt that our sex life will be the topic of discussion at the knitting group, the book group and the conservation commission meeting. If we're lucky, it might not be on the agenda for the annual town meeting."

"Do you think she'll mention it to my mother?"

"Given that your mother is a member of both the book group and the conservation commission, not to mention numerous other committees on this island, I think the answer to that is yes. But so what?"

"It will be another transgression to add to a very long list."

Jenna had once overheard her mother say *Lauren never gave me any trouble, but Jenna*— She'd paused at that point, as if to confirm that there were no words to describe Jenna's wayward nature.

"Whenever I'm with my mother I still feel as if I should be sitting in the naughty corner."

Greg gave a slow smile. "What happens in this naughty corner? Is there room for two?"

"She thinks you're perfect. The only thing I've ever done that has won the approval of my mother is marry you! It drives me batshit crazy."

"Batshit—" Greg arched an eyebrow. "Is that today's word?"

"If you're not careful I'll tell her what a bad influence you are."

"We're married, Jenna. We are allowed to have sex wherever and whenever we like as long as we don't get arrested for public indecency."

"I know, but—you know my mother. She'll sigh the way she does when she despairs of me. She'll be wishing I was more like my sister." Although Jenna adored Lauren, she had never wanted to be her. "My mother is the beating heart of this island. If anyone is in trouble she's there with her flaky double-crusted pies and endless support. She's closer to Betty at the store than she is to me." And it was a never-ending source of frustration and hurt that she and her mother didn't have a better relationship. ✓

Jenna considered herself easygoing. She got along well with pretty much everyone.

Why did it feel so hard to talk to her mother?

"Parent-child relationships are complicated."

Dysfunctional: relationships or behavior which are different from what is considered to be normal.

"I get that. What I don't get is why it still bothers me so much. Why can't I accept things the way they are? It's exhausting."

"Mmm." Greg glanced at his watch. "Happy to deliver a lecture on the latest research into mother-daughter relationships, but I charge by the half hour and you can't afford me." He kissed her again. "Get dressed, or the next thing they'll be discussing at the annual town meeting is the fact that their first-grade teacher was standing in front of the class wearing her dinosaur pajamas. Want me to cook tonight?"

"It's my turn. And speaking of my mother, I'm visiting her later."

"Thanks for the warning. Better pick up a bottle of something strong when you pass the store."

"Visits were so much easier when my dad was alive."

Greg raised an eyebrow. "He was always on the golf course."

"But he usually wandered in at some point and he was always pleased to see me. Mom still thinks I'm a wild child."

"It's the reason I married you. I'll see you tonight, and

you can be as wild as you like." He tucked a strand of hair behind her ear. "Text me later to let me know how you are?"

"Only if you promise not to give Pamela your phone."

"Or you could stop sexting." He pulled her against him. "On second thoughts, don't stop sexting. I like it and it's great for my reputation."

"Oh please—your island approval ratings are already through the roof." She shoved at his chest. "Go."

"I'll see you later." He scooped up his coat and car keys and made for the door. "Oh and, Jenna—"

"What?"

"Try to relax." He winked at her and was gone before she could throw something.

Shivering in the blast of cold air he'd let into the house, she walked back into the bedroom and glanced out of the window.

Despite everything, he'd made her smile. He always made her smile.

Then she noticed him standing by the car, his shoulders slumped, and her smile faded.

He was always so upbeat about everything, but right now he didn't look upbeat. Was he putting on an act for her sake?

She waited until he drove away, then swapped pajamas for her smart black pants. Last year they'd fitted perfectly but now they were tight around the waist and she knew that had nothing to do with being pregnant and everything to do with the fact she'd started using food as a comfort.

Greg had left coffee for her and she poured herself a cup, reached for the oatmeal and then changed her mind and took a cupcake from the tin instead. She'd made them the day before and decorated them with sugar icing. They were supposed to be a peace offering for her mother, something she could take to her book group, but she wasn't going to miss one, was she?

Not the healthiest breakfast, but the negative pregnancy test was enough to make her want to fall face-first into the nearest source of sugar.

She sank her teeth into the softness of the cake and closed her eyes.

Baking soothed her.

If she'd had a child, she would have baked with them. She would have had the softest buttercream, the lightest sponge cakes and her cookies would have been the envy of every-one. She could imagine all the kids saying *I wish my mom could cook as well as yours*.

As Jenna didn't have any kids to eat the cupcakes, she ate most of them herself. She ate to fill a big hole in her soul, but unfortunately it filled other things, too, including her fat cells.

She stared at the crumbs on her plate, drenched with re-gret and self-loathing.

Why had she done that? It wasn't as if she didn't under-stand what was going on here. She was married to a thera-pist. She felt a rush of frustration that she didn't have more control. She knew that smothering her emotions with sugar wasn't going to solve anything, but she didn't seem able to stop it. Her desperation for a baby had snapped something inside her.

She felt as if her life was slipping out of her grip and it was terrifying.

She had a sudden urge to call her sister, but that would make her late for work.

Would her sister even understand? Lauren had the perfect life. She had a beautiful house, no money worries, a great husband and a beautiful daughter.

And she couldn't exactly talk to her mother.

Nancy Stewart was the sort of person who had time and sympathy enough for everyone. Unless you happened to be her daughter.

Jenna drove to school along empty roads. In the summer months, her journey took at least twice as long. From late May through to early September, the Vineyard hummed with visitors, both summer residents and day trippers. They came to savor the "escapist" feel of the island, but did so in such large numbers that they inadvertently turned it into a copy of the places they'd left behind.

Jenna parked in the school parking lot and was caught at the gate by Mrs. Corren, who was anxious about Daisy, her daughter.

Andrea Corren gave her a wobbly smile. "Hi, Jenna. How was your weekend?"

I found out I'm not pregnant. "Good, thanks, Andrea. You?"

"Not good." The wobble in her smile moved to her voice. "Do you have a minute?"

She didn't. She had twenty hyperactive children waiting for her and she needed to keep them busy, occupied and entertained. That, she'd discovered, was the way to achieve a happy, harmonious classroom.

What she didn't need was to arrive late.

But she was also a little worried about Daisy.

"Of course." She saw Andrea Corren's eyes fill. "Let's find somewhere more private." She opted for the gym, which would be quiet for at least another half hour.

"How can I help, Andrea?"

She sat down on one of the small chairs. It forced her knees up at a strange angle, one of the reasons she rarely wore skirts or dresses to work. Dignity went out of the window when you taught six-year-olds. Sitting in this awkward position, she was horribly aware of the waistband of her pants biting into her stomach.

Why had she eaten that cupcake?

Andrea sat down next to her. "Things have been unsettled at home. Tense. We— Things are a little—rough—right now between Daisy's father and me. Our marriage isn't great."

Jenna stopped thinking about cupcakes. By "rough" did she mean something physical? This was a small community. Everyone knew Todd Corren had lost his job before Christmas and been out of work since. And everyone knew he'd punched Lyle Carpenter in an altercation on New Year's Eve.

"Do you think the problems in your marriage are having an impact on Daisy?"

"He's having an affair." Andrea blurted out the words. "He denies it, but I know it's true."

"I'm sorry." And she was. A fractured marriage was an injury to the whole family. Children limped wounded into her classroom, trying to make sense of the change in their world and she did what she could to create an environment that felt safe and secure.

"I haven't said anything to the children, and I'm trying hard not to show how upset I am because I don't want to confuse them. They don't know what's going on, and I'm afraid if I say something he'll make me seem like the bad guy. *Mom is having one of her moods again*, that kind of thing. I don't want to bring the kids into this. How does Daisy seem to you?"

"She's been a little quieter than usual, but she hasn't said anything specific." Jenna made some suggestions, careful to keep the conversation focused on the child. It wasn't her job to fix their marriage or pass comment, although invariably when you were a teacher, you became involved with the whole family. The fact that she'd been at school with the mothers of half the kids in her class, and some of the fathers, occasionally complicated matters.

Andrea pulled a tissue out of her bag. "I don't want this to harm my kids. If he stops right now, maybe we can fix this. Maybe they never have to know. But I'm not good at keeping secrets. I'm an honest person and I've raised them to be honest, too, so by making me do this, he's tainted our family. It isn't just his deception, it's mine, too, because now I'm lying to my kids."

Jenna understood how heavy a secret could be, especially when you carried it for a long time. "I really hope you manage to work out your problems, Andrea."

"We used to be so close. Known each other since we were kids, like you and Greg. Maybe that's the problem. We've been together so long, he never sowed his wild oats."

Jenna had never sowed wild oats either. Neither, to the best of her knowledge, had Greg.

"Have you thought about talking to someone?"

Andrea's eyes filled again. "I've been seeing Greg."

That didn't come as a surprise. Half the island had seen Greg at one time or another. The other half had seen his partner in the practice, Alison.

"I'm glad you're talking to someone."

"Greg is wonderful. You're lucky being married to him." Andrea reached for her purse. "He has this way of talking, sort of quiet but firm. Makes you think there's hope and that you're going to be able to fix whatever the problem is."

That voice hadn't managed to fix the fact that she couldn't get pregnant.

"He's good at what he does." That was true. Greg made a difference to the island. And so did she. Community was important to both of them. Jenna often wondered how her sister could live in a big anonymous city. She knew she wouldn't be happy doing that. With the exception of a few vacations and her time at college, Jenna had lived her whole life here. She'd married Greg in the Old Whaling Church in Edgartown in the presence of half the community. Her oldest friend had made the cake and Lauren had done her makeup. She'd known most of the guests her whole life.

Jenna stood up. "I'll keep an eye on Daisy."

"Thank you. Daisy adores you. You're all she talks about. Mrs. Sullivan said this, Mrs. Sullivan said that."

Thank goodness Mrs. Sullivan hadn't said the *F* word.

"Daisy is smart."

"Too smart sometimes. I'm worried she'll see things I don't want her seeing." Andrea stood up, too. "You're very good at your job, Jenna. You're going to be a wonderful mother when you eventually decide to have children."

Jenna managed to keep her smile in place.

She walked Andrea back to the school gates, promised to keep an eye on Daisy and then made her way back to the classroom.

The wind was biting and most of the islanders were longing for spring. Not Jenna. Spring meant buds on the trees and lambs playing in the fields. Everywhere you looked there was new life. This time last year she'd been sure that by now she'd be pushing a stroller along the streets. Instead she was back in her classroom teaching other people's kids.

Of course it was still possible that spring might be lucky for her, too.

If she and Greg had nonstop sex over the next few weeks she could potentially be pregnant by April or May. That would mean a Christmas baby.

She allowed herself a moment of dreaming, and then snapped out of it.

All she thought about was babies.

Obsess: to worry neurotically or obsessively.

Her obsession had even entered the bedroom. When she and Greg made love she found herself thinking, *Please let me get pregnant.*

Maybe she'd cook a special meal tonight. Open a bottle of wine. Try to relax a little. She could greet him at the door wearing nothing but a smile and hope Mrs. Pardew across the road wasn't looking out the window.

She reached the door of her classroom and winced at the noise that came from inside.

Bracing herself, she pushed open the door and the noise dimmed to a hum.

"Good morning, Mrs. Sullivan." The chorus of voices lifted the cloud that had been hanging over her.

Maybe she didn't have her own children, but she had them. She loved their spontaneity and their innocence, their bright eyes and smiles. She even loved the naughty kids. Like Billy Grant, who was currently standing on his desk, waiting for her reaction.

He was a rebel with a strong sense of adventure and a cavalier attitude to risk. Fortunately no one knew more about that instinct than Jenna.

"Billy, our classroom rule is that we don't stand on desks."

Billy folded his arms but didn't move. "You're not the boss of me."

Jenna arched an eyebrow.

He lasted two seconds and then scrambled off the desk and plopped onto his chair.

Everyone knew that when Mrs. Sullivan gave you *that look* you did what you were supposed to do or you'd be in serious trouble. He made another attempt to deflect blame. "Bradley told me to do it."

"If he told you to jump off a bridge would you do that?" She straightened her shoulders and addressed the whole class. "One of our classroom rules is that we don't stand on the desks."

"Rules are boring," Bradley muttered. "Why do we have to have them?"

So we can break them.

"Bradley wants to know why we have rules," she said. "Who can tell him the answer?"

A sea of hands shot into the air and she picked the girl in the front. Little Stacy Adams, whose dad had recently run off with another man, giving the island enough gossip to feast on for a decade.

"To keep us safe."

"That's right." Jenna smiled. "Some rules are there to protect us." And if you ignored the rules you could be left with a secret and a guilty conscience.

Maybe it was her fault that she wasn't closer to her mother, she thought. She knew things she wasn't supposed to know and that made things awkward.

Keeping that thought to herself, she moved to the front of the class. "Everyone sit in a circle."

There was a mass scramble as they found their places on the floor.

"Will you tell us a story, Mrs. Sullivan?"

"One of your special made-up ones."

As they sat round watching her expectantly, she felt a rush of pride and affection. Winter would soon give way to spring, and spring to summer and then this group of children would be leaving her classroom for the last time.

When they'd arrived in her class, they'd been a raggedy, unruly bunch but now they were a team. Friendships had formed. Some friendships might even last through to adulthood, as hers and Greg had. Some might fracture.

Not all relationships were easy.

She threw herself into her day, moving from story time to math. Unlike some of her colleagues, she loved teaching first graders. They were curious and enthusiastic. They loved coming to school and they loved *her*. From the moment she stepped into the classroom, she was wrapped in warmth and affection.

Most of all she enjoyed seeing the progress they made. They experienced so many firsts.

Usually she lingered in the classroom after the children had gone, tidying up and preparing for the following day, but today she drove straight to her mother's house.

On a cold January day it was foggy and cold and the roads were quiet.

Her mother lived down-island in Edgartown. Ridiculously picturesque with its waterfront and harbor, Edgartown was one of the more populated areas of the island, which was one of the reasons Jenna had chosen to live up-island with its beautiful beaches and spectacular sunsets.

Even in winter when the town was quiet, Jenna preferred

the wildness of her part of the island. Her drive took her past rolling farmland, stone fences and beaches. Wherever you were on the Vineyard, you were never far from the beach. And when you couldn't see the sea, chances were that you could still smell it.

At this time of year she drove easily through Edgartown's narrow streets.

The Captain's House where her mother lived was set right on the waterfront, close to the harbor and the lighthouse. The house had been in her family forever, since Captain William Stewart had seen fit to build his home on what was arguably the best plot of land in the whole of Martha's Vineyard. When her mother's parents had died in an accident, leaving Nancy an orphan at the age of eight, she'd continued to live in the house with her grandmother.

Money had been tight and they'd rented out rooms to cover their costs.

The house was considered historic, and occasionally Nancy would give a private tour to students or history buffs, and talk about the Vineyard's place in the whaling industry. Jenna's father had been heard to say on many an occasion, usually when huddled in his coat in front of a blazing log fire, that because a person was interested in history didn't mean they wanted to experience it firsthand. The antiquated heating system of The Captain's House counted as history as far as Tom was concerned. In the middle of winter there had been many nights when Jenna had crawled into bed with her sister for warmth.

Two years previously the heating and wiring had been replaced as part of an upgrade and modernization.

Jenna had wondered at the time why her mother had waited until after her father had died to do it.

The door was open and Jenna walked through the entryway with its wood paneling and wide-planked floor. There were bookshelves stuffed with books, and more books piled next to them on the floor. Every surface was covered in the possessions and purchases of previous generations.

Her mother was a hoarder. Jenna had never seen her throw a single thing away.

There were items in the house that had belonged to her great-grandmother and were never used. Some of those things were ugly, but still Nancy wouldn't hear of disposing of them.

She considered herself the custodian of the family's heritage.

Jenna knew that an entire bedroom upstairs was filled with her father's things. Trophies he'd won playing golf, his model boat collection, his clothes. Did her mother ever go in there? Did she cry over his things?

She found Nancy in the kitchen, opening mail. "Hi, Mom. I made cakes for your book group. Cute, don't you think?" She removed the lid with a flourish.

"So pretty! Thank you." Nancy took the tin from her and placed it on the table next to the papers. "How was your day?"

For a wild moment Jenna contemplated telling her the truth.

Not pregnant. Feel crap about it. Any chance of a hug?

She couldn't remember when her mother had last hugged her.

"My day was fine." Holding her feelings inside, she walked to the window and stared out across the lawn to the sea. "It's cold out today. Windy." Were they really reduced to talking about the weather?

"How's Greg?"

"He's great." She turned. Was it her imagination or was her mother looking older? The lines around her eyes were more pronounced and her hair seemed to have lost its shine.

Jenna had seen photos of her mother as a young woman. Her features were too bold to qualify as pretty, but she'd been striking and had her own individual style. That style seemed to have deserted her years before. Gone were the colorful outfits that had raised eyebrows on the few occasions she'd picked Jenna up from school. These days she dressed mostly in black and navy, as if life had drained the brightness from her.

Nancy signed a letter and slipped it into an envelope. "He's a special man. It's good to see you settled and happy, Jenna."

The comment struck her as odd. It bordered on the personal, and personal was a land her mother rarely visited.

She almost asked if something was wrong, but decided there was no point, so instead they had a neutral conversation about a plan to build affordable housing and the challenges of maintaining the rural character of the island while managing the increase in summer visitors.

"The school is at capacity. We can't take any more kids without compromising educational standards." Jenna sat down at the table. It had belonged to her great-grandmother and there were scars and gouges in the wood to prove it. Somewhere underneath Jenna knew she would find her name scratched into the wood.

"Any funny classroom stories for me? I could use some light entertainment."

Jenna often regaled her with stories, although she'd

learned to talk about her day without mentioning anything personal about the kids.

Most of the parents would have been horrified to learn how much their six-year-olds could divulge to their first-grade teacher.

She told her mother about the school trip they had planned to the nature reserve, and about the lesson she'd taught on states of matter where the children had made ice cream in the classroom. The idea had been to demonstrate that a liquid could become a solid, but two of the children had managed to cover themselves in cream.

"And Lily Baker made me a gorgeous card." She pulled it out of her bag and passed it across the table. "Don't shake it. It's heavy on the glitter."

"She's back at school?" Her mother slipped her glasses back on so she could look at the card. "I saw her when she was in hospital. Took her a copy of *Paint with Nancy* and some pencils."

Back in the day when her mother had been something of a global name in the art world and there had been much demand for her work, someone had suggested producing upmarket educational material—*In other words a coloring book*, Jenna had said to Lauren—designed to encourage budding artists. The idea was that children would feel they had been given the opportunity to paint with Nancy.

The project had never taken off and boxes of the coloring books had gathered dust in one of the unused rooms in The Captain's House.

"How did you know Lily was in hospital?"

"Her grandmother is in my book group."

"Of course. Yes, Lily had a few days in hospital with a fever. Fully recovered, thank goodness."

They talked for a while and then Jenna went to use the bathroom, but on the way something caught her eye.

"Hey, Mom." She paused and called out to her mother. "What happened to the painting on this wall?" It was a beautiful seascape, painted by her mother early in her career and one of the few that had never been offered for sale. Her mother's career as an artist could be divided into two distinct phases. Her earlier work was light and bright and her later work was stormy and dark. Lauren called it her depressing phase. The missing painting was one of her early works, painted before her mother had hit the big time. Jenna loved the wild swirls of blues and greens.

Surely her mother hadn't sold it?

Her mother emerged from the kitchen. "I—" She stared at the faded space on the wall as if she'd forgotten about it. "I took it down. I thought I might…redecorate."

"Do you want help? I could come over on the weekend."

Her mother didn't hide her alarm. "I don't think so. I still remember the mess you made of the rug when you decided to paint Lauren's room bright blue. I came back from a day at the studio and spent the next two days painting my own house instead of a canvas."

Jenna remembered that incident, too.

Lauren had redecorated her bedroom at least once every three months. Any money she had, she'd spent on interior design magazines. She'd study them, and then use the ideas she liked best, enlisting Jenna to help transform her room to match her latest vision. They'd dragged furniture from one side of the room to another, painted walls and changed fabrics.

On one occasion Jenna, as dreamy as she was clumsy,

had tripped over a tin of blue paint and sent it flowing over the floor.

With her usual artistic flourish, their mother had turned the streaked floor into a smooth surface of ocean blue. Then she'd diluted the color for the walls until the room looked like an aquarium complete with small fish and plants.

Jenna had loved the newly painted room so much she'd taken to sneaking in and sleeping on Lauren's floor, settling herself between a friendly-looking octopus and a seahorse. She and Lauren had giggled and talked long into the night cocooned in their underwater paradise and when her sister had changed her room three months later, Jenna had felt bereft.

It was at least twenty years since the paint spill episode and yet her mother still talked about it as if it had happened yesterday.

"I've improved since then," Jenna said. "I did most of the decorating in my house." But her mother had already walked back into the kitchen and wasn't listening.

Irritated, Jenna used the bathroom and walked back to the kitchen.

Her mother was staring at another set of papers but she quickly pushed them to one side.

"Have you spoken to your sister lately?"

"Last week. I thought I might call tonight, but then I remembered it's Ed's fortieth birthday party. She's booked caterers and a string quartet." Jenna tried to read the papers, but they were upside down. "If she still lived on island I could have loaned her my recorder group. That would have blown everyone's eardrums." She realized her mother wasn't listening. "Mom?"

Her mother gave a start. "Sorry? What did you say?"

"I was talking about Lauren's party. She was nervous something might go wrong."

"Knowing Lauren, it will be perfect. I don't know how she does it all."

Jenna refrained from pointing out that Ed was seriously wealthy and that they could buy in whatever help they needed.

For the past couple of years Lauren had been studying for an interior design qualification, but study was a bed of roses compared with hauling yourself out of bed every day to deal with a bunch of kids with runny noses.

Her sister's life seemed effortless.

"Mack has big exams this summer."

"She'll fly through them, as Lauren did."

"I guess she will." Did her sister have to be so perfect? Much as she loved Lauren, there were days when Jenna could happily kill her. And then she felt guilty feeling that way because as well as being perfect at everything else, Lauren was the perfect sister and always had been.

It wasn't Lauren's fault that her sister couldn't get pregnant.

Feeling empty, Jenna reached for the tin on the table. The book group wasn't going to miss one cake, were they?

She fought an internal battle between want and willpower.

Willpower might have won, but as she went to pull her hand back her mother frowned.

"Are you sure you need that?"

No, she didn't need it. But she wanted it. And dammit if she wanted it, she was going to have it. She was thirty-two years old. She didn't need her mother's permission to eat.

She took a cake from the tin, so annoyed she took a bigger bite than she intended to. Too big. Damn. Her teeth were jammed together so now she couldn't even speak. Instead she chewed slowly, feeling like a python that had swallowed its prey whole.

Her mother went back to sorting papers. "Mack is doing well. Like Lauren, she is very disciplined."

The implication being that she, Jenna, showed no self-discipline at all.

She swallowed.

Finally. In the battle of woman against cupcake she was the victor.

"Good to know."

"Lauren is lucky Mack hasn't turned out to be a wild child like—" her mother waved her hand vaguely "—some people."

"You mean me." Jenna kept her tone light. "Thanks, Mom."

"You have to admit you didn't sit round waiting for trouble to find you. You went out looking for it and you dragged your poor sister into it with you. You, Jenna Elizabeth Stewart, were enough to give any mother gray hairs."

"I've been Sullivan for more than a decade, Mom."

"I know." Nancy's expression softened. "And you are lucky to have that man."

Annoyed: irritated or displeased.

"He's lucky to have me, too."

"I know. But let's be honest—you stopped getting into trouble the day you married Greg." She glanced at the clock. "It will be dark soon. You should probably leave."

"I can drive in the dark, Mom. There's this amazing invention called headlights."

"I don't like you driving in the dark. Remember when you drove the car into the ditch?"

She did remember, but even smashing her head against

the windshield hadn't been as uncomfortable as this stroll down memory lane. "I was twenty-one. My driving has improved since then." Jenna stood up. "But you're right. I should go. I need to stop at the store to pick up some things for dinner. Take care, Mom. Enjoy your book group."

"I will. Thanks for dropping by."

As if she was a stranger, not family.

There were days when Jenna wondered whether the only way to get closer to her mother was to join the book group.

CHAPTER FOUR

Nancy

> *Secret: a fact that is known by only a small number of people, and is not told to anyone else*

AS SOON AS the door slammed behind her daughter, Nancy grabbed her coat.

She'd been so desperate for Jenna to leave, she'd almost bundled her out of the house.

Pushing her arms into the sleeves, she stepped into the garden.

At this time of year it looked sad and tired. Maintaining a coastal garden was always a challenge, and this one was particularly exposed.

The narrow strip of windswept land was all that separated The Captain's House from the sea. She'd seen this view in every season and every mood. Today the surface of the water was smooth, almost glass-like, but she knew it could change in a moment from deceptive calm to boiling anger. Her seafaring ancestors would have told her that you should never trust the sea.

Like humans, she thought. You shouldn't trust them either.

It was trust that had led her to this moment. The moment she'd been dreading.

She'd let everyone down.

She could refuse to answer the door of course. Pretend not to be home. But what would that achieve? It would only postpone the inevitable. And she'd been the one to call him, so not opening the door would be ridiculous.

She'd been terrified he might arrive while Jenna was here, but fortunately she hadn't stayed long and hadn't seemed to notice that Nancy was almost urging her out of the house.

It was one of the few occasions she'd been relieved not to have a particularly close relationship with her daughters.

Nancy would have to tell her the truth eventually, of course, but not yet.

The worse part was the waiting, and yet the ability to wait should have been in her genes. Her great-great-grandmother might have stood in this exact same spot two centuries before while waiting for her husband to return home after two long years at sea. What must she have imagined, thinking of the tall square-rigged ships out there facing mountainous seas and Arctic ice? And how must the captain himself have felt finally returning home after years of battling the elements?

He would have seen the house he'd built and felt pride.

Nancy's cheeks were ice-cold and she realized she was crying. When had she last cried? She couldn't remember. It was as if the relentless wind blowing off the sea had eroded her tough outer layer and exposed all her vulnerabilities. She was crumbling and she wasn't sure she had the strength to handle what was coming next.

At some point over the past sixty-seven years she was supposed to have accumulated knowledge and wisdom, but right now she felt like a small child, lost and alone. Dread was a lurch in the pit of your stomach, a cold chill on your skin. It was the ground shifting beneath your feet like the deck of a ship in a squall until you wanted to cling to something to steady yourself.

She closed her hand round the wood of the Adirondack chair that had been a birthday gift from her daughters. In the spring and summer months she sat out here with her morning coffee, watching the boats, the gulls and the swell of the tide.

Now, on a cold January afternoon with the dark closing in, it was too cold for sitting. Already her hands were chilled, the tips of her fingers numb. She should have worn gloves but she'd only intended to step outside for a moment. One breath of air to hopefully trigger a burst of inspiration that had so far eluded her.

She desperately wanted someone to tell her what to do. Someone to hold her and tell her everything was going to be all right.

Pathetic.

There was no one. The responsibility was hers.

"Nancy!"

Nancy saw her neighbor Alice easing her bulk through the garden gate. Two bad hips and a love of doughnuts had added enough padding to her small frame to make walking even short distances a challenge.

They'd been neighbors their whole lives and friends for almost as long.

Alice was breathless by the time she crossed the lawn to where Nancy was standing.

"I saw Jenna's car. Does that mean you told her?"

"No."

"Lord above, what did the two of you talk about for an hour?" Alice slipped her arm through Nancy's, as she'd always done when they used to walk to school together.

Nancy wanted to pull away. She'd thought she wanted support, but now she realized she didn't.

"I don't know. Sometimes I wonder how it's possible to talk for an hour and say nothing."

"You'll have to tell her eventually. Our children think we don't have lives, that's the trouble. All my Marion talks about are the children. Does she think nothing happens in my life? My *Rosa rugosas* may not interest her, but they're important to me."

Nancy and Alice shared a love of gardening. Before Nancy had employed Ben, the two women had helped each other in the garden and shared knowledge on which plants could withstand the harsh island weather and sea spray.

"I wasn't there for my girls," she said, "so how can I ask them to be there for me?"

"Nancy Lilian Stewart, would you listen to yourself? When you say things like that after all the sacrifices you made, I swear I want to slap you. You should tell them everything."

Everything?

Even Alice didn't know everything. "It's too late to change the way things are."

"That's nonsense."

"I feel like a failure."

"You give it all you've got. What you've got isn't enough, that's all. Not because you're a failure, but because life can deliver blows that would fell a mountain."

They stood side by side in silence.

"I've failed this place."

"It's a house, Nancy."

"Not to me." The Captain's House was a responsibility, handed down to her by her family. It was the place where she'd grown up and the place she'd fallen in love. The house was large, but Tom had filled it with his personality and warmth. He'd cast light on dark corners and his laughter had blown away dust and cobwebs. Both their children had been born there. And it wasn't only the house that held memories, it was the contents. Every room held pieces passed down through the family. Those pieces had meaning. Those pieces mattered. She was the custodian. A poor custodian, as it turned out.

Alice nudged her. "I'm looking forward to book group."

Despite everything, Nancy smiled. "Why? You never read the book."

"I know. I come for the cake and companionship. Two of the best things in life. You're a good friend, Nancy Stewart, always have been."

Nancy said nothing.

Alice sighed. "You were there for me when I lost my Adam and when my mama died. If I could solve this problem for you, I would and so would anyone in our little book group. Sometimes those women are so annoying I could strangle them with my bare hands, but I also know they'd drop everything to help if they knew about your troubles."

Nancy felt a thickening in her throat. "I should get on. I have things to do. Thanks for coming round."

"I didn't come round. I squeezed through your fence, same way I did when I was four years old, but I'll go if you want me to. You know where I am."

Nancy stayed lost in thought long after Alice had squeezed her way back through the fence.

There were so many decisions to make. So many things to handle.

So many regrets.

She turned and looked back at her home.

The white clapboard house had been built in 1860 and had been in her family ever since.

She knew every shingle and every pane of glass.

This house had seen a lot, and so had she.

Her great-great-grandfather had been captain of a whaling vessel, a master mariner of vast experience who'd held ultimate command of the ship. By all accounts he'd been a difficult man. She knew there were those who thought she'd inherited that trait.

In her own way she was a captain, too, only her vessel was her family. And she couldn't shake the feeling that she'd driven the ship onto the rocks.

What was left? Tom was gone. Her two children no longer needed her and she'd stopped hoping that their relationship could be different. That didn't stop her worrying about them.

She'd worried when Lauren had chosen to marry Ed and move to England instead of taking up her college place. It had seemed so out of character. But love did strange things to people. Nancy had often wondered if Lauren had been pregnant when she'd married Ed, but they seemed happy, so what did it matter?

Her younger daughter had caused her more anxiety. Jenna had bounced through life with an almost exhausting enthusiasm. Growing up, Jenna had dragged Lauren into all sorts of scrapes, but the two of them had somehow survived and Nancy suspected that was down to her eldest daughter, who had always watched over her sister.

She heard the sound of a car and then the crunch of footsteps.

With a last look at the sea, she walked back toward the house. Every step was an effort. She felt as if the house was watching her with accusing eyes. She smelled the sea, felt panic close over her head and wondered if this was how it felt to drown.

She stepped through the door and saw the place as a stranger might, battered and battle weary, revealing every scar and wound.

The rooms were crammed full of furniture, ornaments, books, old maps.

Nancy couldn't bring herself to throw anything away.

Some of the windows were rotten, the paintwork in the entryway was chipped and there was a large empty space on the wall where she'd removed that damn seascape.

She'd told Jenna she'd taken it down so she could decorate. The truth was she loathed that painting. Perhaps it would be more accurate to say she loathed what it represented. She would have burned it if it hadn't been for the fact it might still have a purpose.

She opened the door and looked at the man standing there. She had to tilt her head and look up because he topped six feet and dominated her doorway.

She'd first spoken to him five years before on what could, without drama or exaggeration, be described as the worst night of her life. Those years had left their mark on her. Not, it seemed, on him.

She had no idea how old he was, but she would have guessed midthirties.

His eyes were a cool blue and shadowed by secrets. His mouth, well shaped and firm, rarely curved into a smile. His jaw was dark with stubble and the sweater he wore had probably been deep blue at some point but had faded to a washed gray hue.

Had she really expected him to show up in a suit and tie? No. He looked exactly the way she'd expected him to look. Why would he shave before knocking on her door? He wasn't the type of man who was remotely interested in social conventions or the opinions of others. He lived life according to his own rules and that, as it turned out, was lucky for her because five years ago he'd helped her when no one else would.

She felt a pang of envy. What would her life look like now if she'd been more like him? If she'd been braver?

"Thank you for coming."

It was ironic that he should be the one to help her out of her current situation.

She needed him, and yet at the same time she hated him for taking from her the one thing she had left in the world. And truthfully she had no idea how he would respond to what she was about to say. He was unpredictable, a man you could never be sure of.

She almost laughed aloud. Was there a man alive you could be sure of?

"Mrs. Stewart." His voice was somewhere between the rough, sexy drawl of a whiskey drinker and the low growl of a jungle cat. It occurred to her that if that voice hadn't been attached to a man she'd grown to trust, it might have left her feeling uneasy, as would those narrow watchful eyes.

"Thank you for coming. It was good of you."

"I was surprised to get your call. I thought it might be a mistake." His handshake was firm but that didn't surprise her. It had been his physical strength, among other things, that had saved the both of them that night.

"No mistake." The mistakes, she thought, had been made long before. "You'd better come in. There's something I need to say to you."

CHAPTER FIVE

Lauren

> *Party: a social gathering, for pleasure,*
> *often held as a celebration*

LAUREN CHECKED HER list and made a final sweep of the house.

She knew the place looked good.

She'd poured her interest in interior design into her own home, and while Mack was in school she learned trade skills such as paint effects and upholstery. She filled notebooks with photographs and sketches and shopped for fabric and objects. Gradually she'd transformed their London home into an elegant space perfect for family living but also for entertaining.

Occasionally friends asked for her advice on decorating and Lauren was always happy to help. She had an eye for space and color and could see potential in the most run-down, tired property. It wasn't luck or hard work that gave her the ability to see what others didn't, it was an artistic talent no doubt inherited from her mother. Possibly the only trait she'd inherited from her mother.

And finally she had a qualification and could start taking on paying clients.

Her home was the best advertisement for her skills and abilities, and tonight at Ed's party there would be people who might potentially give her business.

She'd already decided to set up her own company but had yet to decide on a name.

City Chic?

Urban Chic?

She took a final glance round the living room, satisfied that everything was exactly as it should be.

She heard the front door slam, signifying Mack's return from school, and unconsciously braced herself.

Her daughter strolled into the room. Mack was tall and did everything in her power to disguise that fact. She was at that age where anything that drew attention was considered embarrassing and to be avoided at all costs, so she slouched to make herself appear smaller.

Lauren had green eyes, but Mack's were blue. Her hair, even with hints of pink blending in with honey and caramel, was her best feature.

Lauren had a sudden vision of Mack lying in her crib asleep, then holding up chubby arms as an adorable toddler.

"Did you shorten your skirt?"

Noticing her mother, Mack tugged her headphones away from her ears. "What?"

"Did you shorten your skirt?" Immediately she regretted making that the first thing she said.

"No. I grew. It happens. I could stop eating, but then you'd nag me about that, too." Mack opened the fridge and stared into it as if something in there had personally offended her. "There's nothing in here."

How could a fridge full of food be "nothing"?

"The caterers are setting up. There are bagels." Lauren opened her mouth to tell her not to keep the fridge door open, and then closed it again. Did she nag? "How was your day?"

"I spent it at school. Enough said." Mack split a bagel and toasted it.

"I had coffee with Ruth and Helen today. They mentioned an ancestry project you're working on. Sounds interesting."

"Interesting?" Mack spread cream cheese on the bagel. "I guess that's one word for it."

What had happened to her eager, enthusiastic daughter?

"Do you need help? You know our ancestors on my side of the family were whaling captains? Martha's Vineyard played an important role in the whaling industry. Nantucket mostly provided the ships, but the Vineyard provided the captains and crews and other support." Seeing that Mack was barely engaged in the conversation, Lauren stopped. She knew she was trying too hard. Maybe she should make it more personal. "Edgartown, where Grams lives, was one of the most important ports on the coast. The Captain's House was built in the nineteenth century. Your grandparents spent a lot of time restoring it—" She broke off, aware that she'd lost her audience. She might as well have been having a conversation with the freezer.

Mack carried on eating, unresponsive.

Lauren slid onto the stool next to her. "Did something happen today?"

"No."

Lauren felt a rush of frustration, and mingled in with the stress of it was sadness because she remembered days when Mack would come running in from school, all smiles, desperate to share something that had happened during the day. *Look, Mommy, look at this.*

Those days had gone.

"Mrs. Hallam called yesterday."

"Yeah? I bet the conversation was thrilling." Mack was careless, but Lauren saw her daughter's cheeks flush.

"She's concerned about you. About your grades. She wants us to set up a meeting."

"Grades. *That's* what this is about?"

"This?"

"When you hijack me in the kitchen, I know there's something. I don't know why you don't come right out with it." Mack put the knife down on the counter, smearing grease.

Lauren sat on her hands to stop herself from snatching the knife up and wiping up the mess. "I didn't 'hijack' you. I want you to know you can talk to me, that's all."

"No, what you want is for me to talk to you whether I want to or not about a topic of your choice. Not the same thing."

Parenting a teenager was like navigating a treacherous swamp. You took a step and hoped you'd plant your foot on solid ground, but it was equally likely you might find yourself sucked under.

"I'm worried about you, Mack. Not speaking up in class? You talk more than anyone I know. And you're smart, and yet your grades are dropping."

"I'm bored, okay? I'm sick of English. And history. What use are those? Why doesn't my school teach computer coding or something interesting and useful that might actually lead to a job?"

Lauren kept calm. "Maybe we can find you a weekend class on computing if that's what you'd like. But school is important, too. And studying. Our choices have consequences."

"Yeah, that's right." Mack gave her a hard look. "They do."

Something about the way her daughter was staring at her didn't feel right.

"Mack—"

Mack slid off the stool and slung her schoolbag over her shoulder. "Are we done here? Because I have a ton of homework."

"We'll talk about this another time."

"Great. Something to look forward to."

Lauren thought, *I don't have the patience for this.* "Guests are arriving at eight. Dad will be home around seven, so I thought we could have a private celebration before the party."

"I have to study. And we both know he won't be home by seven. He never is."

"He's not going to work late on the day of his party." She said it with more conviction than she felt and Mack shrugged.

"Whatever." She sauntered off with an indifference and nonchalance that Lauren could never have managed to achieve at any age, certainly not sixteen.

One teenage girl. How hard could it be to handle one teenage girl?

Lauren went upstairs to change and put on her makeup and tried not to think about the time Mack would have sat in the middle of the bed, watching her mother with hungry, admiring eyes.

It seemed that idolizing your mother had an expiration date.

Before leaving the bedroom she checked her reflection in the full-length mirror.

The dress was new and flattered her slender frame. She was the same size she'd been at twenty. Four times a week without fail she went running. She also did yoga and Pilates and was careful what she ate.

It was important to always have a plan and stick to it. She wished Mack could see that.

She tried to ignore the voice in her head that reminded her what she'd been like at sixteen.

She needed to focus on the party.

Of course the one thing you did need at a party to celebrate a fortieth birthday was the person whose birthday it was, and by seven thirty there was still no sign of Edward.

"Told you." Mack wandered past wearing a pair of skinny jeans that clung and a pair of heavy boots that Ed said made her look like a construction worker.

Don't say a word, Lauren. Not a word.

"Dad probably got caught up at the office." But as soon as Mack vanished into the den to watch a movie, Lauren pulled out her phone and sent Ed a quick text.

Are you on your way?

The doorbell rang and she felt a rush of relief. Maybe he'd forgotten his key.

But no, it was the string quartet arriving early.

She let them in, showed them where to set up and walked back to the kitchen, where the caterers seemed to have everything under control.

The champagne was chilling. The glasses were ready. The canapés were in the oven. Everything was perfect.

The door sounded again and this time when Lauren opened it she saw her mother-in-law standing there.

Maybe not completely perfect.

If there was one accessory she would never choose to have at a party, it was her mother-in-law, but how could she not invite her to her only son's fortieth birthday party?

"Gwen! Wonderful to see you." Lauren always overdid the greeting to compensate for her true feelings. On one occasion she'd leaned forward to kiss Gwen, but the other woman had turned her head sharply and Lauren had ended up pecking her on the neck like a drunken chicken.

Still, Gwen loved her son and that was a quality Lauren could respect.

Gwen was clutching a parcel. "Where's my precious boy?"

He's forty, Lauren thought. *Not a boy.*

"He's on his way home."

Gwen handed over her coat. "He's still at work? On his *birthday*?"

Her tone stung like a jellyfish and Lauren felt her face burn.

Gwen seemed to hold Lauren personally responsible for the fact her son worked long hours. Not that she expressed her disapproval directly, but the pursed lips, sighs and eye rolls conveyed her message with perfect clarity.

Ed was fond of saying that his mother spoke fluent body language.

Privately Lauren had often wondered whether she would have married Ed had she met Gwen first.

"Come and talk to Mack, I know she'll be thrilled to see

you. She's in the TV room." Lauren took the stairs down to the TV room and Gwen followed.

"She's watching American TV?" She said it in the same tone she might have said *taking drugs and having sex?*

Why couldn't she find a single nice thing to say?

Nice dress, Lauren.

House is looking beautiful.

Did you arrange all this yourself?

My son is so lucky to be married to you.

"I don't know what she's watching."

"She could be watching porn. I read that all teenagers watch porn."

"She's not watching porn, Gwen." *Ed, if you're not home in the next five minutes, I'm going to kill you.*

Mack appeared in the doorway. "Mom, that American porn film you suggested I watch is—" She broke off and gave a dazzling smile. "Hi, Nana, didn't see you there."

Gwen swayed and clutched at the wall to steady herself.

Lauren had an inconvenient urge to laugh. There had been a time when she definitely would have laughed, but she'd worked hard to suppress that side of herself. Unfortunately it seemed determined to make a reappearance.

She didn't dare catch Mack's eye, although since Gwen already thought she was the world's worst parent, she probably couldn't sink any lower in the approval ratings.

"Mack, can you come upstairs and help greet people?"

The way Mack sighed you would have thought Lauren had asked her to donate a kidney.

"Can't you and Dad do it?"

"Dad isn't home yet." How could he be late tonight of all nights? As she kept listening for the sound of his key in the door, her irritation became tinged with anxiety. It wasn't like him to be late when there was a reason to be home, and it wasn't like him not to answer his phone, but so far he hadn't responded to a single one of her texts. Maybe his battery had died. "I'd appreciate help."

"Sure. That would be awesome, Mom."

Lauren winced. Gwen hated *mom*, and her daughter knew it.

There was a gleam in Mack's eyes and for a moment it felt like old times when they'd shared a joke.

And then the doorbell rang, announcing the first of their guests, and the moment was gone. Lauren opened the door to their neighbors who were armed with bottles of champagne and balloons with the number forty emblazoned in swirling writing.

The rest of the guests arrived in a steady stream. The string quartet fought valiantly to be heard above the sound of laughter and conversation. Champagne flutes clinked together and sparkled under the lights. The house hummed with celebration. Only one thing was missing.

Ed.

By nine o'clock irritation had given way to anxiety.

She'd left eight messages on Ed's phone, each one more desperate. Their conversation of that morning kept going round in her head.

She's not the problem.

Did the "problem" have something to do with the reason he was late?

An image inserted itself into her head. Ed, with his pants down, pumping into an unknown girl on his desk. *Why did she have to think of that now?* She pressed her fingers to her forehead and squeezed her eyes shut to block it out.

She was wondering about the etiquette of cutting a birthday cake when the birthday boy wasn't present, when the doorbell rang again.

All the guests had arrived, so it had to be Ed.

Weak with relief, she tugged open the door and saw two police officers standing there.

Now what?

There had been a spate of car vandalism in the street, and the Wright family, who lived four doors down, had been burgled the summer before, but generally this was a quiet, safe area of London loved by residents and tourists alike. She'd certainly never had anyone in uniform standing on her doorstep. "Mrs. Hudson?"

"Yes." Lauren smiled her best hostess smile. "How can I help?"

The younger of the two officers looked sick, as if he was suddenly wishing he'd picked any job except this one, and she knew then that this wasn't about a neighborhood crime.

Her legs turned to liquid. "What has happened?"

The older policewoman took charge, her eyes kind. "Do you have somewhere quiet we can talk?"

Quiet? Lauren gave a hysterical laugh. "I have thirty guests in the house, all celebrating my husband's birthday, so no, not really. I'm waiting for him to come home."

One look at their faces told her everything she needed to know.

Ed wouldn't be coming home tonight, or any other night. He wasn't going to eat his cake, nor toast his birthday with champagne.

Ed wasn't late.

He was gone.

CHAPTER SIX

Jenna

> *Envy: the desire to have for oneself*
> *something possessed by another.*

ON HER QUEST to make a romantic dinner, Jenna stopped at the store on her way home and bought food. While she was there, she paused by the magazines and glanced at the covers.

"How to Get a Bikini Body."

"Beat Those Cravings."

Judging from the covers, she wasn't the only one with a problem.

She glanced over her shoulder to check no one was looking and dropped two magazines into her basket.

"Jenna? *Jenna!* I thought it was you."

Jenna turned the magazines over. "Hi, Sylvia."

She'd been at school with Sylvia, but their lives had diverged. Jenna had gone off to college and Sylvia had stayed on island and proceeded to pop out children as if she was on a personal mission to increase the number of year-rounders. Personally Jenna was relieved when the summer people left. The roads were clearer, the beaches were empty and you didn't have to stand in line for ages at the bakery.

She put field greens, tomatoes and bell peppers into her basket. "How are the children?" Why had she asked that question? The Dentons had six kids. She could potentially be here for hours.

She only half listened as Sylvia talked about the stress of ferrying the children to and from piano lessons, swimming lessons, art class and football.

I'd like that type of stress, Jenna thought.

Sylvia was still talking. "And poor Kaley was in hospital with her asthma again. Your mom was so kind. Visited every day. She's great with the kids. And she loves babies. Isn't it about time you and Greg started a family?" The way Sylvia said it suggested that producing babies was something Jenna might have forgotten to do in the day-to-day pressure of living their lives.

Jenna fingered an overripe tomato, wondering whether the pleasure of pulping it against Sylvia's perfect white shirt would outweigh the inevitable fallout.

Probably not.

She dropped the tomato into her basket and made a vague comment about being busy.

"I must get home." She grabbed a bottle of wine. She probably shouldn't be drinking, but she wasn't pregnant, so why not? Greg wanted her to relax, didn't he? She'd rather drink wine than go to yoga, and after her earlier encounter with her mother she needed it.

"My Alice loves those stories you read to them, *Adventures with My Sister*. Could you tell me the author? Is it a series? I'm going to buy those books for her birthday. Her favorite is the story about them freeing the lobsters."

"They're not published," Jenna said. "I make them up. I used to tell stories to my niece when she was little and somehow I carried on doing it with my class."

"No way! Really? Well you should be writing books, not teaching. Where do you get all those wonderful ideas? You must have quite the imagination."

"Thank you."

That and a colorful childhood to draw on for inspiration.

"If you wrote those stories down, the whole class would buy them, that's for sure."

Write the stories down.

Why hadn't she ever thought of that?

Author: a person who composes a book, article or other written work.

"By the way—" Sylvia's tone was casual "—I was driving through Edgartown half an hour ago and I happened to see a pickup truck parked outside your mother's house. Guess who was driving it? Scott Rhodes." She lowered her voice, as if the mere mention of that name might be enough to get her arrested. "He looked as bad and dangerous as ever. I swear the man never smiles. What is his problem? I didn't know he knew your mom."

She hadn't known that either. Thoughts of a new life as an author flew from her head.

What was he doing calling on her mother? And if Sylvia had seen him half an hour ago then that meant Jenna must have missed him by minutes.

Scott Rhodes?

She remembered the summer she'd first seen him. He'd been stripped to the waist and across the powerful bulk of his shoulders she'd seen the unmistakable mark of a tattoo. That tattoo had fascinated her. Her mother wouldn't even allow her to have her ears pierced.

Scott didn't seem to care what other people thought and that, to Jenna, had been the coolest thing of all.

She was aware that she cared far too much. She was a people pleaser, but in a small island community that ran on goodwill, she didn't know how to be any other way.

Scott Rhodes, on the other hand, answered to no one but himself and she envied that. Even looking at him made her feel as if she was doing something she shouldn't, as if by stepping into his space you made a statement about yourself and who you were. Danger by association. She expected to feel her mother's hand close over her shoulder any moment.

Not that she'd been *that* interested. She was in love with Greg. Greg, who she knew so well he almost seemed like an extension of her. Greg, who smiled almost all the time.

Scott Rhodes rarely smiled. It was as if he and life were on opposing sides.

She'd been studying his muscles and deeply tanned chest with rapt attention when he glanced up and caught her looking. There was no smile, no wink, no suggestive gaze. Nothing. His face was inscrutable.

Scott worked at the boatyard and did the occasional carpentry job for people. He slept on his boat, anchored offshore, as if ready to sail away at a moment's notice.

Why would Scott Rhodes be visiting her mother?

Hi, Mom, I hear you had the devil on your doorstep...

Aware that Sylvia was waiting for a response, Jenna

shrugged. "My mother knows everyone. And she still plays a role in the yachting community. Scott knows boats."

Sylvia nodded. "That's probably it." It was obvious that she didn't think that was the reason at all, and neither did Jenna.

It nagged at her as she drove the short distance home, enjoying the last of the weak daylight.

The cottage she shared with Greg between Chilmark and the fishing village of Menemsha had a view of the sea from the upstairs windows and a little garden that frothed with blooms in the summer months.

It was, in her opinion, the perfect place to raise a family.

Of course, she didn't have a family to raise.

Maybe they ought to get a dog.

She pushed that thought aside, along with all the questions she had about Scott Rhodes, and parked her car.

In the summer this part of the island teemed with tourists, but in the winter months you were more likely to see eiders congregating near the jetties, riding the current and sheltering behind fishing boats. The sky was cold and threatening and the wind managed to find any gaps in clothing.

She loved the place whatever the season, whether she was wrapped up in layers in the winter, or eating a warm lobster roll on the beach in the summer watching the sun go down.

Today there was no sun.

Jenna fumbled her way into the house, grateful for the warmth.

She lit the wood-burning stove in the living room, unpacked the shopping and made a casserole. Beef was Greg's favorite, but she'd read somewhere that red meat reduced fertility, so she used chicken.

While the casserole simmered in the oven, she chopped vegetables.

Then she tidied the cottage, took a shower and changed into a wool dress she'd bought to wear at Christmas two years before. It had looked good on her then. Now, it clung in places it wasn't supposed to cling. She picked up one of the magazines she'd bought and stared gloomily at the slim, toned blonde dressed in leggings and a crop top.

"You are so airbrushed." She flung the magazine to one side and picked up the other one.

This one recommended a diet of raw food interspersed with long periods of fasting.

"If I fast, I faint." What she really needed was the Comfort Eater's Diet. Or the Stressed While Trying for a Baby Diet.

In the meantime she needed to order control underwear.

She stuffed both magazines under the sofa and noticed the notepad on the coffee table that Greg had been using to make a shopping list.

Maybe she *should* write down some of her stories. Why not?

She tore out a clean page and sketched two little girls with a goat, but the goat ended up looking like a pig.

She tapped its bloated stomach. "What you need is a bikini diet."

Throwing down the pen, she slid the paper under the sofa along with the magazines. Maybe she'd think about it another time. Or maybe her stories were better told round a campfire than written down.

Her dress felt uncomfortably tight, so she walked to the bedroom to choose something else.

She pulled on her favorite pair of stretchy jeans and a sweater Greg had bought for her birthday. It was a pretty shade of blue, shot through with silvery thread, and it fell soft and loose to the top of her thighs, concealing all evidence of her dietary transgressions.

She was checking the casserole when she heard the sound of his key in the door.

"Something smells good." Greg walked into the house and dropped his keys on the table. "How's my green-eyed mermaid?"

He'd called her that since the summer she turned eight years old when she'd barely left the sea.

"Mermaids don't have curly hair and freckles." She smiled as he came up behind her and kissed her on the neck.

"You shouldn't stereotype mermaids. You look gorgeous. Is that sweater new?"

"You bought it for me."

"I have great taste. How was your mother? Are you in need of therapy?" He slid his arms round her and she sucked in her stomach to make herself thinner. She liked the fact that he kissed her before he even hung up his coat. Andrea was right—she was lucky to have Greg. So why didn't that feel like enough?

What was wrong with her?

"I decided on the sort of therapy you can pour into a glass. It was that or chocolate chip ice cream."

"That's what I call a dilemma." Greg let go of her and hung up his coat. "Walk me through your decision-making process."

"Wine is made from grapes and grapes are fruit, which makes it one of your five a day. So it's healthy." She handed him a glass of wine. "And if I'm not pregnant, I might as well drink. How was your day?"

"If I tell you my day was good are you going to snatch this glass from my hand?"

She grinned. "No, because by the time I've finished whining you're going to need it."

"Wine for whine. Sounds like a reasonable deal." Greg took a mouthful of wine. "I'm braced. Hit me with it. What was today's gem?"

"Nothing new. She reminded me about the painting incident and held me personally responsible for her gray hair."

"Her gray hair makes her look distinguished. She should be thanking you."

"She praised you, of course." She lifted her glass in a mock toast. "You, Greg Sullivan, are the all-conquering hero. A gladiator among men. A knight in shining armor. I was lucky you were there to save me from my wicked ways."

"She said that?"

"Not in so many words, but she was thinking it."

Greg put the wine down. "Did you tell her you were feeling down about the whole baby thing?"

"No. Our conversations are an exchange of facts."

His gaze was steady. "You're unhappy. That's a fact."

"Not those sorts of facts. Everyone else seems able to talk to my mother, but not me."

Why did it matter? She had Greg. Greg had always been easy to talk to. When people talked about marriage as something that had to be "worked at" she didn't understand what they meant. She and Greg just *were*. They fitted like hand in glove or foot in shoe. They didn't need to work at anything.

They ate dinner at the table in their cozy kitchen while the winter wind lashed at the house and rattled the windows. After they'd finished the meal and cleared up, they curled up on the sofa.

Jenna topped up Greg's wineglass and he raised an eyebrow.

"Are you trying to get me drunk?"

"I'm a wild child, remember? I'm living down to my

reputation." She slid off her shoes, curled her legs under her and moved closer, pressing her body against the solid strength of his.

Unlike her, his body hadn't changed much in the past decade. Greg believed exercise helped control mood and set an example to the community by spending time in the gym and running on the beach. As a result his body was as good as it had been at eighteen.

She thought about what Andrea had said earlier.

Would her marriage to Greg be different if they'd had other relationships? "Do you ever wish you'd sowed your wild oats?"

"Excuse me?" He shifted so he could look at her. "You want me to become a farmer?"

She laughed and took another sip of wine. "You're not a morning person. You'd be a terrible farmer."

"So why the 'wild oats' question?"

"No reason. Ignore me. Let's go to bed."

He looked at her quizzically. "It's not the right time of the month for you to get pregnant, is it?"

She felt a flash of guilt, and that guilt was intensified by the knowledge that she'd done those calculations, too. "It's not the right time for me to get pregnant, but that's not the only reason to have sex."

"Isn't it?"

"What's that supposed to mean?"

"Only that lately that seems to be the only reason you ever want to climb between the sheets with me." He put his wineglass down and then took her face in his hands and kissed her.

Greg had been the only guy she'd ever kissed if you didn't count that one session behind the bike sheds with

Will Jones, which she didn't because that had been part of a dare. Sex had changed over time. Being with him didn't give her the same dizzying thrill she'd had when they'd first gotten together—*Take that, Mom. Saint Greg and I had sex before we were married*—but in many ways it was better. Familiar. Intimate.

As he deepened the kiss, his other arm came round her waist. She shifted closer to him and felt something hard dig into her hip. "Is that your phone?"

"No, it's my giant penis and the reason you married me." He nuzzled her neck but she shoved him away and put her glass down on the table next to his.

"Wait! Greg—why is it in your pocket?"

"My penis?"

"Your phone!"

He sighed. "Because that's where I always carry my phone. Where else would it be?"

"Anywhere else! You're supposed to be keeping your testicles cool and your phone out of your pocket. We agreed."

Greg swore under his breath and released her. "This is crazy, Jenna. You're obsessed."

"I'm focused. Focused is good. Focused gets things done."

"Getting pregnant is all you think about. When was the last time we talked about something *not* sex or baby related? And I don't count talking about your mother."

"Over dinner." She smiled triumphantly. "We talked about decorating the upstairs bedroom."

"Because you want to turn it into a nursery, even though you're not pregnant."

Oops. "Last week we had a long conversation about politics."

"And the impact it might have on any children we have."

That was true.

"It's possible I might be a little overfocused on pregnancy. It's what happens when you really want something you can't have. Like being on a diet. If you can't eat a chocolate brownie, all you think about is eating the chocolate brownie. You dream about brownies. Brownies become your life. You're a psychologist. You're supposed to know this!"

Greg breathed out slowly. "Honey, if you could just—"

"Do *not* tell me to relax, Greg. And don't call me 'honey' in that tone. It drives me batshit crazy."

"I know, but Jenna you really *do* need to relax. If something is taking over your mind, then the answer is to focus on other things. The way to forget the brownie is to think about something else."

"Cupcakes?"

His expression was both amused and exasperated. "One of my clients is opening a new yoga studio in Oak Bluffs. Maybe you should go. You might find it calming."

"I might find it annoying." She thought about the girl in the magazine. "It will be full of serene people with perfect figures who are all in control of their lives. I'd have to kill them, and that wouldn't be calming for anyone."

Greg retrieved his wine. "Okay, no yoga. Tai chi? Kickboxing? Book group?"

"My mother runs the book group, and given that the last book I searched for was *How Not to Kill Your Mother*, I don't think I'd be welcomed as a member."

"Go to a different book group. Start your own. Do *something*. Anything to take your mind off babies."

"You're saying you don't want babies?"

"I'm not saying that." He finished his wine. "I do want babies, but I don't think all this angst is going to help."

She remembered the way he'd looked when she'd glanced out of the window. Thoroughly despondent.

She was about to ask him how he felt about the whole thing when her phone rang.

She ignored it.

Of course Greg wanted babies. Didn't he?

He glanced from her to the phone. "Aren't you going to answer that?"

"This conversation is more important than my phone." Her phone stopped ringing but started again a moment later and Greg reached down to pick it up.

"It's Lauren."

Jenna stared at him stupidly. "What?"

"Your sister." He thrust the phone at her. "We can wish Ed a happy birthday."

Why did she have the feeling he was relieved their conversation had been interrupted?

"But isn't it the middle of the night in London?"

"It was obviously a great party." He rose to his feet and walked toward the door.

"Where are you going?"

He smiled. A normal Greg type of smile. "To pack. If you're going to talk to your sister, it means I have time to take a six-month sabbatical. Your conversations aren't exactly brief."

"We're not *that* bad."

"No, you're right. A two-week vacation should cover it. In the meantime I'll make us coffee." Greg walked to the kitchen and Jenna watched him go.

Everything was going to be okay. Of course it was.

She was married to Greg, and Greg knew how to handle every situation.

Who needed yoga when they were married to their very own therapist?

Picking up her wineglass and stretching her legs out on the sofa, she settled in to have a long chat with her sister. It was true that one call last month had reached the two-hour mark, but she and Lauren lived thousands of miles apart! What did he expect? And she was pleased Lauren had called. She'd be able to tell her about the pregnancy test. "Hi, Lauren. Happy birthday to Ed! How was the party? I was going to call you tomorrow. Did our gift arrive?" Because she was expecting everything to be perfect, it took her a couple of minutes to absorb what her sister was saying. "What? Lauren, I can hardly hear you—are you crying?" She sat up suddenly, spilling her wine over her jeans. "Say that again!"

By the time Jenna ended the call she was in shock.

Her hand was shaking so badly she almost dropped her phone.

Greg walked back into the room and put two mugs of coffee on the table. "Did you lose the signal or something?"

"No."

"Then why so quick? I was going to speak to Ed."

"You can't." Her lips felt strange, as if they didn't want to move. "Ed is—" She broke off and he looked at her.

"Ed is what?"

Jenna felt shaky and strange. Her eyes filled. "He's dead. Today was his fortieth birthday. He was found at his desk by one of the cleaners. They think it must have been his heart. My poor sister." She remembered the agony in her sister's voice and didn't even try to hold back the tears. How would Lauren live without Ed? What would she do? "I have to go to her." She felt her sister's loss as keenly as if it were her own.

Looking shaken, Greg took the glass from her hand and tugged her to her feet. "I'll call the airline while you pack."

Her brain was moving in slow motion. "We can't— I can't—" She couldn't think straight. "There's school, and—"

"I'll call them. I've got this."

"What about the money? We already decided we couldn't afford to go away in the summer."

"We'll figure it out. Some things are more important than money."

She didn't argue. There was no way she wasn't going to be with her sister.

Only hours before she'd been envying Lauren, and now her life was shattered.

It was unbelievable. Unfair.

And to think she'd been about to off-load her own problems.

Jenna sleepwalked to the bedroom and pulled out her suitcase. Without thinking about what she was packing, she stuffed random clothes into it. All she could think about was her sister, her big sister, who had always been there for her through thick and thin.

There was nothing her sister didn't know about her.

Not a single thing.

"It's all booked." Greg appeared in the doorway, his phone in one hand and his credit card in the other. "Take sweaters. And a coat. It's cold in England. And an umbrella, because it will probably be raining. And don't forget to charge your phone so I can call you."

"What? Oh yes." She pushed some thick socks into the case and paused, helpless and more than a little scared. She felt inadequate. "What do I do, Greg? What is the right thing to say to someone who has lost a husband? I wish you were coming with me."

But they both knew he couldn't. He had people counting on him, and no one who could cover for him.

"I'll call you every night. And you can text me. I promise not to give my phone to Pamela."

It seemed like a lifetime ago that they'd laughed at that.

Jenna glanced round her bedroom and tried to work out what she'd forgotten. Lauren would have made a list. She probably had a list already on her laptop entitled "for emergency travel." Everything would be checked off. Red ticks for the outward journey, blue ticks for the return journey.

Jenna didn't have a list to tick.

She was the disorganized one. Lauren was the perfect one.

Except that her perfect sister's perfect life was no longer perfect.

CHAPTER SEVEN

Lauren

Widow: a woman whose spouse has died

SHE'D NEVER EXPECTED to fall in love when she was eighteen. That hadn't been part of her plan. She'd had her life mapped out in her head. She was going to college, and after that she'd get a job in New York City. She was going to soak up bright lights and busy streets and learn everything she could about design until she was ready to start her own business.

That had always been her dream.

And then she'd met him.

Their relationship started with a single look. Until that moment she hadn't realized so much could be conveyed without speech. It was more than interest. There was a connection.

It was the summer before she left for college and she was spending the long, hot humid months doing what all the other local teenagers did, namely working hard to make money for the winter. She had three jobs, one of which included bussing tables at a seafood restaurant.

She was clearing one of the tables on the sunny deck, counting the hours until she could go home, when a man strolled up to the takeout window.

Something about the way he moved caught her attention. He had a quiet way about him, an understated confidence that was lacking in many of the boys her age who were wrestling awkwardly with their own identity.

He was wearing black jeans and a black T-shirt and his cap was pulled down over his eyes.

As he pulled a sheaf of notes out of his pocket, his gaze settled on Lauren.

She had long legs and blond hair. She was used to boys looking at her. They'd reached an age where everything was about sex, who had "done it" and who hadn't.

All her closest friends were having sex and boasting of their experiences. Cassie had lost her virginity in a field near Chilmark and had to explain away poison oak to her parents. Kelly's first experience had been on the hood of her dad's Cadillac in a deserted parking lot.

Because she didn't want to expose her most private fears, Lauren pretended she'd had sex, too. She doubted she was the only one, but her reasons for holding off were probably different from most.

She was afraid she might have a phobia. The thought of sex made her heart race and her palms grow sweaty. That wasn't normal, was it? It was all the other girls talked about, so she assumed it was supposed to be exciting, not terrifying.

Because she didn't trust her reactions, there was no way

she was experimenting with anyone from her school. What if she freaked out and humiliated herself? It would be all over the island in hours that Lauren Stewart was frigid.

This man was different. He was older for a start, and a stranger. Definitely not a Vineyarder. Nor did he look like a tourist. His fingers were stained with oil and his work boots were scuffed. A seasonal worker, she decided, and wondered why her brain was asking a thousand questions about him.

She had no idea how long the moment would have lasted or what might have been the outcome because her imagination chose that moment to conjure up a disturbingly vivid image of what it might be like to be kissed by him. It was real enough to knock the air from her lungs and trigger a curl of heat low in her belly, a reaction she'd never had before. As a result, she stumbled into a chair and knocked over a bottle of beer.

Her face burned with humiliation and by the time she'd cleared up the mess and dared to glance over in his direction, he was gone.

He hadn't smiled at her or nodded. Hadn't acknowledged her in any way. But she knew that if someone had asked him, he would have been able to describe her in detail.

She wasn't sure whether to be relieved or terrified to discover she was in fact capable of experiencing the same feelings as her peers.

Until she'd laid eyes on the unsmiling man in black, she hadn't felt an urge to find out if she really did have a problem. She'd even wondered if she'd go through life without ever having sex.

But suddenly it was all she could think about.

She was still working out how to discreetly discover his identity when she saw him again.

She'd crept out of the house late at night and gone for a walk on the beach.

There was only one other person there, and she'd known even from a distance that it was him.

She'd had a choice to make. She could step forward, or she could step back.

"THANK YOU ALL for being here." Her voice echoed around the cavernous space.

A week before she'd been planning Ed's birthday party. Now she was speaking at his funeral.

She focused on the stained-glass window at the back of the church because that was easier than staring at the people seated in rows. It was bitterly cold. Lauren couldn't stop shivering.

The night of the birthday party was a blur in her mind. She remembered the police stepping into the house, the sound of Gwen wailing, gawping guests slinking from the house muttering condolences instead of birthday greetings.

And now she was supposed to say something meaningful when none of it held any meaning.

"I first met Ed when I was eighteen and I knew right away that he was the perfect man for me."

That was true, wasn't it? The fact that there was one box he didn't tick on the list of ideal attributes for a life partner didn't mean he wasn't perfect.

"We met by chance on the beach in Martha's Vineyard where I grew up, and we immediately had a connection."

I was crying. Ed was drunk.

We were both brokenhearted.

Both of us in love, but not with each other.

Choices, she'd discovered, had consequences.

She stared hard at the floor, terrified that her sleep-deprived brain might confuse her speech with her thoughts. What if she made a mistake and said the wrong thing aloud?

What if, for once in her life, she told the truth?

"Ed and I knew we were going to be together forever." Except that Ed had broken that promise and died. *Why?* He watched his weight and exercised. People like him didn't die slumped over their desks. She felt cheated. Angry. Devastated. It took a sob from someone in the front row to remind her she was supposed to be talking. "It was romantic."

It hadn't been romantic at all.

It had been practical. Sensible. A decision made by two people who favored planning over impulse.

She stared at the extravagant display of lilies at the back of the church and knew she'd never be able to have lilies in the house again.

"Ed proposed to me on the beach at sunset."

There were murmurs of approval and sympathy from the mourners who were listening avidly. She wondered what they'd say if she told them the truth.

There had been no proposal. At least, not in the traditional sense of the word.

Ed had flung an arm round her.

You're in trouble. I'm in trouble. We both chose badly, which is what happens when you let your emotions make decisions. Let's get married. I like you. You like me. That's a better basis for marriage than love. Love is for poets and artists. Getting married because of love is like building your house on quicksand. You never know when the whole thing is going to collapse.

She hadn't been able to disagree with that.

She'd been emotionally numb and frightened about the future.

Lauren remembered Ed hugging her, telling her it was going to be okay, that they'd rescue each other, and the ache in her chest was almost unbearable.

They'd done that. They'd rescued each other. But now he'd abandoned her.

What was she going to do without him?

They'd had a deal—

"We married right away—" Her voice broke slightly and she cleared her throat. "When Mack was born I remember thinking our family was complete. Perfect. Our life together was perfect."

She glanced at Mack, who was seated next to Jenna, her features a frozen mask. Lauren's heart broke for her. She'd done everything she could to give Mack a stable, secure family life but she hadn't been able to save her from this.

She choked out a few more words. How great Ed was as a provider, what a great friend he was and how much he would be missed.

Standing at the front of the church, trying not to look at the sea of faces, she felt lonelier than she ever had in her life before.

No one had ever told her that it was possible to be an adult and still feel as terrified as a child.

She had a sudden yearning for home, for the community she'd grown up in.

When her father had died, Lauren had flown home and stayed three weeks. The fridge had been so full of food, they hadn't had to worry about shopping or cooking for the entire duration of her stay. Casseroles had appeared in their kitchen, along with homemade cake. Neighbors made a support list. Her mother was asked to write down anything that needed doing from mowing the lawn to emptying the trash and the tasks were divided between everyone. They'd felt enveloped by the community.

Lauren didn't feel enveloped. She felt alone and exposed.

She sensed movement and saw her sister reach out and take Mack's hand.

Jenna, who had taken the first flight she could find so she could be by her side. She was wearing a navy coat and her hair was curling rebelliously in response to relentless English rain. Jenna, whose love and loyalty was never in question.

And Lauren remembered that she wasn't alone.

She felt a rush of gratitude. Having her sister there helped her to stumble through the last few lines of her speech without blurting out anything scandalous.

She kept thinking about that last conversation she'd had with Ed.

She's not the problem.

What exactly had he meant by that? She didn't know, and now she never would.

Saying her own silent farewell, she walked back to her seat.

She felt Jenna slide her hand into hers, as she'd done when they were growing up.

Sisters always stick together.

Lauren tried not to think about how she'd cope once Jenna left. Maybe she could persuade her to move in. There were schools in London. Jenna could teach anywhere and Greg wouldn't struggle to find work either. Almost everyone she knew needed a therapist, even if they weren't aware of it themselves.

But she knew Jenna would never leave Martha's Vineyard.

Maybe she'd go back for longer this summer. In the past they'd been restricted by Ed's need to be in London, but Ed didn't need to be anywhere ever again. And if Greg was working then perhaps she, Jenna and Mack could spend some time together.

She was about to lean across and tell Mack she didn't have to speak if she didn't want to when her daughter rose to her feet.

She walked to the front of the church. For once her back was straight, as if she'd finally accepted her height.

Since the night of the party she'd been even less communicative.

Lauren told herself it was natural for Mack to be withdrawn. She'd lost her father. Lauren had already found a grief counselor who specialized in teenagers. She intended to call her as soon as the funeral was over, and she couldn't wait for that moment to come.

Lauren willed her daughter to have the strength to get through the next few minutes.

There was an expectant silence broken only by the occasional cough and a muffled sob.

Mack said nothing.

The silence stretched for so long that people began to fidget. Expectation turned to impatience.

Lauren felt a rush of fierce protectiveness.

Why had she allowed Mack to do this? She was sixteen years old. It was too much.

She was about to stride up to the front of the church like a mother hen reclaiming her chick, when the chick opened its mouth.

"I'm supposed to say a few words about my father."

Mack's voice was clear and steady, cutting through the tense atmosphere of the church.

Lauren relaxed.

Her daughter had aced drama. She could do this.

"The problem is," Mack said, "I don't exactly know who my father is. You'd have to ask my mother about that. All I know for sure is that it wasn't Ed."

CHAPTER EIGHT

Jenna

Startle: to be, or cause to be, surprised or frightened

"WHERE DO YOU keep mugs?" Jenna prowled around Lauren's shiny perfect kitchen. Every cabinet was neat and ordered. She tried not to think about her kitchen at home, where assorted plates nestled alongside mismatched mugs hand painted by the children she taught. Her mugs said things like World's Best Teacher and Superwoman. It was like drinking her coffee with subtitles.

Lauren's mugs were white and they all matched. Not a chip. Not a crack. Not a single accolade emblazoned on the side. Her home looked like something out of one of those glossy magazines she'd been addicted to growing up.

Jenna glanced at her sister. She'd changed into black yoga pants and a black roll-neck sweater. Her hair was twisted into a severe knot at the back of her head and the pallor of her skin emphasized the dark hollows under her eyes.

Her sister could have taken a role in a horror movie without bothering with makeup, Jenna thought. She suspected Lauren spent most of the night crying, although during the day she managed to hold it together.

After Mack's revelation, the gathering had been more farce than funeral. Her confession had shaken the atmosphere so dramatically the resulting shock waves should have been measurable on the Richter scale.

Everyone's mouths had been open, with the exception of Mack's. With hindsight, Jenna wished her niece had closed hers sooner.

At first she'd assumed it was grief talking, but then she'd seen her sister's frozen expression and had second thoughts. She knew that look. It was the same look Lauren had worn as a child when they'd been caught doing something they shouldn't, like the time William Foster had reported them for letting his chickens out.

Jenna considered what she knew about her sister's relationship.

Lauren and Ed had met on the beach and married a month later. It had been a whirlwind, but everyone who met Ed found it easy to understand why Lauren had fallen in love with him so nobody questioned it too deeply.

When Mack had been born barely nine months later, Jenna had wondered if Lauren had already been pregnant when she and Ed had married, but so what?

Now she felt like one of the kids in her class doing a basic math puzzle. *If Jane has four apples and Mary takes one away, how many apples does Jane have left?*

Could she have had an affair? No. Lauren had already been pregnant when she'd come back from her honeymoon.

How could Ed not be Mack's father?

Like Mack and the rest of the people at the funeral, Jenna wanted to know the answer to the key question.

Lauren hadn't spoken a word since they'd left the funeral.

Jenna wanted to call Greg for advice, but since when had she needed Greg's advice on how to talk to her sister, someone she knew almost as well as she knew herself?

She removed two perfect matching mugs from the cabinet, boiled water and made hot tea.

That was what the British did in a crisis, wasn't it? They drank tea. Lauren had lived here for sixteen years, which made her as close to British as it was possible to be without being born here. "Was Mack telling the truth?" She pushed aside a stack of papers and put the two mugs on the table.

Lauren stared at the tea but didn't touch it. "Yes."

Jenna sat down next to her and took her hand. "Why didn't you tell me?"

"I didn't tell anyone."

I'm not anyone. I'm your sister. "Since when do we not talk to each other?"

"I wanted to protect my daughter. I always planned to tell her, but I was waiting until I was sure she was old enough to understand. I wanted her to grow up in a secure, stable home knowing she was loved. I didn't want her to have doubts or fears. I didn't want her to be—" She lifted bruised, exhausted eyes to Jenna. An ocean of memories flowed between them.

"You didn't want her to be like us."

Lauren's eyes glistened. "You're probably the only person who can understand."

Jenna felt sweat prickle at the back of her neck. "Do you want to talk about it?"

Please don't let her want to talk about it.

"No. It's not relevant."

It was funny, Jenna thought, how they'd both managed to ignore the past. It was like being in the room with a wild animal and hoping that if you didn't look at it, it wouldn't bite you.

"If it's impacting the choices you make, then it's relevant."

"Didn't it impact yours?"

Jenna felt her cheeks grow hot. "This is about you, not me. You kept a major secret from your husband and daughter."

"No, I didn't. Ed agreed we should wait until Mack was older. We were planning on sitting her down and talking to her soon."

"Wait—you're saying Ed *knew*?"

"From the beginning."

"And he married you in spite of that?"

"He married me because of that." Lauren let go of Jenna's hand and reached for her tea. "It's complicated."

No kidding.

Jenna was still getting her head round the fact there was a huge part of her sister's life she knew nothing about. "Did you tell him everything? He also knew about—"

"No. Not that. Just about Mack. And she's all that matters now. She's lost her dad, and she can't even grieve properly because she's so confused." Lauren's voice wobbled and she glanced toward the door that Mack had slammed between them the moment they'd arrived back at the house.

"Is she going to be okay? I need you to tell me she's going to be okay."

"She's going to be okay," Jenna said, hoping it was true. "It will take time of course, but she'll figure it out and so will you. And you have each other."

"Right now I don't think she finds that a comfort. She's so mad at me." Lauren blew her nose. "She's obviously known Ed wasn't her father for a while. It explains so much. She's been difficult lately. Moody. I thought there might be something she wasn't telling me—" She glanced at Jenna, who shrugged.

"No one is better qualified to recognize the signs of secret keeping than the Stewart sisters, right? Do you know how she found out?"

"She was doing an ancestry project at school as part of her history coursework. I guess it must have been to do with that. I haven't worked out the details yet. But why didn't she talk to me? Why not ask me?"

"Er—did we ever talk to Mom about things?"

"No, but we didn't talk to Mom about anything. Mack and I talked about everything."

Not quite everything, Jenna thought.

"Did Ed adopt Mack?"

Lauren stared at her tea. "No. We talked about it, but at the beginning it would have meant—" she drew in a breath "—contacting the father, and neither of us wanted to do that. Later it would have meant visits from social workers and they would have insisted we tell her right away. We always planned to tell her, but we wanted to do it when we felt she was able to handle it. And I didn't want that to be when she was young. Also, there was Ed's Mom."

"What about his mom?"

Lauren shook her head. "It doesn't matter."

"She didn't know about Mack?"

"Ed didn't want her to know." Lauren toyed with her mug. "He knew there was no way Gwen would accept him raising another man's child."

Jenna thought about the woman she'd met at the funeral. "Is she always like that?"

Lauren finally took a sip of tea. "Like what?"

"Scary. Fierce. Dragon-like." *Unsympathetic.* She was shocked by the unkindness shown toward her sister. "Don't take any notice of those things she said. She's distraught, and people say things they don't mean in those circumstances. Looking for someone to blame is part of the process." She was pretty sure she'd heard Greg say that at some point.

"She doesn't like me."

"What did you ever do to offend her? Before today, I mean—"

"I married her son."

"That made you her daughter-in-law, not the enemy."

"I wasn't what she wanted for Ed."

"But you're gorgeous, kind, loyal—"

"—and American. It was like Edward and Mrs. Simpson all over again." Lauren put the mug down. "Ed was with someone before me. She was the one his mother wanted him to marry."

"But presumably he didn't want to marry her."

"In fact he did, but she— That situation was complicated, too." Lauren sounded exhausted. "She was there today. Caroline Fordyce Smith. She sat next to Gwen in the church."

The whole event was a blur in Jenna's mind. "The blonde with the dead bird on her head?"

Lauren gave a faint smile. "I think it was supposed to be a hat."

"Yeah? Because if that landed on my head, I'd call pest control. Ed had a narrow escape." Relieved to see her sister come close to a smile, Jenna plowed on. "Why did it end?"

There was a long silence.

"Ed can't have kids." Lauren's eyes filled and she shook her head. "I keep doing that. I keep talking about him in the present tense and then I realize he's gone."

Jenna didn't know what to say, so she simply reached out and took her sister's hand.

Lauren blinked back the tears. "No one knows that. Apart from Caroline of course. Ed didn't want people to know. I'm only telling you because he's gone—" her voice juddered "—and because I trust you. His mom doesn't know. Mack doesn't know either. She used to ask for a baby brother or sister, but of course that was never going to happen."

"Why couldn't he have kids?" Jenna felt cold. The mere mention of someone not being able to have children made her feel unsettled.

"It was something to do with an accident he had in college."

Jenna relaxed slightly. That wasn't something that could apply to her. She could cross it off the list.

"So Dead Bird Caroline dumped him?"

"Yes. And said some pretty awful things. I guess she was upset and disappointed, too, but her words stayed with Ed. His mother thinks they broke up because Ed met me, and Ed didn't want to tell her the truth. He hated the fact that he wouldn't ever be a father." Lauren gripped her mug. "I think for a lot of the time he pretended Mack was his."

"Why were they sitting together in church? She doesn't know Caroline dumped him?"

"No. They've stayed friends. Bizarre."

What a mess. "I know you're upset about what happened, but people will soon forget about it."

"Forget about the fact that Ed isn't Mack's father? I don't think so."

"It's none of their business. The only people that truly matter here are you and Mack."

Lauren rubbed her forehead with her fingers. "I'm being selfish talking about me the whole time. How are you? You thought you might be pregnant—"

Jenna felt as if someone had delivered a light kick to her stomach. "Not this time."

Lauren looked stricken. "I'm sorry—"

"It's not a big deal." She caught her sister's incredulous look and shrugged. "So it's a big deal. Let's talk about it another time. Right now the priority is you, and poor Mack. You should go to her. Does she drink tea?" Mack was more British than American, wasn't she? "You could take her one."

The mention of Mack seemed to rouse Lauren. "I should try to talk to her again, but no tea. She'd probably throw it at me." She let out a long breath. "I thought the day Ed died was the worst day of my life, but this one is coming close."

Jenna didn't know what to say. "I feel helpless, but I'm here for you."

"I'm grateful to you for coming." Lauren gave a faint smile. "If I could have chosen my sister, I would have chosen you."

Hearing those words from their childhood tugged at Jenna's heart. "We'll get through this."

"I hope so." Lauren didn't move. "There's something else. That morning before he left for work, Ed was acting weird. We were talking about Mack, and he said, 'She's not the problem.' The implication being that we had another problem."

"What?"

Lauren shook her head. "Not a clue."

"Forget it. I'm sure it was nothing." Her phone buzzed and Jenna grabbed it, expecting to see Greg's number. "Oh joy—it's Mom."

"I can't talk to her now." Lauren stood up so suddenly she knocked her mug flying. Tea spilled over the table and soaked the papers.

"I've got this—" Used to dealing with overenthusiastic children, Jenna scooped up the papers and threw a cloth onto the spreading puddle.

She shook the papers. "Is this something important?" She squinted at the blurred ink. "Looks like a list."

"I made it the night Ed died. I didn't want to forget anything."

Her sister had been making lists the night her husband died? "This is four pages long."

"There's a lot to think about when someone dies."

Jenna put the papers down away from the wet patch. "If you forget something I doubt anyone will blame you." The phone was still ringing and Jenna leaned across and muted it. "I'll call her later."

Lauren sent her a look of gratitude. "Thanks. She offered to come, but I put her off. I told her it was too far. I—I couldn't handle it. Pathetic, I know."

"You don't have to explain to me." Their mother was great in a crisis, providing that crisis wasn't within her own family. "I'll call her when I've psyched myself up. Do you have anything stronger than tea? Wine? If I have to talk to Mom about something serious, I need to be drunk or medicated."

Lauren didn't seem to hear her. She sleepwalked her way across the kitchen as if someone had programmed her via remote control.

"I'm going to check on Mack. I know she doesn't want to talk to me right now, but she has to have questions."

They all had questions, such as *who is Mack's father if it isn't Ed?*

Lauren paused in the doorway. "I'm glad you came."

"Me, too." Jenna felt a rush of love for her sister. "We'll figure all this out, I promise. Come home with me."

"To the Vineyard? I couldn't do that. My life is here now. And Mack has school and her friends—"

"Is that really why?"

"What do you mean?"

Jenna shrugged. "I always had the feeling there was a reason you spent so little time there." And it had hurt her feelings that her sister, who seemed to have limitless funds, hadn't come home more often. She hadn't come over for Greg's thirtieth birthday party or to attend the wedding of one of her school friends. It was as if something on the island had scared her away.

Now Jenna was wondering if it had something to do with Mack's real father.

"Ed was always busy."

But you could have come without him. "Sure. Forget it."

Lauren's hand tightened on the door. "Don't tell Mom about Mack. Not yet. I need to work out how to handle it."

"No one is better at keeping secrets than I am. You should know that."

But maybe, Jenna thought, they'd learned to keep their secrets a little too well.

She waited until Lauren was halfway up the stairs before calling Greg.

Late evening in London meant late afternoon on the Vineyard. He was probably finishing up with clients, but she felt a desperate need to talk to him. If there was one thing guaranteed to make you appreciate your husband, it was watching another woman lose hers.

Gratitude: a feeling of thankfulness or appreciation.

"Hey, sweetheart." The sound of his voice was as welcome as a cool breeze on a summer's day.

"Hey, you. I love you."

"Love you, too. How's it going?"

"Awful." She gave him an update, skipping the part about Ed not being able to have kids.

"You didn't know? But you two talk about everything."

"Apparently not." And it shouldn't bother her, should it? A person didn't have to know *every* single little thing about another person, even when that person was a sister. "Lauren is talking to Mack now."

"That won't be an easy conversation. Not exactly the kind of information you want to learn when you're heading into adulthood."

"Lauren is a great mom. Whatever you may think of the decision, she did what she genuinely believed was best for Mack." As she jumped to the defense of her sister, she wondered what she would have done in the same situation.

"No one is questioning her intentions. But discovering your parentage isn't what you thought it was is a tough thing to deal with when a child is as old as Mack."

Jenna felt a rush of irritation. "Could you quit being a

therapist for five minutes? This is my sister we're talking about. My family. Lauren had her reasons."

And she knew what those reasons were.

Cold washed over her skin.

Dammit, Lauren, why didn't you talk to me?

But it sounded as if Ed hadn't wanted to tell Mack either.

Feeling the sudden kick of jet lag, she toed off her shoes and went to stretch out on the sofa and then decided the place was too pristine to encourage lounging and slipped her shoes back on. She thought about her own comfortable living room with the sofa handed down from Greg's parents and the dining table they'd had from his grandmother. She felt a wave of homesickness so strong that for a moment she couldn't breathe. "Sorry to be irritable. I miss you. I wish you were here. I wasn't expecting to fly into a storm of drama."

"I'm the one who is sorry. It's been a long day. I guess I forgot to switch off the therapist when I walked through the door. You'll handle this, honey, I know you will."

Her relationship with Greg wasn't something she examined closely or even thought about. Other people said she was lucky and she knew she was, but she didn't wake up in the morning and think *I'm married to Greg Sullivan, lucky me.* But tonight she was thinking it. Tonight what they had felt precious, as if she'd had a piece of china in her house for years and only now understood its true worth.

She tightened her hand on the phone and glanced quickly toward the door to check she was still alone. She felt guilty thinking about her own problems when her sister was going through hell. "I'm sorry if I seem obsessed about this whole baby thing. I promise to relax more. When I'm home I'll go to yoga. Buy me a mindfulness book. I promise not to throw it at you."

They talked a little longer and then said their goodbyes.

Jenna wandered into the hallway and glanced up the stairs where Lauren had vanished an hour before.

It shook her to acknowledge that she and Lauren weren't as close as they'd once been.

But maybe that was inevitable.

She walked back into the living room and stared into the street. Her sister's house was big, but it was still hemmed in by other houses. The house across from them was digging into the basement and there were construction noises and clouds of dust from dawn to dusk.

She'd forgotten what it was like to be in a city, to live with the thunder of noise, the crush of people and so much traffic that crossing the road felt like an extreme sport.

It reminded her of her first few months of college in Boston. At first it had felt exciting to be away from the island, but over time the gloss had faded and she'd missed the Vineyard. She'd missed being able to walk to the beach and chat to the fishermen as they brought in their catch. She'd missed bumping into people she knew when she went to buy a loaf of bread. She missed sunrises and salt air, the feel of sand under her feet and the breeze lifting her hair. Most of all she'd missed Greg, who had gone to college in New York City. It was as if someone had wrenched part of her away.

Was that how Lauren was feeling without Ed?

All it had taken was a few days in her sister's company for her to realize how wrong she'd been to envy her.

You never really knew what was going on in someone else's life.

She, of all people, should have remembered that.

CHAPTER NINE

Mack

*Humiliate: to say or do something which makes
someone feel ashamed or stupid*

I HATE MY stupid life.

Mack lay in the dark, wishing the house would collapse
and bury her in the rubble.

She hadn't meant to blurt it out like that. She'd meant to
say a few nice things about her dad—*Ed? What was she
even supposed to call him?*—and then sit down, but in the
end what came out of her mouth hadn't been what was in
her head. Epic fail. And now she didn't know what to do.
She'd cried herself dry and she didn't know if she was crying for herself or Ed.

She knew she was acting loopy.

She'd felt loopy ever since she'd discovered her dad
wasn't her dad.

That had been the worst day of her life. She'd started to shake like a little kid on her first day at kindergarten. She'd lived in terror of someone finding out and now she'd made the nightmare come true.

Abigail, Phoebe and Tracy had been in the back row at the funeral, supposedly to give her moral support. And David had been there, too. David, from the neighboring boys' school, who she'd been exchanging looks with for a while. Boys didn't usually look at her, but she'd been quietly hoping he might ask her to the movies or something. She'd even tried making herself more "girly," but it had all been for nothing.

It would be round the whole school that Mackenzie didn't know who her dad was. A few of the kids in her class had divorced parents, but at least they knew who they were. No one had identity issues. She'd walk into class and everyone would stare at her. She'd be on display, like some sort of museum exhibit.

An idea formed in her head. Wild, desperate, but possible.

She could run away.

No one could stare at her if she wasn't there, could they? She didn't have to go to school ever again. She had some savings and if she wore a push-up bra and a ton of makeup she could pass for eighteen. She'd get a job. Would she need her passport for that? Her birth certificate?

With a groan, she rolled onto her back and stared at the ceiling. It was still covered in those tiny fluorescent stars her mother had put there when Mack was six. Bookshelves lined the wall above her bed so she could reach out her hand and grab one whenever she couldn't sleep, which was depressingly often. Closest to her was her tattered copy of *Moby-Dick* and next to that *The Old Man and the Sea*. Her

mother wanted to box them up and put them in the attic but
Mack couldn't bear to be parted from them.

She didn't much like English or writing essays, but she
did love reading and those books connected her to her past.
They made her feel as if she belonged somewhere. Not London, where the traffic and the people crammed together so
tightly that there were days when it felt as if there was no
oxygen left, but somewhere by the sea where there was air
and room to breathe. Her favorite place in the world was
The Captain's House on Martha's Vineyard, where her other
grandmother lived. The house had a room on the top floor
where Mack always slept. If you half closed your eyes you
could imagine you were on a ship.

Maybe she could get a job on a boat and spend months
away at sea like her ancestors.

Not whaling like the old days, she'd never do anything
that cruel, but anything that meant not being back on land
for at least a year.

If she got really lucky she'd be shipwrecked like Robinson Crusoe.

Anything was more appealing than going back to school
on Monday.

She wished she'd never done that stupid ancestry project; then she never would have dug out her birth certificate
and found out the truth.

Instead of a name where her father's name should have
been, there was a line. A *line*. Like she'd appeared from nowhere or something.

She'd stared at it for at least an hour, sure there was some
mistake.

Her parents must have filled it out wrong. Some stupid
admin person must have had a hearing problem. *Hello? Why*

*has someone drawn a line? The father's name is Edward
Hudson. Hudson, like the river.*

She'd bombarded a search engine with questions.

What does it mean when it's not your dad's name on your
birth certificate?

Can your birth certificate be wrong?

She'd wanted there to be an alternative explanation, something simple, but the simple truth was she had no idea who
her father was and her birth certificate was no help at all.

Every time she'd looked at it she'd felt a hot flush of embarrassment.

And almost as bad as not knowing the identity of her father was the thought of her mother having sex with someone. If there was one thing no teenager ever wanted to think
about it was parents having sex.

She shook her head, trying to get rid of the vision.

She'd always been close to her mother, but now she
couldn't even be in a room with her without imagining her
with a man. It was hideous.

She'd worried that her dad might find out and leave. Then
she'd be shuttled back and forth between warring parents
like a couple of the kids in her class.

But now Ed was never going to find out.

He was never coming back.

It felt as if someone had thrown her emotions into a
blender. One portion of misery, two of fear, one of anger and
a handful of freshly picked resentment. Pulse on full power
until the whole thing is so mixed up you can't identify any

of it and there you have it—one head case smoothie. Drink
in one gulp and wonder if you'll ever feel normal again.

Her phone lit up and she saw Phoebe's name pop up.

Phoebe the dreamer. Phoebe who, if she knew what Mack
was going through, would probably say, *Are you sure you're
not a secret princess?*

Did her real dad even know she existed? Was he suddenly
going to turn up and try to yank her into a whole new life?
She wanted to know who he was and what happened next,
but it was obvious her mother was freaking so there was no
chance of a proper conversation and honestly Mack wasn't
sure she wanted to talk about it. What if the truth was even
worse? Maybe her dad was an ax murderer or something.
Maybe he'd chopped up old ladies or messed with little kids.

Maybe she'd rather have a line on her birth certificate.

She heard a soft tap on the door and quickly stuffed her
phone under the pillow and rolled onto her side, keeping
her back to the room.

"Mack?"

At least her mom was talking again. When she'd gone
silent in the church, Mack had been scared she'd killed her
or something.

She heard the door open, then footsteps. The bed dipped
as her mother sat down next to her. She smoothed her hair
as she'd always done when Mack was little and it made her
feel like crying again. She was so mad at her mom and yet
she'd never needed her more.

Whenever Mack had a problem, her mom was the person she talked to. She never freaked like all the other moms
she knew. Phoebe's mother lectured her. Abigail's mother
shrieked, sometimes when Mack was there, which was *oh-so*
embarrassing. Her mom listened. They'd always laughed

together. Because her mother was younger than the other moms, sometimes she'd felt more like an older sister. And her friends had all envied her, although not anymore.

But this time her mother *was* the problem. She'd lied. How could Mack ever trust her again?

She jerked her head away from the soothing touch even though part of her desperately wanted it.

"Talk to me, Mack. You're very upset and I understand that."

"You're the one who should be talking." She felt physically sick. What if she threw up in her bed like a little kid?

"Could you at least turn round so I can see your face?"

"Why?" Mack turned, the movement sending her hair whipping across the face. "Checking for something familiar? Trying to work out who my father is?" She hadn't thought it was possible to feel worse than she already did but she saw the hurt in her mother's eyes and realized it was possible.

How could you be mad at someone and feel guilty all at the same time?

Her mother took a deep breath. "I don't need to work anything out. I know exactly who your father is, Mack."

CHAPTER TEN

Lauren

Despair: total loss of hope

LAUREN STARED DOWN at her daughter. How was she supposed to handle this?

This wasn't how today was supposed to turn out.

She'd had a plan for the funeral. Forty-six carefully laid-out points on her list, all with a red tick next to them. Nowhere on that list had been "Tell Mack about her real father."

She'd always planned to do it when the time was right, and that time wasn't now. Mack was hurt and confused, which was the very thing she'd tried to avoid.

She hadn't even had a chance to process her own emotions and now she had to switch off her own feelings so that she could concentrate on those of her daughter. She had to be a mother, not a bereaved wife. A better mother than she'd been up until now. How, when she'd tried so hard to get it right, could it have gone so wrong?

"We always intended to tell you, but we were waiting for the best time."

Mack shot upright. Her mascara had smeared under her eyes and her hair stood on end. "The best time was *a long time ago*."

"Maybe. I don't know. I wanted you to grow up feeling secure and confident. We were waiting for you to be old enough to understand before we told you. Ed was your dad in every way that mattered. I didn't mean for you to find out this way."

"Find out what? That you had an affair? That's *disgusting*."

It had been life changing. On the rare occasions she allowed herself to remember, she could still feel the touch of his hands and the warmth of his mouth. The press of sand against her naked, desperate flesh. When she was with him, she'd felt the electrifying thrill of being alive.

"I didn't have an affair. That's not what happened. I was always faithful to your f—to Ed."

"I can count! No matter how you add it up, you were expecting me when you married Ed."

"Yes," Lauren said. "I was."

"So, what? You had sex with another man on your honeymoon? Ugh."

Lauren clasped her hands in her lap to try to disguise the fact that her fingers were shaking. She hadn't slept for a week. She spent her nights crying by herself, shocked by her own grief. She hadn't known a human being was capable of losing so much water. During the day she mostly held it together but it required such an effort she couldn't touch food. Her head felt as if it was stuffed with wool and somehow in this state she had to have the most difficult conversation of her life. She could barely find any words, let alone the right ones. "That wasn't what happened."

"Then what? You tripped and fell on a guy and you were like, oops, I got pregnant? *What?*"

Thinking about it was one of her banned pastimes. It was all too easy to start thinking, *What if?* But now she was not only going to have to think about it, she was going to have to talk about it, and not only with Mack.

"Before I met Ed, I was—" she wondered how much to say "—in love with someone."

"You're kidding." Mack's eyes flew wide with that teenage incredulity that emerged whenever parents revealed themselves to be remotely human. "Who?"

Did she really have to talk about this? What sort of example would she be setting for her daughter? "He was someone—unsuitable."

"What does that even mean?"

"He was older than me. More experienced." Which wasn't hard, because she'd had no experience at all. "Not the settling-down type. He lived for the moment. He loved boats and the sea, so sometimes he'd skipper a boat for the tourists. And he built boats. He was good with his hands." Very good with his hands. She remembered watching him working on the deck of a boat, sanding down planks while wearing nothing but a pair of board shorts. She'd never seen anyone like him before. She'd been unable to drag her gaze away from his body. Wide shoulders pumped with muscle and gleaming with sweat. Dark curls of hair that covered his chest. Powerful biceps that flexed when he worked. Looking at him had made her think of sex in a way that left her skin hot and prickly. And then he'd noticed her standing on the dock and given her a long look that had stolen her breath. "Sometimes he'd spend the day on the beach surfing. He lived on a boat—" she cleared her throat "—sometimes one that belonged to someone else and he didn't have permission to use. If the owner caught him, he'd sleep on the beach. He wasn't big on responsibility." It was the understatement of the century.

"Whoa—" Mack's eyes were round. "So you're saying you hooked up with a bad boy?"

It was odd what impressed a teenager.

"I wouldn't exactly say—" She reflected on the monumentally uncomfortable reality of having to confess to one's mistakes to an impressionable teenage daughter. *Do as I say, don't do as I do.* "We didn't— I don't know how to describe it."

Mack's mouth was open. "But you're perfect," she blurted out and Lauren gave a humorless laugh.

"I am so far from perfect, you have no idea."

"How did you meet him?"

"He came into the café where I was working."

"And you got talking?"

"No, not that first time."

It had been more than sixteen years and yet she could still remember the way she'd felt that day. The delicious thrill. The intoxicating excitement. The incredible high that came from knowing he'd noticed *her*.

"And then you hooked up. Did Grams know?"

"No."

"You were scared of what she'd say?"

"I didn't talk to Grams much. Not the way you and I do."

Or used to. She knew now why Mack had changed over-night.

Mack looped her arms round her knees. Her face was pale. "How long did it last?"

"The whole summer before I went to college."

It had been the best summer of her life. The summer against which all other happy times that followed would be compared and fall short. It had taken her years to realize that none of it had been real. That even if their relationship had somehow lasted, it wouldn't have looked the way it had then.

"And when Grams finally found out, she freaked?"

"I never talked about it, I never brought him home and she never saw us together." She saw Mack's mouth drop open. "I know, I'm a hypocrite because I expect you to talk to me about everything. I want you to feel you can. But I didn't feel that way with Grams."

"You loved him?"

"Yes." If they'd stayed together, would it have lasted? They'd never had a chance to be bored with each other or challenged. "He loved me, too, but he wasn't the sort who wanted responsibility. He'd had a difficult childhood. I don't want you thinking I was with someone who had no feelings for me. I don't want you to take my experience as encour-agement to be sexually adventurous."

Mac snorted with laughter. "A relationship when you're eighteen isn't exactly sexually adventurous, even if the guy doesn't own a house. So you found out you were pregnant and you panicked because you didn't want me."

Lauren could feel the hurt pulsing from her daughter. "I wanted you. I wanted all of it. Him, you, a home on the island—I wanted a life together." She'd been naive. She'd tried to squash life into a neat package, not realizing that wasn't how it worked.

She hadn't slept. Hadn't eaten. Hadn't wanted a life that didn't have him in it. And because their relationship had been conducted in secret, she'd had to hide feelings too big to be hidden.

It was the only time in her life she hadn't talked to her sister.

Mack tugged the covers. "Did he know you were pregnant?"

"Yes. I didn't feel it was right to keep that from him. Every man has a right to know he's going to be a father."

"So he freaked and you never saw him again?"

"No. He was shocked, that's true, because we had used birth control." She emphasized that and saw Mack roll her eyes.

"Forget it, Mom. You don't ever get to lecture me again on any of this stuff."

Lauren decided that was tomorrow's worry. "For some reason it didn't work. He asked me what I wanted to do."

"He wanted you to get rid of me?"

"No. That option was never discussed. It wasn't something either of us would have wanted. He said he'd marry me if that was what I wanted."

Mack rolled her eyes. "Jeez. Romantic. *Not*. Like you were actually going to consider that."

She'd considered it.

"Exactly. I was in love and pregnant but I still had enough wits to know that to marry a man who didn't ever want to settle down would be a recipe for disaster."

Reliability. That had been the most important thing for her.

"So you turned him down."

"Yes." And seen the relief on his face.

"So you decided to have me on your own. That's kind of brave. And super scary. And he didn't try to talk you out of it? He walked away."

"He sailed away."

Mack gave a snort of derision. "*Men.* What did Grams say? She was okay about it, right?"

"I didn't tell her."

"Wait—you never told her you were pregnant?"

"I was going to. Before I could do that, I met Ed."

"Where? How?"

"On the beach. I was sitting there one evening, trying to work out what to do." Breathless with panic, life in ruins, trying to work out whether to walk into the sea, start swimming and never come back.

"So you were sitting on the beach, and Dad—I mean Ed—" she stumbled over his name "—Ed came along and you hooked up?"

He'd talked her down off the ledge and for that she'd always been grateful.

Kind, patient Ed who had taught her that people's lives were rarely what they seemed. That everyone had a part of himself or herself that they didn't show to the world.

Ed, who had also been nursing a bruised heart and problems of his own.

"We talked. Turned out he was on vacation to get over a relationship that had gone badly wrong."

"With that Caroline woman? Nana talks about her sometimes."

"She dumped him."

"That's not the way Nana tells it."

"Well it's how it was. Ed was devastated. Maybe that's

why the two of us clicked, to begin with at least. We were both hurting and we formed a friendship. Ed told me about his relationship, I told him about mine. And I told him I was pregnant."

"He knew?"

"Yes. I told him I was trying to work out how to tell Grams. He was the one who suggested we get married."

Mack looked taken aback. "But you'd only just met."

"I know it sounds crazy, but I liked Ed a lot. I knew we could be happy together."

"But you weren't *insanely* in love like you were with the other guy?"

How was she supposed to answer that? "I loved Ed. Was it different to the way I felt about your father? Yes, but that didn't make it less real. Ed and I liked and respected each other. Friendship and respect can be an excellent basis for a marriage. And we were honest with each other right from the start. That's what true intimacy is. We told each other everything."

Or so she'd thought. *She's not our problem.*

It had grown dark outside and Lauren leaned forward and flicked on the bedside lamp.

"I'm sorry I blurted it out that way, in front of everyone." Mack's voice was small and threaded with guilt.

"I'm sorry we didn't tell you. It's our fault, all of it. As parents we tried to do what we believed was best, but maybe we got it wrong."

"Why didn't Ed adopt me?"

Regret shot through her. She wished now that they tackled this subject years ago, together. "He always intended to, but it would have meant contacting your real father and neither of us wanted to do that. So we put it off and—" she swallowed "—somehow it didn't happen." She decided not to mention that Ed couldn't have children of his own, or his fears about Gwen not accepting a granddaughter who wasn't her flesh and blood. She didn't need to add to Mack's insecurities. "But the one thing you have to know is that Ed loved you. He couldn't have loved you more even if you'd been his, or if he'd adopted you."

"Yeah, right. So what happens now?"

Hearing the quiver in her daughter's voice, Lauren decided honesty was probably the best approach. "Nana is very upset, but I'll try to talk to her and—"

"I mean, what's going to happen now it's the two of us? What will we do? How will we live?"

She had no idea, and it terrified her. But she was a mother. It was her job to reassure her child and tell her everything would be fine. *But how could it be fine without Ed?*

"Ed made provisions for you in his will, so you don't have to worry about the future. We will carry on living here, in our home, doing the things we've always done."

"Without Ed."

"Without Ed." Her stomach lurched. She felt as if she'd been dropped in a desert with no map and minimal survival skills. "This horrible, horrible thing happened to us, Mack, and we're going to feel sad and it's going to be difficult but eventually, one day, it will get better." *Please let it get better. Please don't let that be a lie.* She desperately wanted her daughter to be okay. *She* wanted to be okay because the thought of feeling like this forever was terrifying. "We have to be strong, Mack, and deal with things a day at a time. We'll do it together. Warrior women, that's us." Wishing she believed it, she leaned forward and hugged her daughter, but Mack pushed her away.

That rejection felt like the worst thing of all.

She wondered what Jenna was doing. Had she called their mother? That was another conversation Lauren wasn't looking forward to. "I'm going to go and check on Aunt Jenna. Will you join us?"

"Maybe later." Mack curled up under the covers. "Have you ever seen him again? My real dad?"

Lauren felt her heart kick against her chest. "No. We've never seen each other again."

"So you don't know where he is or what he's doing? He could be married with six kids."

The thought of it made it difficult to breathe. "I don't think so."

There was a pause. "Am I like him?"

"In some ways. He was very smart, like you. He loved the sea—"

"I love the sea."

"I know." Lauren remembered Ed's mouth tightening slightly when she'd told him that Mack wanted a bedroom like a ship's cabin. It had been an uncomfortable reminder that Mack had DNA that didn't originate from him. On impulse she reached out and pulled Mack's battered copy of *Moby-Dick* from the shelf. "This belonged to him."

"My real father?" Mack took it from her and leafed through the pages, searching. "His name isn't in it."

"He gave it to me at the beginning of our relationship. It was his favorite book."

"It's my favorite book, too."

"I know." Lauren saw the way Mack held on to the book with both hands. "Is there anything else you wanted to ask me?"

"Yeah—" Mack scrubbed her cheek with the palm of

her hand. "The man you loved. My real dad. What was his name?"

There was a tap on the door and Jenna put her head round. "Sorry to disturb you, but there's a friend here to see you. James? He says it's urgent. Said he's your lawyer and the executor of Ed's will."

Lauren sat still for a moment. There was a buzzing in her ears.

She's not the problem.

She rose to her feet, her stomach churning and her instincts telling her that she was about to find out what the problem was.

Had Ed committed fraud? Had he left all his money to a cat's home? Was this something to do with Mack?

Whatever it was, she had a feeling that the worst day of her life wasn't over yet.

PART TWO

PART TWO

CHAPTER ELEVEN

Nancy

Dilemma: a difficult situation in which you have to choose between two or more alternatives

"PEOPLE HAVE NOTICED your car parked outside the house. There's been gossip. I hope it doesn't bother you." She handed him a mug of coffee. Far too strong for her tastes, but it was the way he liked it. It struck her that she knew any number of small things about him—that he liked his coffee black, his beer cold, that he hated mushrooms, rarely bothered wearing a sweater no matter how hard the wind blew, preferred to work with the windows open—but none of the big things.

"Why would it bother me?"

"Most people care what others think."

He took a mouthful of coffee and slowly lowered the mug. It was obvious from his expression that he didn't give a damn.

It was one of the many things she liked and admired about him. "You don't care. I realized that five years ago." At the time she'd thought it strange that he'd been the one to come to her rescue. She'd never been the type to dream about a hero riding to the aid of a damsel in distress, but even if she had, she never would have cast Scott Rhodes in the key role. It seemed more likely that he would have been the one to put the damsel in a state of distress in the first place.

And yet—

"I've never mentioned it to anyone. You're the only one who knows. Unbelievable really that you, a stranger, know my most intimate secret. I protected my family from all of it." She'd always protected them. It was the one thing she'd done right as a mother.

He put the mug down and turned back to the job in hand, restoring her window frames.

There were people on the island who talked so much you wondered if death might come before the end of the conversation. And then there was Scott.

He'd always been more of a listener than a talker.

She'd watched in fascination over the weeks as he'd taken apart the sash frames and put them back together. He'd dug out paint and caulk, oiled wood, and secured the glass in the sash. A surgeon operating on a child couldn't have taken more care.

Not that she'd ever doubted his skills. He knew wood like she knew paint.

He'd built the Morton's boat a few summers before and a library for Sandra Telford. She hadn't stopped boasting about it, although she'd whispered that she'd hidden the silver while he was working.

That comment had annoyed Nancy. To the best of her

knowledge there had been just the one incident, many years before, where Scott had taken a boat that hadn't belonged to him. The boat had been returned without a scrape or a scratch, but the police had been involved.

Everyone made mistakes, didn't they? She'd made major mistakes.

She'd snapped at Sandra and received a curious glance in return.

If Sandra remembered that and happened to notice Scott's pickup parked outside, she'd probably put two and two together and make six.

Funny to think she and Sandra had once been close. They'd sat side by side in school and told each other everything, two people who had naively thought they were confiding in each other but in truth had nothing of importance to share. Then Sandra had married Bill and Nancy had married Tom and they'd drifted apart.

"I'm only mentioning it now because things have happened that will mean it won't stay a secret for much longer. I've never thanked you properly for what you did—" She broke off. "Or for not talking. You could have made things very awkward for me."

He reached up to the window and his shirt pulled tight over the muscles of his arms and shoulders. "Why would I have done that?"

"Because that's what most people would have done. One person tells another, then it trickles through the community and before you know it, the trickle is a stream and the stream flows faster until it bursts its banks. Privacy on an island this size isn't easy." Although it was possible, if you worked at it. "That's probably the reason you choose to live on the water and not on land."

He didn't comment on that, but she saw a gleam in his eyes that could have been humor.

In all the weeks he'd been working on the house, she'd never once found his presence intrusive. She didn't know exactly when he was going to turn up, but she never complained when he did. And it wasn't only because the work he was doing needed doing so badly, it was because she liked having him around. It made her feel less alone, which made no sense at all because she was an intelligent woman and perfectly aware that she'd never been more alone in her life.

Perhaps she felt comfortable with Scott because he already knew everything there was to know about her, all the parts she'd successfully hidden from everyone else. He knew her failures and her weaknesses. Having nothing left to hide was surprisingly liberating.

She stared at the room they'd been working on. "There are so many imperfections in the walls of this place."

"Not every imperfection needs fixing." He wiped his palm on the faded fabric of his jeans. "Sometimes you have to accept the flaw and live with it."

Were they still talking about the house?

One of the reasons she'd employed him was because he understood the difference between restoration and renovation. He respected the unique details of the original building.

"It's old, but it has good bones. Like me." She made the joke, and then felt awkward.

"If you're worried about the walls, you could paint something to hang there."

Her heart bumped hard. "I haven't painted since that night." Something else she hadn't told her daughters. Occasionally she spattered paint on her fingers so that Jenna didn't ask questions. The truth was she hadn't been to her studio in five years. The drive that had powered her whole life, her existence, was gone. And she missed it. She missed its healing powers, its ability to transport her to a different place. Painting had been a sanctuary, and now her life felt bare and cold.

She turned back to him. "I've often wondered why you helped me that night." She knew she'd never forget it. Not a single, hideous moment. It had been a night of surprises, all of them bad.

He wiped his hands on the cloth he kept tucked into his jeans. "I sailed a boat. I didn't save the world."

He'd saved her world.

"You sailed a boat in a hurricane. There was no one else in the air or on the water."

"If I hadn't done it, you would have found someone else to take you."

She knew she wouldn't.

She'd been desperate.

Scott Rhodes had been her last resort and despite his casual, dismissive treatment of the subject, she suspected he knew that.

"Why did you do it?" It was something she'd asked herself repeatedly, mostly when she was trying to distract herself from everything that had happened. She thought about the mountainous seas and the terrifying howl of the wind. At the time it had seemed as if nature had been reflecting her mood. "Why did you risk your life for me that night?"

"You paid me."

"Hardly enough for you to risk your life." She eyed the rip in his jeans. "And you're not driven by financial interests. You have no responsibilities. No mortgage. No family."

"You needed help." He turned back to the wood, smoothing the surface with his hand, his movements slow and sure.

He'd been the same that night. Everything about him had been calm and measured. She'd been terrified, not only by the storm sent by nature but by the one going on inside her, and by the knowledge that the truth was about to be exposed, despite all her efforts. Something about his steadying presence had helped her hold her emotions together.

"You're kind, but you prefer to let people think you're moody and a little dangerous. It's your way of keeping them at a distance." And she could understand it. There were plenty of people she'd like to keep at a distance. Maybe she should start saying less and scowling more.

She sank onto the chair and saw his quick frown of concern.

There it was again, the kindness he tried to hide.

"We might have to postpone some of the work we were planning. My daughter is arriving soon." And because there was no one else she could confide in, she confided in him. "I have to tell her the truth. I've dreaded this moment. I really hoped it would never come."

He put down the plane and straightened. "I assume you're not talking about the state of your window frames."

"I'm talking about the state of my life. It's going to be a shock for my daughters, particularly Lauren. She's been living in England for the past sixteen years." It made her heart ache to think of what her oldest daughter must be going through right now. "It's ironic, don't you think? Just when I think I've reached a stage in life where I have no one to worry about but myself, my daughter's world collapses."

How much should she tell the girls? How much could she hold back?

The truth came in different sizes, didn't it? She could tell an extrasmall truth, veracity's equivalent of a size zero, or she could perhaps offer up a medium. Let's face it, the whole truth and nothing but the truth—*an extralarge truth with a side of blunt*—would swamp everyone.

Scott had stopped work and there was a deep furrow in his brow. "How has her world collapsed?"

She sensed she had his full attention and wondered why.

"Her husband died a few weeks ago. It was sudden. And complicated. Turns out he owed a great number of people a large amount of money." Were they cursed as a family? First she'd been widowed, and now Lauren. How much should she say? What if Lauren didn't want the whole community knowing her private details? Not that Scott could be described as chatty even at the best of times.

"She's coming home permanently?" There was a roughness to his tone that hadn't been there before.

"She needs support." Should she have insisted on going to the funeral? Lauren had put her off and Nancy hadn't been able to decide if her presence would make things worse or better. She'd been in an agony of indecision. "She has a child. My granddaughter is sixteen. It's a terrible age to lose a father."

His jaw tightened and he seemed about to say something.

She waited, perplexed by his response, but instead of speaking he turned away suddenly, leaving her with the feeling that she'd said the wrong thing.

The problem with not knowing someone well was that you had no idea which subjects to broach and which to avoid.

She knew little about Scott's family history, although his lifestyle didn't suggest the presence of a warm, loving family lurking in the wings. She'd heard rumors of foster care and a troubled upbringing.

Maybe he'd lost his father, too. Maybe that was it.

"My daughter is arriving on the ferry this afternoon. Could you give me a ride? I know it's a lot to ask, but the garage still has my car." Maybe she was overstepping, but it seemed like the best solution to her. Greg was working and Jenna couldn't possibly take more time off. "She'll have luggage and you have room in your pickup. I'll pay you, obviously. Or maybe I should get a cab—"

"I'll do it." He picked up his tool belt. "I don't want payment."

"I insist that—"

"I don't want payment." Something in his tone stopped her arguing.

"In that case, thank you."

Once again Scott would be by her side while she tackled something she was dreading.

This time they weren't sailing into a hurricane, but she knew there was every possibility that the landscape of her life would be entirely altered by what was about to hit.

CHAPTER TWELVE

Lauren

Sanctuary: a place of refuge

LAUREN STOOD ON the observation deck of the ferry and stared across the choppy sea. The water reminded her of grief, slapping at the boat, pummeling, swirling.

The other passengers, less preoccupied by their own problems, had chosen warmth over the view and long since vanished below deck to the snack bar to avoid the frigid squalls of air.

It was like a slap in the face, and Lauren needed that.

"Marriage can be whatever we want it to be," Ed had once said to her. "There are people who believe in fairy-tale romance who end up in the divorce court a few years later crushed under the weight of crumbling expectations. Then there are people like us who are honest about what we want."

How about the debts, Ed? Why didn't you mention those?

How could there be no money? Ed had been good at what he did. The best, some had said, and yet somehow he'd managed to lose everything he'd ever worked for.

She'd tried to concentrate as words and phrases floated past her, although the look on James's face had been enough to tell her how bad the news was.

Trying to get higher returns for the fund.

Acquired several private companies.

Lack of liquidity.

All the money tied up in the company.

Lost all his capital.

It had been Jenna who had pointed out that she still had the house, and Lauren who had to confess that Ed had taken another mortgage. He'd mentioned a temporary lack of liquidity. What he hadn't mentioned was how serious it was.

According to James, there was unlikely to be anything left when the debts had been paid. It would take a while to untangle everything, but right now it seemed they would be lucky for the estate not to be declared insolvent.

Apart from that last day, there had been no signs that anything was wrong.

She hadn't known the person she'd lived with for more than sixteen years.

The cold wind whipped at her hair and slid down the collar of her coat, but she didn't notice. In the long list of things wrong with her life, being cold was right at the bottom. The feeling of numbness that spread through her had nothing to do with the weather.

She'd had to borrow money from Jenna to cover their journey from England to Martha's Vineyard and right now she didn't have the means to pay her sister back.

The seesaw of emotions was making her dizzy. One minute she was angry, the next she was devastated. Anxiety formed a tight band around her chest.

She missed Ed horribly, but she'd barely had time to process her emotions. Life was sweeping her along like a river in full flood. She was gasping for air, swirling, grabbing at anything she could but still couldn't reach the safety of the bank.

She hadn't only lost Ed and the house and the life she'd had, she'd lost her vision of the future.

Only now was she realizing how excited she'd been about this new phase in her life.

To support her daughter she would need to find a job that paid immediately. But what could she do?

"Do we have to stay with Grams?" Mack was slumped over the rail, watching the sea churn beneath them. "How long for?"

Until I can't stand it any longer.

She killed the thought because she was truly grateful to have somewhere to go. Staying with her mother might drive her insane, but it would give her a chance to regroup and plan her future.

"I thought you loved The Captain's House and Martha's Vineyard?"

"This is different. This isn't a holiday."

And didn't she know it.

"I know you're coping with a lot. First Dad—"

"Ed." Mack had refused to call him anything but Ed since the night of the funeral and it made Lauren feel sick with guilt.

"He was your dad."

"I don't have a single morsel of his DNA." Mack glared fiercely at the water. "Does he have blue eyes?"

"Excuse me?"

"My real dad. Blue eyes?"

Lauren swallowed. "Yes, but being a father is about more than DNA. Ed was your father in every single way that mattered." She was too tired for this conversation. Her head throbbed from lack of sleep and too much crying.

"Newsflash—the whole egg being fertilized thing matters, Mom, otherwise the rest doesn't happen."

"Your dad loved you. Love is showing up, honey. Sticking around." *Do you hear that, Ed? It's about sticking around. Checking that your heart is working okay. Going to the doctor.* She knew it was irrational to be angry with Ed for dying, but that didn't seem to help. The words *if only* were stuck in her brain like an earworm. "He was there when I was pregnant with you, when you were born, when you cried in the night. He was the one sitting at the school concert when you sang solo, and the one who was right there talking to your teachers."

Mack thrust her jaw out. "I'm calling him Ed."

Lauren felt helpless. She was terrified of saying something that would make a bad situation worse. "I know it's difficult for you, leaving London in the middle of a very important school year—"

"Are you kidding? That's the only good thing about this. I don't have to take those stupid exams."

But those "stupid exams" were important.

What if she'd ruined her daughter's life? "You'll go to school here. There are good schools on the island."

"But they don't know, right? They don't know everything that has happened?" Mack's horrified tone said everything about the way she was feeling.

"No. It's up to you how much you tell."

"I won't be telling anyone anything. It's going to stay a secret. It shouldn't be a problem. I learned from the best."

Lauren felt as if her heart was splintering into pieces. "Don't say that. It's important to talk to the people you love."

"You're *seriously* saying that to me? If Aunt Jenna were here right now she'd be doing that word thing she does where she gives you a definition. *Hypocrisy*—when your mom tries to get you to do something she doesn't do herself."

It required superhuman patience to hold on to her temper. If circumstances had been different she would have called Mack out for her brattish behavior, but she knew her daughter was mixed up and miserable and taking that misery out on the person closest to her.

She gripped the railing. She felt dizzy and wasn't sure if it was lack of food or whether she was coming down with something. *Could hypocrisy make you dizzy?*

She'd wanted to be everything her own mother wasn't. Attentive, interested, loyal and, most important of all, present. Why hadn't anyone told her it was harder than it looked? Why hadn't anyone told her that what constituted "good" parenting wasn't always obvious? She'd taken her own mother as an example and promised herself that she'd do everything differently. In the end she'd made her own set of mistakes.

"I know you feel I did the wrong thing. I've made decisions you disagree with, but I do want us to keep talking. I want to know how you're feeling, even if it's hard to hear."

"I feel like crap, okay? And I *don't* want to talk." Mack's jaw lifted and her expression was combative. It had been the same since the night of the funeral.

Lauren wanted to wrap her daughter in her arms and hold

her while she cried and talked it out, but Mack had turned into a porcupine. She had a feeling that if she hugged her she'd be pulling needles out of herself for the next month.

"Mack—"

"A person is entitled to privacy, right?"

"There's a difference between privacy and secrets, Mack. When you make new friends—" *please let her make new friends* "—you might find it helps to talk to them."

"Yeah, like you did? You didn't even tell Aunt Jenna about my real dad. I saw her face the day of the funeral."

"Don't model yourself on me. I'm starting to think I need a complete do-over."

It had been a long and punishing few weeks, most of which had passed in a blur of meetings with lawyers and Ed's accountants. The list of people he owed money to grew every day. She felt stupid for not taking a closer interest, but she knew she wasn't stupid. She'd trusted her husband. Was it naive to trust the man you were married to?

How could he have hidden something so enormous from her? Why? How long had he had problems with the business? When had it all started? What had gone wrong?

Damn you, Ed.

She stared across the choppy sea to the island. Something stirred inside her, a deep unease, as if some part of her sensed that this place could somehow shake the foundations of the life she'd built. She'd always had mixed feelings about Martha's Vineyard. Her visits home brought a rash of memories, many of which she could happily have deleted from her brain. She associated the place with teenage emotions and bad choices.

Most of all, she associated the place with *him* and that one spectacular summer that had never been matched or repeated. She'd experienced heartache and heartbreak and a breadth of other agonizing human emotions in the space of a few short months, and had changed forever.

Jenna had been right when she'd questioned whether there was a reason Lauren hadn't returned often.

He was the reason.

She'd been afraid of bumping into memories. Afraid of bumping into him.

In London she was a different person. She'd reinvented herself. Part of her had always been a little nervous that she might revert to her original self when she stepped off the ferry.

Lauren stared down at the boil and swirl of the waves. For a wild moment she thought about jumping. With her current run of luck she'd probably land on a rock.

She looked away from the water, feeling guilty for even thinking of jumping. She had responsibilities, and now she was facing them on her own. There was no one else.

Had marrying Ed been a coward's way out or the right decision? She no longer knew.

"Staying with Grams will be fun."

"For two weeks in the summer, yes, but *forever*?" Mack turned her head slowly, the look in her eyes pure teenage disdain. "You promised to be honest. That night in my bedroom you said *no more lying*."

"You're right, I did." She rejected the instinct to protect her daughter from the truth. "It might not be that much fun, but we don't have much choice." What could she say? That she wasn't looking forward to it either? That a grown woman of thirty-five shouldn't have to move back home with her mother, especially when they'd never had that great a relationship in the first place? That she had no idea how to talk to her own mother about what was happening in her life? "It's hard, but we need to keep going." She tried to inject some normality. "We'll do some of the things we always do. Beach, bike rides, maybe go shopping—"

"Last time I looked you couldn't buy a new life."

They'd been given a new life whether they wanted it or not. And they couldn't shop for anything until she'd worked out a way to produce income. That was top of her list of problems to solve.

"We're lucky Grams has a big house and can easily accommodate us."

Lauren loved her mother, but the thought of living in close quarters after so many years made her hyperventilate. Her mother didn't really know her, although to be fair that was probably as much Lauren's fault as Nancy's.

Apart from her sister, there was only one person who had truly known her and he'd sailed away from her life a long time ago.

As the ferry docked and people started to disembark Lauren was tempted to stay on board, but she knew she had to start facing her problems. She had to deal with them one by one, the best she could. Lists. Plans. Control.

Her mother had promised to meet her.

Lauren would have preferred it to be Jenna, but her sister was teaching and she'd already missed more than enough classes flying to London to support Lauren.

She held out her hand but Mack shot her a horrified glance and dipped her head.

"I'm not six. Please don't kill my credibility dead before I've even set foot in the place. There's only so many times a person can move, you know?"

Lauren wondered how they were going to get past this.

Ed's death should have pulled them closer, but it had pushed them apart.

Patience and time, she thought. That was all she had.

At least there was nothing more that could happen.

Perhaps the only advantage of being at rock bottom was that the only way was up.

They hauled their luggage off the ferry and she saw the familiar figure of her mother clutching the edges of the same unflattering gray coat she'd worn for the last decade. For someone lauded for her use of color, it had always puzzled Lauren that her mother now showed such a lack of interest in clothing. Despite the fact that her paintings commanded eye-watering sums, she never seemed to spend anything on herself. Her once-blond hair was now a uniform gray and a pair of glasses perched on the end of her nose.

Next to her stood a man. His shoulders were wide and powerful and he hunched them slightly as protection against the relentless buffeting of the wind. His legs were long and strong and his hair was the color of the sky at midnight. Although she wasn't close enough to see his eyes, she knew they were blue. Ice blue, like frost on the water or a pale winter sky.

Lauren stopped walking and Mack bumped into her, almost knocking her off balance.

"Whoa! If you're going to put the brakes on, some warning would be good." Steadying herself, Mack stepped round her mother and kissed her grandmother. "Hi, Grams. Yes, I've grown. Yes, I'm taller. It's an amazing feat of nature."

Nancy gave a distracted smile, either not noticing teenage sarcasm or unfazed by it. "How was the crossing? Lauren, I hope you don't mind that I didn't drive. My car is in the garage. You remember Scott Rhodes? He's been doing some work on the house and he gave me a ride." She gestured vaguely to the man standing next to her and Lauren tried to control the waves of dizziness.

Scott Rhodes.

So in fact she hadn't hit rock bottom yet. She was still falling.

It had been more than sixteen years since she'd seen him, but the recognition was instant and visceral. Heat seared her skin and shot through her pelvis. Her legs started to tremble.

Her gaze locked on his and she felt as if she'd slammed headfirst into a wall.

Her senses felt as if they'd been woken from a long sleep.

Through a cloud of mist she heard Mack say, "Wait a minute, did you say your name was *Scott Rhodes*?"

The world started to spin. No matter how hard she tried, she couldn't suck air into her lungs. Something heavy pressed against her chest. Heart attack?

As if in slow motion, she felt the bag slip from her fingers and her legs start to give way under her.

I'm going to faint, she thought. *Maybe I'll hit my head and all this will be over. Maybe I'll fall in the water and drown*—

But she couldn't let that happen, could she?

Mack needed her—

She crumpled to the ground and through the shadows and rolling gray mist heard Mack's horrified scream.

"You've killed my mom!" Her voice was high and shrill and came from far away. "Thanks a lot. Now I'm an orphan."

CHAPTER THIRTEEN

Lauren

Flashback: a scene that returns to events in the past

MOONLIGHT SPILLED OVER the beach and she lay nestled in the protective curve of his arm, staring up at the stars. The sand was warm beneath her back and she could hear the soft rush of the sea as it hit the shore.

Was there a more beautiful place on earth?

If there was, then she didn't need to see it. This was enough.

"I love you."

"I love you, too." His arms tightened around her. "I've never said those words to anyone."

But he'd said them to her.

It made her feel invincible, as if she could walk on water or leap off a building and fly.

The future she'd envisaged was changing shape. She

wasn't sure where college fit in with the way she felt about Scott. She tried to imagine herself going to classes and never seeing him. How could that option possibly make her happy?

"You could come with me when I leave." She'd been thinking about it, trying to find solutions.

"And do what?" He lay still. "I sail boats. There's not a lot of call for that in a city."

"You'd hate living in a city. Forget it, it wouldn't work." But what would? It made her brain ache, trying to find a solution. No matter how many different ways she tried to assemble the pieces of the puzzle, they didn't fit. "I could come with you. We could live on a boat."

"I don't own a boat, Laurie. I sail other people's boats. I fix other people's boats."

"But Joshua says you're the best he has ever had working for him in the boatyard. He says you have a feel for the sea, and a feel for wood. He has more than enough work for you. You don't have to leave." She was desperate to convince him.

"I can't stay in one place." He let go of her and sat up, his jaw tense as he stared out to sea. "I have to keep moving."

"Why? Because that's what you've done before? Maybe it's time to change that." She was so desperate she decided to be bold. "I know it happened to you over and over again when you were growing up. I know they moved you from foster home to foster home, often with no warning—"

"Laurie—"

"And I know you hate talking about it," she plowed on, "but now you're doing the same thing to yourself! You don't have to move, Scott. You could stay. You could settle."

"You need to stop this." He sounded tired. "You need to stop planning a future."

"Just because you didn't ever dare plan a future when you were growing up doesn't mean you can't now."

"Things change, Laurie."

She wasn't sure what he meant by that. "I'm not going to change. My feelings for you won't change."

"Things happen that are outside your control."

"But we have control over this. Us. We'll find a way." When he didn't even look at her she felt a rush of despair. "I know you don't trust anyone, but I'm not anyone." He was like a stray dog, she thought, afraid to approach any human.

"What you need is to go to college, then get a fancy job in Manhattan and date smart guys who are lawyers or doctors."

"Just because a guy isn't a lawyer or a doctor doesn't mean he isn't smart."

"You're so young, Laurie."

"I am not!" She felt him slipping away from her. She felt as if she was losing him and the one thing she did know was that she didn't want that. What she wanted was love, and she knew she'd never find another love like this. She leaned forward and kissed his jaw, feeling the roughness of stubble beneath her lips. "You're the first man I've ever loved."

"I'm the first man you've had sex with." His voice was rough and she knew he was thinking about it.

She thought about it all the time. His hands. His mouth. "That has nothing to do with my feelings."

"Are you sure? Sex has a powerful effect on some people."

"Until I met you, I never wanted to have sex. You know

why." And it still surprised her that she'd felt able to tell him so much. He was the only person she'd ever told.

She'd been attracted to his strength and quiet confidence.

She knew some people on the island were wary of him, but with her he'd been gentle and patient.

He understood her. He listened. He cared. She felt closer to him than anyone in her family, even her sister. She trusted him completely.

The fact that their relationship was private made it all the more intense and personal. She shared him with no one.

Sometimes she passed him during the day when she was rushing to and from her job at the beach café. Her gaze would meet his and it took all her effort not to race across and hurl herself into his arms.

The only thing stopping her was the knowledge that they'd be together later. She met him every evening, after dark on a private stretch of sand that belonged to a beach house that was unoccupied. They had a place at the far end of the beach, tucked between the dunes, where other people rarely went.

Some people had a bar or a restaurant that was their place.

For Lauren it was a patch of sand sheltered by dunes and seagrass.

"Let's stop talking about the future." The more time they spent together, she reasoned, the harder he would find it to leave her. "We have the whole summer ahead of us. All I care about is now."

CHAPTER FOURTEEN

Mack

> *Remorse: a sense of deep regret and guilt*
> *for some misdeed*

"MOM, WAKE UP." She felt the concrete of the dock pressing through her jeans and the cold bite of the wind on her neck, but the only thing she cared about was that her mother wasn't moving. "Please don't be dead." She couldn't possibly die and leave Mack now, when her life was a disaster and her brain was jammed with so many confused feelings she couldn't begin to unravel them.

The tears she'd been holding back rose like the tide, scalding her throat.

"Mom!" Why had she been so vile? She'd said mean and hateful things and now her mom was going to die, too, and Mack would be alone with a big fat guilty conscience to add to all the other emotions churning uncomfortably inside her.

Worst of all was the fact that she wouldn't have the chance to say sorry.

The thought terrified her so badly she knew she was going to break down and sob right here in front of everyone.

Her mother was pale, and the dark rings under her eyes made her look like something from one of those zombie movies Abigail had made them watch.

Mack felt as if she were being choked. There was no air and her chest hurt. Was she having a heart attack? *She was going to die, too.*

She sent a desperate look to her grandmother, but Nancy was standing immobile.

It was as if she'd been turned to stone.

Mack was trying to come to terms with the fact that she was going to die right alongside her mother when a strong hand closed over her shoulder.

"Breathe out slowly—" The voice was deep and reassuring. "You're going to be all right."

She was not all right.

"Dying—" She gasped out the word and he crouched down next to her, his hand warm and steady on her back.

"You're not dying. You're safe."

Safe? How could he think she was safe?

And why wasn't her grandmother doing something or saying something?

But the feel of that hand on her back gradually calmed her. It soothed and comforted. He didn't talk nonstop, but he was quiet and calm. Perhaps she wasn't dying. Surely no one could be that calm if they were about to witness a catastrophe?

"Keep breathing slowly. I'm not going to let anything

happen to you." Something about that rough, firm voice made it impossible to do anything but respond.

Gradually her heartbeat started to slow. The tingling feeling faded.

"My mom—"

"She's going to be fine, too. She fainted, that's all. I'm going to take a look at her now, so you keep up that slow breathing for me." He shifted away slightly and she resisted the temptation to grab him and yell *don't let me go*.

"Are you a doctor or something?"

"No."

He glanced at her and she found herself staring into eyes exactly like her own.

She swallowed.

Did he know? Did he see what she saw?

She waited for him to say something, but he didn't. Instead he placed his fingers on her mother's wrist and checked her pulse.

Then he let go of her mom's wrist and stroked her hair away from her face. "Laurie—"

Laurie?

Mack stared at him. No one ever called her mother Laurie. She was always Lauren. And she'd never heard anyone use that tone before when talking to her. Not even her dad. Ed. Scott's tone was gentle. Personal. More like a purr than a bark. Like he really *knew* her.

Feeling self-conscious and insecure, she sneaked another look at her grandmother.

Her mom had told her that Grams hadn't known about Scott, but she had to know, otherwise why would she have brought him here? Maybe they'd had a conversation over the phone and her mom had forgotten to tell her. There had been plenty of occasions when her mother had tried to talk to her over the past few weeks and Mack had rebuffed her.

Of course she wouldn't have rebuffed her if she'd known she was going to *die*.

"Should we call 911?" Her grandmother's voice was thready and weak and she was looking at Scott Rhodes as if he was likely to have an answer for every problem.

Mack was surprised by the trust she saw there.

Why were her grandmother and this man so comfortable around each other? Why wasn't she yelling at him for having killed her daughter? Or making her pregnant? It was hard to know which might seem worse to an adult.

"She's going to be fine. Let's get her to the house." He slid his arms under Lauren's limp body and lifted her easily.

Mack knew her mouth was open but she couldn't help it.

Not in a million years would Ed have ever picked her mom up. In fact Mack had never seen a man pick a woman up before, except in the movies. She'd always assumed that in real life you'd probably put your back out. "Where are you taking her?" What if he was going to drop her mom in the cold water or something? Maybe he was angry she'd married Ed.

"I'm taking her to the car."

Mack was relieved to hear her mother give a moan of protest as Scott placed her on the seat of the pickup. If she was moaning, that meant she was alive, didn't it?

Relief turned her legs to water.

She saw her mother's eyes open and widen as she stared at Scott.

In that instant it was as if the rest of the world had vanished.

They gazed at each other for so long that Mack wanted to yell, *I'm still here!*

She felt like crying, and she wasn't sure if it was exhaustion after the flight or relief that her mother wasn't dead.

She wanted to get to The Captain's House before she broke down and embarrassed herself. She was way past the age when it might be considered okay to cry in public.

Scott, however, didn't seem to be in a hurry. He worked at his own pace. He leaned across to fasten the seat belt and Mack saw her mom turn her head away, as if she didn't dare have her face that close to his.

Mack was relieved when Scott opened a door and gestured to the pickup.

She climbed in with a small chin lift of defiance, as if she hadn't almost thrown up on the pier and died of fear. If first impressions counted, then she'd blown it. He was probably thinking she wouldn't have been such a wimp if he'd raised her.

Fortunately it was a relatively short drive to her grandmother's house. Her grandmother started asking Mack about schools, exams and friends—normal stuff. She didn't mention the fact that Ed had died or that her mom had passed out on the dock.

Hello, can we talk about some real issues here?

The weirdness of it couldn't be expressed, but her whole life was weird now.

She missed Ed so badly it made her chest ache, and she didn't understand how it was possible to love someone and be mad at the same time.

Mack stole a glance at her grandmother, trying to work out why she'd brought Scott.

Maybe her grandmother had thought her mom needed a replacement for Ed, although it was a bit quick, wasn't it? And anyway her mom had said Scott hadn't wanted responsibility. Unless something had changed radically he wasn't likely to be interested in taking on a fainting, superskinny broke woman and her messed-up teenage daughter.

Mack didn't know much about relationships, but she suspected they weren't much of a catch.

They arrived at the house and her mother insisted on walking from the car.

"Are you sure that's a good idea?" Mack hovered, trying to prove she wasn't the heartless teen Scott seemed to think she was. "I don't want you to faint again. Let him carry you."

"I don't need anyone to carry me."

That had to be a good sign, surely? Her mother had always been strong, calm and capable. Even when Mack had blurted out the truth about her dad at the funeral, Lauren had stayed calm and together. She'd been calm and together right until the moment she'd stepped off the boat and seen Scott.

Right now she looked pale and frail. Scott obviously thought so, too, because he prowled close to her, presumably ready to catch her.

It was a relief when they finally stepped inside the house.

The Captain's House felt like an old friend and was exactly the way Mack remembered it.

Despite what she'd said to her mother, it gave her a little buzz of excitement to be back. She'd once heard a bunch of tourists talking about its "historic charm," but that wasn't why she loved it. She loved it because you could literally *smell* the sea, not just because the ocean was right there outside the door, but because it seemed to have permeated the walls of the house. The place had nooks, secret doors and balconies, and all the rooms were crammed full of stuff. There were books, old naval charts, objects that had been gathering dust for over a century. Her grandmother never threw anything away, which Mack thought was pretty cool although she knew it drove her mother and Aunt Jenna to despair. There were cracks in the paintwork and character. Like an older person, Mack thought, with plenty of life experience and lots of stories to tell.

On the walls of the entryway there were old black-and-white photographs as well as one of her grandmother's paintings. Except—the painting was no longer there.

She frowned at the faded wallpaper.

"Where's the painting, Grams? The pretty blue one?" It was the only one of her grandmother's paintings that she liked. The rest were gloomy. Looking at them made Mack want to dress in warmer clothes.

Her grandmother looked flustered. "I moved it."

Scott hauled their bags from the pickup and put them in the entryway.

"You must be exhausted after your journey," her grandmother said. "I've made something to eat."

Mack's stomach was still churning. "That's kind, but I'm not that hungry, Grams."

"You must eat something before you take a nap."

Mack opened her mouth to point out that she was sixteen not six, and generally made it through the day without needing a nap, but then it occurred to her that it would give her an excuse to escape from all this stress and be on her own. She could message Phoebe.

Anything to get away from her crazy family. And Scott.

"That would be good, thank you." She felt Scott's gaze settle on her. She had a feeling he could read her mind and it was a little unnerving.

She slumped on one of the kitchen chairs, lack of sleep and jet lag catching up with her.

"Toast," her grandmother said vaguely. "I'll make toast."

"Great." She could probably choke down a couple of mouthfuls to appease her grandmother.

"You've never met Scott, so I should introduce him properly."

"We haven't met in person." Mack looked at Scott. "In case you're wondering, yes, I do know that you're my real father. And I know you basically resigned from the job years ago, which should make me mad at you, but given that I'm low on family right now and can't afford to be picky, you needn't worry about me making trouble."

"Mackenzie!" Her grandmother dropped the cup on the floor, where it shattered into pieces, splashing tea over the floor and the cabinets. "What are you talking about?" She turned to Lauren. "Is this grief talking? I don't understand."

Lauren closed her eyes. "Mom—"

Oh crappity crap. Mack felt a wash of horror as she stared at her mother. "Wait. Are you saying Grams didn't know? I thought you already told her!"

Her mother looked like a ghost. "When would I have told her?"

"On the phone or something! I heard you talking."

"About travel plans. Not about—anything else. I was waiting to do it face-to-face."

Her grandmother hadn't known?

"But why did she bring him to the ferry then?"

This whole situation was starting to drive her insane. It was worse than the Shakespeare play she'd studied, where characters dressed up as different people.

Her grandmother hadn't moved. Tea dripped off the cabinets. "What were you waiting to tell me? That Scott is Mack's father? Where would you ever get an idea like that, Mack?"

Mack said nothing. From now on she was keeping her mouth shut.

First the funeral, now this.

She was never talking again.

Instead she grabbed a cloth and kept her head down as she mopped up tea and retrieved shards of china.

"Scott, I must apologize for my granddaughter." Nancy sounded faint. "I have no idea why she'd say a thing like that. It's ridiculous."

Scott stirred. "Does Lauren have other kids?"

Nancy looked perplexed. "Only Mack."

"In that case, Mack is my daughter."

Her grandmother was clutching the back of a chair and staring at Scott. "All this time you knew and didn't tell me? Why?"

"It was Lauren's decision."

"But if it's true that Mack is your daughter, that would mean you and Lauren—"

"Don't say it!" Mack interrupted. "We get the picture." She saw her grandmother lift her hand to her throat and felt a flash of alarm.

What now?

She stood up slowly and approached her grandmother as she would someone was poised to jump off a ledge. "Grams—"

"But this is Lauren we're talking about. If it were Jenna, I could understand it because she was always a wild one, but *Lauren*—" Nancy shook her head, bemused. "That's not the daughter I know!" She looked at Scott and he returned her gaze without flinching.

"Then I guess we know a different person."

Scott, Mack thought, seemed like the only sane person in the room.

Nancy turned her head to look at Lauren. "But you married Ed, and—why would you keep something like that from me?"

Mack rolled her eyes. "Mom is like a big well of secrets—she's like MI5 or the CIA or something."

"Mackenzie." Her mother's voice sounded strangled. "Go to your room. You shouldn't be listening to this discussion."

"No way. Any discussions are happening right here in front of me, otherwise no doubt something else will emerge that I won't find out for another ten years and by then I'll be psychologically damaged for life." Maybe she already was. Sometimes the stuff going on inside her head scared her. "Whatever happened to telling the truth? Right now I have had enough of my totally fucked-up family."

Lauren inhaled sharply. "Do not use that language." She snatched her bag from the table and pulled out her phone. "I'm letting Aunt Jenna know we arrived safely."

Sending an SOS more like, Mack thought.

Her grandmother seemed to rouse herself. "Aunt Jenna is teaching today."

Mack shared her mother's desperation. "She needs to come over as soon as she's finished. And she needs to bring cookies, or cupcakes—preferably both. And also Uncle Greg because he knows how to fix situations and this situation definitely needs fixing."

She realized her mother hadn't spoken to Scott. Nothing. No words had been exchanged. Just that one look so hot that if you stood in the middle of it you would have come away with seared flesh.

The atmosphere was so still and tight it was as if someone had sucked all the air from the room.

"Scott?" Her grandmother's voice sounded faint. "I wonder if you'd mind leaving us? I think I need to catch up with my family. It seems we have rather a lot to talk about."

Scott eased away from the counter where he'd been leaning and watching Lauren.

"You know where I am."

It was Nancy who answered. "Thank you, Scott."

Mack wondered why her grandmother was thanking Scott when he was, in a way, responsible for this whole mess in the first place.

CHAPTER FIFTEEN

Jenna

> *Revelation: a surprising or interesting fact*
> *that is made known to people*

"ARE YOU SURE it's a good idea to go over to your mother's again? You've been there every day since Lauren and Mack arrived." Greg locked the front door of the cottage and they walked to the car together. "Maybe they need space."

"They don't need space." Jenna thought about the message Lauren had left on her phone that morning. "Lauren needs backup."

"And that's you?"

"Yes. I'm her sister. She keeps telling me she's fine, but how can she be fine?"

"I guess she's doing what she can to hold it all together."

"And that can't be easy. She told me yesterday that the cause of death was heart disease. Damaged valve or something. Can you imagine that? Ed was forty. The whole thing is terrible for her, and she keeps getting these calls from London from that lawyer guy I met, so it never ends." Jenna threw her purse on the back seat of the car and slid behind the wheel. "And living with Mom can't be easy either. She doesn't talk about the big stuff."

Greg fastened his seat belt. "We've discussed this a million times. We both know your mother finds it hard to show emotion."

"I know, but I thought she might have tried a little harder with Lauren. Didn't you see how she was at dinner with Lauren the first night? She barely mentioned Ed." Jenna waved to one of their neighbors who was walking their dog.

"Because she didn't know what to say. A lot of people don't know what to say in difficult situations, Jenna. She's not alone. Not because they don't care, but because they're afraid of saying the wrong thing. Of making it worse. And she was probably stunned into silence by the revelation about Scott. I know I was."

"I still can't believe she took Scott Rhodes to meet Lauren."

"The part I find harder to understand is how he can be Mack's father. If you'd asked me to list all the possibilities, he wouldn't have made the list."

He would have been top of her list, Jenna thought. Why hadn't it occurred to her before?

She drove away from the beach, taking a left and then a right.

"Now I think about it, there *was* something—" she tightened her grip on the wheel "—they noticed each other."

"Evidently. Can you slow down? It's not going to help your sister if you land us in a ditch."

"Sorry." Jenna eased her foot off the accelerator. "I'm worried about her. Do you think Scott's the reason she didn't come home much?"

"I don't know—*slow down*!"

Jenna braked hard. "Maybe she was worried she'd run into him."

"I'm worried we're going to litter the island with dead bodies. Do you want me to drive?"

"No. Sorry. I'll slow down. I'm anxious. From what Lauren told me, she'll have to get a job." Jenna drove carefully through West Tisbury, where the annual fair and livestock show ran for four days every August. She wondered if her sister was missing the city and decided it was probably the last thing on her mind. "Whenever we spent time together, she and Ed always seemed happy, didn't you think?"

"You can never tell from the outside what is going on inside a marriage. We probably look happy, too."

Her heart gave a bump. "We *are* happy."

"You haven't seemed too happy lately."

Why had she started this conversation when she was driving? "I want a baby, that's true, but it doesn't mean I'm not happy."

Was he saying *he* wasn't happy?

She felt a rush of panic. Greg was the one sure thing in her life. Dependable and reliable. She'd built a future with him on solid foundations, and suddenly those foundations had given a warning tremble.

They were silent for the rest of the drive and when Jenna finally pulled up outside The Captain's House and glanced at Greg, his eyes were closed.

"Greg?"

"Mmm?" He opened his eyes. "Are we here?"

"Yes. Wait—" She put her hand on his arm before he could unfasten the seat belt. "Are *you* happy? You talk about everyone but yourself. Tell me how you're feeling."

"I'm tired. Work is busy."

She didn't want to talk about work. She wanted to talk about *them*.

"You do want a baby, don't you?"

He hesitated. "Of course."

"Sometimes I think I want one more than you do."

"I want a family. But it's not the only thing I think about."

Was she that bad?

From now on she was going to stop talking about it all the time, at least to Greg. Now that Lauren was back, she could talk to her.

On impulse she grabbed him and tugged him toward her. "I love you, Greg Sullivan." She pressed her lips to his, feeling the familiar shape of his mouth.

He slid his hand behind her neck and kissed her back. It started slow, but no one knew how to stoke the heat like Greg. With each slide of his tongue and brush of his fingers, he turned the kiss into a dizzying prelude to a greater intimacy. She knew exactly how that intimacy would feel and raw sensation flashed through her. There was a delicious ache in her pelvis and she wished they were back home.

His hand stroked its way under her sweater and up to her breasts and she felt her flesh tighten under the skilled brush of his thumb.

"Greg!" She gasped against his mouth and he eased away just enough to speak.

"What?" His voice was thickened, his eyes sleepy and sexy.

"We can't. Not now."

"You'd rather talk to your mother than do this?"

"I'd rather not get arrested for conducting an indecent act in public." But she was tempted. This felt *good*. It had also felt spontaneous and there had been little of that in their lives lately.

"I guess you're right." He let her go and instantly she felt bereft.

"I love you."

"Love you, too." The sincerity in his voice soothed her.

There was nothing in the world better than knowing you were loved, and nothing that made you appreciate that gift more than seeing someone who had lost that.

"Let's rescue my sister."

She took his hand as they walked into the house, savoring the closeness. How must Lauren have felt marrying Ed when she was in love with Scott? It wasn't something she could imagine.

As they entered the house, she sniffed the air. "Something smells good."

The smells might have been hopeful, but as they walked into the kitchen Jenna felt the tension in the atmosphere. Her mother was lifting a casserole out of the oven and Lauren was setting the table. The look she gave Jenna was one of utter relief.

"Hi."

Jenna walked straight across the kitchen and hugged her, frowning as Lauren's hip bone jabbed her in the side. She could probably give half her body weight to her sister and Lauren still wouldn't be fat.

Lauren's arms tightened around her and Jenna remembered the times they'd done this as children.

When one was in trouble, the other was there.

Jenna noticed Mack slumped at the table. She was focused on her phone as if she was trying to disconnect herself from what was happening in the room. Like her mother, she had dark hollows under her eyes and she looked exhausted.

"How are you doing?" Jenna let go of her sister, checking first that she wasn't about to keel over.

"Good." There was a wild look in Lauren's eyes and she was shivering.

Lie: to speak untruthfully with intent to mislead or deceive.

"Are you cold? This place can be drafty."

Winter in the house was so much harsher, somehow. Summer shone light into dark corners but now, in the depths of February, the whole place felt tired and unloved. Or maybe it was the atmosphere. A house was only as happy as the people who lived there.

"Scott fixed the windows," Nancy said vaguely. "No more drafts."

"Scott?" Jenna glanced round cautiously, half expecting him to be leaning against a wall gazing at them all in brooding silence.

"He was here earlier finishing off some work on one of the doors, but he left."

"Which shouldn't be a surprise—" Mack glanced up from her phone "—given his track record."

Lauren flushed. "It wasn't like that."

Why would her sister defend a man who had left her pregnant?

Jenna wished now that she'd found a way to drag her sister out of here so that she could be on her own with her.

"Sit down. Let's eat." Nancy put plates on the table.

Jenna sat next to Lauren, across from Greg.

Was her mother really going to act as if none of this was happening?

And then she saw Nancy take a deep breath.

"As we're all together round the table, I thought this would be a good time to have an honest talk."

Really? Jenna thought. Did anyone in her family know how to have an honest talk?

"That sounds healthy," Greg said, and Jenna frowned.

It sounded out of character.

Nancy served casserole onto plates and handed them round. "Now that Lauren has had time to recover from her jet lag, we need to talk about what happens next."

Jenna added rice to her plate, appalled by her mother's lack of tact. While she had the spoon in her hand, she added a mountain of rice to Lauren's plate. Her sister needed to eat. "There's plenty of time to think about the future."

"No," Nancy said. "In fact there isn't."

There was an awkward silence and Jenna felt a rush of irritation.

Couldn't her mother just once deliver soothing platitudes as she was supposed to?

"Mom?"

"We need to help Lauren formulate a plan."

"Plan?" Jenna failed to keep the irritation out of her voice. "You mean about Scott?"

"No. I assume there's nothing to be done there or she would have done it years ago."

"I'm here." Lauren hadn't touched her food. "Sitting right here at the table. And I know I need to make decisions. I need to find a job and somewhere to live."

"There's plenty of time for all that, isn't there, Mom?" Jenna tried to smile but only managed to bare her teeth.

"You have ten bedrooms, so the house isn't exactly over-crowded. Lauren can live here while she decides what's best for her and Mack. The rest can wait."

Nancy sat down hard on the nearest chair. "It can't wait."

"It's only until I'm back on my feet again," Lauren said. "We won't get in the way. You'll hardly see us if you don't want to, and we certainly won't stop you painting."

And there it was. The truth.

Because they both knew that was the only thing that mattered in their mother's life. Painting.

"This has nothing to do with painting," Nancy said. "You have no idea how I have struggled with this, but I know it's the right decision."

"What is? What decision?" Jenna realized with a lurch of her stomach that this wasn't about saying the wrong thing at the wrong time. This was something more.

Her mother gripped the edge of the table. "I'm selling The Captain's House." There was a ripple in her voice that almost sounded like emotion. "The place is too big for me now. I'm on my own. I don't need ten bedrooms."

Jenna couldn't have been more shocked if her mother had clocked her with a skillet.

"You said you would never sell it. You said your ancestors would turn in their graves."

"Things change."

Lauren was the color of hospital sheets. "Who are you selling it to?"

Nancy studied her hands for a long moment and then looked up.

"That's the part that might be a little awkward. I'm selling to Scott Rhodes."

CHAPTER SIXTEEN

Nancy

Reflection: careful thought about a particular subject

NANCY AND TOM had been dating for precisely three months when he asked her to marry him. It had been a sunbaked day in the August of 1970 and they'd been watching the *Island Queen* ferry dock in Oak Bluffs.

Even though she was in love, Nancy had no idea that Tom intended to propose. Why would she? She had little experience of relationships. Losing both her parents at the age of eight had taught her nothing was permanent. As a result, she held part of herself back.

Tom, on the other hand, had no problem with relationships. He worked as a salesman, which turned out to be a perfect career for someone with his charm and charisma. The company he worked for was based in Boston, and he often spent weeks off island traveling.

When he returned, it was as if someone had switched a light on.

He turned that beam onto Nancy, who was dazzled.

She'd dated one other man before Tom, and he had claimed he loved her despite her passion for painting. Tom had said he loved her because of it, so naturally when he'd proposed on that sunny day against a blue sky and a calm sea the first thing she'd said was *yes*.

Right there and then he'd slipped a ring on her finger. She would have rather he hadn't done it in full view of the passengers spilling from the ferry to spend the day on the island, but Tom had always been impulsive.

It had been Tom who had suggested she paint the scene of their engagement so that they could remember it forever and she'd enthusiastically recreated the scene exactly as it was and hung it in the entryway at Tom's request.

It had hung there throughout their marriage, the blue skies and sparkling seas a reminder of that day.

She'd been relieved, and also a little surprised, that Tom had embraced the idea of living in The Captain's House.

He was hungry, impatient, always looking for the next thing. He rarely sat still whereas Nancy could spend hours in one position while she painted, losing track of place and time. She'd expected him to try to persuade her to move to Boston or even New York City, but he hadn't.

"You're a Stewart," he'd said, swinging her round as if they were in a ballroom, not on a beach. "The Stewart family has always lived in The Captain's House."

That was true.

After her parents had passed, Nancy had lived there with her grandmother, a woman who had little in the way of a sense of humor but much in the way of possessions.

Each generation of her family had added to the house, until it was crammed with objects from the past. There were days when it felt as if she was living in a museum.

"One day this place will be yours," her grandmother had said, and Nancy had wondered what she was supposed to do with ten bedrooms and seven hundred cobwebs. The weight of responsibility pressed down on her, but she also felt a sense of purpose.

It was her job to keep the house for future generations and it was a relief to have someone by her side while she did it.

It didn't take her long to realize Tom didn't share her emotional attachment to the place.

"It's freezing," he'd say, as they pulled on more layers of clothing and lit another fire in the living room. "We should replace all the windows with something more modern and fix the heating."

He made other suggestions that made Nancy realize he didn't understand the house at all. Her job was to preserve it, not rip out the heart of it. Quite apart from the fact they didn't have the money, she didn't want to do any of those things.

But it was the only thing they argued about. Other than that, they were happy.

When Tom was away, which was often, she had her art and her house.

The artist in her appreciated the graceful lines and the architecture, the woman in her loved the space and the light, and the child in her was comforted by the feeling that generations of her family were somehow there with her. Despite its size, it was impossible to ever feel lonely when your history was stamped in every crack in the wall. It was the kind of house that didn't just belong to a family, but became another member of the family. And maybe a part of her had thought that with a house like this sheltering them, a family would be protected.

It turned out she'd been wrong about that, just as she'd been wrong about so many things.

They lived on Tom's salary, most of which was eaten up by the eye-watering costs of keeping up The Captain's House. She felt fortunate that Tom's career in sales brought in enough that they could at least make ends meet. He traveled a lot, but that was the price they paid for financial security and, given that the house drained money and living in it had been her idea, she wasn't in a position to complain.

Nancy sold the occasional painting, but the money didn't make much of a contribution to their household expenses.

Had she been painting for money she would have given up, but she'd never painted for commercial gain. She painted because doing so made her happy. When she was painting, everything else vanished from her mind. It was art, but it was also a form of meditation. She could no more give up painting than she could give up breathing.

Her sudden and unexpected career success had coincided with the birth of her first child.

Lauren had been two weeks old when a wealthy summer visitor had spotted one of Nancy's paintings in a local café. He owned a gallery in Boston and had a buyer who he knew would devour Nancy's atmospheric seascapes.

He'd taken everything she had, and come back for more.

Her work went from being largely ignored to being much in demand.

Soon she was the one who had to travel. She had exhibitions in New York, Paris, Geneva, London.

With two young children it would have been impossible

but by then Tom had lost his job and failed to get another, which meant that when he wasn't on the golf course he was home. He was a wonderful father to the girls, always playing with them and making them laugh. He held them enthralled in that beam of light that drew everyone to him, while Nancy stood hovering in the shadows.

She tried to feel grateful rather than hurt. She reminded herself that it was because Tom was good with the children that she was able to embark on the tour.

She'd arrive home exhausted, and feel like a stranger in her own house.

Without her there to add structure to the day, the girls were almost feral and any attempt on her part to instill discipline seemed to widen the rift.

The harder she tried, the more alienated she felt.

Tom would scoop up the girls and say, "The three musketeers are off to the beach. See you later."

Nancy felt excluded, but she had no idea how to insert herself into their cozy triumvirate. She loved her daughters. She loved Tom. What was the matter with her? Why did she always feel as if she was on the outside looking in?

And then came that day in June, when she'd arrived home early from an exhibition in Europe and found Tom in bed with a girl he'd met on the beach.

Nancy stared at the tangle of bedding and bare limbs and knew her world would never be the same again.

"It didn't mean anything, Nancy." At the same time as he was throwing the girl out the door, he'd thrown a hundred excuses at his shattered wife.

He was lonely. She was always painting or traveling.

Nancy heard one thing—

It was her fault.

She wasn't good at relationships. She couldn't keep her husband and her children preferred their father.

It was worse than bereavement, because every time she saw him she remembered that she wasn't enough. That girl had turned out to be the first of many. Tom grew more adept at hiding it, but Nancy always knew. There would be late-night phone calls. Nights when he disappeared without telling her where he was going. It grew so bad she found it hard to be in the house with him, and one day she tackled it head-on.

"I think you should move out."

"Why? You're never here anyway. I'm the one who is there for the girls while you're flying around the world being a big star."

Nancy had held the hurt inside. "I'm supporting my family."

"That's right, rub it in. Make me feel less of a man because I'm not earning. There are plenty of women out there who appreciate me."

She knew about those women, and she'd watched as he'd raked his hands through his hair, those same hands that had stroked their way over flesh that wasn't hers.

"I think you should go to them."

This time there was panic in his eyes. "Leave my kids? No. I love them and they love me. We have fun together. They *need* their father."

The implication was that she was boring and that they didn't need her.

My kids. As if Nancy didn't have a role to play.

"They need stability. They don't need a father who spends his life with his pants round his ankles."

"They're not going to know unless you tell them." His

gaze challenged her. "They're having the perfect childhood. Are you going to take that away from them?"

She thought about what it had been like growing up without her father.

At best they'd resent her. Maybe they'd even hate her.

Nancy couldn't bear the thought.

As she was contemplating the horror of that scenario, Tom delivered the final blow.

"If you send me away, they'll blame you." And she knew that what he was really saying was *I'll make sure they blame you.*

It gradually dawned on her that to keep any sort of relationship with her daughters and protect them from being hurt, she was going to have to keep her husband.

It felt as if she was making a deal with the devil.

CHAPTER SEVENTEEN

Mack

*Pressure: trying to persuade or force someone
to do something*

MACK SLAMMED HER locker shut and wished for the millionth time that they'd never left London. The other kids streamed past her in the opposite direction, leaving her feeling like a lone salmon swimming downstream.

If she could have picked a superpower, it would have been invisibility.

It was her third week at her new school and so far it had been a disaster. In London she'd managed to blend, chameleon-like, into her surroundings but here she didn't know the people or the rules well enough to do that. She was terrified of doing something wrong and making herself a target.

They were studying totally different stuff, and the other kids were already in friendship groups. She knew from experience that breaking into those groups and being accepted would be a nightmare. The girl who had been assigned to show her round and support her had vanished back to her friends as soon as her job was done.

The worst thing was lunch in the cafeteria. It was a huge open space where the strong flourished and the weak and vulnerable were exposed. Mack felt like a lone gazelle grazing on the savannah in full view of a pride of lions.

Her mother had encouraged her to join after-school clubs to meet people, but so far she hadn't spoken more than a few words to anyone and all she wanted to do at the end of the day was go home and escape to her bedroom. The thought of extending the torture wasn't appealing.

Across from her a lanky dark-haired boy was pinning up a poster advertising the Coding Club.

Tuesdays and Thursdays from 2:30 to 4:00 p.m.

She felt a thrill of excitement. In London, the focus had all been on traditional subjects and cramming for exams. There was no coding club.

Mack checked no one was looking and glanced again at the poster.

Could she go?

No. Excitement gave way to gloom. She knew from experience that to express interest in computer coding would be social suicide, especially when she was so new.

First impressions counted.

She turned back to her locker, ignoring the yearning inside her. Whatever label she managed to earn in these early days would stick. She didn't want it to be nerd or geek. Bad things happened to nerds and geeks.

She dragged her heels to English. She loved reading, but the essays they were set were so boring.

If she'd been a teacher she would have made it more fun.

On a scale of one to ten, how much do you want to strangle Anna Karenina?

She grinned to herself and then saw a student looking at her and quickly wiped the smile off her face.

She tried not to think about Phoebe back home in England.

Without making eye contact with anyone, she slid into an empty seat and pulled out her books.

She'd already read the book the class was studying. Was she supposed to say so? Or pretend to be stupid?

"Hi." The girl next to her flashed her a smile that almost blinded. "I'm Kennedy. And you're new. I've seen you in some of my classes."

Mack was so relieved that someone had finally spoken to her, she almost melted with gratitude. "I'm Mack."

"You're British? Oh my God." Kennedy pressed her hand to her chest. "I *love* your accent. Where are you from?"

"I lived in London, but my mom is from here. I'm only half-British. She was born on the Vineyard." And if it was going to make her more popular she would be as British as possible.

"But now you've moved back? From London? Why?" Her tone suggested she couldn't imagine why anyone would want to do that.

"My—" Mack stalled. No way was she ready to divulge personal details. "My dad died."

"Oh, that's too bad." Kennedy's brow creased. "So tough."

"Yeah." Mack felt emotion rush at her and dipped her head in horror. If she cried now it would all be over. She leaned down and pulled her pens out of her bag, giving herself a moment to recover. *Breathe, Mack, breathe.*

"So do you want to hang out some time?" Kennedy was open and friendly and Mack had to fight even harder not to cry, but this time the emotion was driven by relief.

It was all she could do not to hug Kennedy.

She'd hoped that she might find some friends eventually, but she hadn't expected it to be so soon. And she hadn't expected the overture to come from someone like Kennedy, the coolest girl in the year.

"Thanks." Humbled and touched, she tried not to choke on the word. "I'd like that."

"Great." Kennedy's smile widened. "A bunch of us go to the beach most days after school. In the summer we swim and stuff, but while the weather is cold we mostly just hang out, chat and do things to keep warm."

Mack wondered what "things" were. "I don't have a car or anything."

"No worries. My brother and a couple of his friends have cars, so we'll give you a ride."

Mack shifted uncomfortably. There was no way her mother would want her to climb into a car with a bunch of older boys she'd never met before.

"I have my bike at school."

"Mitch drives his dad's pickup so you can sling the bike in the back of that. Come this afternoon. We'll meet at the front entrance. It will be good for you to meet a few people." Kennedy's eyes narrowed. "Unless you need to check with your mom or something."

Mack was torn. Now that the first thrill had faded, she was starting to feel uneasy. But Kennedy's smile was like a flickering torch in a dark tunnel and Mack didn't want that light to go out.

She had a feeling this was some sort of test and she was determined not to fail.

It wasn't as if her mother was likely to check up on her. She had too much on her mind to be a helicopter parent right now. And she'd wanted Mack to make friends, hadn't she?

"My mom is cool with whatever I want to do," she said.

"Great." The smile was back to full wattage. Kennedy had perfect teeth, blue eyes and that groomed all-American look that Mack knew she'd never be able to achieve.

Across the room, Mack noticed the lanky, dark-haired boy who had pinned up the advert for the Coding Club. Their eyes met. He gave her an awkward smile and she looked away, embarrassed.

"Ignore him," Kennedy advised. Flicking her hair back, she took her book out of her bag and slapped it on the desk. "He's probably just looked up from his keyboard and discovered girls exist, but he wouldn't have a clue what to do with one of them so don't worry. He's a coding creep."

Mack didn't think he looked like a creep, but to say so would sentence her to a life in teenage exile so she kept quiet.

At that moment the teacher arrived in the classroom and attention focused on work.

Mack kept her head down and said very little.

When they went to the cafeteria for lunch, this time she sat with Kennedy and her friends.

It was obvious that they were the golden group, the elites that others watched with envy.

They laughed loudly and were confident.

Mack saw a few kids sitting alone, and was relieved not to be one of them.

During break she sneaked a text to her mom.

Staying after school with friends. Home late.

The reply came moments later.

So proud of you joining a club and making friends so fast.
Go you! xx

Mack felt a twinge of guilt but told herself it was just
some lighthearted fun with a bunch of cool people.

What could go wrong?

During the drive to the beach she was squashed in the
back seat between two girls she didn't know and a boy who
obviously thought it wasn't cool to shower. There weren't
enough seat belts for all of them, but they'd joked that if
they had an accident they'd be wedged too tightly to be
thrown anywhere.

Mack laughed, too, although it took effort. Some of the
roads on the island were single track and bumpy. She would
have felt better having a seat belt.

Kennedy's brother, Nick, was driving and during the gen-
eral chat Mack discovered he was a senior and off to Har-
vard to study medicine in the fall.

Medicine. He was going to be a doctor. That had to
make him sensible and responsible, didn't it? Mack relaxed
slightly. The feeling lasted until he parked at the beach,
popped the trunk of his car and she saw the booze.

Panic lodged itself in her chest.

If there was one thing that freaked her mom out, it was
underage drinking. The drinking laws were more lenient
in the UK but that hadn't helped her when she'd had her
vodka moment.

The other kids all seemed so confident and comfortable,

and she felt horribly out of place. She didn't want to be here. She didn't want to do this.

She watched as Nick tossed a beer to one of his friends and grabbed one for himself.

Her mom had drilled into her that she should never get into a car with someone who had been drinking, but to refuse a ride home would risk alienating her new friends. It would also mean she'd be stranded at the beach.

She had no idea how to get back to The Captain's House from here and it would be dark soon.

It seemed she was stuck with her new friends.

She glanced desperately at Kennedy, but the other girl was busy laughing and flirting with one of the older boys.

"So, you're Mack?" One of Nick's friends strolled over to her. He was good-looking and his smile was friendly. "I'm Mitch, and you must be new. I haven't seen you around."

Mack relaxed slightly. "I just moved here from London."

She allowed herself a small smile. Mack and Mitch? That was never going to work.

"London, England?" He took a swig of beer. "You ever see the queen?"

Definitely never going to work.

"No," she said. "I never saw the queen." *She lives in a palace, dumbass.*

She glanced across the beach and saw Nick making out with someone she recognized from her English class, a girl who sat next to Kennedy. Even as she looked, the girl fumbled for the zipper of his jeans and Mack looked away quickly.

"Ignore them," Mitch advised. "They need to get a room. Which they probably will later. Help yourself to a beer."

Mack hesitated. If she refused, she ran the risk of being

teased, and if she accepted she ran the risk of being caught drinking under age and that wasn't good either.

In the end she accepted and decided to find a way to spill some of it.

She half wished her mom would call to check where she was, but for once her phone was silent.

Mitch lit a cigarette, took a long drag and then offered it to her.

Mack shook her head. Not even to fit in was she prepared to inhale that noxious stuff.

He shrugged and smoked it himself instead.

She glanced round to see where Kennedy was and caught a glimpse of her blond head inside one of the cars. The windows were steamed up so you couldn't even see inside.

Mack decided that was probably a good thing.

She shouldn't have come.

She definitely shouldn't have come.

The wind was cold and she shivered.

"You're cold?" Mitch crushed the cigarette under his boot and pulled her against him. "I'll warm you up."

She wanted to push him away but she was so cold she was grateful for any warmth she could get.

"How long are we staying?"

"We only just got here." He pressed his mouth to hers and she tasted cigarettes and almost choked.

It was gross. How could anyone think this was fun?

She tried to shove him away, but his arms were like bands of steel.

For the first time since she'd agreed to this stupid trip, she felt a flash of real fear.

Mitch grinned down at her. "You could be a little more friendly."

"I need to get home." She tried to push him away again but the more she pushed the more he tightened his arms.

"Hey, relax. We're having some fun, that's all."

She knew this wasn't fun and she also knew she was in serious trouble. If she ever found a way out of this, she was never, ever making a bad decision again. "Let me go!"

"You heard her." The voice was deep and came from right behind her.

She recognized it instantly. It belonged to the same person who had come to her rescue last time she'd been in trouble. Scott Rhodes.

Relief flooded through her. She knew that later she was going to feel humiliation along with a whole lot of other uncomfortable emotions, but right now all she cared about was that she was safe. It didn't occur to her that Scott might not be able to handle this group. He looked like the kind of guy who could handle anything.

Mitch obviously agreed. He recognized Scott and promptly let go of Mack, thrusting her away from him so roughly she would have fallen if Scott hadn't caught her.

He steadied her, his hand firm on her shoulder. "Are you okay?"

There was a big wedge of tears lodged in her throat but she managed to nod.

Scott's mouth tightened into a grim line. Mack quailed. He was obviously really mad at her.

Mitch must have seen it, too, because he took a step back.

"Hey, she got in the car. She chose to come. There's no law against that."

Scott paused. "Maybe not, but there are laws against underage drinking, drinking and driving, and driving without seat belts, not to mention laws about consent. She told you

to let her go. You need to work on your listening skills."
Dangerously calm, he glanced at Mack and jerked his head
toward the car. "Get in."

"But my bike is—"

"I'll deal with it."

Head down, she walked to Scott's pickup and slid into
the front passenger seat. It had started to rain and through
the misted windshield she could see Scott talking to Mitch.
The boy had his head dipped so Mack couldn't see his face,
but his body language told her it wasn't a comfortable conversation.

Something licked her hand and she almost jumped out
of her skin.

She turned round in her seat and noticed the dog in the
back seat.

She hadn't thought anything could make her feel okay
ever again, but the sight of the dog lifted her spirits.

The car door opened and Scott slid into the driver's seat.

Mack swallowed. "I didn't know you had a dog. He's
gorgeous."

"Fasten your seat belt." He checked his mirror and re-
versed down the track until he reached a turning spot.

Mack reached out her hand to the dog, who leaned forward and licked it again.

"What's his name?"

"Captain. He's a Chesapeake Bay Retriever."

The light was fading fast. His headlights picked out the
track as they bumped their way to the main road. The landscape around them was indistinct. In London the streets
were illuminated so brightly it was like sleeping with the
lights on. Here on the Vineyard there was nothing but stars.

Mack closed her eyes for a moment, relieved to be safe.

She'd worry about the impact of it all tomorrow. For now she needed a rest from it all.

"Thank you for rescuing me. How did you know where I was?"

"I was on the beach with Captain and saw the cars drive past. I recognized that boy you were with." He tightened his grip on the wheel. "It didn't take you long to find the wrong crowd."

"I didn't know they were the wrong crowd." But she had known, hadn't she? Deep down she'd known, but she'd been so grateful to be included she hadn't cared.

She was pathetic.

Scott's gaze was fixed on the road ahead. "Over here, underage drinking is an offense."

"I know."

"That guy who had his hands on you—"

"I met him an hour ago. He's a friend of Kennedy's brother." She glanced sideways and saw that his jaw was tight.

"You do know what he wanted, don't you?" In the fading light he looked rough and a little dangerous. She could understand why Mitch had decided to back away without a fight.

"Yes. I'm not stupid." Or maybe she was. She slumped in her seat. "I don't blame you for being mad. That's twice you've had to rescue me."

"I'm not mad. I am concerned that you didn't know how to deal with him."

"I would have been okay." She tried not to think about that disgusting kiss or those arms like iron bars, locking her body against his. She also tried not to think about what rumors Kennedy and the others were going to spread about her in school, but that was harder.

"You need to learn to take care of yourself and we're going to deal with that, but the first rule of self-defense is not getting yourself into bad situations in the first place."

Mack gaped at him. "You're going to teach me how to fight?"

"Fighting and being able to defend yourself aren't the same thing. Did you ever do any martial arts? Self-defense?"

"I'm not what you'd call a sporty person." Mack kept her hand between the seats so that she could stroke Captain. "If I was, I wouldn't have had problems. Sporty people don't usually get bullied. Don't tell me—you were captain of the football team."

The corner of his mouth flickered. "No ball skills whatsoever." It was only a hint of a smile but it was enough to make her feel better.

"I bet you have like fifteen different black belts and can throw a ten-ton man onto his back with a flick of your little finger."

"No belts of any color. And I was a scrawny kid."

Mack eyed the bulk of shoulder muscle under his jacket. "You're not scrawny now."

"I filled out some, that's true. But it's not what you're like on the outside that stops you being bullied, it's what's on the inside."

"My insides are a mess, too, so I guess I'm doomed."

"It starts with your brain. First you do the thinking. Is this a good situation? Does it feel right?"

Mack huddled in her seat. Nothing about that situation had felt right. "You make it sound easy, but it's not so easy when you're friendless."

"A friend is someone who cares about you. What you had back there was a bunch of teenagers who didn't give jack shit about you." His bluntness made her eyes fill.

"Thanks for not making me feel better *at all*." If she had another way of getting home, she would have taken it. She was already feeling raw. She didn't need any more abrasions.

"You want me to lie and pretend those kids are your friends?"

"Okay, enough! Stop! I don't need this." Mack put her hands over her ears and then let them drop into her lap. "They all hate me. I get it. I'm never going to make friends now and I'm going to be alone for the rest of my life."

He frowned. "All I'm saying is—"

"I know what you're saying! There's no need to hammer it home. Is this what you would have been like if you'd stuck around?"

"Honest, you mean?"

"I was going to say *tactless. Unkind.*"

"We have different definitions of *unkind.*"

"Whatever." She leaned her head back against the seat, wondering if life could possibly get any worse. "Are you going to tell my mom about tonight?"

He slowed down as they approached an intersection. "Why would I do that?"

"Because I made a stupid choice. You probably think I need discipline."

"I think you had a nasty moment and that's going to stay with you longer than anything I, or your mom, might say. If you want to tell your mom, that's your decision." They'd reached Edgartown and he drove slowly along the narrow streets.

She was so relieved to be home and safe she almost cried.

Instead she stroked Captain. He licked her palm again and again, as if he knew she needed comfort. "I love your dog. How long have you had him?" She hoped he'd stick with the subject of the dog. It seemed the safest thing to talk about.

"Couple of years. I found him washed up on the beach."

"Washed up?"

"Someone tried to drown him, but Chesapeake Bay Retrievers are great swimmers. He managed to haul himself as far as the dock and then collapsed with half the ocean in his lungs."

"That's terrible." Mack was horrified. "How can people be so cruel? And he has the nicest face of any dog I've ever seen."

"You don't have a dog?"

"No. I would have loved one, but we lived in London and our house wasn't exactly dog friendly. We didn't have a big yard or anything." But if they were staying on the island, maybe they could get a dog. The thought cheered her, until she remembered that her grandmother was selling the house. To Scott. She decided that wasn't a topic she wanted to raise. She'd had all the stress she could handle for one night. "Dogs are always pleased to see you. You don't have to pretend to be cool. You don't have to try and fit. You can be yourself. You probably have no idea what I'm talking about."

"I know exactly what you're talking about."

He pulled up outside her grandmother's house and Mack found herself wishing the journey had been longer. A few moments before she'd been ready to jump from the car, but with the dog's warm nose nudging her sympathetically she was in no hurry to move.

"When you were my age did you have to move and change schools?"

He stared straight ahead. "All the time."

"How did you make new friends?"

"I got to like my own company." He turned his head to look at her. "That's usually better than the wrong company."

"I know I try too hard, but I want to feel accepted. I guess because things are a bit rough at home." She leaned her head back against the seat, braced for him to say something that would make her feel worse.

"Have you told your mom how you feel?"

"No. She'd worry, and believe me she has enough to worry about. I may not be the daughter of her dreams, but even I'm not going to dump another load of crap on her head. You want to know something crazy? Sometimes I lie there at night and imagine I have superpowers like in the movies."

"Resilience is a superpower." He leaned across her and opened the door. "You have that."

"You think so?" She wasn't sure. She would have liked to talk about it some more, but he'd opened the door so presumably he was done with her. "Are you sure you don't want to come in? The fact that you saved me probably gives you plenty of plus points. I'll be the one in trouble, not you." She shrugged it off, pretending to not care even though she cared very much.

"I don't think it's a good idea." He sprang out of the car and Captain jumped out after him, tail wagging as Scott unloaded her bike. "Do you have a phone?"

"I'm a teenager. My phone is the equivalent of life support."

He held out his hand. "Give it to me."

Was he going to confiscate it? Wary, she handed it over and he tapped the screen and entered a number.

"You're giving me your number?"

"In case you're ever in trouble and you don't want to call your mom." He handed the phone back to her. "I can't guarantee not to say the wrong thing and upset you, but I can guarantee to come when you call."

She felt as if someone had thrown a warm blanket around her shoulders.

For the first time since she'd arrived on the island, she didn't feel alone. There was someone she could call. Worried she might burst into tears, she bent to kiss Captain on the head and then straightened. "Thanks."

Scott reached out and squeezed her shoulder. "Don't beat yourself up. There's not a person alive who hasn't made bad choices at one time or another."

"Did you?"

"I made more than most." With a brief smile he whistled to the dog, climbed back into his pickup and disappeared down the street.

CHAPTER EIGHTEEN

Lauren

> *Reunion: a meeting between people who have*
> *been separated for some time*

LAUREN PARKED HER mother's car and walked down to the boatyard.

It was still early and she'd left everyone else asleep. She'd been awake since one o'clock, which would have been six in the morning in London. It had been weeks since she'd arrived on the Vineyard, and still she wasn't sleeping. The moment she closed her eyes her mind started to race. Her chest felt as if it was being squeezed by metal bands and panic rushed down on her like the tide.

First Ed, then the money, leaving London, her mother selling The Captain's House—

Lauren breathed deeply, trying to find the calm that used to come so easily.

The early morning sky was cloudy, the sea a gunmetal gray. Her coat, which had felt perfectly adequate for chilly coffee mornings in London, was woefully inadequate against the cold bite of the wind that slapped at her face and tugged at her hair. She turned up her collar, wondering if she'd ever feel warm again.

After everything that had happened lately, one more thing shouldn't have had an impact but when Mack had told her about the beach incident she'd felt physically sick.

Part of her was relieved Mack had confided in her, but she knew that for Mack to be so open with her given the current rocky state of their relationship, she must have been very shaken up.

And no matter how much she didn't want to see Scott Rhodes, she owed him her thanks.

On the other hand, maybe it was crazy doing this to herself.

She was already halfway back to her car when she saw his pickup bouncing down the uneven dirt track toward her.

He'd already seen her so it was too late to run.

She was conscious that it was just the two of them, alone on this cold morning, and felt as guilty as a woman contemplating an affair.

I'm sorry, Ed, I'm sorry.

And then she remembered that Ed was the reason she was back on Martha's Vineyard.

If it weren't for him, she wouldn't be standing here now, waiting to talk to her ex-lover.

Ex-*love.*

She'd loved Scott so much she hadn't been able to see further than the end of her feelings.

Her heart accelerated as Scott slammed the door and strolled across to her.

A dog bounded toward her, tail wagging. She might have felt nervous except Mack had talked about the dog nonstop.

It had surprised her to learn that Scott had a dog. Surely a pet was a commitment?

She stooped to stroke the animal, which gave her an excuse not to focus on the man, although she'd already seen more than enough.

He'd filled out. Shoulders wider, chest bigger. Different in every way to Ed, who had grown up pampered and indulged by a doting mother. Scott rarely talked about his past, but he'd said enough. The legacy of his hard upbringing was visible in the way he chose to live his life. He kept himself fit and ready for anything. He was self-contained and self-reliant.

Scott Rhodes needed no one.

And yet he'd understood her as no one else had before or since.

She straightened and forced herself to meet his gaze. The past, blurred and muted over time, sharpened into focus.

The dangerous crackle and snap of chemistry hummed to life inside her.

She tried to shut it down, but looking at him was all it took for her to feel herself begin to unravel. She'd held it together since the fateful birthday party, battling each obstacle that had come her way, dealing with life, teetering on the edge of a deep pool of emotions but too scared to allow herself to tumble in case she couldn't pull herself out again. But now all she wanted to do was fling herself against him. She hadn't felt safe in a while, and she knew those powerful arms would make her feel safe. She knew they'd make her feel other things, too, which was why she didn't step forward.

Ignoring the pounding of her heart, she smiled. "I came to thank you for last night. What you did for Mack."

"She told you?"

His hair was very dark and his features strong. The blue of his eyes was the only thing that softened what might otherwise have been described as a hard face.

"She was very shaken up. And grateful to you."

"Seemed to me I upset her. I'm not used to talking to kids. I don't know the right way."

"She's a teenager. Today's right way is tomorrow's wrong way." Her mouth felt so dry she could hardly speak. Right now she felt like a teenager herself. "She's grateful and I'm grateful, too. If anything happened to her I'd—"

"I don't think she'll be doing it again." He turned back to the truck and hauled some bags out of the back, the muscles of his shoulders flexing. "Are you feeling better? I haven't seen you since that day at the ferry."

Why was she looking at his muscles? What was wrong with her? "I'm sorry Mack blurted it out like that. The fact that you're her father."

"I am her father."

She'd spent so long trying to forget that fact that it was a shock to hear him say it so calmly. "It wasn't the way I would have chosen to spread the news."

"News spreads. The method doesn't generally matter."

She knew it wouldn't take long for it to filter through to the locals, but he probably wouldn't be around long enough for it to bother him. "I didn't think you'd still be living here. I was surprised to see you."

"I gathered that by the way you keeled over on the dock."

She would have felt embarrassed if she hadn't been busy wrestling other feelings. "I assumed you'd be sailing a far distant ocean somewhere."

His face was inscrutable. "No."

"Mom mentioned that you've been doing some work on the house. You're working here full-time?" The boatyard belonged to the company Island Marine and had occupied this corner of the harbor for as long as she could remember. The owner Joshua Roper had died a few years previously and left the business to his son Charlie, who had been a couple of years ahead of Jenna at school. "You're working with Charlie?"

"Sometimes."

Sometimes. When it suited him. Life on his terms.

Some things hadn't changed.

But he'd saved her daughter.

"It's cold. Let's take this conversation inside before you catch pneumonia." He transferred the bags to one arm so that he could unlock the door of the office, and then dumped everything onto the table.

Captain bounded into the room and settled himself on a large cushion in front of the log burner.

Lauren glanced round the place, wishing she could stop shivering.

One half of the room was used as an office, complete with file cabinets. There was a desk, and she noticed a high-spec computer. The other half was equipped as a kitchen. It was surprisingly tidy, every surface clear and shining. She remembered visiting a couple of times with her father when she was young and the place had been a mess. It seemed Charlie hadn't inherited his father's untidy traits.

The walls were covered in maps, some of them annotated with bold black strokes of a pen.

She stepped closer. "What are the lines and arrows?"

"They're the routes I've sailed." He lifted milk out of the bag and stowed it in the fridge.

She studied the map, relieved to have an excuse not to look at him. "You've virtually sailed round the world." Single-handed. Alone.

"There's a lot to see."

"Did you ever find what you were looking for?" Her question was met with silence so she turned her head and met his gaze.

"Did you?" His voice was rough.

What had she been looking for?

At first it had been love, but then it had been security and stability.

She'd lost all three.

Because it was impossible to think when he was looking at her, she glanced back at the maps.

She hadn't imagined that being alone with him would be this hard.

Her feelings unsettled her. She didn't want to be the sort of person who lost a husband one day and then wanted to rip the clothes off another man the next.

Her emotions were so close to the surface she felt like one of those volcano experiments Mack had done at school. Everything was about to boil over.

She studied the lines on the map. He must have been away for a year. More? "Where are you living?"

"On the boat."

Some of her happiest moments had been spent on his boat. There had even been moments when she'd thought they might have a future.

Determined not to think about that, she turned. "Mack said you brought her home. You should have come in."

He glanced at her. "Things were a little tense last time I was in the house. I wasn't sure I'd be welcome."

"You saved my daughter from a difficult situation. Of course you would have been welcome."

His gaze was steady. "Is she doing all right?"

"She's very confused right now." She was desperate to talk about it. The responsibility was a crushing weight to carry alone. "I don't know why she did what she did last night."

"You never did anything reckless at her age?"

Lauren felt herself flush. They both knew the answer to that one.

"It's tough for her, trying to fit in. She had some issues in her old school, too." She wondered why she was telling him this. If he'd been at all interested in being a parent, they might be having a different conversation now.

"Trying to make yourself fit in never works. You are who you are."

Which was why there had never been any hope for them.

"I didn't only come here to thank you. Mom says you're buying The Captain's House." She'd had a few weeks to digest the information and she still couldn't believe it. "Why would you do that?"

When her mother had first announced it, it was hard to know who had been more shocked, her or Jenna. Even calm, unflappable Greg had seemed startled.

Of all the things she'd pictured happening in life, her mother selling the family home had never been on the list. Nancy wouldn't even throw away a photograph. How was she going to dispose of the whole thing?

All that talk about finding it difficult to afford the upkeep made no sense to Lauren because she knew her mother had made a fortune with her paintings.

She was hoping it was all a mistake. Maybe her mother

was having a delayed midlife crisis. The thought that Scott might be buying her home made her want to hyperventilate.

"The house is no longer for sale." The words *especially not to you* hovered on her lips. "I don't know what you said to her to persuade her to sell it but it's not going to happen, and the fact that I'm grateful to you for saving my daughter isn't going to change anything."

He tipped fruit into the bowl on the table. "So you still don't talk to your mother."

"What's that supposed to mean?"

"If you'd talked," he said, "you wouldn't be standing here now trying to find answers to the questions you should be asking her. You're staying in the house, not with your sister?"

"Yes."

"If you're in your old room, which I'm guessing you are because it has the best views and the windows are sound, then that means you're less than five strides away from the room your mother uses."

"I don't see what—"

"Instead of knocking on her door and having a conversation, you chose to drive over here when it's barely light and confront a man you hoped you'd never see again."

She was struggling to close the door on her feelings but they kept finding ways to sneak through the cracks. Her heart started to beat harder, thumping against her ribs like a warning.

"I didn't hope that."

There was an ironic gleam in his eyes. "You took one look at me on the dock that day and passed out."

"I hadn't been sleeping, or eating—"

"And the last person you needed to see was a man you hate with every bone in your body."

"I don't hate you." Her voice gave up on her and emerged as a croak. "I never hated you." Didn't he know her better than that?

He turned away and carried on unloading the last of the bags. "I wouldn't blame you if you did. I gave you reason."

He was pushing against that door and she no longer had the strength to keep it shut.

She felt raw and exposed. This wasn't how the conversation was supposed to go. It wasn't supposed to be about them. "What about you?" She'd seen the effect he had on women. She'd seen the way heads turned. After they'd parted ways she'd occasionally imagined him with one of those women, but the vision was so painful she'd done her best to delete it. "Was there anyone serious for you?"

"No."

"You're telling me you didn't have other relationships?"

"No, I'm not telling you that." He glanced at her. "I'm telling you there wasn't anyone serious."

A warmth spread across her belly. "I thought you'd forget me."

"Forget you? How?" He gave a humorless laugh. "You were the one person who understood me. Certainly the only person I ever trusted. There was never any chance I'd forget you, Laurie."

His use of her name was intimate. Personal.

She thought about the way he'd whispered it against her lips as they'd lain naked.

She'd known, almost from the start, that anything they had wouldn't last. If anything, that had deepened the intensity of their feelings.

It had been years since she'd seen him, but it could have been yesterday. She knew how it felt to be kissed by him.

Touched by him. She knew his lips, his hands, his mind and that knowledge fed the chemistry that still simmered.

"I didn't come here to talk about the past. I want to talk about the present." And the future. If he intended to buy a house, then that meant he'd be a permanent fixture on the island. She wouldn't be able to stand it. "Why would you want our house? You're the man who doesn't want ties or responsibilities. You live on a boat so that you can sail into the sunset at a moment's notice—" She realized she was repeating a conversation they'd had more than sixteen years ago and almost choked on the words. "I don't understand why you'd want to saddle yourself with property when you didn't—" She broke off and his gaze locked on hers.

"When I didn't want a child? Is that what you were going to say?"

"I understood why you didn't want that. I don't understand this." She eyed the rip in his jeans and the battered jacket that seemed to have seen its share of winters. She had no idea what The Captain's House would be worth, but she was pretty sure it would be a small fortune. How could he begin to afford it? "You were never interested in settling down."

"That was more than sixteen years ago. Are you telling me you're the same person you were sixteen years ago?"

At that moment she felt as if they were back where they'd started.

"What are you saying? That you suddenly want a house, a mortgage and a yard where you grow your own vegetables? I know you better than that, Scott."

He ignored that question and spooned coffee into a machine. "When did you last eat?"

"What?"

"You can't stop shivering. I'm asking when you last ate."

Her head throbbed and she lifted her fingers to her forehead, wishing she'd tried to sleep a little longer. Coming here had been a mistake. She should have sent a note. "I don't know—" She rubbed her head with her fingertips. "Last night."

"Not eating isn't going to fix anything." His gaze skimmed over her. "You don't weigh anything."

"You don't know what I weigh."

"I carried you, remember?"

She was trying not to remember. Right now she wished she were back in that semiconscious state.

She also remembered the soft rumble of his voice in her ear. *I've got you.*

In those few moments, she'd felt safe. She'd always felt safe with him, which was ironic given that he'd hurt her more than anyone.

"It's been a difficult time."

"I heard. I'm sorry about your husband. Do you want breakfast?" He pulled open the fridge and pulled out eggs and bacon.

"Is Charlie going to mind your making yourself at home?"

"You can ask him next time you see him." He fried bacon and cooked eggs in a skillet. The smell tantalized and seduced until she almost felt hungry.

When he plated up crispy bacon, perfect scrambled eggs and mushrooms she frowned.

"You used to hate mushrooms."

"Still do. This is for you." He put the plate on the table and pulled out a chair. "Sit down."

She wasn't sure she could eat, but the food looked so good her stomach was sending her mixed signals.

He heaped food onto his own plate and put it on the table along with two brimming mugs of coffee.

She nibbled a piece of bacon. "You always did know how to look after yourself."

"There wasn't anyone else to do it for me."

"Was it a shock, seeing your daughter?"

He spooned sugar into his coffee. "I think she had the bigger shock."

"She only found out about you recently."

"I guessed that."

"I was trying to protect her. I didn't want her to grow up feeling insecure." For the millionth time she wished she could go back and do things differently. "I don't know why I'm telling you this."

"Because it helps to talk to someone." He stirred his coffee. "And you know me."

Scott knew about her past. He would understand, possibly even better than Ed, why she'd made the decisions she had. The fact that Scott knew her so well made her feel uncomfortable. It felt wrong to have that depth of intimacy with someone you weren't married to. "I was determined to be a good mother. Every decision I made, I put her first."

"She's lucky to have you."

"She doesn't think so." Lauren put her fork down. "She's mad at me."

"You can be mad at someone and still love them."

For some reason she found that more comforting than anything else anyone had said to her. "The one thing I really wanted to get right in life, I got wrong."

"You made the decision you thought was right at the time. That's all any of us can do."

"Have you ever made a decision you regretted?"

There was a long silence. "Yes."

The way he was looking at her left her in no doubt about which decision he was talking about.

There had been a time when his confession would have left her dizzy with hope and longing.

Now? She didn't know. Over the past few weeks her feelings had been battered so badly she felt numb, but now something inside her was reawakening. It was a tingle in her skin and a flutter in her belly.

"Eat." He reached across and put the fork back in her hand. "Before you can be responsible for someone else, you have to take care of yourself." The kindness to his tone brought a lump to her throat.

Since Ed had died, her focus had been on everyone else—his mother, her daughter—never on herself.

Lauren hadn't had time to deal with her own feelings. Maybe she didn't want to. She'd rather postpone the moment when she had to deal with the fact that Ed was never coming back. That he'd deceived her.

The thought made her chest tighten.

"Tell me why you're buying the house."

Scott rose to his feet and cleared the plates. "Instead of asking me why I'm buying it, you should be asking your mother why she's selling it."

It sounded so straightforward and obvious when he said it, but he was correct in what he'd said earlier. Talking to her mother had always been the hardest thing in the world.

She stood up and picked up her bag. "Thanks for breakfast and for rescuing my daughter. And for scraping me off the deck that day."

"Anytime."

"There won't be another time. I don't intend to make a habit of passing out."

"Eat more. That helps." He gave her a rare smile and that smile felt like a balm.

Some people never smiled and some people smiled all the time. Scott Rhodes smiled when he meant it, and right now he meant it.

That smile made her feel stronger.

"See you around, Scott." She headed to the door, wondering why he bothered to arrive at work so early when Charlie wasn't even here to see it.

She had one foot through the door when he spoke.

"Laurie—" The urgency in his tone made her head whip round.

She looked at him, mesmerized by the glacial blue of his eyes and the dark shadow of his jaw.

Her heart pounded against her ribs. "What?"

"Nothing." He shook his head. "Forget it."

The reckless, wild side of her that she'd buried a long time ago thought about pushing him to tell her what it was he wanted to say. But what was the point of that? She knew him well enough to know he wouldn't tell her what was on his mind until he was ready.

She also knew that whatever it was he'd wanted to say, it hadn't been "nothing." But whether it was something she wanted to hear was a different matter.

CHAPTER NINETEEN

Jenna

*Confrontation: a dispute, fight, or battle
between two groups of people*

JENNA WALKED INTO the kitchen of The Captain's House
and found the contents of the cabinets spread across the
floor. There were saucepans, skillets, platters, jugs, assorted
dishes that didn't match—it looked like a yard sale, and in
the middle of it all was her sister, wearing black jeans, a
black sweater and a cloak of visible stress.

"Hi." Jenna put the bag she was holding on the table. "I
got your text. Great idea to talk while Mom's out. What are
you doing?"

"Cleaning. Can you believe the amount of junk Mom
has? I can't even get half these cabinets to shut." The frantic pitch of her voice rang alarm bells for Jenna.

Each time she saw her sister she seemed closer to snapping.

"Mom never throws anything away, you know that." She was relieved to see Lauren manage a brief smile.

"Everything in this house has a history," they chorused together and Jenna grinned, too.

"Hey, I have an idea." She wondered why she hadn't thought of it before. "Let's leave all this and go to the beach like we used to."

Lauren's smile vanished. "I don't have time to go to the beach."

"You love the beach. You used to ditch school to go to the beach."

"That was a long time ago. And it's winter. It's freezing out there."

Jenna regrouped. Maybe that suggestion had been asking too much, too soon.

"At least come and sit down. I'll put the junk—oops, I mean family heirlooms—back in the cabinets and then I'll make coffee. Have you had breakfast?"

"I don't know. No, I don't think so. There's no time to sit down. I have so many things to do I don't know where to start."

Jenna noticed the stack of papers on the table.

Lists again, she thought, glancing at the one on top of the pile.

And then she saw a copy of the local newspaper open at the job section. A few of them were circled in red.

Waitress needed for evenings and weekends.

Chambermaid needed for summer season.

"Is this for Mack?"

Lauren was pushing saucepans back into the cabinet. "For me. I need a job."

"But these are summer jobs."

"I'll take whatever I can get."

"Why are you doing this now? Have you had more news from London?"

"I know a few more of the details. Not that it makes much difference." Lauren picked up a jug. "Do you think Mom would notice if we threw this out?"

"Probably. You have details of how it happened?"

Lauren put the jug down. "Ed set up the hedge fund ten years ago. You already know that."

"Yes. I remember you telling us he picked up some big investors from Russia and the Arab states."

"That's right. Well, the fund grew pretty fast, and that was when he decided to take a different path. He acquired a few private companies, including a leisure company. They got themselves into debt." She stared into space, the jug forgotten. "James told me that investors started asking for their money back, and that's when it all fell apart. Almost all the money was tied up and Ed hadn't drawn income for more than a year, something he failed to tell me. He extended the mortgage on our house. James thinks he really did believe he'd figure it all out without having to tell me—" She roused herself and looked at Jenna. "So I need a job."

"What about your plans to start your interior design business? It's all you've talked about for the past couple of years."

"That was a dream. Real life isn't built on dreams."

"Don't say that. Without dreams, where would we be?"

"Living in the land of reality."

Jenna thought about the baby she wanted so badly. "Sometimes a dream can become reality."

"That's in books and movies." Lauren's tone was bleak

and Jenna felt as if someone had wrenched her heart out of her chest.

If her sister wouldn't come to her, then she'd go to her sister.

Pushing the pans out of the way, she sat down on the floor next to Lauren and put her arms round her.

"I'm not going to be one of those annoying people who says 'I know how you feel.' I can't possibly know how you feel. All I'm going to say is that I'm here and I love you. We'll get through this somehow."

"How?" Lauren leaned her head on Jenna's shoulder. "I need a job, Jenna. That has to be the first thing. And I can't be picky."

"You are the smartest woman I know. We'll find a way you can still start your business."

"To do that, I'd need money. Also clients. I always knew it would take time. In England I had contacts and a network. Here, I don't know anyone."

"But I do. And Mom does. Mom knows everyone."

"No one is going to take on an interior designer whose work they haven't seen. My house in London was my showroom."

"Maybe you can use my house as a showroom. It could use the attention. God, this floor is hard. How long have you been sitting here?" Jenna stood up and pulled Lauren to her feet. "Sit at the table. I'll put the kettle on. What time is Mom home?"

"I don't know. She has a conservation committee meeting." Lauren stacked saucepans. "Is she on every committee?"

"Pretty much. Could you eat eggs? I make great scrambled eggs. If it's the conservation committee we have plenty of time." She cracked eggs into a bowl, beat them with a whisk and sizzled some butter in the skillet. "One of Greg's clients has started a yoga class. I thought we could go together."

Lauren started to laugh. "Yoga? You hate yoga."

"But you love it." Jenna tipped eggs into the pan. "The fact that I'm willing to contort myself into uncomfortable shapes is a measure of my love for you. There is no one else in this world who could persuade me to sign up for a yoga class."

Lauren shook her head. "You don't need to go to yoga for me."

"If we did it together, it would be fun. We could giggle in the back row like teenagers and generally be disruptive." She stirred the eggs and lowered the heat. "We could start some serious gossip. I can imagine it now. *Those Stewart sisters.*"

Lauren looked wistful. "It's been a while since anyone called us that."

Too long, Jenna thought.

Nostalgia: a yearning for the return of past circumstances.

"When you texted me, you said you wanted to talk about Mom."

"Yes. I want to talk to her about everything and I thought it would be good if we did it together."

"By 'everything' do you mean the house, or—" Jenna hesitated. There were some things even they didn't discuss. "Other stuff?"

"What? No! The house. That's it." The look of alarm on her sister's face answered her question.

"Right. Wanted to clear that up because we need to agree

on a strategy and normally our strategy is say nothing." She tipped the eggs onto the plate and buttered a slice of toast.

"I want to understand what's behind this decision to sell, don't you? She's obviously been planning it for a while because she had Scott do all that work on the windows and redecorate two of the bedrooms."

"I know." Jenna put the plate in front of her sister. "Eat. No excuses."

"Wait—" Lauren looked confused. "You *knew* she had Scott here and you didn't think to mention that to me?"

"I didn't know it was relevant. You're forgetting that I only found out recently that Scott Rhodes was a person of interest."

Her sister's color rose. "This isn't about him."

"If Mom was selling to a different person you'd be equally wound up?"

"I'm not wound up."

Jenna glanced at the pans still spread across the floor and the lists on the table. "Right."

Lauren ate slowly, as if she was forcing down every mouthful.

When the plate was clear, Jenna reached for her bag. "I made cookies."

"I couldn't eat another thing. I'll save them for Mack."

"Have things settled down at school?" Jenna knew about the beach incident, and also that the other kids hadn't been speaking to Mack.

"Not really. I wanted to go in and talk to the school but she won't let me. Says that will make things worse."

"This is why I teach first grade. They're easier to handle."

Lauren stood up and walked to the window. "I'd forgotten how much I love this place."

"I thought you loved London."

"I do, but this is different. London is like a superficial acquaintance that you know you're going to have fun with if you go out for a night. But the Vineyard is like meeting up with a friend you've known forever, and realizing that time apart doesn't matter because you know each other so well. Does Mom still have help in the garden?"

"Yes. Ben comes a few times a week in the summer. Less in winter. He manages half the gardens in the town. He's been a good friend to Mom."

"Do you remember when they planted that tree?" Lauren stared into the garden across the lawn and the barren flower beds waiting patiently for winter to make way for spring.

Their tree was a direct descendent of the historic and now famous pagoda tree on South Water Street. Thanks to the efforts of a sea captain who had nursed the seedling all the way from China to New England, the tree had been a feature of Edgartown for almost two hundred years.

"I remember." The father of one of the children in her class was the tree warden.

On Martha's Vineyard, the trees were a community. Some were even related.

Lauren turned. "Why didn't she talk to you before now about selling? You visit her every week."

"What are you implying?"

"I'm not implying anything. I thought you might have picked up on something, that's all."

"Since when has Mom been easy to read, and since when is that my fault?" Jenna knew she was being defensive and felt guilty. Her sister was going through hell and she should be supporting her, not introducing her own issues. "Sorry. I'm trying to give up sugar and it's making me bad-tempered."

"You're bad-tempered because we both have mommy is-sues and I'm trying to shift some of my horrible guilt on to you. It's my fault, not yours." Lauren shook her head. "I'm the one who is sorry. I could have tried harder to talk to Mom in one of our calls."

"Wouldn't have made a difference, you know that. If you're worried about having somewhere to live, you can stay with me." But even she knew that wasn't a practical long-term suggestion. She and Greg had a second bedroom, but it was small and not exactly suited to her sister and a teenage girl.

"Thank you, but I hope we won't need to. What we need is an honest talk with Mom."

"Good luck with that." She'd long since given up trying to discuss anything important with her mother. "There's something else puzzling me."

"What?"

"How can Scott afford to buy this house?"

"I don't know. I had a conversation with him but I couldn't work it out."

"Wait—" Jenna thumped her feet onto the floor and sat up straight "—you saw him? You went to see your first love and didn't tell me?"

"I went to thank him for helping Mack. He made me breakfast."

Jenna noticed she didn't deny the "first love" comment.

The sound of the front door interrupted them.

"Damn," Jenna muttered. "This was about to get inter-esting. Don't think the conversation has ended."

Nancy walked into the room. In those few seconds be-fore she noticed both of them sitting there, she looked tired and beaten.

Jenna felt an ache in her chest.

How long had that look been there? Lauren was right. She should have paid more attention. Maybe they weren't exactly close, but Nancy was still her mother. She'd pulled away as a defense mechanism, not because she didn't care.

The look was gone the second she saw them. "Jenna! I didn't know you were visiting today."

"I asked her over," Lauren said. "We want to talk to you, Mom."

Nancy dropped her bags and sat down without bothering to remove her coat. "About what?"

"The house." Jenna noticed that her mother's hands were curled into fists.

Lauren pulled out an empty chair and sat down. "Why didn't you tell us before now that you were thinking of selling?"

"It only came together recently. I don't need a house this size."

Jenna thought that with all the junk around the place her mother probably needed every one of the ten bedrooms. Looking closely at her mother, she realized that her mother's smile was fixed and strained. She wondered if Lauren had noticed, too.

"You *love* this place," Lauren blurted out. "You love it more than—anything."

Jenna knew her sister had just managed to stop herself saying *you love it more than us*.

"It's a house," Nancy said. "One can't have feelings for a building."

"But you do have feelings for it. All those times people wanted you to sell and you never would. 'Over my dead body,' you said once."

"How dramatic. I realize the timing is inconvenient for Lauren, but—"

"This isn't about me, Mom," Lauren said. "It's about you."

Jenna felt a rush of frustration but underneath was compassion. "Why can't you talk to us, Mom? You talk to your friends, to the people you visit in hospital, the mailman, the gardener, but not to your own daughters?"

Nancy sat very still. "I don't know what you mean. We see each other every week. We talk all the time. And Ben is more than the gardener. He's a dear friend."

"We don't talk about the things that matter. We talk about your book group, my class and the weather."

"That's because there isn't much going on in our lives."

"There's plenty going on in our lives!" Jenna almost blurted out the fact that she couldn't get pregnant, but something stopped her. She wasn't ready to discuss something as personal as that with her mother.

Lauren reached across the table and grabbed her hand, squeezing hard. Jenna felt a rush of gratitude toward her sister.

"Talk to us, Mom. We want the truth."

There was a long silence. Nancy cleared her throat. "Are you sure?"

Jenna felt a flash of foreboding. "Yes."

Nancy stood up and paced to the window, keeping her back to them. "I'm selling the house because I can no longer afford it."

"If money is tight then maybe—"

"Money isn't just tight, Jenna. It's gone. I'm broke and have been for a while."

Broke?

Jenna looked at Lauren, who seemed as shocked as she was.

"But—how? You made a fortune with your paintings and it's not as if you're exactly a big spender." She couldn't remember the last time she'd seen her mother wearing anything new.

Nancy dug her fingers into the countertop. "Your father was a big spender."

"Big spender? How big?" How much money could one man spend on the golf course?

"He went through money like water and unfortunately in the latter years of our marriage made none of his own. I didn't realize until it was too late. I left him to deal with that side of things, as I left him to deal with the childcare. I thought we were an unusually modern couple, but it turned out I was deluding myself—something I did far too often. I've known for at least a year that I was going to have to sell, but I've been cowardly. Putting off the inevitable. I didn't want to admit to being a failure."

Jenna couldn't remember ever seeing her mother vulnerable before. "You're not a failure, Mom. Why would you think that?"

"This house has been in my family since it was built. My ancestors protected it, and I'm the one to sell it. I've let everyone down, including my own daughters." She looked at Lauren. "The one time you need something from me, and I can't give it to you. That's not a good feeling."

"I'm an adult," Lauren said. "It's not your role to support me. But are you saying Dad spent *all* your money?"

"I thought of it as 'our' money, but yes. He spent it."

"That's terrible, but surely you could make more? You're a brilliant artist." Jenna groped around for options. "Couldn't you paint something new and sell it for a fortune?"

Nancy picked up a cloth from the side and folded it. "It's been five years since I painted anything."

Jenna felt a flash of shock. Five years? No. That wasn't possible. "Mom?" How could she have not known this? "You stopped when Dad died? You were heartbroken."

Nancy put the cloth down. "I wasn't heartbroken. I was angry. So angry that for the first time in my life it clouded everything. I couldn't see to paint. There was nothing in my head except anger."

If Jenna had been shocked before, she was stunned now.

Lauren spoke first. "We don't blame you for feeling angry, Mom. Dad left you in a bad way financially. I'm angry with Ed for much the same reason. It's killing me because part of me is grieving and another part wants to yell at him. You must have felt the same way."

"I wasn't angry because of the money. At least not at that point. I thought I'd be able to keep the ship afloat, as I always had. It was the one thing I could do. Earning the money was my role. I thought I could paint my way out of trouble. I like to think I was confident, rather than arrogant."

Jenna was confused. "But—"

"I was angry because of the *way* he spent the money. My money. Your money." She grabbed an apron from the back of the door. "I should be cooking, not talking. Mack will be home from school and she'll be hungry. You know what teenagers are like."

"Wait. Mom, sit down."

But her mother was rattling round the kitchen, pulling out bowls and weighing scales. "I thought I'd make a vegetable potpie for supper. Will Mack eat that?"

"Yes, but it can wait." Lauren was on her feet. "How did Dad spend the money?"

Nancy thumped the bag of flour onto the countertop. "He threw it away trying to impress women."

"Women?"

Nancy seemed to deflate. It was like watching the air leave a balloon. "I was never going to tell you girls. I know you adored your father. He had some wonderful qualities."

"Wait a minute—" Jenna didn't dare look at Lauren. "You're saying Dad had another woman?"

"Not one woman. One woman would never have been enough for your father. He blamed me, of course. Said that the fact that I earned the money 'emasculated' him and made him look foolish among his friends. Apparently his ability to pick up women somehow solved that, although I've never understood how multiple affairs made him more of a man."

Jenna saw Lauren glance in her direction.

Knowing exactly what her sister was thinking, Jenna shook her head fractionally. Warning bells were clanging in her head and she wondered why her sister wasn't hearing them, too.

Do not say what you're thinking of saying.

"Why didn't you leave him?"

Nancy gave a wistful smile. "Because of you girls. You, Jenna, in particular, used to wrap yourself around him the moment he came in from work."

Jenna remembered it. *Daddy, Daddy, Daddy*...

"I couldn't take that away from you," Nancy said. "Anyone who saw the three of you together would have understood that. The three musketeers. That's what he called you. Everyone remarked on what a good father he was. I couldn't spoil that for you. And I didn't want to tarnish those memories, but now I have and I'm sorry for it. I want you to forget it."

Forget it?

"We knew," Lauren said. "We knew he had another woman."

Jenna wished she'd gagged her sister.

"That isn't possible." Nancy's face drained of color. "I was so careful. I never talked about it when you were in the house."

"You weren't the reason we knew."

Jenna didn't know how to stop what was coming. "Lauren, don't—" Was she really going to do this after all those years of keeping it to themselves? And now, when her mother was obviously feeling vulnerable? What if telling the truth made their mother feel worse? But then she saw Lauren's jaw lift and knew that nothing she did or said was going to stop what happened next. She recognized that look.

It was a look she hadn't seen on her sister's face in a long time.

She wasn't sure whether to be relieved or nervous.

"We saw him, Mom."

"You saw him with a woman?" Her mother's face contorted. "He swore to me he never brought them to the house after that first time—"

Her mom had caught her dad with a woman in the *house*? Jenna's head was spinning.

"Not the house," Lauren said. "It was at your studio. You were in Europe. We thought Dad was asleep and we sneaked out of the house. We did it all the time. And we saw him through the window."

How could her sister be so calm?

Jenna was shivering as if she had a bad case of the flu. She tried never to think about that day.

She'd pressed her nose to the glass, trying to work out what was happening. She'd seen her father's naked, hairy limbs tangled with those of a woman. For a moment she'd thought they were wrestling, and couldn't understand why her charming, easygoing father would be fighting. Was the woman an intruder? But why would her father be naked?

And then she'd seen something else that she'd never been able to completely wipe from her mind.

She felt hot all of a sudden, and then cold.

Nancy curled her fingers over the back of the nearest chair to steady herself. "What exactly did you see?"

Please don't let Lauren give her the details.

"Far too much," Lauren said. "It put us off sex for a while, didn't it, Jenna?"

"This isn't about us." Jenna felt as if she was choking. "It's about Mom. I can't bear to think you were going through that and you never told us. Did you confide in Alice? Does she know?"

Her mother didn't look at her. "I—I didn't talk about it with anyone."

She hadn't even told her closest friend?

"Who did you talk to? Who was there for you?"

"No one. It was humiliating enough without confessing it to everyone, although I'm sure some of the Vineyarders knew. The ones he slept with for a start."

"Who?"

Her mother shook her head. "It doesn't matter now. But the fact that you saw him—" Her voice was threaded with anger. "If he wasn't already dead, I'd kill him. The philandering waster—" She broke off and breathed deeply. "How old were you?"

"Eleven," Lauren said. "So I guess Jenna was eight. It was

the year Meredith Painter caught her dad having sex with the woman who ran the sailing club. She told her mother and the marriage fell apart. Meredith was distraught. Her father blamed her for breaking up the family and the whole thing was terrible. She told us again and again that she wished she'd never said anything. We didn't want it to happen to us. We thought we were protecting you."

Little white lies, Jenna thought. *So many little white lies*.

"Eight and eleven." Nancy closed her eyes, as if she didn't like the vision she was seeing. "Babies. My poor girls."

Jenna couldn't remember a time when her mother had spoken in that tone, or used words like that. She wasn't sure how to react.

She'd expected to be blamed for leaving the house and going to the Sail Loft, but her mother didn't seem to be thinking about that.

"How many affairs did he have, Mom?"

Nancy looked tired. "I don't know. There are some things you are better off not knowing. I knew about three of them. One of them turned up here one day looking for him. At the beginning I tried hard to fix things. I was desperate not to lose him."

"Because of us?"

"Not only because of that. I loved him, too. Desperately. Tom had this gift of drawing people to him. The same qualities that dazzled you, dazzled me. It makes me feel ashamed when I think back to the things I tolerated. The humiliations I endured."

"I don't know how you stood it." Jenna tried to imagine how she'd feel if Greg had one affair, let alone several. "I would have kicked him out."

"I hope you would. I tried to do that once, and he told

me that if I did that you girls would resent me forever for breaking up the home. I knew he was right." She paused. "Tom was the 'fun' parent. Your father had so much charisma he could make the simplest moment seem magical. You three were a unit, and I wasn't part of it. But I could at least make sure you were well provided for."

Jenna was horrified. "Why did you think earning the money was your role?"

"I was good at it. Not so good at being a mother." Nancy spoke quietly. "I enjoyed being with the two of you, but Tom would always interrupt with an idea that was more fun, more inventive, more crazy, and off you'd all go, the three of you together. It knocked my confidence. That happens when you're not good at something."

Jenna felt as if her heart was being crushed. "Mom—"

"It was my fault. I let Tom make me feel inadequate—and he was good at it. It was as if he was always saying, 'Look how much better at this I am than you.' It was obvious how much you enjoyed being with him, and instead of finding ways we could have our own type of fun together, I retreated and let him get on with it." Nancy blinked and Jenna realized her mother was struggling not to cry.

Never in her life had she seen her mother shed tears and seeing it now tore through the flimsy barriers she'd put between them.

Jenna sprang out of the chair so quickly it crashed to the floor. Crossing the room in three strides, she then wrapped her arms round her mother. "I'm sorry. I'm so sorry." She thought about all the times they'd played with their father. She'd assumed her mother disapproved and had no wish to join in. It hadn't ever occurred to her that Nancy hadn't joined in because she didn't know how. Nor had it occurred to her that her father was being manipulative. Using his children to hurt his wife.

She half expected her mother to push her away and when Nancy clung tightly Jenna couldn't hold back her own tears.

How could she have been so blind?

"I'm the one who is sorry." Nancy patted her shoulder. "I never wanted you to know."

Jenna glanced across the room and saw that her sister was crying, too. It was the first time she'd seen her sister cry since she'd lost Ed.

Lauren cleared her throat. "We're glad you told us."

"You probably think I was a fool." Nancy fumbled in her purse and pulled out a tissue. "If the same thing ever happened to either of you two girls I would be the first to tell you to leave. Walk out. You deserve only the best. You deserve to be treated with love and respect. Anything less than that isn't worth sticking around for. But it's too late to wish I'd made different choices. All I can do is make the right choice now. Selling The Captain's House will mean I have enough money to buy a small place, and give the rest to you girls." She blew her nose hard and looked at Lauren. "I can't protect you from what you're going through, but at least I should be able to help you financially."

All this and sell her home?

Jenna wasn't going to let that happen. There had to be another way.

Lauren obviously agreed. "You're not selling this house, Mom, and that's final. This time you're not the provider."

Nancy swallowed, visibly moved. "We don't have any other option."

It was the first time Jenna could remember hearing her mother say *we*.

The first time she'd ever turned to them for help in solving a problem.

She felt a warmth inside that she hadn't felt before. For once her family felt like a unit instead of the sum of disparate parts.

It was funny how such a low point could also feel like a high.

"Maybe we do." She let go of her mother and picked up Lauren's pad of paper and a pen from the table. "We're going to figure something out. Put the kettle on, Lauren. Let's make a start."

CHAPTER TWENTY

Mack

*Rebellion: organized resistance or opposition
to an authority*

MACK SAT ON the jetty in the marina with her arms looped
round her knees. Her bike was propped against a wall in
the harbor.

She didn't even know what she was doing here. All she
knew was that she didn't want to spend another lonely weekend in the house trapped with her family. She couldn't handle her own emotions, let alone theirs. It was like being
caught in a flash flood. She couldn't get her head above the
surface to breathe. Something else had happened, although
she had no idea what. She'd returned home from school a
few days before to find her grandmother, her mother and
her aunt huddled around the kitchen table. She couldn't remember ever seeing them huddled before. It was clear she'd

interrupted something big. She hadn't hung around waiting for someone to tell her because no one in her family was big on confessions. Instead she'd grabbed milk from the fridge and gone straight to her room.

For once her mother hadn't followed her. She'd told herself she was glad about that, but the truth was that she felt lonelier than she ever had in her life before.

Kennedy had ignored her since the incident on the beach, and because the other kids were terrified of Kennedy, they ignored her, too.

It didn't matter so much during class, but at lunchtime she sat on her own at one of the lunch tables in the farthest corners of the cafeteria, wishing she could wind back time.

It felt as if every part of her life had gone wrong at the same time.

School was a nightmare. Home was a nightmare. She had no friends. No one to talk to. Which was why she was here now, on a Saturday morning, sitting on a dock that smelled of salt water and fish.

She missed her dad. Ed. *She should be thinking of him as Ed.* She missed their Saturday morning bike rides, their visits to the museums and the way he always managed to calm her mother down.

Mack felt desperately sad, and had no idea what to do with all the feelings inside her. And as for school—she had reinvented herself so many times in an attempt to be popular that she no longer knew who she was.

She saw Scott before he saw her. He walked with a loose, easy stride as if he was on the deck of a ship. His arms were loaded with bags and sailing gear and he was aiming for the big black inflatable boat moored right by her. Captain trotted alongside him, tail wagging.

Scott stopped when he saw her, but Captain bounded across and greeted her like a long-lost friend.

Mack buried her hands and face in his warm fur, grateful that at least someone loved her.

As she glanced up at Scott, her heart thumped a little harder.

She probably shouldn't have come. Just because he'd helped her a couple of times didn't mean he wanted her in his life.

It was like asking for rejection.

Because she didn't want to show how vulnerable she was feeling, she went with careless.

"Hi, Dad." She used a don't-care tone that would have earned her a sharp rebuke from her mother, but Scott Rhodes didn't react. He never seemed to react the way other people did.

"You're up early."

"Despite popular belief, there is no such thing as a typical teenager. We're all individual. Some of us are tall, some short, some love Taylor Swift, and some love rock and rap." She scrambled to her feet. "I thought we could spend some quality father-daughter time together. Bonding is important, don't you think?" Because she was scared and stressed, she resorted to verbal sparring and sarcasm, but Scott didn't seem inclined to play that game. Instead he gave her a brief glance and then lowered the ropes and the bags he was carrying into the boat.

His lack of response left her feeling childish.

"Are you going out in that? Can I come?" Now she was definitely acting like a little kid, begging for attention.

"Have you ever been on a boat?"

The fact that he hadn't told her to go away gave her hope.

"Do you count a pedal boat in Hyde Park? If not then no, but I'm a quick learner. What would you want me to do? I don't know a whole lot about sailing in real life, only from books. If you take me on this boat it's possible I could sink it. I read *Moby-Dick*." She shifted awkwardly, aware that she was talking far more than he was. "Mom gave me your copy."

"You read it?"

"Yes. Why so surprised? I hate most of the stuff kids my age are reading. Usually about teenagers who save the world, which doesn't make sense to me. Most teenagers aren't even allowed to go to the bathroom without telling a grown-up. We have to say where we're going, when we'll be back and what grade we got. It's all rules, rules, rules. Who is going to give them responsibility for the world? That's not happening any time soon. I can't suspend disbelief enough to read that type of thing. But *Moby-Dick* was real. I mean the *Essex* sank, I know that. Grams told me about it."

He rearranged everything inside the boat. "It's not going to be like *Moby-Dick*."

"Because there aren't any whales around here. I know. It's tragic. I don't believe in killing anything. I'm a vegetarian, which annoys Grams because she makes these amazing potpies. She's learned to do cheese and leek because of me. It's pretty good." She glanced at the boat and then at the waves. "I don't mean to be offensive or question your skill or anything, but those are big waves out there. Not that I'm an expert, but I've read a ton of stuff and I can tell you that something more robust would be safer. As we're on Martha's Vineyard and everyone knows *Jaws* was filmed here, I'd rather be safe than sorry."

"We have something more robust."

"We do?" She was surprised by how much she liked the *we* in that sentence.

He gestured with his head and for the first time she noticed the yacht bobbing in the bay.

"That's yours? That big white one? Then what's this one for?"

"This is a tender. I use it to get from the yacht to the shore."

It hadn't even occurred to her to wonder how people got to the boats moored outside the harbor. "You go on the yacht most days?"

"Every day. I live on it. It's my home."

"Cool. If someone annoys you, you can sail into the sunset or throw them overboard. Can I come and live with you?" She saw his expression change and her stomach gave a lurch. "I'm kidding. I know I'd be as welcome as a shark in a seal colony. If you'd wanted me in your life, you would have stuck around sixteen years ago. Don't feel bad about it. No one wants me around right now, so you're not alone." Across the dock she saw a tall, lean boy sling a bag into a boat and spring in after it. She recognized him as the boy who had pinned up the Coding Club notice. Saul something. No, Sam. That was it. Sam.

As she floundered for the name, the boy glanced up and saw her.

Mack felt her face burn. This was awkward.

But to her surprise he lifted his hand in a greeting and a smile spread across his face.

It was the first time since she'd arrived on the island that anyone had seemed genuinely pleased to see her.

She hesitated and then lifted her hand and returned his greeting.

Scott glanced over his shoulder toward the boy in the boat. "You know Sam Tanner?"

"He's in my class. He runs the Coding Club after school. Not that we've spoken."

"Perhaps you should. He's a good kid."

"He probably is, but the truth is that he isn't one of the cool ones. Being friends with him would make me a target." But that wave and smile had cheered her more than she would have thought was possible. Maybe life wasn't so awful. "Even if I wanted to risk it, I don't know enough about computers."

Scott wrapped the last of the bags in plastic and tucked it under the seat. "I know a bit about computers. If there's something you want to know, you can ask me."

"You know how to code?"

"I'm not going to put a rocket into space but yes, I know enough."

"And you'd help me?"

"Yes, although you'd probably find the Coding Club more fun."

She was pretty sure she wouldn't. She certainly wouldn't find the fallout fun.

"How about the boat? Will you teach me to sail, too?"

He straightened and his ice-blue gaze fastened on her like a laser. "Does your mom know you're here?"

"Not exactly. I didn't have a destination in mind when I left the house. I needed space. My family drives me crazy. I mean, I love them obviously, but they do crazy things. They're not big on talking about stuff, so there are lots of misunderstandings."

"If you want to come on the boat, you need to tell your mom you're here."

"I don't think that's—"

"Call her," he said, "or she'll worry."

She hadn't expected him to be so protective of her mother. He hadn't exactly stuck around, had he? But he clearly still had feelings.

Mack wasn't sure how she felt about that.

But she knew she wanted to stay.

She pulled out her phone, even though she had no intention of calling her mom. "No signal."

"I'm not taking you on the boat unless you tell your family where you are."

If she called, her mom would probably stop her from going on the boat, but if she didn't call, Scott wouldn't take her out.

She waved her phone in the air and walked up the dock a little way. "Oh wait—success." She held the phone to her ear and waited a moment. "Hi, Mom, I'm at the marina with Scott, so you don't need to worry about me. See you later. Byeee." She ended the "call" quickly, worried that Scott might take the phone from her and try to talk to her mother himself. That would have been awkward given she hadn't actually called anyone. "Everything's cool. So can I come sailing with you?" She saw him hesitate and the feeling of disappointment was like a blow to the chest. "You don't want me. No one wants me right now."

There was a gleam in his eyes. "Are you trying to manipulate me?"

"No. Just telling the truth. I don't blame people really. I'm moody and horrid, but I honestly can't help it. I'm trying not to be, but it's hard. I don't feel like myself anymore. It's been tough."

"Life generally is."

She was surprised he didn't give her more sympathy. "Maybe if I lived on the sea like you it would be easier."

"Life doesn't go away because you're on a boat. It's wetter and colder, that's all." He held out his hand to her and she stepped into the boat before he could change his mind and call her mother himself.

She clutched his hand as the boat swayed on the water. "We're not going to sink, are we?"

"No. Wear this." He handed her a life jacket.

"I don't need—"

"Wear it."

"Orange isn't really my color—" Her voice tailed off as she caught his eye. "Right. Orange is good. Yay orange. Totally my favorite. I wish everything in my life was orange." She put the life jacket on and he leaned forward to secure the straps.

At least he didn't intend to let her drown. That was a start.

"Sit in the middle and don't move around."

"Aye aye, Cap'n." She laughed as the dog jumped into the boat, wagging its tail. "Not you. The other captain." She saluted and watched as Scott sprang onto the dock and did something with the ropes.

Someone shouted something to him and he raised a hand in acknowledgment and then they were motoring out through the harbor toward the sea.

The weather had been gray and murky all week but now, finally, the sun peeped through the clouds. The water sparkled as they bounced over the surface and Mack gasped as seawater showered her face.

She realized she was laughing for the first time in months, and she was still laughing when he brought the boat alongside the yacht.

"That was *so* cool. Can I steer next time?"

"No." He killed the engine.

She waited for him to warn her to be careful climbing into the boat, but he said nothing, simply held the boat steady and waited while she clambered up the ladder and dropped down onto the deck. The wind blew her hair across her face and she felt a sudden lightness. The only sounds were the slap of the sea against the hull, the clink of the mast and the plaintive call of a seagull. The darkness that had engulfed her lifted. The ache in her chest had gone. Here on the boat she felt far away from everything. Grief. Her home. School. *Herself.*

For the first time in a long while she had a feeling that everything was going to be all right. Not right away, but maybe one day.

Grateful for the reprieve, she wiped her face with her palm and then twisted her soaked hair into a tail and secured it under her hat.

"Mack—" He called her name and she walked back to the side of the boat and took the packages he handed her.

"Where do you want me to put these?"

"In the main cabin." He gestured for her to go below and she bounced down the steps into the cabin.

She handed the bags back to him and watched as he stowed the contents. "I'd rather live here than in a house. It's fun."

"It's not much fun in winter."

"Is that why you wanted to buy The Captain's House? I can't imagine why you'd want a place like that when you can have this. But you don't have to talk about it," she said quickly. "There's nothing worse than people wanting you to talk about stuff you don't want to talk about. I get that. It happens to me all the time right now. Mom wants me to talk and I know I'm supposed to say what she wants to hear, but I can't do that so I've been spending too long in my room playing with electronic devices."

He unzipped his jacket. "You seem to be talking plenty."

"You're easy to talk to. You listen." She studied the navigational charts secured to the wall. "Have you sailed all over the world? I'd love to travel. I'd like to go to California because that's where so many of the tech companies are. Have you been to California?"

"Yes."

"It's great that you can sail off like that. You don't have any ties? No one? I mean, until your long-lost daughter showed up." She tried to see his expression but he had his back to her.

"Do you like hot chocolate?"

"I prefer vodka." Her flippant response earned her one of his steady looks and she sighed, wondering what it was about him that put the brakes on her need to be outrageous. "Is there anyone alive who doesn't like hot chocolate? That would be great, thanks." The spray from the short boat ride had penetrated her coat and she realized she was cold.

Scott opened a cupboard, pulled out a clean dry towel and threw it across to her. "Take your coat off. Dry your hair. I'll fetch you a sweater."

"I'm fine."

"When you're on board this boat, you'll do as I say." He disappeared through a door and emerged a moment later with a soft sweater that looked as if it had been washed a thousand times.

Grateful for the warmth, she slipped it on without argument. The sleeves fell past the ends of her fingers and she pushed them back and took the hot chocolate he handed her.

"Thanks." She slid her hands round the mug for warmth.

Hot chocolate. She remembered Ed making her hot chocolate when she was very young. The ache in her chest came back. "So this boat has sails, but also an engine? You know about engines?"

"I know enough."

"I like physics. And I'm pretty good at it. Last year I wanted to do engineering, but now I'm not sure. I might like to be a computer scientist, but most of what I know is self-taught. I guess I don't really know what I want to do. I'm supposed to have it figured out, but it's hard to have it all figured out at sixteen. Did you?"

"I still don't have it all figured out."

She found that reassuring. She sipped her drink and discovered hot chocolate could be as delicious at sixteen as it was at six. The creamy warmth spread through her, heating her insides. "So far I've done most of the talking. Tell me something else about you."

"What do you want to know?"

"Do you have any other relations? Cousins? Aunts?"

"No."

"No one?" She felt a stab of shock. "I'm all you've got? That's bad."

A ghost of a smile touched his mouth. "I'll let you know."

"Now I feel a huge responsibility to be perfect. That's a lot of pressure for one person."

"I've yet to meet a perfect human."

"In case you're worried, don't be. I don't have expectations. So far when it comes to fathers I haven't exactly hit the jackpot."

"I'd say you hit the jackpot." He took the steps back up to the deck and she finished her chocolate and followed him, curious.

Something about the way he moved around the boat made her think he was annoyed.

Probably with her. Annoying people was her specialty.

"You think you're up for father of the year?"

"Not me. Ed."

It was the last thing she'd expected him to say. "Ed?"

He lifted the lid on a locker and pulled out a rope. "Do you know how to coil a mooring line?"

"What? No, of course not." The wind turned the surface of the water choppy and she braced her legs to help balance against the roll of the boat. "You think my da—I mean, Ed was a good father?"

"Forget it."

"I don't want to forget it. I want to know why you said that. You didn't even know him."

"How about knots? Can you tie a bowline? Figure eight? Reef knot?" He closed the locker with such force she jumped.

"I was born and raised in London. It's not exactly a necessary life skill in a city. He lied, you know."

"You've never lied?"

Mack turned pink. She'd lied a few minutes ago, back on the dock. But that was different. That was a small lie. "He and my mom basically lied my entire life."

Scott didn't respond to that. "You should learn. Knowing how to tie a secure knot might come in useful one day."

Mack tried to work out when. Maybe she could tie a knot in Kennedy's neck.

"Did you know Ed?"

His grip tightened on the rope. "No."

"Then why did you say I'd hit the jackpot? And how

would you have felt if you'd discovered the man you thought was your dad wasn't really your dad?"

"I never knew my dad so I can't answer that."

"Oh." She stared at him. "He died when you were young?"

"I don't know anything about him. I was raised in foster care."

Mack was mortified. Her big mouth again. "I'm sorry."

"You don't need to be sorry. It's not your fault."

"But I said the wrong thing. I hurt your feelings."

"My feelings aren't that easily hurt. And everyone says the wrong thing sometimes. It's part of being human."

Her feelings were easily hurt. Far too easily hurt. "I'm feeling weird right now. Ed's gone and I'm never going to be able to ask him any of the things I want to know."

"What do you want to know?"

Feeling the boat rock, Mack sat down on the locker. "I want to know why he didn't tell me. Finding out that there's no Santa Claus or Easter Bunny was bad enough, but this is so much worse, don't you think?"

"I never believed in Santa Claus or the Easter Bunny." He flicked her a glance. "Decisions aren't always simple. Life isn't always that easy to figure out."

Well *that* was true.

Scott had a quiet way about him that made it easy. He didn't tell her what she should be thinking or feeling, and he didn't nag at her or make her feel stupid. "I want to know if Ed really loved me."

"That's an easy enough question to answer."

"What do you mean?"

Scott tightened his hands on the rope. "Did he leave you? Did he walk out?"

"No. He had a heart attack." And she couldn't get it out

of her head. Had he known he was going to die? Had he
had pain? What was the last thing she'd said to him? She
couldn't even remember and she felt awful about that.

"He was by your side for sixteen years." Scott placed the
rope on her lap and dropped to his haunches next to her. "I'd
say the signs are that he loved you a hell of a lot."

She gripped the rope. "I wish I'd known I wasn't his,
that's all. I would have been okay about them telling me
when I was young."

"You don't know that. No one knows for sure how they'd
react if circumstances were different."

"You're on my mom's side."

"I don't take sides." He took her hand and placed it on
the rope. "This is a mooring line. You're going to learn to
coil it ready for stowage. Are you right-handed or left?"

"Right."

"So make the coils with your right hand, hold in your
left." He showed her and then handed the rope back to her.
"Keep the coils the same length."

She tried it, but her hands were cold. "The rope keeps
kinking up—"

"Twist your hand out as you make the coil. That will stop
it happening. That's good—" he watched as she coiled the
whole rope "—now finish it off and we'll stow it in the locker."

She did as he said and handed it over, wondering why coil-
ing a rope could feel like an achievement. She gobbled up
crumbs of approval like a starving bird. "So does this make
me your crew?" She saw the corners of his mouth flicker into
a smile and felt a sudden high. "Can I ask you something?"

"If I say no, will it stop you asking?"

"Probably not. And we can both agree that you've had
an easy time of parenting me so far."

"If it's a parent you want, you should talk to your mom."

How could she explain that she couldn't talk to her mom right now? "I'd rather talk to you."

"I don't know anything about kids."

"I'm not a kid. I'm a teenager. We're much trickier. And don't bother looking for advice on the internet."

"I take it the advice isn't good?"

"It says things like, 'Try to maintain a channel of communication.'" She used her best TV anchor voice. "'Try to avoid confrontational language and talking in absolutes. Encourage dialogue.'"

"Sounds complicated."

"You have no idea." She took a deep breath. "Did you love my mom?"

He went so still she wished she hadn't asked.

It was like opening up a box and showing someone something awful.

"I'm sorry," she said. "Forget I asked that. Thanks for the chocolate and the rope lesson." She took the steps back down to the cabin, grabbed his mug and washed it up.

She was relieved when he followed her down. At least he wasn't ignoring her.

"Thanks for bringing me on the boat and giving me my first sailing lesson." What if Scott *had* loved her mom? What if this was difficult for him too? "Scott—"

"We should get back." He left the cabin in two long strides and she stood for a moment, wishing yet again that she'd kept her mouth shut.

She hoped she hadn't ruined what was turning out to be the best day she'd had in a long time.

CHAPTER TWENTY-ONE

Lauren

Anxiety: a feeling of nervousness or worry

LAUREN WALKED INTO the garden room where her mother was reading. "Have you seen Mack?"

Her mother glanced up from her book. "Not since last night. Why?"

"I can't find her anywhere."

"Have you tried her room?"

"Yes. She's not there." In normal circumstances she wouldn't have worried, but circumstances hadn't been normal in a long time.

"Maybe she has gone for a walk."

"It's the weekend. She doesn't normally get out of bed until eleven, but I checked her room at eight and it was empty." Where would her daughter be going at eight o'clock on a Saturday morning?

Nancy put her book down. "Call her. One of the advantages of today's technology-addicted youth is that you can always contact them."

"I tried that. Her phone is switched off." And she was trying not to panic.

There was no reason for anxiety.

Mack was probably with a friend.

Except she didn't have any friends.

The anxiety was louder now. More insistent.

Mack was unhappy. She didn't have anyone to turn to. And Lauren hadn't managed to persuade her to open up and talk. Her mind raced ahead.

What if she'd done something awful?

Nancy removed her glasses. "Could she have gone to see Jenna?"

Lauren frowned. "How?"

"The same way she gets everywhere. On her bike."

"That's a long cycle. It would take her hours." Still, Lauren texted her sister. "Did she seem quieter than usual to you last night?"

"Not that I noticed. She never says much."

She used to talk all the time.

Lauren's phone pinged. "She's not with Jenna. I'm going to see if her bike has gone." She hurried outside, trying not to let herself overthink.

Mack's bike wasn't there.

So she'd gone for a bike ride. That was fine.

But why hadn't she told anyone where she was going?

Lauren tried calling again but it went to voice mail.

"What can I do?" Nancy's voice came from the doorway. "Do you want to go looking for her?"

"Where?" Lauren's mind was blank. She had no idea where her daughter was.

She could have been knocked off her bike.

She could be lying dead in a ditch.

Why hadn't she at least left a note saying where she was going?

This was all her fault. She'd known Mack was miserable, and had failed to reach her. She should have tried a different way. She should have tried a million different ways.

"I'm a bad mother." If someone had warned her parenting was this hard she would have insisted on using ten condoms every time she had sex.

"Stop it," Nancy said. "Stop beating yourself up. You're the best mother any child could have."

"My daughter left the house without telling me where she was going. I have no idea where she could be. What does that say about me?"

"It doesn't say anything about you. It says she's a teenager going through a tough time."

Lauren thought about all the things she and Jenna had done as children.

But they'd done them *together*.

That was different. Mack was alone. Grieving. Confused. Depressed?

"I'm going to look for her."

"Where?"

"I don't know, but I can't sit around here doing nothing. Can I take your car?"

"Yes. But, Lauren—"

"Keep your phone on. If she comes home, call me."

She tried to think about all the places Mack liked on the

island. There was that little boutique close by. She liked the beach. But which beach?

She drove along the road that bordered the cycle trail, looking for signs of her daughter. It was still cold and the beaches were empty apart from a couple of people walking their dogs.

She slowed as she passed the entrance to one of the large houses.

Could Mack be on one of the private beaches?

The houses rented for exorbitant sums during the summer, but were often empty at this time of year.

She drove on, occasionally glancing at the beach when the road allowed.

Mild anxiety thickened into dread.

Should she call the police?

What would she say? *My daughter got up unusually early. I think something is wrong.*

They'd think she'd lost her mind. And then they'd want to know all the reasons she was scared for her daughter, and Lauren would have to relive the horror of the last few weeks.

Still, better that than find Mack's body washed up on the beach.

She reasoned with herself as she drove. Mack wouldn't have hurt herself. If she were that unhappy she would have said so.

Wouldn't she?

Just how well did she know her daughter these days?

She wasn't sure whether it was instinct or impulse that made her drive to the marina, but as she drove through the entrance the first thing she saw was Mack's bike propped against the wall.

What would she be doing here? Flooded with panic, Lauren started to shake so badly she almost drove the car into that same wall. She pulled up and was out of the car in a flash.

The bike was there, but there was no sign of Mack.

Her imagination was already in overdrive, and she glanced at the water, terrified of seeing clothes floating or, worse, a body.

And then she heard the sound of an engine.

A boat was chugging into the marina. Scott was at the helm and there, sitting in the front, laughing as if she didn't have a care in the world, was Mack.

A sweet rush of relief—*thank you, thank you*—turned to anger.

She strode down to the jetty on legs so shaky that she stumbled twice.

The moment Mack noticed her, the laughter stopped.

Lauren struggled to speak. She couldn't get air into her lungs.

Finally she managed to make a sound. "Do you have *any* idea how worried I've been?"

Mack stepped out of the boat cautiously. "Worried?"

"You weren't in your room. You didn't say where you were going. *You didn't answer your phone.*"

"Okay, calm down." Mack backed away but her escape was blocked by Scott.

"She called you, Lauren. I heard her do it."

"Is that what she told you?" Lauren stuck out her hand. "Give me your phone, Mack."

"But—"

"Now."

Mack handed it over and Lauren checked the calls and held up the evidence. "She hasn't made a call this morning."

Mack shrugged. "I wanted to go on the boat with Scott and I thought you might say no."

"Do you have any idea how worried I've been?" She was shrieking. She knew she was shrieking but she couldn't control it. Worry had ripped through the last layers of control, exposing everything she was feeling.

Mack shifted uncomfortably. "Calm down."

"I'm angry, Mack."

"Yeah, I'm getting that."

"Do *not* use that tone with me. You can't do this! You can't wander off, not come home and not say anything about where you are, not call, not text—" She snatched in an unsteady breath. "It is selfish and thoughtless and—cruel."

"Cruel?" Mack stood frozen to the spot. "How is it cruel?"

"I thought you might have done something, Mack. I thought you might be lying dead in a ditch or drowned or—"

"Dead?" Mack gaped at her. "Why would I be dead?"

"You're unhappy! I know you're unhappy."

"Maybe, but I don't want to be dead. You know that."

"No, I don't know that because *you don't talk to me*. All I know is that every day you vanish to your room and slam the door. You're upset about Dad—Ed—but you won't talk about it. I know you hate school but you won't talk about that either. You don't talk about anything. If I had facts to go on I might not have been so anxious but you don't give me facts so my imagination is all I have left."

"I didn't think."

"Then it's time you started thinking, Mackenzie!"

Mack pressed herself against Scott. "Okay, but could you calm down? You're going to blow a blood vessel or something."

She wanted to calm down, but she couldn't.

Scott stepped forward and closed his hands over her arms. "It's my fault. I should have called you myself. I should have known."

"Why would you have known? You don't have any experience of teenage girls."

"She's okay, Lauren. And she's learned a lesson. Enough now."

"I decide when it's enough. You don't get to tell me how to parent my child." She stepped away from him and looked at Mack. "I know you're sad. Confused. Grieving, but there still have to be boundaries and today you stepped right over that line. From now on I want to know where you are and who you're with at all times. If you're going to be late home from school, I want to know. Is that clear?"

Mack's eyes were swimming. "What's clear is that my life sucks."

"Maybe, but it's going to suck in a place where I can see you." She turned to Scott. "And The Captain's House is no longer for sale."

"Because I took your daughter out on the boat?"

"Because we have other plans for it."

He raised an eyebrow. "We?"

"The Stewart family." She turned back to Mack. "Get your things."

"I'll cycle home."

"I'm putting your bike in the trunk." She jerked her head toward the car. "Move!"

CHAPTER TWENTY-TWO

Jenna

Tension: mental or emotional strain

"THAT WAS INCREDIBLE." Greg lowered his head and kissed her.

"It was." Jenna slid her arms round his neck. Did incredible sex increase your chances of conceiving? *Please let them have made a baby.*

Greg stroked her back. "Give me five minutes to recover and we'll do it again."

She was tempted, and not just because she wanted to get pregnant. "We don't have time."

He rolled over, taking her with him. "We don't need long."

"It's going to take a couple of hours."

"We could make it a quickie this time."

"I'm talking about getting ready for dinner. My family is coming over. Had you forgotten?"

"Strangely enough the last thing I'm thinking about when you're naked and writhing underneath me is your mother."

Jenna grinned. "Good to know." She glanced at the clock and shrieked with horror. "Is that really the time?" She sprang out of bed so fast she knocked Greg in the jaw. "We need to get going."

He sat up, rubbing his jaw. "Why? Your mother is coming to dinner, that's all."

"All? Greg, *my mother is coming to dinner.*" *And my sister*, she thought, *whose house in London looked like something from a designer magazine.*

"I don't have time for a shower." She pulled on her clothes, hopping round the room like a circus performer. "Get up, Greg. Why are you smiling?"

"Because I love your hair like that."

"Like what?" She glanced in the mirror. "I look like I just got out of bed after having wild sex."

"That's my favorite hairstyle."

Jenna grabbed a hairbrush but in the end gave up and scooped her hair into a ponytail. "Get dressed. I need help with the living room."

"What's wrong with the living room?"

Muttering protests, he pulled on jeans and a fresh shirt and followed her. "I get that your mother is coming to dinner. What I don't get is why that necessitates a complete house makeover." He watched as Jenna tugged cushions from a bag and ripped off the price tags. "Are those new cushions?"

"They are."

Her sister always had cushions and they never looked as if someone had sprawled all over them, marking children's work while drinking wine at the end of a long day.

"I hate cushions. Cushions were invented to give men something to throw across the room."

"They were invented to make the house look cozy and comfortable. *Dressed* is the word I saw used in a fancy house magazine."

"That explains it. I like my houses the way I like my women—undressed."

Jenna dropped to her knees so she could check under the sofa. "Don't ever say things like that in public. It makes you sound—"

"How does it make me sound?"

"I don't know—" Jenna sat up and strands of hair tumbled over her face, half obscuring her vision "—unreconstructed." She shoved her hair back, wishing it was smooth like her sister's.

"Me Tarzan. You Jenna." Greg gave her a suggestive smile. "And if you want me to behave like a modern man, don't throw yourself at my feet, woman."

"I'm not at your feet. I'm looking for my thong. Remember that night we had sex on the sofa?"

"No." Greg was deadpan. "No recollection."

She hauled herself upright and flung a cushion at his head.

He caught it one-handed. "Thank you for proving my point. Cushions are for throwing. They're the soft furnishing equivalent of a stress ball. And of course I remember your thong. I was the one who removed it."

"And now I can't find it." She stuffed her hand down the back of the sofa cushions. "If my mother finds that thong, my life is over."

"If she finds that thong it shows you *have* a life. A sex

life. And I thought you were getting along better with your mother."

"I am, but I'm not at the stage where I want to discuss my sex life. Do you have a paintbrush?"

Greg blinked. "Before I answer that I have to ask what you want to do with it. My mind is working overtime."

"There's a mark on the kitchen wall where I tripped carrying that glass of wine."

He shook his head in disbelief. "So use a cloth to clean it off."

"I tried that! It stained the wall."

"Let me get this straight—your mother is coming to dinner and you want me to repaint the house. You don't think you might be taking this whole thing a little too seriously? Anyway, you're the one who does the painting in this family."

Jenna arranged the cushions the way she'd seen Lauren do it, but somehow her house still lacked the "put together" air that her sister seemed to achieve effortlessly. Maybe she had to accept she wasn't a very "put together" sort of person. "When did my mother and sister last come to us for dinner?"

"I don't remember." Greg shook his head as she threw another cushion onto the sofa.

"I want the place to look good."

Greg sighed. "This is crazy. This is our home. Don't you love our home?"

"Of course." And she did. It was theirs. A comfortable nest they'd built over the years, packed with things they'd chosen together. "But Lauren is an interior designer. She told me her house was like her showroom."

"You're a first-grade teacher." Greg picked up one of the

paintings a child in her class had made for her. "Your home is your showroom, too, but we're showing different things."

She snatched it from him and tucked it in with the magazines. "We don't even have kids, and our home is covered in kids' drawings."

"I like it. We could stick some of these paintings over the stain in the kitchen."

"Or you could paint the wall. There's still time."

He pulled her against him and kissed her. "I am not painting the wall."

"If my mother notices it, I'm blaming you."

"I'll tell her you strolled into the kitchen wearing your thong and I walked into the wall." But his gaze was gentle. "Your mom has a lot on her mind right now. She's confessed to her daughters that she has no money and that her marriage was miserable. I think she's going to have more important things to think about than the state of the cushions on our sofa or a mark on the paintwork. Lauren, too."

"Lauren has barely answered her phone for the past few days. It keeps going to voice mail, and when she calls me back she always seems to be anxious to keep it short. She and Mack had a big fight. Lauren yelled, and was upset about that. I'm worried about her. I hope Mom's confession didn't tip her over the edge. It was a bit of a shock."

"I'm sure. You both found out your dad had affairs. That's a lot to adjust to."

Jenna felt her cheeks heat. "Actually that wasn't the part that was a shock. We already knew about that. At least, we knew about one of them." She felt him still and then he eased her away from him.

"What are you talking about?"

"We knew about Dad."

"What? How?"

There wasn't much point in keeping it a secret now, was there? "Lauren and I saw him—"

"With a woman?" He released her suddenly and dragged his hand through his hair. "When?"

"Years ago. Mom was away. We went to the Sail Loft and he was there—with her." And even now, so many years later, she could picture it as if it had happened the day before. The two of them had peered through the window, shocked and disbelieving.

"Who was it?"

"I don't know. We didn't see her face. Just—well, you don't need the detail." She didn't want to think about the detail.

Greg said nothing for a full minute. "How old were you?"

"Eight." She saw a muscle flicker in his jaw.

"You saw your father screwing another woman when you were eight years old and you never told me?"

"I never told anyone."

"I'm not anyone, Jenna."

"I know, and you have no idea how much I wanted to tell you, but we had to keep it a secret. We knew that if anyone found out, we wouldn't be a family anymore. They would have split up and it would have been like Meredith." At least, that's what she'd believed at the time, but now she wasn't sure. What if they'd got that part wrong?

Greg ran his hand over his face. "This is a huge thing, Jenna."

"That's why we didn't tell Mom. We didn't know what to do. I guess we hoped it was a one-off. Turned out it wasn't, but we had no way of knowing that."

"I'm not talking about the affair. I'm talking about the fact that in all these years together, you never once mentioned it to me."

Her heart started to pound. Damn Lauren and her sudden revelations. "Everyone has things they don't like to talk about, Greg."

"Not you. You're an open book, or so I thought."

"Are you saying there isn't a single thing in your past you haven't told me?"

"You were there for almost all of my past. You witnessed it firsthand." He looked shell-shocked. "Our lives have been tangled together for as long as I can remember, which is why I don't understand why you wouldn't have mentioned it. I didn't think we had secrets, and now I discover that you've had a massive secret for a long time."

Her palms grew clammy. "Please don't make a big deal out of this."

"It's a big deal, Jenna."

"It isn't! It—"

"It's a big deal to me." His voice had thickened. "A very big deal. You didn't trust me enough to tell me."

She stared at him, helpless. A few minutes ago they'd been locked together naked and intimate and now it was like looking at a stranger. "Don't be mad. I can't believe you're reacting like this. It was a million years ago. Why do you even care?"

For once he wasn't smiling. "Excuse me for being human." He strode away from her to the kitchen and slammed the door.

Jenna flinched.

She'd never seen him like this. If they ever had a disagreement, he was rational and calm. She'd never seen him withdraw from her.

What she'd said had upset him, she knew that, but she'd spent her life trying to forget having seen her father that day. Surely Greg could understand that?

She opened the kitchen door tentatively. "Greg—"

"I'm cooking."

Rejection: to rebuff a person.

She bit her lip. "I could help."

"I don't need help."

"But—" The sound of the doorbell interrupted her and Jenna wanted to scream with frustration.

Talk about bad timing. Maybe she should have canceled on them. She could have claimed some vile sickness. But then she wouldn't have been able to check on Lauren.

With a last look at Greg's rigid shoulders, she went to answer the door.

"Something smells wonderful." Lauren was carrying a large portfolio case. "You're such a wonderful cook."

"Thanks." Jenna was relieved that at least her sister seemed buoyant. That was one less thing to worry about. "What's in the case?"

"The result of my light bulb moment. I'll show you in a moment." Lauren slipped off her coat with that elegance of movement that characterized everything she did.

"Is it the reason you've been difficult to get hold of the last few days?"

"I've been busy, that's true. Where's Greg?"

"He's in the kitchen." Jenna hoped her smile didn't look as fake as it felt. It probably wouldn't fool her sister, but hopefully it would work for her mother.

Nancy stepped inside after Lauren. After a moment's hesitation she reached out and hugged Jenna, too. "It's kind of you to invite us over, especially when you've been working all day."

Enveloped by warmth, Jenna closed her eyes, glad she hadn't canceled the evening.

Then she eased away and saw that her mother looked tired, defeated, and she stopped thinking about her own problems.

She'd never seen her mother anything other than fully in control, but it was as if letting out her confession had severed a string that had been holding everything together.

"Can I take your coat, Mom?" And now when she looked at the gray coat she realized that the reason her mother hadn't replaced it was because she hadn't been able to afford a new one.

How could she have missed so much?

She'd been upset that her mother hadn't known the big things about her, but she hadn't known the big things about her mother.

Mack was hovering behind them.

"Hi, honey. How's it all going?"

"Great." She sounded unusually subdued and Jenna gave her a tight hug, surprised when Mack hugged her back, almost clinging.

She knew her niece had been having trouble at school and Lauren had called her, racked with guilt, to tell her how she'd "lost it" with Mack a few days earlier.

Privately Jenna had been a little relieved to hear Lauren had exploded. Her sister's almost unnatural level of control had been starting to worry her and in her opinion Mack had been pushing boundaries a little too far.

"Come on in. I made all your favorite things to eat."

"This room is looking cozy, Jenna," her mother said, and Lauren nodded.

"It's so you."

"Messy, you mean?"

"Comfortable." Lauren glanced around. "A house should

feel lived-in and loved. With yours I immediately want to kick off my shoes and lounge on the sofa with a book."

Jenna was about to reply when Greg appeared from the kitchen, his emotions carefully concealed beneath charm and warmth.

She tried to catch his eye, but he wasn't looking at her.

He poured everyone a drink and after an exchange of small talk, they moved to the table.

Jenna served the soup, along with crusty bread rolls flavored with sea salt and rosemary that she'd baked herself. All she wanted to do was be alone with Greg to talk, but there was no chance of that.

"Did I ever tell you my book group loved your cakes?" Nancy reached for one of the rolls. "They were gone in a moment. Everyone was talking about them."

"I'm glad. And I forgot to mention that I bumped into Sheila. She told me you'd been to visit Kaley in hospital and given her one of your coloring books and pens. That was kind of you."

Nancy gave a short laugh. "I have boxes of them gathering dust."

Lauren picked up her spoon. "You have a lot of things gathering dust in that house, Mom."

"As my grandmother said, you never know when a thing might become useful. I'm not good at throwing things away."

Jenna had learned not to question her great-grandmother's wisdom, particularly as she was no longer around to defend herself. She'd died before Lauren was born, leaving responsibility for the house, its contents and the entire Stewart heritage with Nancy.

"I think you might need to learn." Lauren put her spoon

down and pulled a sheaf of papers from her bag. "Take a look."

Jenna was confused. "A look at what?"

"When I was driving round the other day, I noticed one of those huge beach houses for rent. It gave me an idea," Lauren said. "I want to know what you think."

Nancy raised her eyebrows. "Since when did we work at the dinner table?"

"Since we had a family crisis. If this works out the way I hope it will, we're going to need to use every minute of every day." Lauren opened the file, pulled out a spreadsheet covered in numbers and slid it across the table. "I've talked to a few people in town and run the numbers."

Jenna looked at the spreadsheets and floor plans. "You've been busy." She picked up the sheets closest to her. Each room in The Captain's House was carefully mapped out by hand on graph paper. "Can't you do this on a computer?"

"Yes, but I prefer the old-fashioned way."

It must have taken hours, but that was good, wasn't it? Finally her sister had a focus and a purpose.

Jenna glanced at Greg, but he was silent.

She was surprised no one had sensed the tension between them. Or maybe no one thought to look.

Jenna took a closer look at one of the sheets of paper. "What is that long line?"

"This is the garden room, and the line is the window." Lauren turned the paper round. "You can see door openings, and how that's going to work with the space."

Jenna had never considered how a door opened when she'd planned her decoration. "And those small squares?"

"Side tables. This room has the best views in the house. People are going to want to sit there with drinks."

"People?"

Lauren drew in a breath. "That's the part I wanted to talk about. Look at this, Mom." She handed the spreadsheet to her mother, but Nancy barely glanced at it.

"I appreciate all you're doing, but I can't afford to keep the house, Lauren."

"You can if you rent."

Nancy looked at the paper in front of her. "How would renting help? We still wouldn't be living in the place."

"But it would belong to you. You'd own it." Lauren leaned across and circled a number. "Look at that. It's what we could get for a long summer rental, providing we target the luxury market."

Jenna thought about the rattling windows and the drafts in the winter. She thought about the peeling paint and the way the downstairs bathroom coughed out water as if it were dying. She thought about the possessions her ancestors had accumulated over the years.

"Are you sure we'd be at the luxury end? Maybe we should aim a little lower."

Lauren shook her head. "That wouldn't bring in enough money. The house needs work, that's true, but the position is unbeatable. That's our real advantage over other properties. That and the history of the place. We need to use that history to our advantage."

"Just because people are interested in history," Jenna said, "doesn't mean they want to be living in the middle of it. Hot and cold running water is a must."

Nancy straightened. "Scott refitted two of the bathrooms upstairs."

"If you're renting out the whole house, all the bathrooms need to work."

Lauren scrawled *call plumber* on the top of another piece of paper. "The whole house needs work, but much of it is decorative. We have ten bedrooms—"

"Nine," Jenna said, eyeing her mother. "Dad's hobby room is crammed with things. Model boats, his golf clubs and all those trophies he won. No one would want to sleep in there."

Nancy finished her soup. "He wouldn't ever let me in the room even to dust."

"It must be like something from *Great Expectations*," Mack said, "covered in cobwebs."

It was the first thing she'd said since they'd sat down and Jenna saw Lauren give her a warm smile.

"I bet you're right."

Greg stood up and cleared the plates.

Jenna watched as he disappeared into the kitchen. She desperately wanted to follow him, but she knew their problems were going to have to wait until later. "I suppose we could lock that door."

Lauren tapped her pen on the table. "Let's worry about that later. We have three months to turn The Captain's House into luxury accommodation that people will be prepared to pay good money to rent."

"Three months isn't very long," Nancy said. "Is that possible?"

"Yes. I need to talk to the planning people and all the necessary officials to make sure we can rent the house out, but I've been doing some thinking and drawn up some plans—" Lauren reached down and opened the portfolio she'd been carrying. "Structurally the place is sound thanks to Scott's work over the winter. We can't change the space, so it's about making sure that the decoration makes the most of it.

We are going to enhance all the best things about the house, and reflect the coastal position. I've had some ideas."

She put a stack of mood boards in the middle of the table.

"This takes me back to our childhood when you redecorated my bedroom." Jenna picked up one of the boards. It was covered in images and fabric swatches. She immediately recognized the layout of the master bedroom suite, but not the style. "I love this. But won't it cost a fortune?"

"No. I intend to do all of it myself."

"All of it? We need new sofas in the living room."

"We can't afford that. We'll reupholster the old ones. I can do that."

Jenna looked at her. "You know how to upholster a sofa?"

"I know a lot of things. I've just never had the chance to do them before." Lauren handed the board across to her mother, who studied it for a moment.

"I love this." Nancy reached into her bag for her glasses and took a closer look. "The colors are light and fresh. You have a good eye."

"We'd need to refit a couple of the bedrooms. We need more closet space, maybe some bookshelves. And I have some ideas for the kitchen that shouldn't cost a fortune. And I intend to turn one of the downstairs rooms into a media room." Lauren picked up her phone and showed them some photos.

Nancy flicked through. "I don't have the funds for anything this elaborate."

"I've looked at the costs and I think we can make it work." Lauren's cheeks were flushed. "I've become something of an expert on managing money lately. I had a baptism of fire. Providing we can rent the place for the whole summer season, we can make a profit. Enough for you to live on in the winter, although I have ideas for that, too. And what I have in mind isn't going to cost that much. But it would require you to go to work with your paintbrush."

Jenna wondered if that plan was really about cost saving, or whether her sister was trying to get their mother to paint again.

"Where are we going to find someone to rent it? Are we going to list it with someone on the island? Won't we need a website?"

Lauren retrieved her phone. "Yes, and that's one of the things I can't do myself."

"I could do it," Mack said. "I could build a website if you tell me what you want it to do."

Jenna could almost feel her sister's mood lift.

"That would be great. Are you sure?"

"Yes. I'll figure it out." Mack toyed with the bread on her plate. "Maybe I'll join the Coding Club at school. Someone there would probably be able to help me."

Lauren nodded. "That sounds great. Thank you."

"It's probably suicide, but everyone's got to die, right?" She flushed. "Sorry, Mom. I didn't mean to say that."

"It's okay." Lauren stretched out her hand and squeezed Mack's. "I don't want you to feel you have to watch what you say."

Jenna wished she'd watched what she said.

She glanced toward the kitchen, wondered why Greg was taking so long. "If this works and you rent it out for the summer, you still won't have anywhere to live."

Lauren let go of Mack's hand. "There is somewhere, but I don't know how you're going to feel about it."

Nancy sat up straighter. "Go on."

"The Sail Loft." Lauren passed another mood board across the table. "We could live there."

Jenna was relieved she didn't have food in her mouth at that moment because she would have choked.

The Sail Loft?

Lauren met her gaze and then looked away again. Color streaked across her cheeks, but her chin angled in a way that told Jenna she wasn't going to be dissuaded.

"There are only two bedrooms." Jenna tried logic first.

"Yes, but the master is huge. I've thought about the space and it would be easy to build a partition and divide the room into two, temporarily at least. It would be small, but I think it would work."

Jenna wondered why she felt sick. It wasn't as if she was going to be the one living there.

"Why not use the top floor?"

"Because it's Mom's studio. She needs it for when she starts painting again."

She was making an assumption, Jenna thought. "When" not "if."

Nancy frowned. "I haven't been there since your father died." Her voice sounded strange. "The place could be flooded for all I know."

Jenna knew her mother hadn't painted, but she hadn't known that she'd stayed away from the Sail Loft.

"I wish you'd told me. I could have supported you."

"You're supporting me now."

"Yes." And it would mean she'd have to go back to the Sail Loft. She'd have to walk up that path and look through that window.

"And I couldn't have told you without telling you everything else." Nancy sent a glance in Mack's direction.

"Anything you have to say, you can say in front of Mack," Lauren said.

Nancy looked unconvinced. "I'm not sure if I think it's appropriate to—"

"Mom—" Lauren's tone was sharp "—we've all tried the approach where we keep things to ourselves to protect each other, and where has that gotten us? From now on everything is out in the open and we'll deal with it together."

Jenna knew Lauren was still getting calls from London about Ed's estate. Each time she'd come away several shades paler.

She knew her sister had been hoping Ed had some money put aside that she didn't know about, but so far there had been no good news.

Nancy glanced between them. "You have no idea how much I wish you'd told me you knew about your father."

"We only saw him that one time," Lauren said. "We had no idea he did it more than once."

Once had been enough, Jenna thought. "Could we get rid of the honeysuckle? I can't stand honeysuckle."

Her mother gave her a steady look. "I've been thinking of doing it for a while. It's invasive and competes with native plants. It will be the first thing to go."

"Wait a minute—" Mack stared. "Gramps had an *affair* and you saw him?" Her expression was so comical it even made Jenna smile.

"At the time I thought adults only did it to have babies. For a while I was worried I was going to get a baby sister." It was the first time she'd ever joked about it and it might have felt like a step forward if Greg hadn't chosen that moment to walk back into the room with the main course.

He was the only one who didn't join in the awkward laughter.

The look on his face made Jenna uneasy. Greg was the master of his emotions but right now he didn't seem to be doing so well.

Mack shuddered and Nancy shook her head.

"It's a wonder the two of you weren't put off sex for life. I hate to think of you girls in that position. Of course if Jenna had been a little less adventurous, instead of always leading you into trouble—" Nancy's gaze shifted to Jenna and Lauren stood up to help serve the casserole.

"It wasn't Jenna, it was me."

Nancy looked confused. "You were by her side whatever she did, Lauren. I knew I could trust you never to leave her, however adventurous she was."

"She wasn't," Lauren said. "I was the adventurous one."

It seems so long ago, Jenna thought. She hadn't seen that side of her sister for a long time. Not since she'd left home.

From the moment she'd moved to London, Lauren had been transformed.

It was as if she'd been determined to stamp out her former wild self.

"You reinvented yourself," she said and Lauren handed her a plate.

"I guess my last adventure was getting pregnant, and that scared me. It's pretty sobering to realize you're in charge of another life."

"Wait—" Nancy's voice was faint. "I always thought it was Jenna. I thought you were protecting her."

Lauren shook her head. "The times we went skinny dipping at night, when we jumped off the Jaws Bridge, when we crept to your studio the night we saw Dad—all me. I was the ringleader. And I didn't protect her, she protected me."

"My nerves were continually shredded," Jenna confessed.

Mack was staring at her mother. "You went skinny dipping? Like, no *clothes*?"

"Yes."

"And you jumped off the Jaws Bridge? You always tell me not to do that!"

"Which makes me a raging hypocrite, I know. My only excuse is that I have firsthand knowledge of how much trouble teenagers can get themselves into. There's a part of your brain that doesn't make great decisions."

"Yeah," Mack muttered, "I think I already found that part."

Nancy looked stunned. "I can't believe I got it so wrong."

"I wasn't exactly a saint," Jenna said. "I was pretty accident-prone. The paint incident really was me."

"And the goat," Lauren said.

Jenna frowned. "The goat was *you*. You felt sorry for it. You thought it should be liberated from that post where it was tethered all day."

Mack choked. "The story about the sisters and the goat is *true*? I thought it was made-up?"

"I thought it was made-up, too." Nancy shook her head. "I can't believe I didn't know this about my own daughter."

"Mothers never know everything about their daughters," Mack said kindly. "Don't beat yourself up, Grams. And there are some things you're better off not knowing."

Was that true?

Jenna glanced at Greg, but he wasn't looking at her.

She had a feeling he didn't agree.

CHAPTER TWENTY-THREE

Nancy

Purge: to get rid of undesirable things

"Thank you for coming with me." Nancy stood on the overgrown path in front of the Sail Loft.

She really didn't want to be here.

Behind her she could hear the sea. Now, in March, the unloved garden was a wilderness, but she could see the possibilities.

"It's what friends are for. I can't believe you haven't been here in five years, and I can't believe you didn't tell me." Alice put her hand on Nancy's arm.

"After Tom died something changed for me. I suppose I turned away from the life I had when he was alive."

"I understand. You don't have to go inside, Nancy. Tell them you don't want to. Come and live with me instead."

That was out of the question, but the suggestion gave her

the strength she needed. "I have to do this. Lauren is right, it makes sense."

"Not if it upsets you."

How much should she say? "If it means I don't have to sell The Captain's House, then it's worth it." Why hadn't she considered this option herself? *Because she was a coward.* "My daughters are smart, both of them."

And brave.

She couldn't bear to think what they probably saw that night. Damn Tom and his libertine ways.

Alice was staring at the Sail Loft in silence. "Are you sure about this?"

Nancy paused. "Anyone would think *you* didn't want to go inside."

Alice gave a wan smile. "I hate seeing you hurt, that's all."

Nancy patted her on the shoulder and walked ahead. She could have done this on her own, but inviting Alice had been the right thing to do.

If she was really going to move forward, then she needed Alice here.

The key didn't turn easily in the lock, but whether that was because it was rusty from lack of use or because her hand was shaking, she wasn't sure.

Finally she unlocked the door and pushed it open.

The shutters were closed and the place smelled of dust and paint, although how it could still smell of paint after so long she had no idea. Dust sheets covered the sofas and there was a lace of cobwebs high on the ceiling. Other than that not much had changed.

An image appeared in her head, disturbingly clear.

She saw Tom, leaning over a dazzled woman, his laughing blue eyes charming her the way he'd charmed Nancy. Had he made promises? Had he lied? Or had he told her that this was the way he was, that he did this with every-one and that although she might feel special now, he would have forgotten her by tomorrow?

She turned and saw Alice sitting on the dusty sofa. "Alice? Are you all right?"

Alice stood up suddenly. "I'm worried about you. Let's leave right now."

"We only just got here. Why would we leave?"

Alice's eyes filled. "You're my dearest friend. I hate to see you putting yourself through this."

Nancy felt something stir inside her.

She made a decision.

"Let's clear him out, Alice. We'll do it together." It was time to get rid of the man, starting with his things. Nancy walked through to one of the bedrooms and pulled out a box of Tom's things. "We should sort through this."

There was a box of his clothes tucked in the spare room and she dragged it out and flung it into the garden. The feeling of satisfaction was astonishing. It was like shooting adrenaline into a vein.

Alice flinched as if she'd been struck. "Don't you want to sort through them? There might be things here you want to keep." She walked into the garden and retrieved a jacket that had spilled onto the overgrown grass. "Are you sure this is the right thing to do? Don't you want to hold on to a few memories?"

Nancy wished she could rid herself of the memories as easily as she could rid herself of his clothes. "That's a jacket, and it's taking up space. He's gone, Alice. Keeping his clothes isn't going to change that."

She flung open shutters and windows, letting in sea air. The breeze flowed through the rooms, sending a few stray pieces of paper fluttering across the dusty floor.

Today the sky was blue with a promise of summer and she remembered how much she'd once loved being here, in her beach sanctuary.

Why should Tom continue to contaminate a place that had once been special to her?

She was going to strip the whole place back until it was an empty shell, and then she'd build it up again the way she wanted it.

Reaching into her bag, she pulled out a scarf and tied it around her hair to protect herself from dust and cobwebs. Then she got to work.

She emptied cupboards, flung clothes into bags and tipped away the contents of drawers. She moved through the rooms like a whirlwind, with Alice shadowing her like a startled rabbit saying things like, "Nancy, are you sure?" and "You're really throwing this away?"

Nancy continued to pile things in the garden.

When the ground floor was finally empty, she rolled up her sleeves and reached for the bag she'd brought with her. It was going to take more than a bucket of bleach to get Tom out of her life, but at least it was a start.

Cleaning turned out to be therapeutic. She scrubbed and rubbed until sweat clung to her body.

She was aware of Alice next to her, dusting surfaces and shaking out rugs in the garden.

She threw out the old mattresses and scrubbed the floor and the walls.

They needed painting. Maybe she could do that. She hadn't painted for five years, but a wall was different, wasn't it?

Finally, when the downstairs rooms were as clean as she could make them, Nancy turned her attention to the top floor.

She'd bought the place for the upstairs studio, with its acres of glass and north light. That was all that had ever interested her. If there had been a whole football team living in the downstairs bedrooms she wouldn't have known. That must have been where the girls saw Tom if they'd been peeping through the window. What a stupid man he was for not closing the shutters before he did the deed.

Still, at least it meant her precious studio remained uncontaminated.

She took the stairs slowly, almost afraid to reach the top. The first time she'd seen the place she'd gasped aloud and then realized that the Realtor didn't seem to know what a gem he had on his hands. Because she didn't want him to push up the price, she'd muttered a lot about rotten rafters and the number of dead mice and then made him a low offer. The previous owner had died, and fortunately the family were keen for a quick sale.

Now, of course, it would be a different matter. Land this close to the beach was at a premium.

The moment Nancy stepped out onto the wide floor boards she felt the same rush of excitement she'd felt when she first saw the place. How could she have stayed away so long? She felt as if she'd neglected a friend.

I'm sorry I abandoned you.

No one had touched the place since her last visit. There was her kettle, still perched on the table in one corner where she'd left it alongside half a jar of coffee, the contents of which had solidified. When she was painting she'd gone hours without taking a break, oblivious to the world around her. She'd finish when the light started to fade and then she'd make herself a drink and sit in the garden on her favorite rickety chair and listen to the sea.

The tide came and went, washing away the debris from the previous day and depositing more, licking at the sand, changing the shape of the landscape.

She imagined herself as the tide, washing Tom out of her life. It was a surprisingly satisfying exercise.

Alice had followed her upstairs but Nancy ignored her, lost in the moment.

Her footsteps echoed as she walked the length of her studio. This room soared up into the rafters, giving a feeling of space and light. She glanced up, checking the place was still fundamentally sound. There were no signs of water damage. No ominous stains on the wall that might have suggested a deeper problem.

Her paints were where she'd left them. She checked them and saw that although some of the watercolors had dried up, the oil paints were fine.

Now, with distance, she could barely remember that burning desire and elemental excitement that had driven her to put paint on canvas.

The fire was gone and there was no longer a need to escape, so what reason was there to pick up a brush?

She heard the sound of an engine and then the slam of a car door and female laughter.

Lauren and Jenna.

Jenna had been teaching, and Lauren had spent the day scouring the island for bits and pieces that she could use to transform the house.

Nancy moved closer to the glass and watched as they

walked together up the overgrown path. She saw Lauren pause to point something out and Jenna nod in agreement.

Sisters.

Would life have been easier if she'd had a sister? It would have been good to have someone to share things with. Someone you could trust no matter what. Someone by your side through thick and thin.

She'd been wrong to worry about her children so much. They had each other, and they always had. Who would have guessed that it had been Lauren who was the ringleader? The adventurous one?

Did you know that, Tom?

She was certain that he hadn't known. He'd spent his life thinking about himself.

She saw them pause in the doorway, as if they were afraid to enter.

Jenna said something and Lauren pulled a face. Then she took her sister's hand and they vanished from view as they stepped into the house.

"Mom?" Jenna's voice floated up the stairs.

"Up here." Nancy cleared her throat and pulled herself together. If the girls had bad memories, then she'd find a way to put new ones there.

She heard the clatter of their feet on the stairs and they appeared in the loft room, so alike and yet so different.

Her girls.

For years she'd bracketed them with Tom. Because the three of them had spent so much time together, she'd been unable to separate them in her head. She'd allowed that feeling of being excluded to persist when they'd reached adulthood, but she saw now that if there had been a rift then, she'd been the cause of it. She'd been afraid that confessing the truth would drive them further apart, but it had brought them closer.

"You were supposed to wait so we could do this together," Jenna said as Lauren put her bag down on the floor.

"You shouldn't have done this on your own." And then she noticed Alice. "Oh, you had Alice with you. That's good."

It was good, Nancy thought. Bringing Alice had been the right decision.

"There's still plenty to do," she said. "Getting this place habitable isn't going to be easy. And that's before we get started on The Captain's House." The thought of it should have exhausted her, but she felt energized. Instead of feeling defeated, she felt hopeful.

She felt like flinging open the upstairs windows and yelling, *Do you see me, Tom? You didn't crush me.*

Lauren pulled out a sketchbook. "You've done a wonderful job of clearing out downstairs. It makes it easier to visualize everything. If three of us are going to live here we are going to need closet space, but I don't want to overcrowd the rooms."

"If it's carpentry you need, then we should ask Scott." Jenna strolled over to the canvases stacked against the wall. "He did a great job on the house."

Lauren said nothing.

Nancy studied her daughter, noticing the shadows under her eyes.

It was still early days, of course, but they needed to do what they could to reduce those shadows. "I can't ask Scott for any more favors."

"You mean because Lauren told him you're no longer selling the house?" Jenna glanced up from the paintings.

"House sales fall through all the time, Mom. Fact of life. I'm sure he understood."

"Not because of that. Because I owe him enough already."

Lauren grabbed a bag and started clearing out the old coffee jar and other detritus that had been sitting gathering dust for years. "What exactly do you owe him, Mom?"

Nancy hesitated. She could have brushed it away. Scott wouldn't say anything, she was sure of that, but it was as if her first confession had opened a door she couldn't easily close.

Might as well empty the closets of all the skeletons, she thought.

Did it matter that Alice would hear?

No. It would probably be a good thing if she knew the truth.

"I owe Scott," she said, "because he was there the night your father died. He helped me. Risked his life."

Jenna paused with her hand on one of the canvases. "Risked his life how?"

"There was a hurricane—"

"We know. That was why the tree came down on his car."

Nancy stared out the window, surprised by how vivid a memory could be. "The call came late afternoon. By then no one was on the water. Houses and business were boarded up. The ferry had stopped running hours before, and the airport was closed. There was no way to get to the mainland. I asked a couple of people if they'd take me, but they refused." She remembered walking past the harbor and feeling the force of the wind tearing at her. It was like nothing she'd ever experienced. "Then I saw Scott. I knew him by sight. We'd never spoken. But everyone knew he was the best sailor around. I asked him if he'd take me to the mainland and he agreed."

Lauren looked stunned. "In a hurricane?"

"I expected him to refuse. I wasn't sure which of us was most crazy. I'll never forget that crossing."

"I remember that night." Jenna said. "It was terrifying. When I called to check on you, you told me you were safe. I assumed that meant you were home. So Scott dropped you off and then came back to Martha's Vineyard?"

"No. By the time we arrived, the storm was much worse. Maybe Scott thought he'd diced with death enough for one night, but I don't think it was that. I think he didn't want to leave me. His kindness is something I'll never forget." Nancy stared out over the sea. Today it was calm. It was hard to imagine it could ever be as angry as it had been that night. "Scott came with me in the cab to the hospital, and I was too pathetic and grateful for the support to send him away."

"Why didn't you call me?" Jenna let the paintings fall back against the wall. "I hate the thought of you going through that alone. I would have been there for you, Mom. I would have gone with you."

"And risk your life in that terrible storm? One dead family member was enough. And anyway, the police had already told me your father wasn't alone in the car. I didn't want you to know about that."

She heard Alice make a small sound. Surprise? Shock?

Jenna crossed the room in two strides and wrapped her arms around her. *"Mom—"*

Alice sat down hard on the one chair in the room. "Oh, Nancy—"

Nancy leaned on Jenna, breathing in the soft floral scent her daughter always wore.

She was so affectionate, so warm, *so like Tom.*

No, not like Tom. Tom had used warmth as a snare, and affection as currency.

Jenna gave freely.

"Wait—" Lauren rubbed her fingers over her forehead. "Dad was with a woman the night he died?"

"Yes." Nancy gave Jenna's shoulder a squeeze and stepped away. "She worked in the hotel he often stayed in when he was off island. One in a long line of women who rode in that car with him." She noticed that Alice's face had lost all its color. "Are you surprised? You shouldn't be. That was my Tom. That was who he was, although of course not many people knew that side of him. That was probably my fault."

It had been her private shame and humiliation.

Maybe she should have hung him out to dry and let him deal with the fallout, but if she'd done that, her girls would have been hurt.

She felt Lauren's hand on her arm. "Scott stayed with you that night?"

"Through all of it. The hurricane, the hospital, the police, arrangements to return the body to the Vineyard— We stayed in a motel and he listened to me storm and rage. He didn't leave my side. Then he brought me home and we never mentioned it again."

"And you never told anyone."

"No. Tom died in the car the night of the hurricane. As far as anyone knew, he was on his own. It was considered a tragedy and half the island were at his funeral, but you know that part of course."

She saw that Alice's cheeks were wet.

Jenna must have seen the same thing because she rushed

across with tissues. "Oh, Alice, you're such a good friend. Mom is so lucky to have you. And Scott." She turned to her sister. "Can you believe he did that for Mom?"

Lauren was staring into space, lost in thought. "Yes," she said. "Yes, I can."

Nancy wished she knew what her daughter was thinking. "I wouldn't have made it through that night without him."

Lauren took a deep breath. "Is that why you were selling Scott the house? Because you felt you owed him?"

"I was selling because I needed the money and he was willing to pay my price. Scott never had a home of his own. I felt as if I was giving something back to him." But in the end her feelings for the house had proved more powerful. It seemed that obligation and responsibility couldn't be so easily overridden. She felt a twinge of guilt. Scott had been good to her.

Family might be complicated, but not having one seemed a worse option to her.

Lauren was suddenly very quiet. It was Jenna who spoke.

"Will you be all right living here, Mom? I'm worried it will be hard for you. Not only because of the limited space, but the memories."

It should have felt hard, but it didn't.

Shedding secrets had lightened the load she'd been carrying. She felt ready to sprint forward with her life instead of trudging.

"It won't be hard." Nancy glanced down at the garden. She already had plans for it. They would need plants acclimatized to wind and salt. Instead of a lawn, she was going to have a wildflower meadow. Cosmos, poppies, daisies and lupines. She wanted to look out her window and see birds and butterflies. She'd call Ben and ask him to help. He had more knowledge about coastal planting than anyone, except perhaps herself. Together they could transform this small perfect patch of land into something as spectacular as the garden at The Captain's House. It would be different, of course, but different was good. The thought of working side by side with him lifted her spirits. She enjoyed his company, his smile, his calm manner.

"I can't believe the pile of stuff outside the house," Jenna said. "I was worried we'd have a fight on our hands to persuade you to throw anything away. Did Alice do it for you?"

"No, I did it." Nancy smiled. "It turns out it's never too late to learn new skills."

CHAPTER TWENTY-FOUR

Lauren

> *Progress: to move forwards or onwards
> towards a place or objective*

THE WEEKS PASSED in a blur of activity and while Lauren busied herself with clearing, sewing and painting, the island shook off the freezing cloak of winter and spring emerged. Forsythia bloomed, brightening the garden with a burst of gold, the streets grew busier and the air warmed.

On a sunny Wednesday in mid-April she was awake early and making cushions for one of the upstairs bedrooms when she heard the kitchen door open.

Jenna came in wearing shorts and running shoes. "Are you ready?"

"Ready for what?" Lauren put the fabric down and rolled her shoulders to ease the ache. Her head hurt and her fingers hurt. "I'm ready for strong coffee, a hot shower or maybe even wine."

"At six in the morning?"

"Is that the time? The hours are merging." And she was using every one of them, partly because it helped to bury her emotions under layers of hard work, but mostly because she was enjoying thinking about something other than her own problems. "Why are you dressed in running gear?"

"Because I'm ready for our run." Jenna picked up the fabric. "I love this color. Very beachy."

"It's for the master bedroom. What run?"

"The one we're about to go on. I need to run off my stress." She fiddled with the fabric. "Is Mom in?"

"Upstairs. Still asleep I think. Be careful with that. There are pins in it. What's up?" She knew her sister well enough to know when something was wrong.

"I haven't been sleeping." Jenna handed the fabric back. "I keep thinking about Dad and all those women."

"Me, too." Lauren threaded a needle. "I'm trying to put it out of my mind."

"Do you think it would have made a difference if we'd told Mom what we saw?"

Lauren shook her head. "None."

"I hope you're right."

"I know I'm right." She stabbed the needle into the fabric. "Dad couldn't help himself. Expecting him to ignore women would have been like putting an alcoholic in charge of a bar and asking him not to drink."

"Did you know he had other affairs?"

Lauren focused on her sewing. "No. I didn't know for sure. I suspected. I saw him at a couple of summer picnics, talking and laughing with women. He was a flirt."

"I didn't see that."

"You were younger than me. You probably didn't notice."

"Has it changed the way you feel about him?"

Lauren snipped the thread. "Seeing him that night we were together changed the way I felt about him. When I wasn't with him, I was always wary. Didn't quite trust him. But when I was with him he always made sure we had so much fun I forgot that I didn't trust him."

"I was the same. And I feel guilty," Jenna confessed. "I feel like I'm being disloyal to Mom by not hating him."

"He was our dad. Little girls are allowed to love their dad even if he's flawed. Mom wouldn't want us to hate him."

Jenna flopped down on the chair next to her. "You look exhausted. What time did you get up?"

"Five." And she'd been upholstering a sofa until midnight. "Since when have you been a keen morning runner?"

"I will never be a keen runner at any time of the day, but that doesn't mean I can't run when I have to. I'll run for cookies, I'll run for ice cream and I'll run for my sister." Jenna waved her hand toward the door. "I'll give you four minutes to get changed. I can't be late for school."

Lauren was touched. "I appreciate the sentiment, but I have a ton of things to do to get this place ready for the rental."

"An hour out of your day isn't going to make a difference. What's all that?" Jenna frowned at the boxes stacked against the wall in the kitchen.

"That," Lauren said, "is just some of the junk Mom cleared out yesterday."

Jenna opened the box on top and peeped inside. "Dad's trophies?"

"She's taking them to the Goodwill store."

"She opened up his man cave?"

"Not only did she open it up, she cleared it out."

"And she didn't seem upset?"

"She was energized. Once she started, there was no stopping her. I helped her. I think she found it cathartic."

"A month ago, I never would have believed it possible." Jenna closed the box back up. "So now we have a tenth bedroom."

"I still need to clean it up and decorate, but yes. Eventually." Would they get it all done in time? She'd been working nonstop since they'd agreed on their plan.

She'd thrown herself into the redecoration of The Captain's House, relying more on creativity than cash. She spent her days trawling thrift stores and yard sales, and was consistently surprised by what people were prepared to throw away.

She bought wooden crates cheaply, painted them and used them as side tables in the children's bunk room. She sewed pretty patchwork quilts for the beds in coastal colors, using scraps of fabric that had been discarded. She'd picked up an outgrown beach dress in bold blue-and-white stripe and used it to recover cushions in the garden room. She had to pay more than she'd planned for the perfect rug for the living room, but she'd found bargain lighting that had helped rebalance her books.

Every night at dinner she showed off her fabric finds to her mother and they discussed colors and textures. Her mother was painting the rooms, mostly in white to reflect the light and space. Lauren used the furnishings to add color.

She sewed late into the night and started again early in the morning. Their deadline hung over her. She knew she needed to get a few rooms finished so that they could photograph the house and advertise it, but she'd underestimated how long it would take to transform a house as big as this one. And they still had the Sail Loft to tackle.

"You've been busy," Jenna said and Lauren nodded as she folded the quilt.

"It stops me thinking about Ed, and Scott. And takes my mind off worrying about Mack."

Jenna grabbed an apple from the bowl on the table. "How is she?"

"Happier I think." Which was a relief. Lauren wasn't quite sure what had brought about the change and assumed it was school. She was too relieved to question it too closely. "We don't talk much but she seems to have stopped treating me like the enemy."

"That's a start." Jenna finished the apple. "Come on. It's low tide. We can run along the beach."

It had been years since she'd run along the beach.

Lauren was tempted. "A short one."

They ran along the bike path that led between Edgartown and Oak Bluffs, and then dropped down to the beach.

The moment her feet hit the sand, Lauren found her rhythm. She wondered why she hadn't done this before now. She'd forgotten it. Forgotten how much she loved it.

Her stride lengthened and her running shoes were virtually silent on the sand.

The fog that had shrouded her brain cleared. Her dark mood lifted.

Her mind focused on running and only running and it was a few minutes before she thought to glance over her shoulder, and realized she'd left her sister behind.

She turned and Jenna finally caught up with her.

"How can you be that fit when you've been sitting down for months?" She doubled over, panting. "I hate you."

Lauren grinned. "I've done a lot of pacing." She took a sip from her water bottle. "This was a great idea."

"Glad you think so." Jenna heaved air into her lungs. "I hate running. It's boring."

"Not when you run with someone."

"Maybe not, but I wasn't running 'with' you. I was in your slipstream."

Lauren felt the wind feather her face and pull gently at her hair.

How was it almost May? It felt like yesterday that the police had knocked on the door, and yet it also felt like a lifetime ago. A different life.

The days had passed, hour by painful hour, and somehow while she'd been wrapped up in layers of wool and grief, the weather had become kinder. The wind had lost its bite and sunlight danced across the surface of the water. It was early spring, and the air was already filled with the promise of warmer months, of a lush hot summer, as if the Vineyard was stretching sleepily after a winter of hibernation.

Jenna stretched. "We should turn back or I'll be late for school and my little monsters will be uncontrollable. I have to be ahead of the game."

"You love it, don't you?"

"Teaching? Yes. There's nothing I'd rather do. Once I close that classroom door, everything in my world feels right."

Lauren glanced along the beach in the direction she'd been running. Another twenty minutes and she'd be at the boathouse where Scott worked. "Would you hate going back without me?"

Jenna followed her gaze and smiled. "No. Go."

"First tell me how you are." She never knew whether to mention the baby or not. "How are things?"

"I'm not pregnant, if that's what you're asking." Jenna shrugged. "I need to get back." She turned but Lauren grabbed her arm.

"Are things all right between you and Greg?"

"What do you mean?"

"The last few times you've come round to the house, you've come alone."

Jenna shrugged her off and stooped to adjust her running shoes. "He's busy, that's all. And we're working on the house, not socializing, so there didn't seem much point in bringing him."

"Right." Was the whole baby issue creating a problem for them? Lauren made a note to pay closer attention to her sister. "Thank you for making me do this. I owe you."

"This is just the beginning. Today a sedate run along the beach, tomorrow jumping off the Jaws Bridge."

Lauren laughed. "It's low tide, so no thanks. Let's take it a step at a time."

She watched her sister lope slowly back along the sand.

If she could have willed her to be pregnant, she would.

When she'd discovered she was expecting Mack, she'd felt nothing but terror. She'd felt desperately unready to be a mother.

Jenna was more than ready and she and Greg would make great parents.

As the sand grew softer and grainier, Lauren returned to the bike path and ran in the shade of the trees, her pace steady as she closed in on the marina.

By the time she arrived, she was out of breath herself.

And sweaty.

Great. Why hadn't she thought of that?

Scott was painting the underside of a boat, music playing in the background. The moment he saw her, he stopped what he was doing. The distance between them shrank to nothing until she could no longer hear the call of the seagulls or the background buzz of a drill. There was only the intense blue of his eyes, the insane pounding of her heart and the way he made her feel. It was as if some magnetic force connected them, able to pull them back together wherever they were.

He walked across to her, using the rag in his hands to wipe the oil from his fingers.

He was wearing faded Levi's that molded to every muscle, and the sleeves of his shirt were pushed back to the elbows. She caught a glimpse of tanned throat and, thanks to a few open buttons, a hint of dark hair through the open neck. A sheen of sweat clung to his skin and the smudge of grease on his cheek made her think of war paint.

Sixteen years and he was still the sexiest man she'd ever laid eyes on.

Lauren felt a hot flush of guilt. She wasn't supposed to find other men sexy, but it seemed her body hadn't got that message. Sexual attraction was no respecter of social conventions.

Her mouth felt dry and her stomach dropped as if she'd missed her step.

How? How could there be anything left after so many years?

She didn't understand it. She certainly didn't want it.

He studied her for a long, lingering moment and then without shifting his gaze called to the teenager he had working alongside him. "Cal?"

"Yeah, boss." The boy was there in an instant, eagerness and respect visible in his body language.

"Would you fetch us some coffee?"

Cal looked at him blankly. "Coffee?"

"Hot. Wet. Full of caffeine. You'll know it when you see it." Still holding the oily rag in one hand, Scott dug the other into his pocket and pulled out some notes. "Head to the Marina Café. It's going to take you thirty minutes."

Cal glanced at the office. "But there's a kettle in the—"

"Marina Café. Thirty minutes."

"Thirty—" Cal opened his mouth and closed it again. "Right, boss." He took the notes from Scott and scampered off, leaving them alone.

Lauren felt ridiculously self-conscious. "You've taken on an apprentice?"

"He helps out from time to time."

"Local boy?"

"Yes. Life hasn't exactly gone his way lately."

And he knew all about that of course. No one knew more about the challenges life could send than Scott. What she'd known about his past had broken her heart, and when she'd realized that his past was going to stop them having a future her heart had broken all over again.

"What happens when you move on again?"

"Who said I'm moving on?"

"It's what you do."

He rubbed at a stubborn stain on his fingers. "If that happens, then I guess he'll have to find someone else to work alongside."

"From the way he was looking at you, he thinks you're a hero."

His mouth curved. "We both know it won't take him long to get over that."

That smile still had the ability to cut her off at the knees. As a vulnerable eighteen-year-old his smile had made her feel special and it still did.

She shouldn't have come. It was too hard, standing here in front of him as if he was no more than an acquaintance. As if there hadn't once been a world of feelings between them.

They'd been good together. More than good.

Hope and possibilities had been spread like a feast in front of them, but instead of gorging themselves they'd walked away leaving all that potential untouched.

She'd tried hard to let him go and live the life she'd been given.

"The first time I saw you, you were running along the beach."

She frowned. "The first time we saw each other was in the café. You came in that day and I was bussing tables."

"I'd seen you before that," he said. "I used to watch you run every morning. You were fast. And light on your feet. You ran like an athlete. This is the first time I've seen you run since you arrived home."

"It felt good. I have Jenna to thank for it." She saw him glance over her shoulder. "She turned back. She's teaching. It's a school day."

He nodded. "How's Mack?"

"Doing better, I think." She wished she knew for sure, but she and Mack still hadn't returned to their old relationship. Things were less tense, but Lauren had a feeling that was because Mack was spending most of her time at school or in her room.

"She's smart. I'm glad she finally joined the Coding Club."

"You know about that?"

"Yes. She said something about setting up a website for The Captain's House so I suggested she join. It took her a while to find the courage. She was afraid of being teased." He rubbed his fingers across his jaw. "She's the only girl in the club, but she seems to be handling that."

"You know a lot about what's going on in her life." The fact that Mack was telling him more than her own mother, hurt. "You've been seeing a lot of her?"

"Her cycle route home from school takes her past the boatyard. She calls in sometimes. You know that. After last time, I made sure she told you."

"She said she was helping. I didn't realize the two of you were having long, meaningful conversations."

"Is that a problem?" He tucked the rag into the back pocket of his jeans while she struggled for a response.

"What do you want me to say? That it hurts my feelings that she'll talk to you, when I've spent the last sixteen years caring for her and putting her first? Yes, it hurts. And I hate myself for that because I'm worried about her and as long as she is talking to *someone* that's good."

"But you'd rather it wasn't me."

"She recently lost someone she loved very much, even if she's forgotten that right now." She heard the edge in her own voice and hated herself for it. "What happens when she gets attached and then you move on again?"

"You're making a lot of assumptions."

"I know you, Scott."

He gave her a long look. "I'm not going anywhere."

"Not today, but we both know you'll move on at some point."

"Maybe I won't."

There was no way she was going to allow herself to believe he might have changed. "Let's not talk about it."

"If that's what you want." His gaze held hers. "Now that the weather is warming up I thought I could take her sailing. Would you object to that?"

"No. If she wants to go on the boat, then you should take her." She didn't want to give Mack another reason to be angry with her, and it wasn't as if she was worried about Mack's safety. No one knew more about the sea than Scott.

"You could come, too." Something in his tone made her heart rate pick up.

"No time. We're working hard to get The Captain's House ready for rental." The moment she said it she felt like a coward.

They both knew her refusal wasn't only because she was busy.

"How's that going?"

"It's a lot of work, but we're getting there. We're going to move in to the Sail Loft for the summer."

"And you're fine with that?"

She wasn't fine with that. Every time she stepped onto that wretched path she imagined her father's white, hairy buttocks pumping into some woman. It made her feel physically ill, but that wasn't something she intended to tell her mother. There was a limit to how much sharing was appropriate.

She smiled, aware that it was a thin, unconvincing effort. "I'm fine with it."

Scott didn't return the smile. "Are you sure? Because you had quite a phobia about—"

"That was a long time ago. You cured me of that." She interrupted him before Cal could arrive and the details of her sexual hang-ups could be broadcast around the island for everyone to chomp on. "And by the time I've finished with the place, it won't look anything like it does now. Mom has cleared it out, but we haven't started making it habitable. We need a new kitchen and a partition in the main bedroom."

"I could build that kitchen for you."

She'd rejected the idea when her sister had suggested it because she didn't particularly want to be working in such close quarters with him, but now she realized that if he started work immediately he'd be finished before she was ready to begin work on the furnishings. "Would you have time?"

"I'd need to juggle a few things here but yes, I could do it."

However mixed up she felt, she recognized the generosity in that gesture. "You've been kind to my mother. I haven't thanked you for that."

"I didn't do it to earn your gratitude."

"Why did you do it?" It was something she'd wondered about.

"She needed help."

He had an affinity for people in trouble, she knew that. It was a trait that made it inconveniently hard to hate him.

She wondered why he hadn't noticed she needed help when she found out she was pregnant.

"I'm glad you were there for her." She paused. "There was so much I didn't understand. So much I didn't know. I wish she'd told us."

"I guess most of us have things we prefer to keep to ourselves."

She knew he kept plenty to himself. "I should go—"

"You're looking better. You've put on a little weight since

I saw you last." His gaze shifted from her face to her body and she felt the atmosphere snap tight.

He hadn't touched her, and yet her skin tingled with awareness.

"You're telling me I'm fat?"

"No, but it's good to know the wind isn't going to blow you away. That first day at the ferry—I was worried about you."

"I'd lost my husband, and my home."

There was a long silence. "Was he good to you?" His tone was raw. "Did you love him?"

At eighteen she would have thought that question would have a yes or no answer. Now she knew differently.

There were so many different types of love. There was the love she felt for her child, so intense she knew she would die for her if necessary. Then there was the love she had for her sister, a bond so powerful that nothing would ever break it, and the love she had for her mother.

Her love for Scott had been something different again. Fiery, intense and all consuming, it had burned up everything else in its path. It was as if every feeling she was capable of had been channeled into that one relationship and when it blew apart she'd been empty.

She'd sleepwalked into marriage with Ed, grateful for the safety and security. She hadn't loved him in the early stages because she hadn't had a single emotion left to give beyond trust and friendship. Gradually she'd healed, and those feelings had deepened.

Her love for Ed had grown over time like a plant that had flourished when it was watered and tended. It wasn't what she'd felt for Scott, but it had been what she needed.

She'd had no wish to ever feel that depth and intensity of emotion again.

"I loved him."

He pushed a strand of her hair back from her face, his fingers gentle. "You used to wear it loose."

"I used to do a lot of things I don't do now." *Like love you.* "I have to go."

"Why? What's the hurry?" His gaze was steady. "What are you afraid of, Laurie?"

She almost laughed.

The answer to that could easily have been everything, and she realized she was tired of living with that feeling. She'd been afraid since the police had knocked on the door, since Mack had discovered who her father was, since she'd discovered there was no money. And maybe she'd even been afraid before that. Afraid that she wasn't really living the life she could be living.

Either way, she was done with being afraid and that included being afraid to say the things she wanted to say. "At least I stand my ground when I'm scared. You walked away from fatherhood because you were afraid. Because your own childhood was so difficult, you were afraid you didn't have the skills you needed. You were afraid you'd let her down. Screw her up. And I tried to understand that. I told myself you were being selfless, but over the years I've come to the conclusion that you weren't being selfless, you were being selfish." It felt good to say it. Good to stop making excuses for him, for pretending to accept something she'd never truly accepted.

She was aware of the beating of her heart and the soft lap of the water against the dock.

A seagull passed overheard with a shriek and a beating of wings.

It took Scott so long to respond she started to think he wasn't going to and then finally he stirred.

"I came to that conclusion long before you did."

It wasn't what she'd expected him to say. "You were afraid to be a father, but I was scared, too, Scott. I was terrified, and you left me with it."

Emotion flickered across his face.

He opened his mouth to say something and then his gaze shifted from her face to a point over her shoulder. "Cal is coming back." There was frustration in his voice. "We need to take this conversation somewhere more private. My boat is on the water."

"You're inviting me sailing? Now?"

"Yes. There are things I need to say to you."

For a moment she yearned for it. For being back on the water, feeling the roll of the boat as it skimmed the ocean, the wind in her hair, *the freedom*. And Scott, with his hat tugged down over his eyes and his legs braced against the roll of the boat. Sailing would mean being on the boat with him. Just the two of them.

That wasn't going to happen. Being close to him made her feel things she didn't want to feel, and nothing he said was going to change the past.

"We can't turn the clock back, Scott. We can't undo what was done."

"No, but we can move forward. If it helps your decision making, I promise not to put my hands on you."

She still remembered exactly how it had felt when he put his hands on her.

It made her legs weaken to think of it.

Her gaze met his and the tension in the air almost suffocated her.

Then she saw movement out of the corner of her eye and Cal approached. She thought that this was not the conversation to be having when they were about to be interrupted, and then realized that what she should be thinking was that they shouldn't be having this conversation at all.

What was she thinking?

"My husband died, Scott. And whether you believe it or not, I loved him."

Before he could respond, Cal approached carrying two coffees.

"Er—here." He handed them both to Scott, flashed a quick smile to Lauren and vanished back to the boat out of earshot.

Scott handed her one of the coffees. "If you change your mind about sailing, let me know."

She felt temptation tug at her and settled her feet more firmly on the ground.

The tension in the atmosphere had lessened and she felt back in control.

"I won't be changing my mind."

"You never used to be afraid of your emotions."

"We both know that my emotions only ever got me into trouble." Still holding the coffee, she turned and walked back toward the beach.

CHAPTER TWENTY-FIVE

Mack

> *Brave: having or displaying courage,*
> *resolution or daring*

MACK KEPT HER head down as she walked into the cafeteria.

It felt like jumping into a shark tank.

Hello, eat me now.

She picked up her tray of food and walked to an empty table, trying to look as if being on her own was a choice and not a sentence.

She could see Kennedy watching her. Then she murmured something to the girl next to her and stood up.

Mack felt her stomach lurch.

When Kennedy sauntered across to her, she had to fight the impulse to stand up and run.

Instead she thought about Scott.

A friend is someone who cares about you.

"Hi, Kennedy." She produced a smile that Kennedy didn't return.

The other girl put her hands on the table and leaned in, her eyes hard. "How does it feel to be hanging out with the losers?"

The losers.

That was her name for the kids who were part of the Coding Club.

The club was run in the IT room, which was at the other end of the school.

The first time Mack had walked into the room she'd almost turned and walked right back out again.

There had been ten boys huddled around a laptop, arguing about something called Java. Mack had always thought it was an island in Indonesia, but it had turned out that Java was also a programming language.

She'd felt as if she'd parachuted into a foreign land without a phrase book and beat a hasty retreat to the door. She fully expected to see a sign saying Girls Keep Out that she'd missed on the way in, but there was nothing and before she could make it into the corridor, Sam had appeared in front of her.

She hadn't even noticed him among the group until he stepped in front of her.

"Hi. Good to see you." His smile was friendly and Mack had seen so few friendly smiles in the time since she'd started at the school, she decided she couldn't afford to ignore this one.

"Hi."

"You're Mack. I've seen you around the boatyard with Scott."

It was on the tip of her tongue to say *he's my dad*, and

then she decided there was no point in inviting more abuse. For all she knew Sam might have reason not to like Scott.

"Yeah, he's kind of a family friend." She hoped her mom would forgive her for saying that. Truthfully she had no idea what Scott was really, but she was pleased he was around. After that time he'd taken her sailing, she'd taken to dropping round on her way home from school. Sometimes he let her help in the boatyard, so she'd left an old pair of jeans and a shirt there.

"He's cool. He fixed my dad's boat." Sam scratched his head. "So what are you doing here?"

"I need to build a website. I thought I might try coding," Mack said awkwardly. "This is the Coding Club, right?"

Sam stared at her.

"Hello?" Mack waved a hand in front of his face. "Coding Club? Tuesdays and Thursdays?"

"Sorry. We don't get that many girls who want to code."

"How many?"

"You're the first. But that's cool," he said quickly. "Really great."

It didn't sound cool or great to Mack. She didn't mind being in a minority, but did she really want to be the only one? "Maybe this isn't going to work."

"Hey, more girls should be able to code. Why not? It's the future and there's a huge gender gap in the tech world. It's crazy. Coding is a basic life skill. I mean, you couldn't imagine living in a world where you couldn't read, could you?"

Mack flattened herself against the wall, slightly alarmed to be on the receiving end of such evangelical belief. "Well, I—"

"Exactly. Reading is something everyone should be able to do. It gives you access to opportunities. And so does coding. Technology is everywhere. Don't you want to be part of it?"

She wanted to be part of something, that was for sure.

She had no friends at school and home was still pretty tense. Her mom was always sewing, or there was some new drama. Mack couldn't handle her own drama, let alone extra. Sometimes she hovered in the kitchen for a few minutes, evading questions like *how was your day?* (answer: totally crap), but mostly she went straight to her room, where she sat on the bed and messed with her phone or stared out the window.

She missed the old days when she'd been able to talk to her mom about anything and everything.

She missed her old school and her friends.

She wanted to belong.

"I'll think about it."

"If you leave, you'll think of a million reasons not to do it. And if *you* join, other girls might follow."

Mack wondered whether she should break it to him that her influence wasn't exactly impressive. Most days she ate her lonely sandwich by her lonely self in the cafeteria. The number of people lining up to spend time with her amounted to zero. If she was a role model then she knew nothing about it and she certainly didn't see herself as a trailblazer.

This whole thing was a bad idea. Another bad choice among the millions she'd made lately.

She should have tried to teach herself to build a website by watching a video on *YouTube*.

"I don't think this is for me."

"One session," Sam begged. "Stay for one session, and if you don't love it I'll never ask you again."

"I have to build a website."

"Not today."

"Excuse me?"

"If I've only got one session to convert you, you're not going to use it up on that."

"But—"

"If you never want to come again I promise I'll help you build your website anyway. It's easy. Today we're doing something way more exciting."

Mack looked at the boys huddled round the laptop. "What?"

"Does that mean you're staying?"

Was she?

At least Sam seemed genuine. He wasn't trying to stuff beer into her hand or force his tongue down her throat.

"I guess."

"Great. Come and see." He half dragged her across the room before she could change her mind. "Guys, this is Mack. Give her some space."

The boys shuffled awkwardly to one side and she found herself staring at a screen covered in incomprehensible letters and symbols.

She had no idea what this was about. She was going to look stupid and they were all going to laugh at her.

She was good at math, but this wasn't math.

"Sit down." Sam pulled out a chair. "I'm going to show you something."

He tapped the keys and covered the screen in lines of incomprehensible code. Then he hit enter and a robot on the desk moved toward Mack.

She laughed. "Seriously? You made it do that?"

"I can program it to bring you the remote control. Or your phone. You name it."

How about a new life? Can you program it to bring me one of those?

"That's cool. So that's what you do in here?"

"We do everything. Sometimes we're working on an app, sometimes we build a new game. We've done some white hat hacking."

"Hacking?"

"Hey, we're the good guys. But today I'm going to teach you to program that robot to bring you something. After that we'll talk about this website you want."

That had been weeks ago.

Mack hadn't missed a session of the Coding Club since.

She knew all their names now. There was Tyler whose younger sister was in her Aunt Jenna's first-grade class, Max who thought he was terrible at English (Mack had agreed to help him in exchange for help getting the photos to rotate on her website) but could program anything. Curtis, Bradley, Sam—she knew them all.

Better than that, she considered them friends and she loved everything about the club.

Her enthusiasm had surprised even Sam. "I wasn't sure you were going to come back after that first time."

"I wasn't sure either, but here I am."

He grinned. "Not a lot of people know this, but computer programmers rule the world."

She was starting to believe him.

She felt an excitement she never felt when she was starting an English essay.

She was going to change the world. Maybe she'd get a job with NASA. She was so excited by what she could do with computers that there was no way she was giving it up.

They were people, she thought. Not geeks or nerds.

People.

Unfortunately they rarely ventured into the cafeteria for lunch, which was why she was still eating alone.

Mack forced herself to meet Kennedy's gaze.

Her palms were slippery and her heart was bashing hard against her ribs. "I don't know any losers. Only a bunch of really smart guys."

"You're new here and you just lost your dad." Kennedy spoke with exaggerated kindness. "So I'm going to help you out for your own good. Maybe you don't realize it, but those kids you're hanging out with are nerds. Geeks. They are not, and never will be, part of the cool crowd."

"Got it." Maybe she could program a robot to smack Kennedy across the head.

The other girl's mouth tightened. "Do you know what it's going to mean for *you* if you carry on hanging out with them?"

Mack looked at Kennedy and saw that her makeup was so thick it looked like plastic.

This close up she could see the bumps on the skin that the other girl was trying to conceal.

Everyone had insecurities, she thought.

She stood up so that she was eye to eye with her nemesis. She kept her hands on the table in case her shaking knees gave way. "It's going to mean I have good, genuine friends."

"Oh *please*—" Kennedy stared at her and gave a short laugh. "So basically you're a nerd, too."

"No." Mack discovered that her knees weren't shaking anymore. "I'm a girl who can code. And do you know what that makes me? It makes me smart, Kennedy."

CHAPTER TWENTY-SIX

Nancy

> *Purpose: the feeling of having a definite aim*
> *and of being determined to achieve it*

OVER THE NEXT few weeks Nancy's life took a direction she hadn't anticipated.

With Lauren's encouragement, she made appointments with a Realtor who specialized in renting to the luxury end of the market. Lauren went along to the meeting, too, and Nancy had been impressed by her daughter's sharp, businesslike approach.

Nancy herself made long lists of things that needed to be done and people she needed to contact. It helped that she knew almost everyone on the Vineyard. If she didn't know the right person, then she undoubtedly knew someone who did.

She woke with a feeling inside her that she didn't even recognize.

It was excitement, she realized. Anticipation for the future. The feeling was so fresh and new she barely recognized it.

She no longer felt like a passenger in her own life, clinging for dear life in the back of a runaway car. She was the one in the driver's seat and right now she was speeding along with the wind in her hair. There was still one more issue to be dealt with, of course, but she wasn't ready to face it yet.

Humming to herself, she went through the house room by room with Lauren, making plans. Together they stripped the place back and built it up again. It had taken very little time for Nancy to realize that her daughter had inherited her feel for color.

It was Lauren's idea to mix inky, cobalt blues with a blend of Mediterranean shades. In each room she included quirky touches like coastal motifs and found beautiful pieces of driftwood and shells. Some of it cost little, some nothing at all and yet it blended together seamlessly. The result was a house that felt as if it was part of the landscape.

Some of the biggest changes she made were to the room overlooking the water that they'd always called the garden room.

Lauren had removed the old faded drapes and polished up the windows, allowing the light to stream in.

"It makes the room seem bigger." Nancy surveyed the changes to her home. "Those wretched things have been gathering dust for years and obscuring the light. I wanted to take them down, but Tom said the sunlight would fade the furniture."

Lauren was filling a large glass vase with seashells. "He's gone, Mom. You can do whatever you want to do."

Whatever she wanted to do.

Nancy wasn't sure if the thought was exciting or terrifying, and she realized her daughter was in much the same position.

"You can do whatever you want to do, too."

"Not quite." Lauren placed the jar on a low table. "I have Mack to think about."

Lauren instinctively put her daughter first, Nancy thought.

If she had her time again, would she make different choices?

"You're a wonderful mother."

Lauren gave a tired smile. "I don't think Mack would agree."

"Children never agree with their parents. It's part of the development cycle. You swear you'll do things differently when you have your own, and then you make your own mistakes. But there is no doubt that you're a much better mother than I was." Nancy paused. Why did she find this type of interaction so hard? Maybe it was because her own mother had died when she was so young. And there was no way she ever would have talked to her grandmother. "I'm sorry for that. Sorry for the fact that you knew about your father and didn't feel you could tell me. Sorry that when you were pregnant, you didn't feel you could talk to me."

Lauren added another shell to the collection. "Don't be sorry. I wish you'd told us what you were dealing with."

"I believed I was protecting you. I thought that was the right thing to do."

Lauren took a deep breath. "I wish I'd known how you felt. You so rarely joined in, I guess Jenna and I both assumed you didn't want to. We only thought about you in the context of us. You were our mother. I didn't think about your life beyond that, who you really were or what you might have wanted. I certainly didn't consider what sacrifices you might be making."

"I doubt any child ever does that." Nancy's arms ached to reach out and hug Lauren, but she didn't know if it was the right thing to do or not.

Jenna was the hugger of the family. Lauren was more reserved.

Protecting herself again? Nancy didn't know.

And she wanted to. She wanted to know her daughter.

"One of my happiest childhood memories was being sick that time with chickenpox," Lauren said. "Do you remember?"

"You were miserable with the spots and the itching. How could that memory possibly be happy?"

"Because you used to come and sit with me. Dad was never interested unless we were running around doing crazy, exciting things. When we were sick, he ignored us, but you used to come armed with piles of paper and paints and crayons, and we'd draw and color. I remember you taught me to draw a cat."

"I remember that." Nancy felt the hot sting of tears. It was funny how wrong you could be. "I thought all your childhood memories would have your father in them."

"Not all of them." Lauren settled herself on the sofa and picked up the quilt she'd been stitching. Every time Nancy saw her, she seemed to be sewing something. This one was destined for one of the bedrooms.

"How are you doing? Not with the redecorating, but with everything else."

"I'm fine, thanks."

She could have left it at that. Until recently she wouldn't

even have entertained the possibility of going deeper. But that was then and this was now.

Determined, Nancy took a step forward and put her hand on Lauren's shoulder. "Are you really fine? I want to know."

Lauren stopped stitching. "I'm up and down. Sometimes it feels as if this is happening to someone else and I'm watching."

"You must be angry." She remembered that feeling. The searing heat of it burning her up inside.

"About the money?" Lauren stabbed the needle into the fabric. "I was, but more because he didn't tell me the truth. When we got together we agreed that we'd never lie to each other. Our honesty was the one thing we shared that was real."

"You were in love with Scott, but you married Ed." Even though she'd never considered herself to be particularly romantic, the thought tore at her.

"Life doesn't always send you easy choices, Mama."

Mama.

Nancy felt her throat constrict. She'd only ever heard that word a few times, when Lauren was very young. As a toddler, she'd been bright and bubbly. *Look at me,* Mama.

When had they lost that?

"I wish you'd felt able to talk to me."

"I didn't talk to anyone. Not even Jenna. The only person I ever told everything to in my whole life was Scott." She measured a new length of thread. "You're probably wondering why I fell for him."

"I don't wonder that." That, at least, was easy to answer. "Scott is troubled—complicated—but the way he has pushed forward through his terrible childhood to become the man he is—" she paused "—there's strength there. So much strength. And integrity. Maybe you sensed something in him that you didn't see in your father."

"Plenty of the islanders were suspicious of Scott."

"Humans, as you discovered early in life, are deeply flawed. Scott doesn't stick to the rules. He doesn't always conform, and instead of embracing different, we're suspicious."

"Not you." Lauren stabbed the needle into the fabric and put it to one side. "After he took you on the boat that night, you became friends? He talked to you?"

"I'm not sure I'd call what we had friendship." What would she call it? She thought about the members of her book group. She thought about Alice. "On the other hand he was there when I needed him and he has never once disappointed me. If that's not friendship I don't know what is. We saw each other from time to time. When he was on the island, he did work for me on the house. He's skilled. I trust him, which is more than can be said for some of the people I've had here in the past. I know he wouldn't believe it, but he would have made a good father."

"I thought so, too." Lauren paused. "Mack is confiding in him a lot."

Nancy hid her surprise. "She told you that?"

"He did. She barely says anything to me, although she did at least tell me where she was going this time."

Nancy wanted to help, but she was so afraid of saying the wrong thing and bruising this new, tender relationship.

"How do you feel about her seeing Scott?"

"I'm not sure." Lauren stood up and walked to the window. "To begin with I was hurt that she'd talk to him and not me, but now I feel grateful that she's talking to anyone. I don't want her to be on her own with all of this. I miss our chats. At home we used to sit at the kitchen island and talk while she ate a snack. I miss knowing what's going on in her life. I miss the laughs and the closeness."

"You'll get that back."

"Will we?"

"I know it. And in the meantime, if you need someone to listen, I'm here."

Lauren glanced at her and there was surprise in her eyes. "Thanks, Mom. And how about you? We're stripping away your old life and you're throwing away things you thought you'd be keeping forever. How does it feel?"

How did it feel?

Nancy looked around her transformed garden room.

She'd hold her book group in here, she decided, at least until they moved out for the summer. Usually they gathered in the kitchen, but this room was light and airy. Now that the weather was warmer they would be able to throw open the windows and let in the sea air. It would be a glorious space in which to meet friends and enjoy good wine and conversation. "It feels good. I feel like a teenager. And it's all down to you and Jenna. The house feels different."

"Being a teenager isn't all it's made out to be, Grams." Mack strolled into the room, her laptop under her arm and her phone in her hand. "It's not all carefree dancing in the streets you know. If you've got five minutes, I have something to show you." There was a bounce in her step, and an excitement in her eyes that hadn't been there before.

This was the first time Mack had come in from school and not gone straight to her room.

Progress? Nancy glanced at her daughter, saw tension in her slender frame and knew she wasn't the only one afraid of doing, or saying, the wrong thing.

Nancy suspected that Lauren was now so busy being careful, she'd lost the ability to know how to respond. According to Jenna, Lauren had been so adventurous there had been times when her youngest daughter had been nervous. What had happened to that woman?

Life had changed her, but change could happen in more than one direction.

If Lauren had been adventurous once, then she could be adventurous again.

"I'd love to see the website," Nancy said, "as long as I'm not expected to understand technology. You know I can't even get the printer to work."

"That's because it wasn't connected to the Wi-Fi, Grams. I've fixed that. Hit Print now and you should be fine." Mack tapped a few keys and then handed over her laptop. "What do you think?" Her tone was casual but Nancy could feel her granddaughter vibrating with anticipation and pride.

She sank onto the sofa that Lauren had reupholstered in pale blue stripes and balanced the laptop on her knees. What she saw took her breath away. There, across the top of the screen, was her beloved house. Flowers tumbled, pink and mauve, against the white clapboard. The words *The Captain's House* were picked out in bold letters. "Oh, Mack—" Memories surged up, thickening in her throat. "Where did you find this photo?"

"It's one of Mom's, taken way back. It's a good one, isn't it? I fiddled with it in Photoshop."

"There is a photo shop on the Vineyard?"

Mack grinned. "It's a computer program. Lets you manipulate images. One of the boys in the Coding Club showed me a few tricks. I could superimpose your head on a unicorn if you like."

Nancy laughed. "Maybe another day." She turned back to the screen. The picture alone would be enough to attract interest. People would fall in love, as she had. The house stole your heart. How could anyone, looking at this, fail to understand why she'd found it so hard to let it go? "That sky is so blue. The colors are intense."

Mack shrugged. "I added a couple of filters to make the colors pop a bit."

"Clever. Lauren, would you look at this? The house looks just dreamy."

Lauren leaned over her shoulder. "Oh, Mack! It's like a postcard." She leaned forward and tapped a key. "This is incredible. You did this?"

"Yes." Mack gave a careless shrug that was supposed to say it was nothing, even though they all knew it was a very big something.

"Stunning." Nancy added her praise to the pile already out there. "I'd rent it in a flash. These pictures are wonderful. You have a good eye. Oh, you're a Stewart, no doubt about that." Mack had artistic talent, too, she realized. In each generation it had manifested itself in different ways.

"I'm half Rhodes, Grams."

"Yes." Nancy looked at her and smiled. "Yes, you are, honey. Have you shown him this?"

"He helped me with it." She eyed her mother cautiously. "He knows a bit about computers. I wanted his opinion."

Nancy felt for Lauren. Whatever her own feelings for Scott, he hadn't stuck by her daughter when she was pregnant.

If she'd known about that, would it have made a difference to the way she felt about him?

Maybe not. She'd been desperate enough the night of the

hurricane to ask the devil himself for help. But that didn't mean she couldn't understand how difficult this whole situation must be for Lauren.

Nancy let her finger hover over the keyboard. "I want to click on the part that says Rooms. Will I delete the whole thing?"

Mack laughed. "No."

Nancy clicked. "Seaspray?"

"I gave the rooms names. To make them more personal. But you can change them. Most sites just call the rooms 'premium double' or whatever, but that's boring."

"It is boring and I love Seaspray." Nancy reached for her glasses and peered at the screen. "Oh, you've used naval terms. The Anchor Suite. That's the master bedroom? What a smart idea. And you've managed to take photographs that make them look fabulous."

"It wasn't hard. The rooms look great since you've done them up, but that's not surprising because Mom's good at that."

Nancy saw Lauren flush at the unexpected praise and warmth.

"Thank you, Mack."

Nancy explored the rest of the website and handed the laptop back to her granddaughter. "This is excellent. I'm impressed."

"I've set up a Facebook account, too," Mack said. "We'll post pictures of Aunt Jenna's amazing food because nothing makes you want to move in to a place like a pile of cookies, and I'll take the view from the garden down to the ocean. I'll add some video of various places around the Vineyard."

"Sounds good. As long as you don't expect me to update this site. I'm too old for Facebook."

"I don't think you are, but one thing at a time. And we have an Instagram account, too. I've already posted some shots."

"I don't know what that is."

"It's an app, Grams." Mack pulled her phone out of her pocket and showed her.

Someone was as fired up as she was, Nancy thought. The house was becoming a family obsession.

"Now it's nearly finished, you could add in some shots of this room." Mack stood up and took a few photos with her phone. "This place is special. If I was staying here, I'd be tempted never to leave it."

Lauren had given away the old rattan furniture and replaced it with deep, overstuffed sofas she found in a boutique hotel that was closing down. The covers were stained, but she'd replaced them, upholstering long into the night until the light had cheated her.

She'd ripped up the carpet that had seen better days, polished up the boards until they shone a rich earthy tone and found a rug in a thrift shop.

Bowls of seashells and a profusion of plants brought the outside into the house.

Nancy would never have thought her home could have felt so calming.

Lauren, apparently, wasn't satisfied.

"That wall needs something." Her daughter stared at the blank space on one of the walls with narrowed eyes. "I don't know what. It needs to be large."

Mack checked the photos she'd taken. "How about a photograph?"

Lauren pondered. "Maybe."

Nancy stared at the space, too.

Why not?

"That painting I used to have in the entryway would work in the space."

Something dragged in the base of her stomach. Could she look at that painting without sadness? Would adding that single drop of poison from the past contaminate everything?

But it was too late to change her mind because Lauren was nodding.

"If I remember the colors correctly then it would work perfectly. Let's try it."

"I'll fetch it now." Wishing she'd never suggested it, Nancy left the room, missing the look her daughter and granddaughter exchanged.

"That was pretty cool, Mom," Mack muttered, her gaze fixed on the door as she waited for her grandmother to re-appear. "Think she'll go for it?"

"I really hope so, because the painting would look perfect here."

"Do you know why she took it down?"

Lauren hesitated. "I'd be guessing."

Mack shrugged. "Go for it."

"Everything Grams painted used to be bright and cheerful and then suddenly it all changed."

Mack frowned. "You think it was when she found out Gramps was—" she broke off and flushed "—having affairs? I can't even say it, it's so gross."

"It is gross," Lauren said calmly, "and yes, I do think that."

"Men," Mack said sagely and Lauren nodded.

"Absolutely."

Oblivious to the conversation going on in her absence,

Nancy retrieved the painting that she'd stored in the back of a closet in a spare room.

She'd put it there because she could no longer bear to look at it. Because it jarred with her mood and reminded her of a time in her life when she'd been happy and hopeful. A time before the dark clouds had set in.

The painting had mocked her from the entryway. *Life used to be like this.*

But why couldn't life be like that again?

As Lauren hung it on the wall Nancy could immediately see how well it fit in. And how different it looked here in this sunny room.

The painting brought the ocean into the room.

Mack came and stood next to her. "How much is it worth?"

"Mack!" Lauren sent Nancy an apologetic look but Nancy shook her head.

"It's a good question, but I don't know the answer. A few years ago, probably a stupid amount." She'd never quite got used to the idea that people were prepared to pay tens of thousands of dollars for one of her paintings. "Now? I don't know. Tastes change. Fashion changes. The market changes." Not that she'd ever painted for the market. She'd painted for herself.

"If you hate looking at it, Grams, you could sell it and use the money to buy yourself something you really want."

Nancy put her arm round her granddaughter. "That," she said, "is an excellent idea. But the strange thing is, I don't hate it. I used to, but now I think I like it. What do you think, Lauren?"

"I think it looks good there, providing you're happy to have it on the wall."

Mack stepped closer to the painting. "Why did you never sell this one, Grams?"

"Your grandfather made me promise never to sell it."

Of course he'd made plenty of promises to her that he hadn't kept. For richer or poorer. He'd made sure it was poorer. Forsaking all others—thinking it made her want to laugh.

Mack was frowning. "Why would he care about this one in particular?"

"I painted this the day we got engaged. He wanted to remember it." But did she?

"Does it make you uncomfortable, Mom?" Lauren had finished the windows and through the gleaming glass Nancy could see the garden and, beyond that, the ocean.

Ben was in the garden, his familiar figure bending and straightening as he tended to her beds. Although he did most of the physical work required to maintain the garden, the ideas were hers. They made a perfect team.

A perfect team.

She saw his muscles flex as he stamped his foot on the shovel and dug deep. His shoulders were broad and his physical job kept him fit. How had she not noticed that before?

Something unfurled slowly inside her, a feeling so unfamiliar she didn't immediately recognize it. Realizing that it was sexual attraction gave her a jolt.

She was too old to have feelings like that, surely? She'd assumed those days were long gone.

In all her years of marriage, she'd never strayed. She'd been too bruised from the fallout of her one relationship to even contemplate another.

"Are you okay, Grams?" Mack was frowning. "You're flushed. Are you sick?"

Nancy dragged her gaze back to her granddaughter and then to the painting. If they could read the thoughts going through her mind, they'd be shocked. *She* was shocked. And goodness only knew what poor Ben would say. She was going to have to be extra careful around him. Imagine how embarrassing it would be if he guessed she was having wildly improper thoughts?

"Is it the painting that's upsetting you?" Lauren looked concerned. "If you decide you don't like it, then we can sell it."

Nancy stared at the painting, remembering not the scene in front of her but everything she'd felt at the time.

She'd been so in love.

Life had stretched before them, as inviting as a summer meadow. She'd been excited by the seemingly endless possibilities, by the thought of sharing a life with Tom.

Over the years she'd wondered if she'd imagined the emotion she'd seen in him that day.

Had he ever loved her? Had she ever been enough?

But now she realized that no one would ever have been enough for Tom.

The happiness she remembered had been real, she was sure of it, and was there anything wrong with remembering happier times?

Glancing out the window, she saw Ben drop into a crouch to plant something in the bed he'd prepared.

He was so careful, treating each plant as if it were made of glass.

Ben's wife had died around the same time she'd lost Tom. Had he seen anyone since? Had he frozen that side of his life as she had?

Maybe she'd invite him for a meal. As friends. Obviously she'd be careful not to let him know she had feelings that went beyond that. Those were, and always would be, her secret.

The prospect cheered her.

She'd thought that her best years were over, but now she was starting to wonder if they were just beginning.

"I don't want to sell it," she said. "It can stay right where it is on the wall."

CHAPTER TWENTY-SEVEN

Jenna

> *Hope: a feeling of desire and expectation*
> *that things will go well in the future*

"I'M GOING INTO school early today, and I'll be late home because I'm going over to the house to help Mom with a few final things because Lauren is at the Sail Loft." Jenna pushed her feet into her shoes. "How's your day looking? Busy?"

"Yes." Greg was seated at the kitchen island, drinking coffee.

He looked exhausted. There were smoky shadows under his eyes and he sat slumped, as if crushed by a heavy weight.

"You were up early." She'd woken early, too, and reached out to him for a cuddle, only to discover that his side of the bed was cold and empty.

It had been a few weeks since they'd last made love. She'd

been nervous to suggest it in case he thought she was just trying to make a baby.

"We're fixing up the last bedroom. The place is looking great. You should see it. Come with me tonight. It would be fun." It had been a while since they'd had fun, she thought. A while since they'd laughed. How had that happened? They used to laugh all the time.

They were Jenna and Greg.

He didn't look up from his coffee. "Not tonight."

"Are you sure? It won't be awkward. Finally my family is working together, instead of against each other. I thought maybe we could invite Lauren and Scott for a meal some-time. Or do you think that would be tactless?" She grabbed her purse, wishing he'd say something. "I'm not sure whether there's anything going on between them or not. I mean, I'm sure there *is* something there, but I'm not sure if they plan on doing anything about it. What do you think?"

"I don't know."

That statement was so ridiculous she almost smiled. "You always know. You always understand what goes on in peo-ple's relationships."

Greg wasn't smiling. "Maybe I'm sick of other people's relationships. Maybe, for once, I'd rather focus on my own."

His tone shocked her as much as his words.

She didn't know him like this. It was like living with a stranger.

As her relationship with her family was improving, it seemed her relationship with Greg was deteriorating. "What's that supposed to mean?"

"Nothing. Forget it."

"How am I supposed to forget a comment like that?" There was an uncomfortable feeling behind her ribs. Panic?

"Is this still about the fact I didn't tell you about my dad?" She was feeling guilty about that, but where was the rule that said a person had to disclose *everything*?

"I guess that's part of it." He rubbed his fingers over his forehead. "I'm tired, Jenna. I can't do this now. I have to go."

"But we're talking, and—"

"I don't want to talk."

She was left floundering like a fish in shallow water. "But you're the one who always says you can sort most things out by talking about them."

"Yeah, well it turns out that's not as easy as it sounds." He scooped up his jacket and his car keys and strode out the door, slamming it behind him.

Jenna flinched.

She stood staring at the door, her stomach clenched.

He'd left the house without kissing her goodbye. He always kissed her before leaving the house. Always.

But not today.

When something was wrong in her life, she talked to Greg, but this time she and Greg were the problem. Who was she going to talk to?

This was too personal to discuss with just anyone. She hadn't even mentioned it to Lauren, despite the fact they'd been running together almost daily for the past few weeks. It felt disloyal. Also her sister finally seemed a little better and Jenna didn't want to burden her with anything else.

Maybe she'd give Greg a few hours to calm down and then call him.

Maybe when she told him the news she'd been holding inside her, he'd be so thrilled that everything would be forgotten and forgiven.

It was early May and the mornings were lighter and

brighter. She drove with the windows open so she could smell the sea air.

Despite her unease about the situation with Greg, happiness bubbled inside her.

She was late.

Not late for school. The other type of late. The type of late that made her heart beat faster and made her glance in store windows at baby clothes. The type of late that insulated her from all external assaults on her happiness. Nothing could destroy her mood right now. Nothing.

She'd been trying not to get excited, but she wasn't only a day late, or even two.

She was five days late. *Five days.*

She lifted her hand and pressed her boobs. Was she imagining it or were they a little more tender than usual?

The thought that she might be pregnant filled her head and made her float along like a helium balloon. If she was right, she'd soon be the same shape as a helium balloon. She didn't care. She wasn't going to complain if she had stretch marks. She was too grateful to be pregnant. If all she did for the next nine months was vomit and sleep, she wasn't going to complain about that either.

A baby.

Whatever was wrong between her and Greg, she was sure that once she told him her news it would all be fixed. He'd be as thrilled as she was. She'd already done the calculations and their baby was due on January 21. The downside was that it would be born right in the middle of a harsh Vineyard winter. On the plus side she'd be able to snuggle up in their cottage and focus on being a mother.

There was a pregnancy test sitting in the bottom of her purse, but so far she'd resisted the temptation to use it. She'd bought in bulk from the internet to avoid giving fodder to the island gossips, but going through so many was costing her a small fortune. At this rate the tests were going to cost her more than putting a child through college, which was why, this time, she'd waited until she was *sure*.

She parked in the school parking lot, aware that she had a silly smile on her face.

She was tempted to call Greg and tell him, but they'd waited so long for this she wanted to break the news in the most exciting way possible and standing in the school parking lot didn't fit that brief.

Maybe she'd put a fluffy toy in his cereal bowl and see if he guessed.

Or perhaps a romantic dinner would be best.

We're going to be a family.

The smile stayed with her as she walked into school.

Nothing, not even the situation with Greg, could put a dent in her happiness.

"Good morning, Mrs. Sullivan." Her class chorused her name as she walked into the room and she reflected on how far they'd come since that first day.

Tansy Wilkins put her hand up.

"Yes, Tansy."

"You're smiling, Mrs. Sullivan. Did someone tell you a joke?"

"No one told me a joke. I'm happy, that's all."

She set them a task, half her mind on her own situation.

Boy or girl?

They hadn't even chosen a name.

Maybe that's what she should do. Leave a book of baby names in his cereal bowl. She liked Darcy for a girl. Darcy

Sullivan. It had a nice ring. And maybe Adam for a boy. Had there ever been an Adam in the family?

She floated through the day and was clearing up the classroom after the children had left when she made up her mind.

She was going to do the test. Right here. Right now.

Impulse: a sudden desire to do something.

She walked to the restroom and locked herself in the cubicle.

The test was right there, in the bottom of her purse, where it had been for weeks.

She ripped open the packaging and then paused, nervous, as if delaying it might change the result. As if nature hadn't already decided.

A few minutes later, she had her answer.

She stayed in the cubicle for ten whole minutes. During that time two people came and went but Jenna stayed silent, her shoulders pressed against the cold tiled wall, her eyes squeezed shut against the scalding sting of despair. She knew she needed to leave the cubicle and get herself to her car but she was scared someone might talk to her and she knew she couldn't handle that. She wasn't sure she could walk as far as her car without breaking down.

Why had she done the test here?

Why hadn't she waited until she was home?

Because she'd truly thought that this time—

She covered her mouth with her hand, holding back the emotion that threatened to hemorrhage out of her.

She wasn't going to be a mother. Not this time and probably not ever. She was never going to give birth, feed her child, pick her up when she fell, listen to teenage woes, be present at her wedding...

Grief ripped through her, the raw pain of a loss so intense that she couldn't breathe.

She fumbled for her phone, intending to call Greg, but then remembered the slammed door.

If it had been good news, she would have called, but how could she call him with this?

The last thing he'd want was her dumping her baby misery on him again. Their relationship felt too fragile to withstand the extra load.

She slid her phone back into her purse and stood in the impersonal cubicle feeling empty and alone.

She needed to get out of here before someone started to ask questions, but where could she go?

Not to The Captain's House, and not home because Greg might be there. She wasn't ready to talk to anyone.

The beach.

She could walk on the sand, breathe the air and cry as much as she liked. Once she'd got it out of her system, she'd be able to face people again.

Confident that she'd composed herself sufficiently to walk out the door, she left the bathroom and immediately bumped into Heather Summer, the principal.

"Jenna! I've been looking for you. I wanted to talk to you about the summer show."

Jenna knew that if she opened her mouth the only thing that was going to emerge was emotion.

She needed time on her own.

"I have an appointment." She pushed the lie through the thickness in her throat. "Could we talk later in the week?"

"Of course." Heather looked at her closely. "Is everything all right?"

"Everything is fine."

Two lies in quick succession.

They made a date, which Jenna immediately forgot as she stumbled the distance to her car.

It would take her ten minutes to drive to the beach, that was all.

Luck wasn't on her side.

She reached her car and saw Andrea Corren strapping Daisy into her own car.

"Jenna!" She emerged from the car, red faced and smiling. "I've been meaning to catch up with you. I wanted to thank you for listening that time a few months ago."

Not now, not now.

"No problem."

"Things are *much* better."

"Great news." Jenna fumbled with her keys and dropped them. Shit. *Shit.*

Andrea closed the car door and lowered her voice so that Daisy couldn't hear her. "Todd and I—well we're trying again. He said it was a mistake. He said he was sorry, and I believe him."

Jenna wondered how many times her father had said that to her mother. "Glad it's working out for you." Her hand closed over the keys and she gripped them so hard they marked her flesh.

"There's something else—" Andrea leaned in closer. "I haven't told anyone else this yet, but I'm pregnant."

Jenna felt the world around her fade slightly. There was a buzzing sound in her ears. "What?"

"Pregnant. I guess it must have been that one episode of makeup sex." Andrea was scarlet. "But I'm happy. I think this will be a new start. It's what we need."

People didn't always get what they needed, Jenna thought. Nor did they get what they wanted.

Devastated: very shocked and upset by something.

She managed to push out some words. *Pleased. Congratulations.*

Andrea looked at her oddly. "Are you all right?"

"I ate something," Jenna said. "Bad seafood. Must go."

She slid into her car and drove toward the exit, braking to allow a mother and her toddler to cross the road.

Jenna stared at the blond curls and the smile, the chubby hand curled around her mother's.

Her child probably would have had curls exactly like that, and maybe freckles.

Except there was no child and maybe there never would be.

The emptiness felt like a giant crater and she was teetering on the edge, trying hard not to fall into it.

Tears blurred her vision and she blinked rapidly, forcing herself to concentrate on the road. A few more minutes and she'd be able to give in to her emotions. A few more minutes.

But the tears weren't willing to wait that long.

She knew she should pull over but there was nowhere safe and her destination was only five minutes away.

Half-blinded, she misjudged the edge of the road as she made the final turn.

She spun the wheel hard, trying to compensate, but the tires hit soft ground and she slammed hard into the ditch and rolled. She screamed, knowing for sure that this was the end. Her bag flew and hit her on the cheek, her head smashed against the window hard, and then there was a sickening crunching sound and the car settled on its roof.

The seat belt kept her trapped there, suspended upside

down as she tried to work out if she was dead or alive. Her head throbbed and her vision was blurry.

Still gripping the wheel with one hand, she reached to open the door with the other, but it had buckled during the impact and wouldn't budge.

She was trapped.

Panic ripped through her. Now what? Did cars catch fire in real life as easily as they did in the movies? Was she about to be burned alive?

Her survival instincts kicked in and somehow she undid her seat belt and landed in an ungainly heap on her back. The pain made her cry out and the only thought in her head right then was relief that she wasn't pregnant.

Of course if she *had* been pregnant she wouldn't be in this situation now.

She'd be at home with a smile on her face waiting to break the news to Greg.

Greg.

He'd be driving home around now but he wouldn't be worried about her because she'd told him she was going to be late. No one knew where she was.

She felt something warm flowing over her cheek and realized she was bleeding. She felt dizzy and sick.

She needed to find her purse.

She wiped the blood away with her palm and forced herself to stay calm as she looked around the car. It had to be here somewhere. Could she smell gas or was it her imagination? *Oh God, oh God*—she found her purse half-hidden under the blanket she always kept on the back seat.

She grabbed it, opened it with shaking hands and pulled out her phone.

Please let there be a signal.

Please don't let the car catch fire.

Mercifully the phone was still working and she dialed 911 and then made one more call.

The moment she heard her mother's voice, it felt like coming home.

Emotion filled her throat, tears filled her eyes and suddenly she was a child again.

"Mom." She could barely get the words out. "Help me."

CHAPTER TWENTY-EIGHT

Lauren

> *Test: to put under severe strain*

"LAUREN?" SCOTT'S VOICE came from the kitchen, where he'd been working all week. "I need to show you something."

Lauren carried on painting the wall. She'd postponed working on the Sail Loft, hoping that Scott would have finished before she started but in the end she'd had no choice. The Captain's House was all but done and they needed somewhere to live. Unless she wanted to share living space with chipped paint, she needed to get to work.

She'd started at the top with her mother's studio, a whole floor away from Scott. Not that it made much difference, because she was constantly aware of him. The knowledge that he was a mere turn of the stairs away from her made her skin tingle and her heart beat faster. And every time she felt that heady rush of desire, she also felt guilt.

To stop herself thinking about him, she focused her attention on the work she was doing.

Her plan for the Sail Loft was to keep it simple, in keeping with the casual beachfront setting.

She'd contemplated using a fashionable gray on the walls, but in the end had opted for a soft white that reflected the intensity of the beach light. She'd painted the wide planks on the floor white, too, and had already found a blue-and-white-striped rug in a thrift shop. The place felt calming. Relaxing.

"Lauren?"

She closed her eyes. The place would never be relaxing while Scott was working in it, and yet she also found herself dreading the moment he finished because then he'd be gone.

"I'll be there in a minute. If I stop now, I'll have streaks."

"That's today's excuse?" His voice was closer this time and she glanced over her shoulder.

"Excuse me?"

He was leaning against the door frame. His eyes were hooded and watchful, but there was a hint of a smile on his mouth that told her he knew exactly how she was feeling.

He claimed he wasn't good at intimacy and yet every look and every word that passed between them was threaded with meaning.

"I worked here for two weeks before you showed up at all."

She put the brush down. "I was busy—"

"And then when you did show up, you made sure you were never in the same room as me."

"We're working on different things. You're fixing up the kitchen." And the kitchen was the smallest room in the house, which was another reason she'd been avoiding it.

She caught a glimpse of herself in the large mirror she'd hung on one of the walls. Instead of wearing her oldest clothes, she'd chosen jeans that skimmed her hips and a tailored shirt that nipped in slightly at the waist. Common sense might have abandoned her but it seemed vanity hadn't.

"Did I do this to you?" His voice was rough. "Is it my fault?"

"Do what?"

"Make you so cautious and careful you no longer dare be who you are."

She didn't want to have this conversation. "This is who I am. None of us are the same person at thirty-five that we were at eighteen."

"I think you're the same person, but you haven't let that person out in a long time."

Was he right? There were days when she couldn't remember the person she'd been back then.

"Life changes all of us, Scott. When you and I were together I was a teenager. Now I'm a mother and a wi—" She'd been about to say *wife* and then realized she wasn't a wife anymore. She was a widow.

She hated that word so much.

"When did you last jump off the Jaws Bridge?"

The question made her laugh. "It's been a couple of decades since I talked my sister into that one."

"Let's do it."

"You have to be kidding me."

"I'm not kidding." He strolled toward her and she felt her heart beat faster.

"Scott, I'm not jumping off the Jaws Bridge. I'm thirty-five years old and I just lost my husband. Can you imagine what people would say?"

"You never used to worry about what people thought."

"Life seems a lot simpler when you're eighteen."

"If not the bridge, then come sailing with me."

"I'm not going sailing with you either."

"Why not?"

Because she'd found a way to live without him. What she hadn't worked out was how to let him back into her life in a way that didn't destabilize everything.

"I have a house to decorate, a child to raise—"

"A life to live."

She straightened her shoulders. "This is my life now."

"You make it sound like a sentence."

There were days when it felt like a sentence. Days when she dragged herself out of bed and pushed herself from one job to the next. She'd read somewhere that if you gave your brain tasks to do it stopped overthinking. She'd given herself a lot of tasks. Sometimes she felt like a robot.

It seemed like a lifetime since she'd felt human. A lifetime since she'd been hugged and held. It wasn't just Ed's arms that she missed. She missed Mack's. She missed the laughter, and the female bond they'd shared.

Things had improved a little between them but it was still a long way from the relationship they used to have, and even her bond with Jenna and her new relationship with her mother didn't fill the void.

She rarely slept through the night and was constantly tired. She woke running numbers in her head, wondering how she could make enough for her and Mack to live on. In the winter the population of the island dwindled, and so did the opportunities for employment.

In those solitary moments, lying in the dark, she'd contemplated moving to a city, maybe Boston or even New

York, but then her living costs would rise and it would mean uprooting Mack yet again. Her daughter needed stability.

"Life can be tough," she said. "You know that better than anyone."

She thought about her mother, living with a man who had affairs, her sister, who couldn't have a baby, her daughter, who had lost a father, and Gwen, who had lost a son.

Lauren had written to her twice and received no response.

Why that should hurt her, she didn't know. It wasn't as if she and Gwen had been close when Ed had been alive.

She felt hurt, but most of all she felt lonely. Lonely for someone who understood her and cared for her. Lonely for someone she could confide in.

Which made it dangerous for her to be around Scott.

She glanced hungrily at his wide shoulders and muscular arms. It would be so easy to slide into those arms and lean for a moment. She didn't want him to fix her life. She just wanted to absorb some of his strength so that she could fix it herself. It was the closeness she missed.

"You've changed so much. I'm sorry." His voice was thickened. "I didn't only kill us, I killed you."

The emotion moved from her throat to her heart. "That isn't true."

"Isn't it? You're gripping life so tightly there is no chance it's going to get away from you. You're afraid to let go of the reins."

"Last time I let go of the reins I found myself pregnant." She'd also found herself in love, and that had been worse. She didn't ever want to go there again. Love had been the most adventurous thing she'd done and also the most terrifying.

"That was my fault, too."

"That was no one's fault. An accident. They happen." The paint was drying on the brush. "You say I've changed, but isn't that what growing up is all about? Learning from mistakes? Making better choices?"

"You used to be happy. You laughed all the time. I'd never met anyone who laughed as much as you did."

"My happiness isn't top priority right now. There's Mack to think of, and my mother. She deserves some happiness after everything my father put her through. And my sister—" She knew Jenna was suffering, and she felt helpless. "You wouldn't understand. You've never stayed in one place long enough to learn about responsibility or commitment." She realized how that sounded and felt instantly guilty. It wasn't his fault that his childhood had been like an ill-fitting jigsaw puzzle. A series of disconnected pieces. "I meant that as a statement of fact, not a criticism. I know how tough it was for you." She knew that the repeated rejection had gradually eroded his belief that he could be loved. And why wouldn't it? No one had stuck with him.

"My childhood taught me plenty about survival."

It was a depressingly bleak summary.

Shouldn't there be more to life than survival?

He was silent for a moment, as if there was something he wanted to add. Then he turned away. "Come and look at the countertops."

Countertops?

She followed him into the kitchen, wishing it wasn't such a tight space, and saw how much progress he'd made in the two weeks he'd been here.

He'd worked miracles. Because Nancy had chosen the place for the upstairs room with its flood of natural light, she hadn't cared about the kitchen. That hadn't mattered too much when it was used as a studio, but they had all agreed that if the Sail Loft was going to become a home, then the kitchen needed serious attention.

Scott had ripped out the old kitchen and replaced the old cheap cabinets with hand-painted custom cabinets he'd built and fitted himself. The countertops were white granite and the result was stylish and sophisticated.

"You've done a great job. It's beautiful." She stroked her hand over the wood, admiring his skills. "Maybe you should do this instead of working at the boatyard." He'd told her once about one of the foster families he'd stayed with, who had given him back because they couldn't handle him. She imagined him as a child, scared and traumatized, waiting for the next rejection. "Will you look for another house for yourself?"

"Not right now."

He stood right next to her and his arm brushed against hers. She felt the tension in him and sensed he was exercising superhuman restraint. For weeks they'd been dancing round the chemistry and it was becoming harder to ignore.

It had been too long. She still wanted him, and want and denial together created a particular type of agony.

She turned her head and met his gaze. Her heart fluttered and her stomach dipped. She wondered what it was about him that made her feel as if she'd missed a step.

The air was so thick with tension she could taste it.

She wasn't sure who made the first move, or if they moved at the same time. All she knew was that one minute she was standing there fighting her feelings, and the next she was in his arms.

They came together hard and fast, his hands cupping her face as he kissed her with a raw, savage need. She kissed him back with the same desperation, her hands digging into the hard muscle of his shoulders as she tried to pull him closer. She felt the strength of his hands holding her head, the erotic slide of his tongue and the intimate pressure of his body against hers. He tugged at the clip holding her hair and she felt it spill over her shoulders and down her back.

Sliding his fingers into the heavy mass, he muttered something indistinct against her lips but she couldn't make out the words.

They kissed with undiluted, unashamed urgency and she felt her body flood with sensation and her muscles weaken.

Without breaking the kiss, he ripped at her shirt and she wrenched at his, sliding her hands over taut muscle until she reached the waistband of his jeans. Her hands brushed against his abdomen and he powered her back against the wall, pinning her there. His arms were either side of her and she was grateful to be trapped between him and a solid surface because her legs didn't seem to want to hold her upright.

She fumbled with the buttons of his jeans and felt the hard, rearing shape of him beneath her fingers. He was brutally aroused and he covered her hands with his as they stripped off her jeans first, and then his.

When he lifted his mouth from hers, she protested.

"Don't—"

"In my pocket…" He kissed her mouth and then her jaw. "Condom."

She let him go long enough for him to retrieve it from his wallet, and then she felt the coolness of the air on her skin, the gentle slide of his palm against her thigh and the slow, skilled stroke of his fingers against aching flesh. She almost sobbed with relief, burying her face in his neck as she gasped out his name. His touch became more intimate and she brought her mouth back to his, restless, fitful and needy as he found the most sensitive part of her with breath-stealing accuracy.

There was a brief pause as he dealt with the condom and then he lifted her in a single easy movement. Keeping her mouth on his, she wrapped her legs around his waist and dug her hands into the solid bulk of his shoulders to steady herself. Her head was spinning and she felt as if she was falling, falling.

"I missed you." He breathed the words against her mouth again and again, *missed you, missed you*, and each time the words were interspersed with slow carnal kisses that sent her heat levels soaring.

She'd missed him, too.

The world around them faded and her thoughts slowed even as her heart rate increased. The past ceased to exist and so did the future. There was only the slow pulse of awareness and the dizzying thrill of anticipation as she felt him brush against her intimately. His hands locked on her hips and his breath was warm against her mouth as he murmured her name, soothing, seducing. He entered her with a smooth thrust and she gasped at the feel of him, the sweet pressure, the power, the intoxicating combination of silk and heat. He drove deeper still and then held still for a moment, his breathing unsteady as he struggled for control. She closed her hands round his arms and felt the tension in his muscles.

"I want you." She whispered the words against his ear, against the roughness of his jaw, against the heated curve of his mouth. "I want you."

He lifted his head and she saw that his eyes had darkened. He moved slowly, his gaze locked with hers as he rocked into her with a slow heated rhythm. He built the tension with long, easy, expert strokes that sent pleasure rocketing through her. Suddenly it wasn't enough. She needed more, *more*, but he refused to alter the rhythm. Each sensual glide was so maddeningly slow she wondered if he even knew what he was doing to her, but then she saw the wicked glint in his eye and the sexy slant of his mouth as he lowered his head to kiss her and realized he knew exactly what he was doing.

She scraped her nails over his shoulder, felt him smile against her mouth and then gasped as he thrust deep, the delicious friction almost too much to bear. The tension built and built, higher and higher until finally she came in a rush of pleasure that dragged a sob of relief from her throat. The ripples of her body took him with her and she felt him shudder as he held her, his mouth taking hers so there wasn't a single part of them that wasn't connected. Locked together intimately she felt every spasm, every vibration, every heated pulse.

Afterward neither of them spoke.

There was only the unsteady rasp of his breathing and the pounding of her heart.

She had no idea how much time passed but eventually he lowered her gently to the floor, his arms still locked round her. She stood for a moment, unsteady, her head resting against his shoulder. She felt the warmth of his hand on the back of her head, cradling her there, and it felt good. So good she didn't want to move away, because once she stepped out of this cocoon she knew she'd have to face reality.

"Scott—"

"Hush—" he covered her lips with his fingers "—don't say anything."

She cupped his cheek with her hand, feeling the roughness of stubble scrape against her palm. His gaze held hers and she hoped he wasn't going to ask her, *What next? What does this mean?* She wouldn't be able to answer him. There were so many reasons why they shouldn't have done this.

"We can forget this happened," she whispered. "We can leave here and never mention it again."

"What if I don't want to forget it?" His mouth was so close to hers there was barely a breath of separation. "I'm not losing you again, Laurie. Not again."

"Oh, Scott—"

He wasn't supposed to say things like that. He was the practical one, and she was the dreamer. What did he think could happen? She couldn't let anything happen because she knew that each new tear he put in her heart would reduce the chances of her ever healing.

He took her face in his hands. "This isn't over."

It had to be. It hadn't even been five months since she'd lost Ed.

And this was Scott. Scott, who had walked away from her. Scott, who in all probability would walk away from her again.

What was she doing?

She knew they needed to talk, but instead of talking they were kissing again and his hands were under her shirt, his thumbs grazing the sensitive tips of her breasts. They were lost in each other, insulated from the outside world, and they might have stayed that way if it hadn't been for the intrusive buzz of Lauren's phone.

Scott tightened his grip on her. "Leave it."

"It might be Mack."

He released her instantly and she searched blindly for her purse. Where was it? Why wasn't her brain working?

As she hunted for it, as she dragged on her shirt, her fingers were shaky and useless. She pulled on her jeans next, disoriented. She couldn't see properly through the tangle of her hair and she swept it away from her face, wondering what had happened to the clip.

By the time she found her phone, it had stopped ringing but it started again immediately, shrill and urgent.

She pulled it out of her bag. "It's my mother."

If there was one thing guaranteed to kill sexual attraction it was a call from your mother.

She answered, relieved it wasn't a video call. Her mother would have seen her flushed cheeks and that would have required an explanation she wasn't able to give. "Is everything all right?"

It took only a brief conversation for her to realize everything was far from all right.

"How bad? How bad is it?"

She ended the conversation and hunted wildly for her shoes.

"Here—" Scott held them out to her. "What's happened? Is it Mack?" His voice was sharp with anxiety and Lauren shook her head.

"Jenna had a car accident. She's in the hospital."

Her mind conjured up hideous images of Jenna being cut out of a car wreck. Her mother hadn't been able to tell her how bad it was.

The phone slid from her fingers and bounced across the floor. Her sister. Her sister was injured.

She thought about the way Jenna had stayed glued to

her side through all the adventures Lauren had dragged her on. Jenna, watching over her as she'd jumped off the Jaws bridge. Jenna tugging her away from the window of the Sail Loft. Flying to London after Ed died. "I have to go to her."

Scott slipped the phone into her purse. "That was Greg?"

"My mother." And only now did Lauren pause to wonder why it had been Nancy who had called her and not Greg. Presumably Greg was pacing the corridors while Jenna was in surgery. "I have to go." She tried again to button her shirt, but her fingers fumbled and slipped. "Dammit—I lost a button."

Scott helped her. "Tuck your shirt into your jeans and it won't show."

She tried to smooth her hair. "I look a mess."

"You've been decorating. You look fine."

She was pretty sure she looked like she'd been having crazy sex.

"I'd never wear my hair down for decorating."

Jenna would take one look at her and know.

Except Jenna was in surgery.

Scott turned his attention to his own shirt, and reached for his jacket and his keys. "I'll drive you. You're upset, and one car accident in the family is enough for one night."

"I'll be fine."

"I'm driving you."

She was shaking. She knew she wasn't safe to drive the car. The last few months had stripped away all her reserves of strength. She'd handled everything life had thrown at her up until this point, but she couldn't handle losing her sister.

The room spun around her and she felt Scott's hands on her shoulders.

"Breathe," he said and she closed her eyes.

"If she—"

"That's not going to happen." Swift and sure he propelled her out of the Sail Loft and into his pickup. He opened the door for her and she slid inside, conscious of the delicate ache in certain parts of her body.

"I feel guilty." Because of Ed or because of her sister? She didn't know.

"Don't." He started the engine and glanced at her. "We *are* going to talk about this, but not now."

"Scott—"

"For the record, this isn't over. And I don't regret what we did."

Did she regret it?

She didn't know. All she knew was that her life was a complicated mess, and she'd just made it a whole lot more complicated.

CHAPTER TWENTY-NINE

Nancy

> *Maternal: feelings or actions typical of those*
> *of a kind mother towards her child*

EARLIER THAT DAY Nancy had loaded the last of the boxes into the trunk of her car and driven them to the Goodwill store.

She'd found Susan round the back, sorting through another load of donations.

"Here's a few more for you." Nancy dumped the boxes by the door and resisted the temptation to kick them.

"Good gravy, Nancy." Susan counted the boxes. "Are you clearing out your whole life?"

"Something like that."

Susan opened the first box. "Oh, Nancy—these are Tom's things."

"They are. Twenty-seven boxes of junk."

Susan checked the box underneath and pressed her hand to her chest. "You're giving away his precious golf clubs. Is that a mistake?"

As if all Tom's possessions could have fallen neatly into the boxes by accident.

"No mistake," Nancy said. The mistake had been hanging on to them for this long. Or maybe the mistake had been not swinging one of his precious clubs into his head after he'd confessed to his first affair.

"Are you sure? I know how particular he was about his trophies. He had a real talent for the sport."

Yes, he was good at getting his balls into a hole.

Nancy gave an unladylike snort, which she turned into a cough.

Susan looked at her nervously. "You told me once that he didn't even allow you to dust them."

"And that was a relief because I never was much of a housekeeper."

"It must break your heart to give them away."

"It doesn't. I should have done it a long time ago." Tom had been taking up space in her life for far too long. She almost shared that thought aloud, but then decided there were some things better left unsaid. Not because it was a secret, but because if she started talking about it everyone would start sympathizing. They'd expect her to talk and the last thing she wanted to do was talk about Tom. He'd had enough of her time and energy.

Are you watching this, Tom?

I'm living my life without you, and it feels good.

Susan pulled out a starched linen tablecloth. "Did you know this was here? Didn't this belong to your grandmother?"

"Yes, but she's been dead more than forty years so I can't imagine she'll have a use for it."

"You don't want it for sentimental reasons?"

"I have all the memories I need stored safely inside me, thank you."

And not all of them were good.

Nancy had been grateful to her grandmother. After all, she'd raised her when she'd lost her parents. Maybe she'd even loved her in a way. But had she been a kind woman? Loving? No, certainly not.

Did a hard life have to make you a hard woman?

Nancy wasn't sure, but she hoped not.

Susan folded the linen tablecloth carefully. "I hear you and Lauren have redecorated The Captain's House."

"That's right. It's stunning. My daughter is incredibly talented. She's going to set up her own design business. We're doing it together." Pride filled her, pushing out all thoughts of Tom. "She has a brilliant future ahead of her."

"Still, it must seem strange, letting someone else stay in your home. Must feel as if it doesn't belong to you anymore."

"It still belongs to me and I have the ridiculous bills to prove it." Nancy was beginning to wish she'd chosen somewhere else to disgorge the trappings of her life. She hadn't realized each box would require a running commentary.

Mack had told her there was a way to call yourself on your phone.

She wished she'd paid more attention.

She was fingering the cellphone in her pocket, trying to remember how to make it ring, when it rang.

Nancy was so shocked she almost dropped it. Had she done that?

Maybe she had more technical expertise than she thought.

She pulled the phone out of her pocket and saw Jenna's name.

Thank God! Maybe her daughter was telepathic.

"Excuse me, Susan—" she tried to sound regretful "—it's my daughter. I need to take this. It might be an emergency."

The last thing she'd expected was that it was in fact an emergency, so when she heard Jenna's breathless, panicked voice her heart almost stopped. "What, honey? I can't hear you—you're not speaking clearly, or maybe it's a terrible signal—" She was aware of Susan listening avidly, her hands still on the box. Wishing people were better at minding their own business, Nancy moved toward the door of the store. "Jenna?"

Finally she was able to understand and her body turned cold.

"I'm on my way."

"You're leaving?" Susan looked at her bemused. "But we have all these boxes to sort through. What if you decide there's something here you don't want to give away?"

"Take whatever you like and dispose of the rest. They're just things, and who cares about things? It's people that matter." Nancy was already halfway out the door. "My daughter needs me."

My daughter needs me.

When Lauren had passed out on the dock Nancy had been unable to move, frozen by what she believed to be her inadequacy as a mother. In the past her girls had never seemed to need her, but they needed her now.

She rushed to her car, brushing past two people who tried to talk to her.

"Can't stop now. My daughter needs me."

I'm coming, Jenna, I'm coming.

She drove as quickly as she could within the limits of safety, half hoping she'd be pulled over so she could ask for a police escort. No one stopped her and she parked and stormed through the doors of the hospital like a hurricane. "I'm looking for Jenna Stewart. I mean Sullivan."

It was only when the woman at the desk gave her a startled look that she became conscious of her disheveled appearance.

Clearing cupboards and loading the last of the boxes had been dirty work. Her skirt was thick with dust and she knew she probably still had that smudge of dirt on her cheek.

She didn't give a damn. All she cared about was her daughter.

"Jenna Sullivan. She was brought in a few minutes ago. Car wreck." Saying the words made her mouth dry. She knew it would be a long time until she forgot the moment she'd picked up the phone and heard Jenna's trembling voice.

Mom, help me.

When had Jenna ever asked her for help?

"The team are with her now. If you'd like to take a seat, we'll—"

"I would not like to take a seat. I need to see my daughter." She felt like a lioness and she was ready to use her claws if she had to. She knew enough about people to know that aggression wasn't going to help her, so she kept her voice well modulated but firm. If the woman couldn't see Nancy meant business, then she needed a sight test.

"As soon as she has been assessed you'll be able to—"

"Now," Nancy said. "I'd like to see her now. It's important that she has family with her."

Her daughter had called her for help, and no way was she letting her down. Not this time.

Not ever again.

The woman at the desk eyed her warily, clearly wondering if she should call security. Keeping her eyes on Nancy, she picked up the phone and moments later an ER nurse appeared.

"You're Jenna's mother? I'm glad you're here. She's asking for you. She's very upset. You can have a few minutes with her before we take her to the OR."

Nancy's stomach flip-flopped. "She needs surgery?"

"Her blood pressure is low and the scan we did shows that she's bleeding into her abdomen. We think she might have damaged her spleen. It's not uncommon after blunt trauma like a motor vehicle accident."

That wasn't the news Nancy had been hoping for and her legs shook as she followed the nurse through into the department. Spleens were important, weren't they? Something to do with protecting you from infection? Mack would have instantly found the answer on her phone, but Nancy was a dinosaur and restricted to the limitations of her memory.

Jenna was lying on a gurney, an IV in her arm and a dressing on her head. There was a livid bruise on her cheek and her eyes were red from crying. When she saw Nancy, more tears spilled down her cheeks. "Mom? I'm so glad you came. Don't leave me, will you? Promise you won't leave."

Nancy stepped forward, hiding her shock.

"I'm right here, honey. I'm not leaving." She wrapped her arms around her daughter as carefully as she could, hoping she wasn't making anything worse. "There. Everything is going to be all right."

"Everything is awful," Jenna hiccupped and Nancy rocked and soothed her.

"I know you're scared, but the doctors here are wonderful. They're going to fix this."

Please let them fix it, please let them fix it.

"It isn't just the accident. That's one more thing to pile on to all the other things. Things they can't fix." Jenna sobbed harder and the nurse monitoring her blood pressure glanced up and frowned.

Nancy ignored her. "What do you mean? What can't they fix?"

"The baby." Jenna's words were disjointed and jerky. "They can't…fix…the baby."

Nancy smoothed away Jenna's tears with her thumb. "You're pregnant? Have you told the doctors?"

Jenna shook her head, her face swollen with crying. "I'm not pregnant. I've never been pregnant." She choked out the words. "I'm never going to be pregnant."

Nancy struggled to keep up. Her daughter was badly injured, bleeding and about to go for an operation, and all she could talk about was the fact that she wasn't pregnant? Why would that be top of her mind? Unless—

"Have you been trying for long?"

Jenna clung to her. "Feels like forever."

"Oh, sweetheart." Nancy stroked Jenna's hair away from her face, trying to ignore the blood streaks that made her want to panic. Scalps bled a lot. It was one of the few things she remembered from when the girls were little. "These things can take a while."

"We've been trying awhile, Mom."

The *Mom* almost undid her, as did the knowledge that this was the first time Jenna had mentioned this to her.

Nancy stood feeling helpless, buffeted by the pain that flowed off Jenna in waves.

Why was it that you felt your child's pain more acutely than your own? She could bear anything that happened to her, but she couldn't bear anything bad happening to her girls.

What could she say that might help?

She so badly didn't want to get this wrong, but they had a matter of minutes before Jenna was taken into surgery. It was hardly the best time to be having this conversation.

"It took me two years to get pregnant with Lauren."

Jenna sniffed. "Really?"

"Yes. Nature is a funny thing, that's for sure. What does Greg say? Have the two of you talked to a doctor?"

"He doesn't want to. He says I need to relax."

Oh, you silly man. "Have you called him?"

Jenna burrowed her face into Nancy's shoulder. "Not yet. Lately we haven't been getting along so well."

Nancy stroked her daughter's back gently, hiding her shock. She decided this was one of those moments where it was probably better to listen than talk. And she was absolutely *not* going to deliver an opinion as her grandmother would have done.

Well, Nancy, of course it's your own fault for—

It's up to you of course, Nancy, but if I were you—

"Tell me what happened today."

"I was five days late and I've never been five days late." Jenna hiccupped, her words disjointed. "I was sure I was pregnant, so I did a test at work. I didn't want to wait. And I thought it might fix things with Greg."

"And the test was negative." Nancy imagined Jenna in the

cold, impersonal school bathroom. She wished she'd thought to pack tissues in her bag. "No wonder you were upset."

"That's not all." Jenna's breathing juddered as she told her mother everything.

Nancy held her close and listened, trying not to react as Jenna described the car accident.

She wasn't going to think about what might have happened.

It was hard to hear, but hardest of all was Jenna's anguish about her lack of pregnancy.

"I want to be a mom. It's all I want. And it's never going to h-happen—"

Nancy held on to Jenna's trembling frame, terrified that so much distress might make the bleeding worse. "You don't know that, honey. We'll figure it out. We'll figure it out together. We should call Greg. He needs to know you're here. He'd want to know."

A woman appeared next to them. "Mrs. Stewart? I'm Gail Johnson, the surgeon. We need to get Jenna to the OR right away. We're prepping for that now."

Jenna's eyes filled. "Could I have a minute more with my mom?"

The doctor smiled. "Sure. We're not quite ready for you. But it will only be a couple of minutes." She adjusted the flow of the infusion and walked out of the cubicle, giving them privacy.

Nancy tried to ignore the sterility of their surroundings. "Can I call Greg for you?" It didn't seem possible that Jenna and Greg were having problems. They were inseparable and always had been.

"This whole baby thing—and what happened with Dad—"

Jenna scrubbed at her face again. "Greg has been weird about it. I'm starting to think he doesn't want kids as much as I do."

"Maybe he is finding it hard to deal with, too."

"Greg knows more about dealing with problems than anyone."

"There's a difference between dealing with other people's problems and dealing with your own." She stood back as the staff came to wheel Jenna to the OR. "Can I call him?"

Jenna hesitated and then nodded. "Will you be here when I wake up?"

"Yes."

"Do you promise? You won't go away?"

"I promise I'm not going anywhere." Nancy reached out and squeezed Jenna's hand. "It's going to be fine. All of it."

She hoped she was right, and she was sure of it when Greg arrived less than fifteen minutes later and she saw his face.

He was ashen, his concern for his wife visible from every angle.

"Where is she? How is she?" Normally calm and contained, Greg looked stressed out of his mind.

"She's in surgery."

He sank heavily onto the nearest chair. "They said she crashed the car on the beach road. What was she doing up there?"

Should she tell him? No. It wasn't her place to do so. "You can ask her that as soon as she wakes up from the operation."

"Why didn't she call me?"

Because sometimes a girl wants her mother.

"You'll be able to talk to her soon."

"Is she—will she—" He ran his hand over his face and Nancy sat down next to him.

Whatever problems her daughter and her husband might have, they would eventually be solved.

"They think she'll be fine. The doctors said they wouldn't remove her spleen unless they had to because that would make her more vulnerable to infection. They'll repair it." Nancy hesitated. "She hit her head when she crashed. Her face is bruised. You should probably be prepared for that. It's a little shocking to see." Should she mention the baby conversation? No. The poor man had enough to deal with right now.

Greg sat with his elbows on his knees and his hands jammed into his hair. "She could have been killed. Oh God, I'm sorry. I didn't think—" He glanced at her, contrite, and she knew he was thinking about another car accident. The one where the occupants didn't get to walk away.

"It's all right."

"It's not all right. It was the wrong thing to say."

"You don't always have to say the right thing, Greg." She hadn't thought about it before, but now she realized what a burden that must be, believing that everyone expected you to have the perfect words to heal all emotional hurts.

It must be exhausting. An extra pressure in a life that was already full of pressure.

She put her hand on his shoulder. "You spend your days dealing with other people's feelings. Make sure you don't neglect your own."

Lauren arrived then, breathless and disheveled. Nancy noticed that Scott was with her.

She stood up. "Jenna will be glad you're here."

"I came as soon as I got your message." Lauren's jeans were spattered with paint. "How is she?"

Nancy wondered why her daughter would be wearing

designer jeans to paint a house and then saw the way Scott hovered protectively.

Interesting.

"She's in surgery." She saw Scott place his hand on Lauren's back in a gesture of support and was engulfed by a wave of maternal anxiety. She loved Scott and she admired what he'd done with his life, but was he about to hurt her daughter a second time? What exactly was their relationship? Lauren was vulnerable. Too vulnerable to withstand another blow.

Nancy sat back down on one of the hard plastic chairs and reminded herself that her role wasn't to make decisions for her daughters, but to support their decisions.

Whatever happened, she'd be there for them. That was a mother's role, wasn't it? And if it gave her heartburn then that was her problem.

They sat together, side by side, drinking vile-tasting coffee from disposable cups.

There was something about the sterile atmosphere of hospitals that could make a bad situation feel a hundred times worse, Nancy decided.

Greg looked haggard and could barely hold the coffee cup Lauren pressed into his hand. Every time someone wearing scrubs walked past he sprang to his feet, his face bone white.

By the time the doctor arrived with news, Nancy was as jumpy as Greg.

"Mr. Sullivan?" Gail Johnson, the surgeon, walked toward them and Greg was on his feet again.

"Is there news? Is she—" His throat worked and Nancy put her hand on his arm.

"Jenna is doing well," the doctor said. "As you know she had a small tear to her spleen—"

"Did you have to remove it?"

"We try very hard not to do that now. In Jenna's case we were able to suture it. We're going to need to observe her for a few days and we'll be doing a follow-up CT scan, but we're optimistic that there won't be long-term problems."

Greg sat down hard on the nearest chair as if someone had cut him off at the knees. His elbows rested on his thighs and he covered his face with his hands.

Nancy put her hand on his shoulder. "She's going to be all right, Greg." He was a good man, she thought. Such a good man.

Greg took an unsteady breath. "I want to see her."

The surgeon frowned. "She's only just woken up from the anesthetic. You should wait until—"

"Now," Greg said hoarsely. "Please."

The doctor hesitated but then saw something in Greg's face and nodded. "You can see her briefly. But just you. Come with me."

As Greg followed the doctor, Nancy remembered she'd had an arrangement to meet Ben to talk about the garden.

He'd be wondering where she was.

Should she call? No, she was already so late it was hardly going to make a difference. And Ben would understand. He was patient and unselfish. So unlike Tom in every way.

They all stayed until the medical staff relented and allowed them to see Jenna. She'd been transferred to the ward, a bright sunny room with windows overlooking fields and trees.

Greg was sitting by her side, holding her hand.

Nancy thought that the chances of the medical staff persuading him to leave at any point in the near future were zero.

Jenna's eyes were closed but she opened them when she

heard footsteps and her eyes brightened when she saw her sister and her mother.

"Hi." Her voice was a croak, and Greg tightened his grip on her hand protectively.

"Don't talk. You're supposed to be resting."

"We wanted to see you for a moment." Nancy leaned down to kiss her. "How are you feeling?"

"Great," Jenna croaked. "Never better."

Lauren stepped forward and kissed her, too. "Next time you want to get into trouble," she said, "call me. I'm the ringleader, not you."

Jenna gave a weak smile. "It wasn't exactly planned."

Nancy saw the look they exchanged.

Thank goodness they'd always had each other.

She gestured to Lauren, who nodded agreement.

"You're going?" Jenna held out her hand. Her face was pale and the livid bruise had spread across her cheekbone.

"I'll be back tomorrow." A good mother, Nancy thought, should know when to stay and when to leave. "I'll bring food, because what they feed you in here will poison you."

Greg stood up, too. "Thank you, Nancy." He hugged her, something Nancy couldn't ever remember him doing before.

He and Jenna had things to talk about. They didn't need her.

She walked back to the car with Scott and Lauren. Now that the worst of the panic was over, she felt drained and exhausted. "How is the Sail Loft coming along?" She made an attempt at normal conversation. "When can I see it?"

"Not until it's finished." Lauren was flustered. "Scott's done a great job."

"I'm sure." Nancy studied her daughter's flushed cheeks and almost smiled.

Whatever the future held, she liked the idea of someone

else having a romantic relationship in the Sail Loft. It might stop her thinking about Tom whenever she walked in there.

Lauren put her hand on Nancy's arm. "It's going to feel different, Mom, I promise."

Nancy was touched by her daughter's sensitivity. "I'm looking forward to seeing it."

Hear that, Tom? We've painted you out of the place. I'm building a new life and your humping, faithless ways aren't going to stop me.

"All your art equipment is safely stored, but I boxed up everything else that was in the cupboards, so you'll need to sort through it at some point and decide what you want to keep."

"I don't want to keep any of it."

Lauren looked doubtful. "Don't you at least want to look?"

They'd reached the parking lot and Nancy saw Scott's pickup parked on the far side.

"I want to start fresh." She reached for her keys. "Now that I've discovered the cleansing properties of clearing out, I'm finding it surprisingly therapeutic."

Lauren grinned. "Who are you, and what have you done with my mother?"

"Your old mother is buried under all the rubbish she held on to for decades. Your new mother is about to go back to The Captain's House and work on the garden until it's dark. I have some planting to do. Ben promised to work on the place this evening, and I plan on helping him. We're giving the place a final makeover. Drive carefully."

A FEW HOURS LATER, Nancy eased upright and her back screamed a protest. She'd worked hard, but work was the only way she knew to handle stress and anxiety, and she was stressed and anxious about Jenna. Had she talked to Greg?

Wincing, she rubbed her hand over her spine.

Ben was next to her, jamming the spade into the ground as he planted out the last of the shrubs they'd bought.

He glanced at her. "You should take a break."

"We still have a lot to do." It was surprisingly companionable, working on the garden as the late evening sun spread across the garden.

Ben pushed the brim of his hat back. "She's going to be all right, Nancy."

"I hope so." She'd never be able to describe how it had felt to get that call from her daughter, knowing she was trapped in the car. At that moment in her life nothing else had mattered. Not the house, not the state of her finances. Not even Tom. "How did you know I was thinking of her?"

"You've called the hospital twice in the last hour." His eyes were gentle and Nancy thought how calming it was to be with him.

"I guess I'm feeling a little overprotective." She pulled off her gardening gloves. "I wasn't a good mother, Ben. I don't need to talk about it and I don't need you to tell me all the reasons I'm wrong. I know it's true. I'm trying to make up for it now."

Ben put his hand on her shoulder. "I'm glad you have your girls."

She was glad, too. She was lucky.

The girls were the one thing she and Tom had done well together. Possibly the only thing.

She turned back to the garden. "We've given this place quite a makeover. The house and the garden. It's looking good."

"Good? It's spectacular. Your garden is beautiful." Ben removed his cap and wiped his brow. "A work of art."

A work of art.

And Nancy realized that was exactly what it was. She'd stopped painting, but instead of using oil and canvas, she'd used flowers and plants to create great swathes of color that drew admiring glances from everyone who passed.

Her garden was a living, breathing work of art.

"You're right," she said. "It is." There was more than one way of creating something that was visually pleasing. "I'd like to do the same with the garden at the Sail Loft. Will you help me?"

"You know I will."

"We need to start by digging out that damn honeysuckle."

"Is it going to upset you moving out for the summer?"

"No. The Sail Loft is closer to Jenna. I'll be able to drop in and visit without getting stuck in hideous tourist traffic."

His gaze was steady. "You haven't been there in so long, I thought you hated it."

"Lauren has redecorated. I'm quite sure I won't recognize the place."

"I'll miss you."

His comment confused her. "I'm only moving a few miles away."

"I'll miss working on this garden with you." They'd agreed that he would continue to maintain the garden throughout the summer. Because the coastal garden was an important part of the house, Nancy had deemed it a necessary expense.

"Will it be too much for you to handle by yourself?"

Despite being the wrong side of sixty, Ben was lean and fit. It hadn't occurred to her for a moment that he wouldn't be able to cope. If he couldn't then it gave her a problem, because her finances wouldn't stretch to another gardener. "Do what you can, Ben."

His eyes gleamed. "You think I'm breaking up under the pressure? I still have some good years left in me. That isn't why I'm going to miss you, Nancy."

"Oh! Well then, what—" She broke off, stumbling over the words, remembering how she'd felt that day when she'd glanced through the window. "But—Ben Winter, are you *hitting* on me?"

"I'm not sure if that's what it's called when you pass sixty, but yes, I'm hitting on you. Why so surprised?"

Nancy almost dropped the plant she was holding.

Her mouth moved but no words came out. Ben had been married to the same woman for forty years. Lucille had died five years earlier, and now he lived alone in one of the smaller houses on Main Street. She knew there were plenty of women on the island who were interested in him. She'd never seen him interested in any of them. Nancy suspected he'd buried his pain under work, as she had.

Never in a million years had she suspected his feelings might go beyond friendship.

He was waiting for her to say something, and she had no idea what to say. She clutched the tomato plant like a lifeline.

"I'm not exactly relationship material."

"You only think that because he crushed your confidence." Ben picked up the spade and rammed it into the ground so hard Nancy expected the earth to shake.

"It isn't about confidence. I'm too old and cynical to even think about love, Ben."

"So let's not fall in love." He winked at her. "We can have sex until our bones crack."

Suddenly she was laughing uproariously. She couldn't remember when she'd last laughed so hard.

"Oh, Ben—"

"I'm not joking, Nancy."

"Well you should be." She felt flustered. Flustered and flattered. Sex? It was ridiculous to even think about it. But his eyes were so *blue*. And the way he was looking at her made her feel like dragging him inside the house and locking the door. "Imagine what people would say."

"I don't give a damn what anyone says. And you shouldn't care either. This is *your* life, Nancy, not theirs. You should be living it."

She felt as if she was teetering on the edge of something desperately exciting. "I value our friendship. I wouldn't ever want to lose that."

"Who said anything about losing it? Not all relationships go wrong, Nancy. Not all men are like Tom."

Somehow he knew, and she was surprised to discover she wasn't embarrassed. If anything she was relieved they had no secrets. Secrets, she'd discovered, were clutter. They filled a space inside you and gathered dust. They stopped you connecting fully with people.

She should say something. But what? Her feelings were unfamiliar and she wasn't sure she could put a name to them.

Ben waited a moment and then turned away. "It's getting dark. We should finish up here."

She felt a flash of panic.

He thought she was rejecting him.

"Ben! Would you—" She stopped. *How should she put this?* "Would you like a drink? The house is empty." Obviously. He already knew that. *Oh, Nancy, you're a fool. A fool!*

"Are you really offering me a drink?"

"No."

He smiled and cupped her face in his hands. "You can say what you mean, Nancy. You don't have to choose your words with me, second-guess what I'm thinking or keep secrets."

Secrets. Oh, how she hated secrets.

"Are we being hasty, Ben? Maybe we should—"

He kissed her.

She'd thought that part of her life was over and yet here she was being kissed in a way she wasn't sure she'd ever been kissed before. His hands held her face while his mouth slowly seduced hers and it felt incredible. It felt right.

A thick, syrupy pleasure heated low in her pelvis and spread through her limbs.

Ben Winter. Kissing her. She felt strangely vulnerable and yet at the same time she knew Ben would never hurt her.

Hot tears scalded her eyes. *Who would have thought it?*

At her age, when she'd thought this aspect of her life was over and done.

She swayed against him but he held her firmly, a rock on which she could safely lean.

When he finally released her, she felt dizzy and heavy with longing. "You don't want to wait?"

"The good thing about maturity is that you've learned there is no point in waiting around for something you already know you want." He took her hand and led her toward the house.

"My daughter is in hospital—"

"And she's safe. But if you'd rather wait—" He paused, ever thoughtful. Ever caring.

Ben.

"No." Life was short, and she'd already waited long enough.

As the sun dipped below the horizon, she gazed at the house.

A light glowed in the kitchen and she could hear the call of seagulls.

"It's looking good, isn't it?" As far as she was concerned, The Captain's House had never looked better. Who would have thought that a big clear out and some love and attention would make such a difference? It was as if it had shaken off the tiredness. "It's been given a new lease on life."

Tightening her grip on Ben's hand, she walked into the house, hoping the same thing was about to happen to her.

CHAPTER THIRTY

Jenna

*Resolution: determination to do something
or not do something*

"CAN I GET you anything else?" Greg hovered over her like a drone. "More soup? Another drink? Painkillers?"

"I'm fine." Truthfully she wasn't fine. She felt exhausted. The doctor had said that was normal, but she was worried about taking so much time off from work. Lindsey Hanks, one of the other teachers, was covering her class but she knew how much stress that would cause. "Maybe I can go back to work Monday."

"No way. You had surgery and spent five days in hospital. I saw Jed Andrews this morning when I went to fill your prescription, and he gave me a vivid description of how they had to cut you out of the car. You could have been killed."

"But I wasn't."

The doorbell rang and Greg went to answer it.

He returned with armfuls of flowers and a stack of cards. Jenna opened them one by one, tears in her eyes.

To Mrs. Sullivan. You are the best teecher. Come back soon.

Mrs. Sullivan, we miss you. Miss Hanks shouts more.

Mrs. Sullivan, sorry you broke your car.

There were paintings, heavy on the glitter and glue, and she examined each one carefully, imagining the children sitting quietly, their little faces set in concentration as they splashed paint and sprinkled glitter.

A painting session was not for the fainthearted. She made a mental note to thank Lindsey Hanks.

"They love you." Greg moved the cards carefully and sat down on the bed. "I saw Lindsey in the store yesterday and she said they're making you a class video."

"I love them, too."

Maybe it would be enough, she thought. She could shower other people's children with love. Be the best teacher ever. At least that way she was making a difference.

"I keep thinking about you rolling the car." Greg's voice was hoarse. "It's giving me nightmares."

"Me, too. It wasn't my finest moment. I'd be a terrible getaway driver." She tried to make a joke, but he didn't laugh.

"The fact that you called your mom and not me wasn't my finest moment either."

She'd hurt his feelings. "Everyone wants their mom when they're sick or injured."

"You don't. You've never had that kind of relationship with her."

"We do now. We're getting along well." She'd never be able to describe the feeling she'd had when her mother had rushed into the emergency room to be by her side. That gesture of love and support had been everything she'd needed.

"A few months ago you would have called me the moment you did that test. You would have talked to me, instead of driving to some lonely spot on the beach road to suffer on your own." He was pale. "Getting that call from your mother was bad, but seeing you in that hospital gown with all those tubes and doctors round you was the worst moment of my life."

"I planned to call you with the good news of my pregnancy, but when there wasn't one—" Her voice wobbled. "I'm sorry. I should have called, but you were so mad at me."

"I wasn't mad at you. I was mad at myself."

"You were upset that I didn't tell you about seeing my dad when I was young, and you were tired of me being fixated on babies. And I don't blame you."

"That isn't what was going on, Jenna."

She felt exhausted. Too tired for the conversation she knew they should be having. "It doesn't matter."

"It matters. I was hurt that you didn't tell me about your dad, that's true. It was such a big deal for you and your sister, I couldn't understand how you could have kept it from me. Don't—" He pressed his fingers to her lips when she tried to speak. "Let me say this. I was afraid that what happened to you had something to do with the reason you chose me."

"It did." She saw his expression change and grabbed his hand. "Please listen! I loved my dad, but I never trusted him after that night. Even though I didn't know he had other affairs, maybe some part of me knew that if he'd done it once he could do it again. I didn't want that. I wanted a man I could trust. You were that man."

"You've only ever been with me." He slid his fingers under her chin and tilted her face. "Was it because you were too scared to spread your wings?"

"The reason I've only been with you is because you're the only man I ever wanted. I was with you because I loved you. And I'm with you now because I love you. I always knew you were nothing like my father."

He bent his head and kissed her. "I'm sorry. I'm sorry I made you feel you couldn't talk to me." He spoke between kisses. "I don't ever want you to feel that way again. There's nothing we can't talk about."

"I know." She put her arms round his neck. "And I'm going to stop being boring and fixated on babies and pregnancy." Somehow, she had to. She knew she'd never forget how low she'd felt when she'd done that test. "I know you don't want a baby as badly as I do—"

"That's not true." Greg took her hand and laced his fingers through hers. "I want a baby every bit as much as you do."

"It doesn't seem that way."

He stared down at their joined hands. "Don't you get it?" His voice was husky. "I love you, too. I loved you before I was even old enough to understand what the word meant. All I've ever wanted is for you to be happy, Jenna. I want to make you happy. But I can't give you the one thing you want most. How do you think that makes me feel?"

She stared at him.

It hadn't occurred to her that he might be thinking that way.

"You told me you were tired of baby sex."

"Because every time we have sex and we don't make a baby, I feel like a failure. It's hard to keep trying at something if you're always failing."

Jenna felt hot tears sting her eyes. "It isn't your fault. It isn't failure."

"It feels that way to me. And I haven't been handling it well." He gave a faint smile. "I'm used to being top of the class, remember? I have to win at everything. Even in my job, I have to be the best." There was a self-derision there that she hadn't heard before. Greg was a winner. The golden boy.

"You're good at what you do, Greg. You've made a huge difference to many people's lives."

"I'm fine at handling other people's life problems, but not so good at my own it seems. With my wife, who is the most important person in my life, I've been inept. The truth is—" he paused "—I've discovered that I can be detached with everyone except myself. Every time you have a negative test I drive by the gym and take it out on the punching bag."

"Seriously?"

"Seriously. It's my kind of therapy. The gym has had to replace it twice in the last year."

She'd had no idea. "Why didn't you say something before now?"

"Because I was trying to be your rock. Steady. I thought if you knew how bad I felt, that would make you feel worse."

"Oh, Greg—" She'd taken his answers at face value when she should have delved deeper. But because this was Greg, and he was so good at articulating feelings, it hadn't occurred to her that there were things going on that he wasn't saying. "Whenever I asked how you felt about it, you said you were okay."

"I lied. It doesn't matter now. That's the past and we should be focusing on the future. On what comes next." He lifted her hand and pressed a kiss to her palm. "Next time you do a test, I want to know. We'll do it together."

"I'm not sure I'll ever do another test again. The g-force of being on a high and then plunging to the pits of despair might kill me."

"I love you." He let go of her hand and wrapped her in his arms, holding her tightly. "You're my love and my life. I love you so much and I wish I could fix this."

It was such an unspeakable relief to be held. Such a relief to feel close to him again. It felt right and natural.

"You're my life, too. We're lucky to have each other." She tugged at the buttons on his shirt. "I missed you when I was in hospital. Come to bed."

He groaned as she kissed her way from his jaw to his mouth. "Jenna, we can't. You're tired and in pain."

"So you'll have to be extra gentle."

"No way." He caught her hands in his. "It's too soon. When that doctor asks me why your stitches have opened up, I'm not taking the blame."

She grinned. "You're no fun, Greg Sullivan."

"Take a couple more days to recover and then I'll show you just how much fun I can be."

Happiness: feeling, showing or expressing joy.

Jenna and Greg.

They were going to be all right. Somehow, in some way, they'd find a way to be all right.

He eased her away from him. "We'll see a doctor. Talk to someone. I'm sorry I didn't agree to it before."

The doorbell rang and Greg raised an eyebrow. "Now are you pleased we're not both naked?"

"In fact, no. But since we're both decent, you might as well answer it."

He stood up reluctantly. "If it's another delivery of cards and chocolates we're going to have to move house."

But it wasn't chocolate.

She heard voices and laughter and moments later Nancy, Lauren and Mack crowded into her bedroom.

Lauren was wearing her hair loose. She looked younger and more relaxed. She was holding a massive bouquet and Nancy had an envelope in her hand.

"Gorgeous flowers," Jenna said, "but you shouldn't be wasting our limited funds on flowers. I still have the last bunch you brought me."

"These are from Mrs. Hill's garden."

Jenna raised her eyebrows. "You didn't—"

"Not this time," Lauren laughed. "Ben works for her, and he picked them with her permission because we know how much you love flowers. Everyone I pass asks after you. Every trip to the store takes five times as long." She glanced at the cards open on the table and then back at her sister. "How are you? You have a little more color."

"I'm better, thanks." Much better since her conversation with Greg.

She still had no idea what she was going to do about getting pregnant, but at least they were talking again.

Greg cleared a pile of books off a chair. "Sit down wherever you can find a space. I'll make some drinks."

Nancy handed Jenna the envelope. "This is to give you something to look forward to when you're better."

Jenna opened it while marveling at the novelty of having her entire family crowded into her bedroom. "Seasalt Spa?"

She studied the embossed card with its lavish silvery print. "Is that the new place near Chilmark?"

"Yes, and we're going together, the four of us. We deserve it after all the work we've put in over the past few months. Manicure, pedicure—it's a makeover." Nancy made it sound as if it was something she did every day of the week, but Jenna couldn't remember a time when her mother had done anything like this for herself.

"You can't afford this!"

"I sold a painting," Nancy said. "Which surprised me, to be honest."

"It didn't surprise me." Lauren leaned in and adjusted Jenna's pillows. "Can I get you anything?"

"No, I'm good, thanks. Stop fussing." But it felt good to be surrounded by people who cared. "Which painting did you sell?"

"The stormy, moody seascape that used to hang in the master bedroom."

"I know the one you mean." Jenna put the vouchers on her lap. "That painting always terrified me. It's so—pessimistic."

"Yes, but fortunately for us, pessimism is selling right now and if people want dismal on their wall, who are we to argue with them?"

Jenna fingered the glossy voucher on her lap. "If you made money, then you should keep it. You'll need the savings to get you through the winter in The Captain's House."

"Some things are more important than savings. We've all had a grim year so far. It's time we had some fun as a family. We deserve some joy."

When had they last had fun together?

Jenna couldn't remember.

"So now you know there's a market for your work, will you start painting again?"

"I'm enjoying creating art in different ways, particularly the gardens. Ben and I have some exciting ideas for transforming the garden of the Sail Loft. But the priority is to focus on our new design business, Coastal Chic. Lauren has an appointment at the bank to talk about a loan, and then we're on our way. I'll be helping her! It's exciting to have a new outlet for creativity. Mack can help out when she's not at school. Has Jenna seen the business card? Lauren, do you have one?"

Jenna shifted position in the bed. She couldn't remember the last time she'd seen her mother this fired up about anything. She wondered if she was the only one who had noticed that Ben's name came up frequently in conversation. "You have a business card?"

Lauren dug her hand into her purse and produced one. "Mack made them. Designed the logo and everything."

Jenna took the card from her. "'Coastal Chic,'" she read. "I love it. And the silver shell logo is perfect. Classy. I'd employ you in a heartbeat."

Mack flushed with pleasure. "I love coding, but I also love the design side of things."

"Which is why the website for The Captain's House looks so good," Nancy said. "Have you seen the design for the pages you wrote, Jenna? Mack has managed to put a whaling ship in the background behind the text. It looks fabulous. Maybe we could set up a property rental business, too."

Lauren looked alarmed. "One thing at a time, Mom."

But Jenna was relieved to see the excitement on her mother's face. "I'll take a look at the website later."

"What are these?" Nancy picked up the sketches by Jenna's bed.

"Those?" Jenna wished she'd hidden them. "Those are my feeble attempts at drawing. I have no talent."

Nancy sat down on the edge of the bed and studied it. "Is it a pig?"

"It's a goat. See what I mean? I should give up." She made a grab for the pages but Nancy held them out of reach as she flicked through the text.

"*Adventures with My Sister.* You wrote down one of your stories?"

Jenna felt her cheeks burn. "I've been writing down a few of them. Some of the parents in my class wanted them to read to the children so I thought I might as well. I haven't decided what to do with it yet."

Mack peered over her shoulder. "My favorite was the one when the two sisters disrupted the ballet class." She took the papers from her grandmother, kicked off her shoes and sprawled on the bed next to Jenna. "Your stories are great. Remember Fred and Alfred? Fred and Alfred were hilarious. And the dinosaur who was a fussy eater. Are you going to write them all down?"

"I don't know. I hadn't thought about it."

"You should." Lauren sat on the bed, too, and Jenna shifted gingerly to make room.

It seemed her entire family was now on the bed with her, crowded either side of her like bookends.

Greg walked back into the room and she met his gaze.

The worried frown on his face made her heart warm. "Mom is seeing if she can rescue my terrible drawing. Or maybe it would be easier if I changed the goat in the story to a pig."

"You have talent. I've always said so." He put a mug of tea on the nightstand next to her.

"She has." Nancy was reading over Mack's shoulder. "Why haven't any of us encouraged you to write them down before? These are engaging, funny, emotional. You make the reader *care* about these girls."

Jenna felt herself flush. "Thanks, Mom. Shame I can't illustrate to save my life."

"You don't need to be able to do both." Nancy took the pages back from Mack. "They can partner you with an illustrator."

"They?"

"A publisher."

"You think someone might want to publish my stories?"

"I do. I know there are plenty of children out there who would enjoy them." Nancy turned the pages over and picked up the pencil. "I've never drawn a goat either." She sketched rapidly, eyes narrowed, her hand free and relaxed. Then she laughed. "Yours might look like a pig but mine looks like a unicorn."

Mack leaned over her shoulder and studied it from every angle. "It's not completely awful, Grams."

"Thank you, honey. You're so kind."

Mack grinned. "We're all about honesty now, remember?"

"I do. And I approve. Also, I agree. I don't think I'm going to be illustrating your aunt's books, but let me think about it. It's a different art form. It isn't as simple as drawing an excellent goat, it's about conveying the movement, the naughtiness, the sense of adventure. The two girls getting themselves into trouble and then getting themselves out. Always together. That closeness has to be on the page."

She eyed Jenna and then Lauren. "Was this Mrs. Fallowfield's goat?"

Jenna shrank against the pillows and Lauren blinked innocently.

"We have no idea what you mean, Mom."

Nancy shook her head. "I'm not even going to ask how many of these stories are true. Instead let's return to plans for our spa day—it's safer. Let us know when you're feeling stronger, and I'll book a date."

Greg eased himself away from the wall where he'd been leaning. "Jenna needs to keep things quiet for a while."

"Greg the dragon." Lauren smiled her approval. "Protector of my sister."

"Don't ask me to draw a dragon," Jenna said.

Pain nagged at her side and she shifted slightly to make herself more comfortable.

Greg frowned. "Do you want meds?"

"No, but thank you." She loved the fact he was so protective. For a short time they'd lost that closeness and now it was back. Love could be intense and passionate, but it could also be warming and comforting, like curling up in front of a log fire with a mug of hot chocolate.

She glanced at her sister. "So when do you move in to the Sail Loft?"

"Next week. We need time for the smell of paint to fade."

"I can't believe it's the middle of May already." It felt strange to think of them living there. "Will you be okay, Mom?"

"Yes. I have my final book group at The Captain's House the night before we move out. After that, someone else will have to host it if the group is to continue." Nancy stood up and walked to the window. "I've been in charge of canapés and conversation for far too long." She gazed down into Jenna's garden.

"You're going to miss having Alice for a neighbor. She's been such a great friend to you. Still, it's not as if you're leaving the island," Jenna said. "It's going to be a big change for you, Mom."

Was this change going to be too much? Impossibly hard?

Nancy turned. "Sometimes change can be good. Out with the old and in with the new—that's what I say."

Jenna gaped at her. "You don't say that at all! You always say, 'Let's store it for now. You never know when you might need it.'"

"I never liked throwing anything away, but it turns out I have a skill for it. I can be ruthless when I need to be."

Jenna exchanged looks with Lauren. "I think I might have banged my head harder than I first thought. I could have sworn I heard Mom say she likes throwing things away."

Lauren stretched her legs out and lay back next to Jenna. "I suspect she might have banged her head and none of us noticed. I don't want to panic you, but she also took the entire contents of Dad's hobby room to the Goodwill store."

Jenna wanted to cheer.

Instead she glanced at Greg. "Honey, could you please explain to us less qualified mortals what is happening to my mother?"

"No idea. I've given up presenting myself an expert on emotions. And if you're going to be planning spa days, I'm going to need more coffee." He kissed Jenna and walked to the kitchen.

Jenna watched him go. Then she caught her mother's eye. She thought about that conversation in the hospital, and how her mother had listened. "Before you say anything, I know I'm lucky to have him."

"I was going to say that he's lucky to have you," Nancy said. "Now, about this spa day. What exactly do they do during a facial? It isn't Botox, is it? I don't think I'd like Botox. I want my face to move."

CHAPTER THIRTY-ONE

Nancy

*Confide: to disclose secret or personal matters
in confidence*

THE NIGHT BEFORE she moved out of The Captain's House, Nancy held her last meeting of the book group.

Whether or not it continued would be up to other people, she thought, as she set up in the garden room. She always loved the garden in May, and this room offered the best view.

From next week the house would be the summer retreat for the Brown family who lived in Manhattan on the Upper East Side. They'd taken it for the whole summer, from Memorial Day to Labor Day, at a cost that had made Nancy gasp aloud. She never would have believed it had the money not already been in her account.

Lauren had handled the negotiation. If it had been up to

Nancy she would have asked a lower price, but Lauren had studied the market carefully.

"It doesn't surprise me," Jenna had said when Nancy had mentioned Lauren's sales skills. "You should have seen how persuasive she was whenever she wanted me to do something we weren't supposed to do."

So the deal was done, and this would be her last night in the house until the winter.

Nancy poked at her emotions carefully, searching for tender places. Sadness? No. She felt nothing. No regret. No guilt for letting her ancestors down.

Instead she felt pride at what they'd achieved, and not only because they'd done it on a shoestring budget. What really made her proud was the teamwork. They'd combined their skills. Who would have thought that at her age she'd be going into business with her daughter? That was something she hadn't anticipated.

Lauren Stewart. Nancy Stewart.

Coastal Chic.

The garden room was a perfect example of the design style they hoped would become their trademark and now it was all ready for her group. Three bottles of white wine were chilling in the fridge and Jenna was in the kitchen making canapés while Mack worked on her laptop at the kitchen table.

Nancy plumped a couple of cushions and decided not to admit that she'd abandoned tonight's book halfway through. It hadn't been her selection, and she'd known immediately that she was going to hate it. The book had hit all the bestseller lists, but she'd chosen to avoid it because of the subject matter. As she was going to be forced to endure a discussion about it, she decided she should at least read a few chapters, and reading it had made her feel every bit as uncomfortable and unhappy as she'd anticipated. It was about the decline of a marriage, and she'd empathized closely with the heroine. The book had felt too much like real life for the reading experience to be described as enjoyable, not that she was about to admit that to anyone in her group because none of these women knew anything about the reality of her life with Tom.

Tonight, she'd let others do the talking.

Mary-Beth arrived first, armed with a bottle of wine and a notepad covered in her sprawling handwriting. "Wasn't sure about this book—" She dropped her bag on the floor, put her notepad on the table and handed Nancy the wine.

Nancy was about to agree when the rest of her friends walked into the room.

"Your daughter let us in. Lauren." Sophie kissed Nancy and then Mary-Beth. "She hasn't changed since she was eighteen."

Nancy suspected her daughter had changed a great deal. Being a widow tended to do that, particularly when there were unresolved issues.

One of the reasons she'd been so angry that Tom had died in that car was that she'd been deprived of the opportunity to tell him what she thought of his lying, cheating ways.

She'd visited his grave a few times recently and told him what she thought of him, although she had at least checked no one was within earshot. She'd found the experience therapeutic. Maybe it was because he no longer responded with lies and excuses. She had her say and he was forced to lie there and listen.

"I confess I didn't love the book." Margie selected a chair by the window. "The heroine was a doormat."

She'd been a doormat, Nancy realized. She'd allowed Tom to behave the way he had. She'd enabled him.

"I agree." Sophie took the glass of wine Nancy handed her. "She should have kicked him out and changed the locks."

Yes, that would have been a good plan.

Nancy imagined herself doing it, maybe swinging one of his precious golf clubs instead of her foot.

Goodbye, Tom. Have a nice life.

Jenna walked in, carrying the canapés. The bruise on her head was still visible if you looked closely, but other than that she seemed back to her old self.

She put the plates down on the low table to a chorus of appreciative gasps.

"Well look at that—" Mary-Beth leaned forward to examine the contents of the plates more closely "—it's art on a plate. How did you make the pastry look like a seashell?"

"Trade secret." Jenna handed out napkins and Nancy helped herself to a canapé, agreeing that the food was indeed art on a plate.

She'd always thought Jenna was 100 percent Tom's child, but now she realized she'd been wrong about that. She'd inherited his warmth, that was true, but she also had Nancy's creativity and appreciation of the visual.

Why had it taken her this long to truly know her daughter? The acid burn of regret over the past was soothed by the balm of the present and the future.

It was never too late to move forward.

She thought about Ben, and smiled. It definitely wasn't too late.

"I don't agree with you about the heroine." Angela helped herself to a pastry seashell. "She did it to protect her daughter. And kicking someone out isn't the only valid response to infidelity. She loved him, so she forgave. You need forgiveness in a marriage. Being able to forgive doesn't make her a doormat."

Mary-Beth pulled a face. "You also need respect. Where was that? It was missing. And speaking of things that are missing, where's Alice?"

"She couldn't make it." Nancy studied the plate of canapés. Bacon or shrimp?

"Alice has never missed a book group. Is she ill?"

Nancy settled for shrimp. "I don't think so."

Mary-Beth reached into her bag for her reading glasses. "Maybe she felt bad because she hadn't read the book."

Margie shook her head. "What's that got to do with anything? Alice comes for the gossip and the company."

Nancy was fairly sure the reason Alice hadn't joined them was because she *had* read the book.

She caught Lauren's puzzled glance but nothing more was said on the subject until everyone had left and the four Stewart women were clearing up.

Mack's approach to clearing up was to eat the rest of the canapés. "They won't keep," she mumbled, brushing crumbs of buttery pastry from the corner of her mouth.

Jenna took the plate from her. "They won't keep with you in the house, that's for sure."

"I'm a starving teenager." Mack grabbed the last one and Nancy carried the empty plates into the kitchen.

"What's going on with Alice, Mom?" Lauren took the plates from her and stacked the dishwasher. "Should we call? Go over there and check on her?"

"No. Don't do that."

"Do you know what's wrong?"

How was she supposed to answer that?

The simplest thing was not to.

"I need to finish clearing up—" She turned to walk out of the kitchen but Lauren caught her arm.

"Are you upset? Has something happened?"

"No. Not in the way you mean. I can't—" Nancy paused, torn by loyalty to an old friendship and concern for her girls. "It's something I'm not able to discuss with you. It wouldn't be fair."

"Fair?" Jenna blocked the doorway. "Fair on you or fair on us?"

Lauren frowned. "Or fair on Alice?"

Nancy foundered. "It's complicated."

"So you *do* know the reason Alice wasn't here tonight?"

"Yes, I think I do." Nancy picked up a cloth and started wiping down surfaces.

"Leave the cleaning." Lauren took the cloth from her and put it on the countertop.

"We said no more secrets," Jenna said. "Whatever it is that's bothering you, we'll handle it. And we won't mention it to Alice, if that's what's worrying you. Why didn't she come tonight? Is it something to do with your leaving The Captain's House?"

"No. I'm sure it was because she didn't like the book."

"How do you know she didn't like it?"

Oh, Alice, Alice. "Because the book was about infidelity."

Jenna opened the fridge and stowed a half-empty bottle of wine. "What does that have to do with Alice?"

Everything.

And it felt overwhelming. The emotion, the indecision, the heartache, it all felt like too much to contain.

"I'm guessing she found the subject matter uncomfortable."

"Alice has a thing about infidelity?"

"Not exactly." Nancy picked up the cloth again and twisted it in her hands. "Alice was having an affair with Tom. I suspect she was the one you saw him with in the Sail Loft that night."

CHAPTER THIRTY-TWO

Lauren

> *Setback: something that reverses progress,*
> *hinders, or thwarts*

LAUREN WALKED OUT of the bank and kept her head down.
She was grateful that the bright sun gave her an excuse to
slip on dark glasses. As long as no one spoke to her, she'd be
all right. All she had to do was put one foot in front of the
other and walk back to her car. Keep moving. It wasn't as
if she hadn't had practice. Wasn't that what the past months
had been about?

Thirty more steps to the car, that was all.

"Lauren!"

The voice came from behind her. She wanted to ignore
it, but good manners forbade it, so she stopped and turned,
grateful that her eyes were shielded.

"Alice. How are you?" She wasn't in the mood to speak to anyone. She particularly didn't want to speak to Alice.

After her mother's revelation, she had no idea what to say to her.

You were supposed to be my mother's best friend.

But she understood the guilt her mother had felt in telling them and her concern that it shouldn't affect Lauren and Jenna's relationship with Alice, so she made a supreme effort to act normally.

"You've moved out of The Captain's House," Alice said.

"A few weeks ago." It was already June. How had that happened?

"Your mom must have been so busy with it all she forgot to say a proper goodbye."

Lauren thought it more likely that her mother hadn't yet decided how to handle the situation.

How *did* you handle a situation like that?

"She's only moved a few miles away," she said. "It's not as if she's left the island."

"It must be hard for you all living in such cramped space after having so much room."

"It isn't," Lauren said. "We're all enjoying being close to the beach."

She'd been surprised by how comfortable Nancy seemed in the Sail Loft. Her mother had undergone something of a transformation over the past few weeks. Her clearing out had extended to her closet and she'd thrown out all the drab clothes she'd been wearing for the last decade. In a storage bag she'd discovered clothes she'd bought years before on trips to Europe and worn for the openings of her exhibitions and for city tours. Her old look became her new look. Instead of blacks and grays, she wore white and teamed it with flowing scarves in bright jewel colors. There was a Pucci silk she'd picked up in Florence, and a Chanel jacket from Paris. Bold silver bangles decorated her wrists and Lauren noticed that she'd taken to wearing a touch of discreet makeup.

"You look like an artist," Jenna had said when she and Greg had visited on their first night there. "I hope you're not going to wear that to paint someone's house. It's asking for trouble. If you don't believe me you need to read *My Sister's Adventures with Paint*."

Lauren and Jenna had both agreed that something was going on between Nancy and Ben.

The two of them were often together in the garden of the Sail Loft, heads together as they studied something.

Nancy had laughed off their comments on her appearance.

"I decided that if I'm going into business with my daughter I need to upgrade my look."

If I'm going into business with my daughter.

Lauren blinked. "I have to go, Alice."

"I'll visit soon." There was a note of desperation in Alice's voice. "Tell Nancy to call. I'm going to miss squeezing through that gap in the fence. We've been doing that since we were four years old."

"I know."

Years of friendship. One betrayal.

Lauren had no idea what she would have done in her mother's position, or whether she would have been able to hold on to that particular secret for so many years.

Nancy had told them that she'd suspected for a long time, but hadn't been sure until that day she and Alice had visited the Sail Loft.

"It's the reason I took her," Nancy had confessed one night as they'd all shared a bottle of wine. "I wanted to see her reaction. I needed to know for sure."

And now she knew.

"I heard you're starting your own business." Alice wasn't in a hurry to let Lauren leave.

"Yes. It's all very exciting." And frustrating. And impossible. Why had she thought anyone would give her a loan? She was a terrible risk.

"I heard from Mary-Beth that you even have your first client."

"Yes."

Miranda Hillyard, a lawyer from Boston who had moved to the Vineyard permanently a few years earlier, and was in the process of renovating a $8.8 million waterfront home near Chilmark. She'd happened to be walking her dog along the beach path one day when Lauren had been painting pallets to use as nightstands.

Miranda had stopped to talk. Within minutes, Lauren had found herself showing her round the Sail Loft. Miranda had fired questions at her and later, when Lauren had typed her name into a search engine, she'd seen that Miranda had a terrifying reputation as the lawyer who never lost a case. It was easy to see why. She was nothing if not persuasive and when Miranda had asked to see The Captain's House, Lauren had agreed. She was proud of what they'd achieved there, although she'd kept details of the budget to herself. Turned out she was the queen of recycling and repurposing, but that didn't mean she wanted to do that with every job.

Finally, after Lauren had bitten her nails to the quick, the woman had called and asked Lauren to come and look round her house and give an opinion.

Lauren had spent half a day with her, walking through the place room by room, absorbing Miranda's vision for the place and translating that into ideas. It had been exciting to think about decor without first thinking about whether they could afford to do it. Miranda was wealthy and had big plans.

Lauren had left with her first client and a major problem.

The Hillyard project promised to be huge and Lauren had no capital with which to fund her new business.

Her mother couldn't contribute because she needed all the rental money from The Captain's House to get through the winter.

If Miranda had been more approachable, maybe Lauren could have discussed it with her, but the other woman was so terrifyingly competent, Lauren didn't want to reveal the horrible mess that was her life.

She'd worked into the night drawing up business plans and Mack had helped her produce a professional-looking document, but it hadn't been enough to satisfy the bank who had turned down her request for a loan. Although she was deeply disappointed, she could hardly blame them. She had no collateral and no business track record. Given the facts, she probably wouldn't have loaned herself money either. They'd suggested she talk to her mother about either loaning her the money or acting as guarantor, but Lauren knew neither was an option.

She was going to have to call Miranda back and say she couldn't take on the project.

That was a call she was dreading on so many levels.

"I should go, Alice." She turned away, holding back the emotion that threatened a serious assault on her dignity.

The sun was hot and the streets were noticeably busier.

The island smelled of summer. The thick scent of colorful blooms mingled with the smell of sunscreen. Summer on the Vineyard meant the shrieks of happy children, strawberries piled like jewels in the farmer's market, the slow drip of ice cream melting in the heat. It meant cooling dips in the sea, a barefoot run on the beach with a salt breeze cooling your face. It meant sitting on the harbor's edge eating lobster claws while butter dripped down your chin.

There was a buzz in the air and an energy that was absent in the winter. The population of the island exploded and people moved at a slow summer pace. The locals would mutter and complain and some would secretly wish for the season to be over, but Lauren didn't wish that.

The Captain's House had been rented for the whole summer right through until Labor Day and the amount they were earning would enable her mother to stay in it for the winter.

The place wasn't going to be sold. It was still the Stewart residence, as it had been for well over a century.

She would have felt hopeful for the future, if it weren't for the meeting she'd had at the bank and the phone call she'd had the night before from London.

What was she going to do if she couldn't get her business off the ground?

Blinded by the combination of dark glasses and misted vision, she walked slap into someone.

Strong hands clamped her shoulders to steady her and she muttered an apology.

Instead of releasing her, those hands tightened.

"What's the rush?"

Scott.

Of all the people she didn't want to bump into right now he was probably top of the list.

"Sorry. I wasn't looking where I was going."

Since that day at the Sail Loft, she'd carefully avoided him, timing her visits so they weren't ever alone together. Every time she thought about that evening in the kitchen she felt remorse, and not only because she'd been having wild, abandoned sex while her sister was trapped in her car in a ditch. She knew that by allowing herself to get close to Scott again, she'd opened a door that was going to be hard to close. The realization that she wanted him badly was as frustrating as it was unsettling. Not only was it the wrong time, but he was also the wrong person. She was smart enough to know that Scott had an effect on her that no other man did. That hadn't changed, but neither had he and she wasn't going to allow herself to believe differently.

"How's Jenna doing?"

"She's good, thanks. Almost back to her normal self."

"And you?" His voice was low and intimate and stirred memories she didn't want in her head.

"I'm good, too. We've moved in to the Sail Loft. The kitchen is great. The countertops are—" She gasped as he lifted his hand and gently removed her glasses. "What are you doing?" She snatched at them but he held them out of reach with one hand and cupped her face with the other.

He angled his head and studied her, his gaze searching. "What's wrong?"

"Nothing. Can I have my glasses back?"

"Not until you tell me why you're upset."

She was conscious of her reddened eyes and the flow of people who passed them. "Scott, please—we're in a public place."

"Then we'll go somewhere less public. I'm parked across

the street." He slid her glasses back onto her nose and took her hand. "Come with me."

"People will talk."

"Yeah, they have a tendency to do that. Doesn't mean you have to listen." He tightened his grip on her hand and led her to his truck.

Too despondent to argue, she slid inside.

She'd be okay. This was a setback, that was all, and she'd become an expert on dealing with setbacks. Fall over, get up again. She hoped her thigh muscles were strong enough to take it.

She heard a panting sound behind her and turned her head to find Captain wagging his tail so hard it smacked against the back of the seat.

It was impossible not to smile. "Your dog is adorable."

"Yeah, he's a keeper." Scott slid into the driver's seat and pulled out of the parking space. "No one can resist him."

And she'd never been able to resist Scott.

She shouldn't have climbed into a car with him. That had been a mistake, but it was too late to do anything about it now.

No matter how bad she felt, she wasn't about to throw herself from a moving vehicle.

She found a tissue and blew her nose. "I'm being stupid."

"I doubt that." He took the road out of town. "Start by telling me why you're all dressed up in your smart London clothes."

"I had a meeting at the bank."

He frowned. "They made you cry?"

"I wasn't crying."

"You couldn't see where you were going."

"I had things on my mind, that's all."

He said nothing else until they reached the boatyard.

He parked the car and killed the engine. "Tell me what's on your mind. I want to know."

She remembered the first time she'd confided in him and the way he'd sat so still and attentive as he'd listened carefully to everything she'd said. No one had ever listened to her like that before. And she remembered the first time he'd kissed her. It had felt as if someone had lit a firework inside her. That feeling had burned up all her doubts, her hang-ups and her inhibitions.

She stared out over the water, watching people come and go. "It's busy. I hadn't realized the business had grown so much."

"Tell me what happened at the bank."

"They won't give me a loan. Without the loan I can't start my business, and it's frustrating because I even have my first client ready and waiting. Do you know Miranda Hill-yard? She wants me to work on her beach house."

"I know the place. That would be a pretty big project."

"Beyond my wildest dreams. Unfortunately the bank thought my dreams were a little too wild."

Scott tapped his fingers on the wheel. "Did you tell them you had a potential client?"

"Yes, but I have no track record and no collateral. I don't blame them really. I wouldn't lend me money either. I'm as upset for the others as I am for myself. We've all contributed something and Mom was going to help me with the design elements. She's excited about it. The last few months we've all had a common purpose. And the best thing is that it was doing something I've always wanted to do." She tried to explain. "Ed was always the one who earned the money and I stayed home with Mack, but I'd reached the stage where

I was ready to work and do something for myself. Finally I got the qualification I needed and it felt like a new phase. I'd already made plans to set up my own business back in London."

"You always had a glossy magazine in your hand, usually covered in pen marks to show what you'd do differently."

She was surprised. "You remember that?"

"I remember all of it."

So did she.

"Ed died and the 'new phase' turned out to be something I hadn't planned for. And then it seemed that maybe I might get to live out that dream after all. It almost makes it harder to handle this time because it was snatched away at the last minute." She closed her eyes, embarrassed. "Sorry."

"Why are you sorry? When life is hard sometimes all you have to keep you going is dreams, and yours have been crushed. You have a right to be disappointed and upset."

That was how she felt. Crushed. First by the phone call from James and then by the meeting at the bank. "Life doesn't turn out the way you plan, does it?"

"Rarely, but in this case it can. How much do you need?"

"Excuse me?"

"Money. How much?"

She'd run the numbers so many times, she knew the answer without looking. And then she realized he wasn't asking the question out of interest. "I don't want your money, Scott."

"Why?"

"Because I need to do this by myself."

"You want to make life as tough as possible, is that it? If you land with your face in a puddle of water be sure to inhale?"

"I can't take your money. And you shouldn't be offering. I'm a risk. If you don't believe me, ask the bank."

"The bank has boxes to tick. I don't. You have a talent and skills that are going to be in demand. The way I see it I'd be making an investment."

"Don't talk to me about investments. It was Ed's investment business that got me in this mess." She pulled another tissue out of her bag and blew her nose. "I had a call yesterday from the executor of Ed's estate. He's a friend."

"And?"

"It's all finished. The bank has repossessed the house, the cars have been sent back to the lease hire companies and the furniture has been sold." There were times when it felt surreal, as if it was happening to someone else. "It's as if that life I had in London never existed."

Scott covered her hand with his. "That's tough."

"I knew it was going to happen, so I don't understand why that call made me feel so bad. I suppose it was a sharp reminder of reality." She should probably pull her hand away, but she couldn't bring herself to. "And a reminder that I was foolish. I trusted Ed. I should have looked more closely at the financial aspect of our lives."

"It's not foolish to trust someone you love, Laurie."

"What did I do to make him think he couldn't tell me? We were supposed to be a team." She sniffed. "I can't believe I'm discussing my marriage with you. Doesn't it bother you, talking about Ed?"

There was a pause. "Honestly? It makes me want to break something."

She gave a shocked laugh. "I'm sorry. I'll stop."

"Don't. Whatever else we were, we were always friends. I hope we still are. You were telling me about your finances."

"Things could be worse. James said we narrowly missed having to make the estate insolvent. We owned some artwork that did well at auction. Because of that, I have money coming to me. A sum total of £1,655. By the time I've paid Jenna back for the flights, I reckon Mack and I can treat ourselves to a small ice cream."

Scott's hand tightened on hers. "No wonder you're upset."

She gave a watery smile. "At least I'm not bankrupt, right? Still, it wasn't enough to make the bank believe in me."

"I have money, Laurie, and I believe in you."

"Oh, Scott—" She felt as if someone was squeezing her heart. "Don't."

"Don't what?"

"Don't give me sympathy."

"I'm not giving you sympathy. I'm giving you money. Or I'm trying to."

She blew her nose again. "I can't take your money, Scott. And you shouldn't be offering."

"How I spend it is my decision."

"I'm looking out for you, that's all. You'll need every cent to fund yourself next time you decide to sail into the sunset."

"You still believe I'm going to sail into the sunset?" There was an edge to his tone that hadn't been there earlier.

"I know you, that's all."

"If that's what you think, then you don't know me." He removed his hand from hers. "You see what you want to see. I hurt you, and you can't see beyond that."

She turned her head. "What's that supposed to mean?"

"Sixteen years is a long time. People change. I've changed."

"But you don't want responsibility. You never have."

There was a pause as he drew in a slow breath. "How

do you think I have built up the capital to make an offer on The Captain's House? You haven't asked me where I got the money."

"Capital?" She swallowed. "I assumed you were taking out a big loan. Is Charlie helping you? I'm sure he's a generous boss."

He rubbed his hand over his jaw and gave her an exasperated look. "Charlie's not the boss, Laurie, I am."

She stared at him. "I don't understand."

"I'm the boss. I own the business. Joshua sold it to me a long time ago."

"You *own* it? But what about Charlie?"

"Charlie didn't want the responsibility."

"But neither do you!" She was confused. None of it made sense.

His jaw tightened. "You don't know what I want. You haven't asked me."

"But if that's true, why didn't you say something before now?"

"I don't know. I don't find these things easy to talk about. I guess I was hoping you'd see it for yourself."

She'd been blind. Self-absorbed. "You sailed round the world—"

"You left," he said flatly. "It seemed like the best option at the time."

She couldn't breathe. "Are you saying you sailed round the world *because of me*?"

"Being here without you drove me crazy. And sailing was always what I did to escape from problems." He gave a humorless smile. "Except that in this case I was the problem, so I took it right along with me. Maybe I should have thrown myself overboard."

She didn't laugh. How could she have gotten it so wrong? "So you came back?"

"Having no roots didn't seem to work, so I thought I'd try something different. Living on the boat was my compromise. I slept at sea and worked on land. The only thing I knew was boats so I figured that was what I should do. Joshua let me use the boatyard, and I built a racing yacht. She was fast. Sold her to some guy from California with more money than sense. Then I built another one. When I wasn't busy, I helped out at the boatyard. And then Joshua had his first stroke. Charlie spent most of his time with his mother or at the hospital. I took over the boatyard for him until he was back on his feet, but when he recovered enough to make the decision, he decided he was done with it. He asked me to take over."

She was stunned. How could she not have known this? "The business is doing well?"

"Yes. We have workboats, trucks and a couple of hydraulic trailers. We have customers on the cape and the islands. It's not easy finding and keeping skilled staff, but we've managed it. And living on the water, my outgoings have been low. So, I'll say this again—let me give you the money. If it makes you feel better we can call it child support. You've raised our daughter for the last sixteen years with no help from me."

Our daughter.

"She wasn't your responsibility."

"She should have been." His tone was rough. "I had no trouble walking away from relationships, Lauren. It was something I was good at. I didn't have any regrets either. Until I walked away from you."

It felt as if there was a lump in her chest. "Scott—"

"I can't fix what happened in the past, but I can fix this. Say yes, Laurie. You're smart. Smart people know when to accept help." He breathed deeply. "Take the money."

"I—can't. It doesn't feel right."

He swore under his breath. "You were mad at me for not stepping up, and I don't blame you for that. But now I *am* stepping up and you won't you let me. I should have done this years ago, I know that. That day on the beach when you told me you were pregnant I should have kissed you and put a ring on your finger the way he did. I should have been the one to give you that safety and security. I should have been there for you, but I wasn't and I have to live with the knowledge that I messed up badly. And I paid the price for that decision, every time I thought of you with Ed. Laughing with Ed." His voice thickened and his hand curled into a fist. "Sharing secrets with Ed. Sharing our daughter with Ed." The way he said it made it sound as if he was chewing on ground glass. "I've learned to live with that, but what I can't live with is the knowledge that you're struggling now and you won't let me help you."

"You thought about me with Ed?"

"Every damn day." He turned to her. "You think I sailed into the sunset and forgot about you? It didn't matter where I was, you were still there with me along with the knowledge that I screwed up the most important decision of my life."

She couldn't breathe. "Scott—"

He reached out and slid his hand behind her head. "Nothing is going to erase the guilt I feel for not being there for you then, but at least let me do this for you now." His voice was raw pain and she looked into his eyes, as rocked by emotion as he was.

Life with Ed had been simple and easy. If she'd had to

find a word to describe their marriage she would have said *content*. There was none of the wild seesawing of feelings she experienced with Scott. None of the highs, but none of the lows either.

"I didn't know," she said. "I assumed—"

"You assumed I was the same person I was seventeen years ago, but I can tell you that screwing up the most important decision of your life does tend to shake a person up."

"I loved you." The words didn't begin to describe the depth and intensity of her feelings.

He rested his forehead against hers. "I loved you, too. I loved you so much I didn't know what to do with all those feelings."

Her cheeks were wet with tears. "I kept hoping you'd wake up one morning and realize you'd make a great father. Better than most because you'd lived alongside so many examples of bad parenting. I kept watching the harbor, hoping to see your boat. Hoping you'd change your mind."

There was a long silence.

She could hear him breathing and see the indecision in his eyes.

"Scott?"

He released her suddenly and leaned his head back against the seat. "I did, but by then it was too late. You were already with Ed."

"What do you mean?"

"Two weeks after you told me you were pregnant, I came back. I intended to talk to you, to see if we could find a way to make it work, although I don't know what the hell I thought would happen. Fatherhood isn't exactly something you try on for size and if it doesn't fit you get to give it back."

"You came back, but you didn't come and find me?"

"I did." His voice was thick. "You were on the beach with Ed."

She tried to remember, but those early days after Scott had left had been a blur. What had he seen? What had he thought? "Why didn't you come and talk to me?"

"Because the two of you were holding hands and someone nearby said wasn't it romantic because it had been such a whirlwind. By the time I'd worked out what I wanted, it was too late."

She felt a rush of despair. She hadn't been holding hands with Ed, as much as clinging. She'd been drowning, and he'd been the only solid thing within reach. "So you decided on the strength of that one glimpse not to even let me know you'd had a change of heart?"

"You'd already agreed to marry Ed. I assumed you were in love with him."

"I was in love with *you*. How could you have thought that would change?"

He stared straight ahead. "I guess I got used to people leaving. Not wanting me. My birth mother, and all the foster families I lived with afterward. My whole life, all I saw was people changing their minds about me. I didn't know what permanence was. I didn't know what commitment was. I did know it was a hell of a lot easier to walk away than to stay. When I saw that you'd moved on, I guess in a way it was what I'd expected."

She lifted her hand to her throat, finding it hard to breathe. *He'd come back. He'd changed his mind.* "I hadn't moved on. I was right there."

"With him. And that was a good decision. And the fact that you didn't see me was probably for the best, too." He put his hand on the wheel and gripped it tightly even though they weren't going anywhere. "If you'd seen me that day, you might have walked away from Ed and that would have been the wrong thing to do."

"How can you say that?"

"Because you needed security. You deserved that. You would have been giving up a sure thing for a bad risk."

She saw the tension in his shoulders.

"You weren't a bad risk. We could have—"

"No." He pressed his fingers to his forehead and shook his head. "We're not doing this. We will never know how that would have turned out and there's no point in guessing. If I'd stayed, I might still have messed it up. Mack had stability. You gave her that. We're going to accept that and move forward. I want to lend you money. I want you to take it."

How could she say no? How could she possibly say no when there was so much emotion behind the gesture?

"I'll take it." She choked out the words. "Thank you."

"There's something else I want."

Her heart kicked against her ribs. "Scott—"

"Not that." His gaze dropped to her mouth. "At least, not yet. I want to be part of Mack's life. I want to play a proper role. I want to share her with you. I want to be there for the bad bits and the good bits."

She managed a laugh. "Are you sure? Be prepared to have your heart ripped open on a regular basis."

A shadow crossed his face. "I've had practice."

"We'll have to talk to her about it—"

"Could we do that together?" He sounded unsure and she felt her heart break all over again.

Rejection was all he'd known.

"Whatever happened to sailing the world in your boat, relishing having no ties or responsibilities?"

"Some ties are good."

Did he mean that? And would he still mean it in a week or a month?

Ignoring the questions in her head, she leaned in and wrapped her arms round him. "I didn't know you came back. I can't bear that you thought I rejected you." She buried her face in his shoulder and he cursed softly.

"Don't cry." He cupped her face in his hands. "I hate it when you cry."

"I can't bear the thought of you torturing yourself imagining me with Ed."

"I'm glad you had a good relationship. A good marriage. I mean that. I wanted only the best for you. It's what you deserved. It's what you still deserve."

His generosity humbled her. "I loved him, but I loved you, too."

"I know." He brushed her tears away with his thumbs. "I wish this hadn't happened to you."

She'd wished that, too, but of course if it hadn't happened she wouldn't be here now, with Scott. She was so confused it hurt.

He lowered his head and kissed her. What began as a gentle, exploratory kiss soon turned hotter and more demanding. She lost awareness of her surroundings. There was only the thrum of blood in her ears and the heat of his mouth on hers. It was a kiss filled with regret, hope, love and promise.

Rocked by emotion, she wrapped her arms round his neck and wriggled closer.

They were so absorbed by each other neither of them heard the car door open.

Through a mist of head-spinning desire Lauren heard Mack's voice, shrill and shocked.

"Mom? Scott?"

Startled, Lauren jumped away from Scott and turned to face her daughter.

How could she possibly be here? Why wasn't she at school? How long had she and Scott been sitting in the car talking?

"You're—" Mack choked out the word. "Ed just *died*, Mom. You loved Ed. How can you kiss another man? It's disgusting. And you, too—" She glared at Scott. "You made me trust you. You made me *like* you! And the whole time you were using me as a way of getting back into my mom's pants. I hate you. I truly hate you." She turned away, stumbling over her bike and almost falling. It took two attempts but finally she climbed onto it and cycled away at a furious speed.

Lauren felt physically sick. Finally, after so many long difficult months, their relationship had reached a new place. And it had been a good place.

And now this.

Scott looked white and shaken. "She hates me."

"She doesn't hate you," Lauren said. A terrible weariness descended on her.

"You heard her. She said—"

"That's a teenage thing."

"Hating?"

"Using words like stones."

"She said I was using her to get into your pants. What you and I have—that's separate. I wanted her to trust me.

I wanted her to like me. Not because of you, but because she's my daughter."

"I know. You need to not pay too much attention to what she said."

"What? How?" There was a sheen of sweat on his brow. "That's a terrible accusation and she is wrong."

"Teenagers say that kind of thing sometimes. *I hate you. No one loves me. I hate my life.* She doesn't hate you. That's not what's going on here."

He ran his hand over his face. "How do you deal with it?"

"I lie awake at night anxious. Long after she has forgotten it, I'm still worrying about it."

Scott shook his head in disbelief. "So what are we supposed to do? I need to tell her she's wrong."

"Let me talk to her first." Lauren fastened her seat belt, her hands shaking. "Can you drive me home?"

"Shouldn't we talk to her together?"

"Scott, she saw me kissing you. Talking to her together would be the worst thing we could do right now. She's feeling vulnerable and isolated. She feels as if I've betrayed her. And Ed."

His gaze met hers. "I was the one who kissed you."

"That makes no difference."

"What are you going to say to her? You can't tell her there's nothing between us, Laurie, because that wouldn't be true."

"She isn't ready to deal with the idea of me diving into a new relationship. I'm not ready for it either!" What had she been thinking?

"This isn't a new relationship. I'm her father, Lauren. It can hardly come as a surprise to her that we have feelings for each other."

What *were* her feelings? She didn't even know. "What we feel doesn't matter. She isn't going to be able to handle it."

"Wait—" his voice sounded hoarse "—you're saying you're never going to have another relationship in case it upsets our daughter?"

"Eventually, maybe, one day—" she faltered. "I don't know. I don't know what I'm saying. I feel guilty and confused and right now like a seriously bad person. I can't see you again, Scott. I mean, of course I'll *see* you—this is a small island—but I can't—we shouldn't—not like this—"

Of all the things she'd thought about over the past six months, plunging into another relationship hadn't even been on the list. But he was right of course. This relationship wasn't new. Feelings had been stored deep, lain dormant, but they were still there. There was a deep, unshakable connection between them that was impossible to ignore.

She'd been worried she might fall in love with him again, but she realized now that she'd never fallen out of love.

She knew exactly what her feelings were and the reality filled her with despair.

He clearly felt the same way. "So that's it? This is it?"

She was trembling.

"I guess it is." She'd let him go once before and that had been hard. How much harder was it going to be this time? "It has to be."

CHAPTER THIRTY-THREE

Mack

Contrite: full of guilt or regret; remorseful

MACK ABANDONED HER bike in the garden of the Sail Loft and ran through to her bedroom, slamming the door behind her.

She flung herself down on the bed and sobbed.

She was crying so hard she didn't hear the door open, but she did feel the bed dip as her grandmother sat down next to her.

"Go away," Mack hiccupped. "I want to be on my own."

"Is that really what you want? Personally I hate being on my own when I'm upset. Every time I discovered another of your grandfather's affairs I used to lock myself away, when what I needed to do was have a good vent with someone who loved me."

"No one loves me." Mack choked into her pillow. "I don't matter to anyone. I want Ed. I wish Ed hadn't died."

"Oh, honey—"

Mack felt her grandmother's hand on her head. Part of her wanted to push her away, but another part wanted to fling herself into her arms and be held.

"I wish we'd never come here. I want my old life back."

"Change is always hard, especially when it wasn't your choice. Do you want to tell me what happened?"

Mack discovered she did, and in halting, choppy bursts she told her grandmother about going to visit Scott after school and what she'd seen.

She'd expected to see her shock reflected in her grandmother's face, but Nancy didn't react the way she'd expected.

"You saw them kissing."

"It was more than a kiss. It was like one of those movie kisses where the people look desperate. Kiss or die, that kind of thing." She brushed the tears away from her eyes and stiffened defensively. "You look pleased. How can you be pleased?" Her voice rose. "No one understands. I hate everyone. I hate my mom, I hate Scott and most of all I hate my stupid life."

Instead of reacting to this dramatic announcement, Nancy patted the bed next to her.

"Sit up. It's time you and I had a talk."

"We're talking."

"No. You're sobbing into a pillow and giving me teenage drama, but I have no idea how to deal with teenage drama because I skipped that part of parenting, so I'm going to have to treat you as an adult. You did say you wanted to be treated like a grown-up, didn't you?"

Had she really said that?

Right now she wished she were back in kindergarten waiting for her mother to pick her up.

Mack hauled herself upright. Adult. Right. She wasn't feeling it, but she could probably fake it. "What do you want to talk about?"

She noticed that her grandmother was wearing another of her brightly colored scarves. This one was a swirl of turquoise and green. Mack wasn't used to seeing her so glamorous. Everything and everyone was changing round her.

"Why don't we start with your telling me why it upset you seeing your mom and Scott together."

Wasn't it obvious? "Dad just died! I mean Ed. Ed died. Mom was supposed to love him and now she's kissing some guy—"

"She was kissing Scott."

"Sure, Scott, but—"

"Scott who is, in fact, your father. A man she also loved very much."

"You can't love two people! That isn't how it works."

"Welcome to adulthood." Nancy's voice was loaded with sympathy. "It's messy, complicated, the pieces don't fit and the picture rarely looks the way you want it to. It's called real life."

"Real life sucks." *Oh yeah, very adult, Mack.*

"Quite often it does. And other times it's wonderful. Light and dark, like one of my paintings. Don't you like Scott?"

Mack sniffed. "Of course. He's cool. And he's a great listener, but that doesn't mean I want him and Mom to—you know…" She couldn't bring herself to say it. She couldn't work out what it would mean for her. In that car neither of them had been thinking of her, that was for sure. "I'd like

life to stay the same for five minutes. Is that so hard to understand?"

"No. I understand how you feel, but have you thought
about how your mother might feel?"

"About what?"

"Life. Your mother has gone through hell and back the
last few months. The man she spent more than sixteen years
with and loved very much—" Nancy raised her hand as
Mack opened her mouth "—yes, loved very much, died.
That's tragic and difficult, and the whole thing was made
even more difficult because of the mess he left. Your mother
had no cushion to protect her from that blow. She's been
weathering the anxiety of that alone, along with managing your grief and her own. She's been worried about how
she'll support the two of you, how she's going to give you a
good life, how she's going to fix things so that I don't have
to sell The Captain's House. She's been focused on her own
survival and on being a mother, a daughter and a sister. It's
about time she thought about being a woman."

"I get that, but it's like she's forgotten Ed." Fear made
Mack defensive. *She* hadn't forgotten him. She thought
about him all the time. She carried his photo with her, although that wasn't something she'd told anyone. What would
happen if her mom loved another man? Where would she
fit in that? She couldn't see, and that scared her. "It's like
he never existed."

"She hasn't forgotten him. She's trying to find a way of
living without him. Ed's gone." Nancy said it gently. "And
no matter how much we want things to be different, he isn't
coming back. Once a person is gone, they're gone. You can
wait six weeks, six months or six years but that isn't going
to change a thing. Your mom can waste years of her life

locked in a cycle of grief, looking backward as I did, or she can pick up those memories and carry them forward into a new life. I'm hoping that's what she'll do, and the sooner the better as far as I'm concerned. She's my child. No one wants their child to be unhappy. It's the reason she puts you first in everything. One day, when you have a child of your own, you'll understand that."

"She didn't seem to be thinking about me when I saw them together." Mack knew she sounded petulant and self-ish and felt a flush of embarrassment. "Sorry. I don't know what's wrong with me. This adult thing isn't as easy as it looks."

Nancy smiled. "I suspect that for that short time she wasn't thinking about you, but that doesn't mean she doesn't love you very much. She'll always be your mother. Nothing is going to change that fact."

"I won't stop talking about Ed. I'm not going to pretend he didn't exist."

"Of course you're not. You can talk to me about Ed any time. *All* the time, if that's what you'd like. And I'm sure you can do the same with your mom. She isn't trying to forget him, Mack. She isn't trying to push you out. She's trying to find a way to move forward and that's healthy. She deserves to be happy. You don't want her to be sad, do you?"

"No." Mack felt smaller than an ant. It wasn't that she wanted her mom to be *sad*, of course it wasn't. But nor did she want her life to be rocked by another major change. "I just— I felt as if I was losing my mom, too."

"Oh, Mack." Her grandmother wrapped her in a hug. "I don't know how your mother feels about Scott, but I do know how she feels about you. She loves you, and nothing is going to change that. As for Scott, let's assume for a moment that she loves him—maybe she never stopped loving him—that doesn't take anything away from what she felt for Ed. There are different types of love, and not every marriage looks alike, but that doesn't mean they're not real."

It felt confusing to her. Scary. "I'm not sure I can handle it."

"You will. People are capable of so much more than they think they are. It's possible to rekindle relationships you thought were lost, build a new life when the old one was dead, learn new habits, break old ones." She eased away from Mack. "It's possible to forgive a friend a grievous hurt."

Mack felt another flicker of guilt that she'd been only thinking about herself. "What are you going to do about that?" She wiped her eyes on her sleeve. "Are you going to kick Alice's butt?"

Her grandmother stirred. "What do you think I should do?"

Mack was surprised. No one ever asked her advice. No one asked her opinion. She thought about it hard before she answered.

"I guess it depends. I mean, Alice was your best friend, which kind of makes the betrayal worse—"

"That's it *exactly*."

Mack felt her confidence grow. "—but also it sounds like Gramps was—" She pulled a face. "Actually do you mind if we don't think about that part?"

"Not at all. I'd rather not think about it either, but you're right—he was. He had a way of dazzling the people around him."

"I know." Mack tucked her legs up and leaned back

against the pillows. "When he was in the room you kind of only noticed him."

"Yes. Alice had lost her husband. It was tragic. She was alone and vulnerable. I suspect, for her, it wasn't so much an affair, as a moment of madness. But there comes a point where you have to make a decision. You can carry anger and hurt round with you and keep stoking it and keeping it alive, or you can choose to let it go and build something new."

"Is that what you did with Gramps? I mean, you cleaned him out of your life like dust bunnies." She wondered if that was a tactless thing to say, but then she saw her grandmother smile.

"I did. And I said things I should have said years ago. Unfortunately he was too dead to hear them. But now that's done." She gave a burst of laughter and Mack looked at her anxiously.

"Are you okay, Grams?"

"Never better. Talking with you made me realize that I really have put it all behind me. Maybe it was all the clearing out. Maybe it was the yelling."

"Maybe it was Ben." Mack watched as her grandmother's cheeks turned pink.

"Ben?"

"Come on, Grams. I know you're really into him. And he's into you." She nudged her grandmother. "You should see your face. You're blushing."

Nancy put her hands on her burning cheeks. "It's been years since I blushed." She gave Mack a naughty look. "And years since I did other things."

Mack felt a flash of panic.

Teasing was one thing, but this— "It's okay," she said. "I don't need the details."

"Good, because I have no intention of giving you details." Her grandmother seemed almost playful and Mack decided it was definitely time to move the subject away from Ben.

"What are you going to do about Alice?"

"I'm going to talk to her. It's time we were honest. Secrets are like walls. They stop you getting close. If our friendship is going to endure and be something worth having, we need to break down those walls."

Mack pulled a face. "That's going to be awkward."

"Life is full of awkward, but this thing with Alice is like having a stone in my shoe. I can keep walking, but I know it's there. We can't move forward comfortably until it's out in the open, so that's what I'm going to do. I'm hoping we can start over. That's all you can do, isn't it? Give up or start over, and we Stewarts aren't good at giving up."

"That's brave. And forgiving." Mack felt something else was needed. Something grown-up and worthy of the conversation they'd been having. "I guess love is complicated." She couldn't even imagine it, but judging how so many adults made crazy decisions she had to believe it was true.

"It is complicated."

Mack relaxed. It was good to know that in the world of adult conversations, she wasn't a complete failure. "But it must be worth it, or people wouldn't keep doing it, right?"

"I suppose so."

Mack wondered if her grandmother was in love with Ben. "Do you think Mom is in love with Scott?"

"Why don't you ask her?"

"Because that would be awkward, too. Also, I've probably already messed it up." Now that the shock had faded, Mack wished she could turn the clock back and react differently. Why did her feelings always explode out of her?

She wished there was a pause button she could press to give herself time to think before reacting. "Scott is probably relieved I'm not his responsibility. After the way I yelled at him he's probably already planning his next sailing trip round the world to get away from me."

Although he was her biological father, he wasn't really tied to her in any way, was he?

He'd walked away once before. He could walk away again.

And after she'd been so rude, he probably would.

She thought about the sailing lessons and about Captain and the fun of helping out in the boatyard. She thought about how Scott had encouraged her to talk about Ed even though it must have been hard for him and how patient he'd been with her.

Her heart started to pound.

Tears stung her eyes. "She's going to tell him they can't be together because of me, isn't she?"

"Is that what you'd want?"

"No! I don't know. I don't know what I want. It's not like it's my choice." She didn't want to forget Ed, but nor did she want Scott to sail out of her life.

"That's where you're wrong. You've made excellent choices since you've been here. You settled into a new school, and you've grabbed opportunities that came your way. You joined the Coding Club. Because of that you found yourself some friends, a new passion, maybe even a future career."

She hadn't thought of it like that.

"I guess some things have turned out okay."

"How about I pour us both some lemonade?" Nancy

reached out a hand and pulled Mack to her feet. "We can sit outside in the garden."

Mack was sitting in the garden with delicious lemonade and one of Jenna's cookies when her mother arrived home.

The guilt returned with a rush.

Her grandmother was right about one thing. Her mom was always there for her. No matter how much Mack yelled or stomped off or said mean things. Her mom was always in her corner.

Mack noticed she had her "London look" about her. She wore tailored pants, a silk shirt and a simple gold necklace Mack recognized as one Ed had given her at Christmas.

She remembered her grandmother's words about how hard things had been for her mom since Ed died.

"Hi, Mom." She saw anxiety in her mother's eyes and felt guilty because she knew she was the one responsible.

"Hi, sweetheart."

The endearment almost cracked her heart open. "Grams made homemade lemonade. Do you want some? There's more in the fridge." She was going to do better, she promised herself. She was going to stop thinking about herself all the time. She wanted to start by saying sorry, but she didn't know where to begin. "I'll fetch you some."

"I'll fetch it," Nancy said, "but first tell me how your meeting with the bank went." She stood up and gestured to her chair. "Sit down. You look exhausted."

"The meeting with the bank didn't go so well," Lauren said and Mack noticed her mom's mascara was smudged.

"They said no?"

"Oh, those stupid people." Nancy sounded cross. "How long have the Stewarts lived on this island? I've a mind to call them up myself and give them my opinion."

"Don't. It isn't necessary."

Mack wondered how her mother could possibly think that. "Without the money, you can't start the business. And that business is your dream." Suddenly it mattered very much that her mom had a dream, too. "Maybe we could call Aunt Jenna. Four heads are good, right? We have to find another way."

"There is another way. Scott wants to loan us the money." The look she gave Mack was cautious, even a little nervous. "It's his way of stepping up and helping."

Nancy nodded approvingly. "I hope you said yes."

Lauren didn't answer right away. "Do you mind if I talk to Mack for a minute?"

Mack's heart sank. Her mom was going to lose it with her, and she deserved it. Was she going to tell her that Scott had been so appalled by her childish explosion he'd set sail to the Bahamas?

"I'll fetch that lemonade," Nancy said and Mack waited, miserable, as her grandmother vanished into the Sail Loft.

Her mother was twisting the ring on her finger. Ed's ring.

"Mack, there's something I need to—"

"Me first." Mack blurted the words out. "I'm sorry. I'm sorry for all of it. For yelling at you. For yelling at Scott. For behaving like a brat when you were dealing with so much, for being so difficult and h-horrible to you—" Tears started to fall, flowing like a river in full flood. She gulped and swallowed, tasting salt on her lips and on her tongue and then her mother was hugging her tightly, rocking her as she'd done when Mack was a child.

"Don't cry, sweetheart. Don't cry."

The love in her voice made Mack cry even harder.

How could her mother possibly forgive her so easily?

"I've been *h-horrid*, and you keep forgiving me and being there and trying to help and I'm such a mean person."

"You're not a mean person. It's not you that's horrid, it's the situation." Lauren smoothed Mack's damp hair away from her face and kissed her forehead. "You're a good person, and you've had to deal with more than any person should."

"But you've had to deal with it all, too, and you've had to deal with *me*, and I made it worse instead of better." She was choking on her tears, gulping air in between sobs, breathing in the mix of her mother's floral scent and the sea breeze. There was nothing on earth that smelled as good as her mother. She smelled like home and safety. She smelled like love.

"Oh, Mack, you make everything better. All of it. If it weren't for you, I don't know how I'd carry on."

Mack clung to her mother. "How can you say that after the things I said earlier?"

"You were upset. Understandably so. And I'm sorry you saw that because I wouldn't have wanted you to."

Mack noticed her mother didn't say she was sorry she'd kissed Scott.

She eased away and took a juddering breath. "Has he gone?"

"Gone?"

"Scott. He's probably packing the boat right now so that he and Captain can sail to a place that doesn't have a teenage population."

"Is that what you want him to do?"

"No." She rubbed her hand over her face. "I like him, but I'm sure he hates me now. He's probably thinking he did the right thing leaving before I was born."

"He's not thinking that, and Scott's leaving had nothing to do with you. He's never been part of a family the way we have. He doesn't know what it's like to have people stick by you, no matter what. To be able to be yourself and make mistakes and know you'll still be loved. He was scared out of his mind."

Mack couldn't imagine Scott being scared of anything. "He's very strong. He can do a hundred push-ups without breaking into a sweat. And he has this quiet way about him that makes you pay attention. Cal in the boatyard told me he once broke up a fight just by walking into the bar. He didn't say a word, but they all took one look at him and backed away. I get that. What I don't get is him being scared of anything."

"There are different types of scared. Scott was terrified of letting me down, and terrified of letting you down but most of all terrified of letting himself down and finding out he couldn't be the person he was trying so hard to be."

"That's crazy. Scott is great. He's so calm."

"He wasn't calm after you yelled. He was worried he'd messed it up and driven you away."

Mack sniffed. "He's worried about driving *me* away?"

"Yes, so I don't think you're going to be able to shake him off that easily. He is trying very hard to get it right this time."

The relief was enormous. "I am sorry, Mom. I should have thought more about you. I should have made you tea in bed and stuff."

Lauren laughed. "No, not that!"

Mack eased away and gave a watery grin. "What's wrong with my tea?"

"You make terrible tea."

"Sometimes I boil the water and forget about it, so by the time I make the tea the water isn't hot but I wouldn't call it terrible exactly."

"It's terrible. Even thinking about it makes my stomach roll." Lauren leaned in and gave her another hug and Mack closed her eyes.

"Mom?"

"Mmm?"

"If you and Scott—well, you know—I mean that's okay."

"We're not anything. I was upset because of that meeting at the bank and other things and Scott is a good listener and somehow things—" There was a pause. "Believe me, Mack, there is nothing that you're thinking that I haven't already thought. It's too soon, all wrong. How could I do this to Ed? It's not fair to you."

Her grandmother was right. Her mom thought about everyone but herself. "How about you?"

"What about me?"

"You're thinking about Ed and you're thinking about me—but what about what you want? You're important, too. What you want matters." Mack felt her cheeks burn. "You have a right to be happy, Mom. I want you to be happy and Ed would have wanted that, too." And she was going to find a way to get that pause button installed on her feelings. "And while we're on the subject, the things I said about Ed not being my dad. I didn't mean that. He was totally my dad. I mean, he took me to swimming lessons every Saturday and that must have been pretty boring." She was relieved to see her mother smile.

"He loved you. He would have done anything for you. You were the child he'd always wanted." Lauren paused.

"Ed couldn't have children of his own, Mack, and he wanted them badly. He wanted you."

Mack felt a stab of shock and sadness. "He couldn't have them? That's why I never got a baby brother or sister?"

"That's right." Her mother rubbed her arm gently. "But it didn't matter because we had you. Ed thought of you as his daughter in every way."

Mack felt as if a big lump had lodged itself behind her ribs. "It would have been nice to have known that, so I could have been better at it." It made her feel bad to think about the times she'd been less than perfect.

"Oh, honey, you were you and he loved you. He wouldn't have wanted you to be different."

Mack felt her eyes sting again. "I wish now that I'd made him breakfast on his birthday. I was difficult to live with," she muttered. "Do you think it was my fault he had a heart attack?"

"What? No!" Her mother sounded horrified. "Is that what you've been thinking?"

"Occasionally." Mack gave an awkward shrug. Her mind was such a mess these days she couldn't untangle any of it.

"Ed had heart disease. A damaged valve. That was what the report said. Nothing you said or did had any influence on what happened. The doctor said he was a ticking bomb." Her grip on Mack's hand tightened. "Sometimes, when someone dies, we blame ourselves. We're trying to find a reason, but not everything has a reason. I blamed myself, too."

"You?"

"Yes. For not insisting that he go to the doctor when he said he felt tired all the time. I should have made the appointment myself."

"Dad was always useless at going to the doctor." They exchanged a look of shared understanding.

"He really was."

"I wish now I'd talked to you right away when I found my birth certificate."

"We shouldn't have kept it from you."

Mack thought about what Nancy had said about never wanting your child to be unhappy. That made sense to her. And even if she might have argued that it was the wrong thing to do, she couldn't argue with the sentiment behind the decision. Love. Who could argue with that? "You were trying to protect me. I get that. You wanted me to feel secure. I guess decisions aren't always black-and-white." It felt like an epiphany. Maybe it wasn't so awful that she didn't know what she wanted to do with her life yet. Maybe it was unrealistic to expect an answer to pop into her head. And maybe she wasn't as bad a person as she thought she was.

Lauren sighed. "I loved Ed a great deal. I want you to know that. We had a good marriage and I have no doubt at all that if he hadn't died we would have stayed married. I loved Ed, but I also loved Scott. I loved him in a way I didn't think it was possible to love. I loved him so much that I couldn't even be angry that he didn't want us to be together. I understood him. I understood why. But I also wanted the best for you. I wanted you to have a stable home and love. After what I experienced with my own father, I wanted yours to be reliable."

But he hadn't been reliable, Mack thought. In the end Ed had let her mother down.

"Did everything in London have to be sold?"

"Yes. James called last night. Everything has finally been tied up."

Mack wondered if that was another reason her mom was so upset. "So the house is gone and everything?"

"All of it."

"That sucks."

Her mother gave a tired smile. "It does, although part of me is pleased it's over. It's been hanging over me."

Mack ached inside. She'd had no idea her mom was even thinking about that. "You must feel terrible. What about Nana? Has she been in touch?"

"No. I think she's still very angry with me. And hurt."

"But Ed knew everything, and Ed loved you. I mean, she could have blamed him for keeping it a secret. Why you?"

"She's grieving. I hope that in time she might soften a little. This is tough on everyone."

"Do you think I should write to her?"

"Would you like to?"

Mack thought about it. "I guess I would. I think Dad would have wanted me to."

"I think so, too. I'll give you her address."

"She was so mean to you and you lost everything."

"Not everything. I have you and Aunt Jenna and Grams. I have this place, this island. I still have hopes and dreams."

And Scott, Mack thought. They still had Scott.

Mack thought about the life she had here. She thought about waking up in the morning to the sound of the ocean and the call of the birds. "I guess the life we have here isn't so bad." You virtually had to write a suicide note before you went cycling in London, but here she cycled everywhere and it gave her a sense of freedom. "Mom?"

"Yes, honey."

"I think Grams might be in love with Ben." She saw her mother smile.

"I hope you're right."

"You wouldn't mind?"

"Mind that my mother finally finds happiness? I think it would be great, don't you? They have been seeing a lot of each other, that's true. I wonder if they're—"

"No!" Mack held up her hand. "Don't go there, I beg you."

"You're right. It's never a good idea to think about one's parents having sex."

"And for me it's grandparents, so—enough said." Mack shuddered. "As long as I don't bump into him in the night on my way to the bathroom."

Nancy appeared at that moment with a jug of lemonade in her hand. "So are you going to take Scott up on his offer?"

Lauren held a glass steady while her mother poured. "Taking a loan from him ties him into our lives."

"That's good, isn't it? It will stop him sailing off when I say the wrong thing and irritate him." Mack flushed as her mother looked directly at her. "And anyway he's already in our lives."

"He wants to be more involved. He'd like to see more of you."

"After what I said to him earlier?"

"Yes. What do you think?"

Mack tested the idea out in her head and decided she liked it a lot. "I guess that would work. Maybe the three of us could go sailing together. If you could handle that."

"She'll handle it." Nancy topped up Mack's glass. "And you'll take that loan. To Coastal Chic and the future. And speaking of the future, I have news, too."

"What news?"

"I've decided to sell The Captain's House after all."

Mack saw her mother frown.

"You're selling to Scott?"

"I offered it to him, but he has other plans now so I'm going to talk to a Realtor. After all our hard work someone might like to buy it as a rental property. I wanted to discuss it with you first. I told Jenna this morning while we were making adjustments to the website."

"Why wouldn't Scott want it?" Mack sipped her lemonade. "Or maybe he can't buy it *and* loan you the money."

"Are you sure, Mom?" Lauren said. "After all these years of battling to keep it in the family?"

"Exactly. I'm tired of battling. Where does it say that life has to be a battle? I want a more peaceful existence, and I want my life to be full of the things I want, not the things I'm keeping out of obligation to others or some ridiculous sense of responsibility. That house is too big for me. It doesn't fit with this new phase of my life. I'm going to live right here in the Sail Loft. Ben is going to help me design a garden that is going to be the talk of the island."

Ben.

Mack caught her mother's eye.

It was difficult to imagine people falling in love when they were as old as her grandmother, but it probably happened, didn't it?

Did people of that age still have sex or did they just hold hands?

Scarlet faced, she drank her lemonade.

Being an adult was one thing, but some thoughts were definitely off-limits.

CHAPTER THIRTY-FOUR

Jenna

> *Acceptance: an attitude or feeling that you*
> *cannot change a difficult situation and that*
> *you must get used to it*

"WE SAW THE DOCTOR." Jenna pressed her hands to the floor, wondering why she'd agreed to yoga. "Is this something I should be telling you while I'm doing downward-facing dog?"

Ungainly: lacking grace when moving.

Lauren glanced at her. "You're not supposed to be talking," she whispered. "You're supposed to relax."

"Talking relaxes me. She wanted to know everything about our sex life. It was a bit kinky." She stopped talking as the yoga instructor came up behind her.

"Press down into your hands. Keep your breathing steady."

Jenna's legs were starting to cramp.

No matter how hard she concentrated, she always seemed to be half a move behind everyone else. She was only here because she'd promised Greg she'd give it a try, and she enjoyed spending time with her sister.

As the instructor moved back to the front of the class, Lauren turned her head. "Have you lost weight?"

Jenna eyed her reflection in the huge mirror. "I have."

"Diet?"

"No. I stopped comfort eating." She gave a wicked smile. "I'm finding comfort elsewhere."

"Shh!" The woman closest to them sent them an incinerating glare and Lauren rose elegantly out of the position she'd been holding.

"Let's go."

"Go?" Jenna's untangling was less elegant. "Go where?"

"We're breaking out of here." Lauren gathered up her mat, sent a look of apology to the instructor and strode out of the room.

Torn between embarrassment and relief, Jenna grabbed her things and slunk out behind her. "I can't believe you did that. You love yoga."

"But you hate it and life is too short to spend it doing something you hate. I couldn't bear the look on your face. It's not supposed to be torture."

Jenna slung her bag over her shoulder. "For a moment there you actually sounded like my sister. Do you want to go skinny dipping? Or we could help ourselves to strawberries from Mrs. Maxwell's garden?"

"Don't push me. We need to take this a step at a time." Lauren pulled the band off her ponytail and let her hair flow. "Let's go for a walk on the beach. You can tell me about your appointment."

"Nothing to tell. They're going to run some simple tests first, so we have a long way to go before we have to start making decisions about anything. But I'm glad we finally went." It had made her feel less helpless. As if they were doing something. "Greg handled it well."

"If Greg can't handle stuff like this, there's no hope for the rest of us."

"It's different when you're dealing with your own problem." She understood that now. "It's personal. You can't be neutral when it's personal. I promised I'd relax more and go to yoga, but yoga doesn't help me relax."

"But eating ice cream on the beach does, so let's go do that." Lauren slipped her arm through Jenna's and they walked across the parking lot.

Jenna thought about all the times they'd done this as kids. "Thanks for helping me escape. If you ever get put in prison, I promise to dig a tunnel and get you out."

"You'd probably be the reason I was in there in the first place."

Jenna tugged at her sister's arm. "Hey, you're the ringleader, not me."

"If I were to ever find myself in prison, I'm sure it would be because I was covering for you, but don't worry. No matter what they did to me, I'd never give you up."

They were both giggling. "They'd find a way of making you talk. They'd wave a pair of great shoes under your nose and you'd yell, 'Hell yes, she's guilty now give me those Jimmy Choos.'"

"I would not give you up for great shoes. I'm not that cheap."

"Lipstick?"

"No way."

"Salted caramel ice cream?"

"That's not fair." Lauren stopped dead. "No one can resist that."

"So if I was standing on the edge of a cliff with a tub of salted caramel ice cream and you could only save one of us, it would be the ice cream?"

"I'd push you off to get to the ice cream."

"How did I get stuck with you as a sister?"

Lauren grinned. "I guess you got lucky. But now you've made me think of salted caramel ice cream. Where's the nearest source?"

"We'll pick some up on the way to the beach. But don't you need to get back to spend time with Mack?"

"She's sailing with Scott."

"Again?" Jenna unhooked her arm from Lauren's and stooped to tie the lace on her running shoe. "Is that a regular thing now?"

"Yes. Turns out she's pretty good at it. She's inherited Scott's feel for the sea. And she's been helping him in the boatyard, too."

"And how about you? Are you seeing him?"

"He loaned me the money, so naturally I feel an obligation to keep him updated on my business."

"When I asked if you were seeing him, that wasn't what I meant. I meant, *are you seeing him*? As in, are you having clothes-ripping, breath-stealing sex?"

"Of course not." Lauren walked away from her toward the car.

"Wait!" Jenna sprinted after her. "Why 'of course not'?"

"It's only been six months since I lost Ed."

Jenna stopped dead. "Lauren Stewart, what is this crap?"

"I'm not Ste—"

"You broke me out of a boring yoga class and threatened

to push me off a cliff. You're definitely a Stewart. So what I want to know is how my ballsy, adventure-seeking sister who has basically been in love with the same guy *her whole life*, isn't having sex on every available flat surface. It doesn't matter that it's only been six months. Where's the rule that says you have to be miserable for a certain length of time?" Across the parking lot a couple climbed out of their car and glanced in their direction.

Lauren rolled her eyes. "If you speak a little louder they'd maybe hear you on Nantucket. It would save me sending out a bulletin. I definitely think you should repeat the part about sex on every available flat surface."

"How long are you going to wait? Ed wouldn't want you to wait, I can tell you that."

"It's not only that I feel guilty about Ed, there's Mack to think about."

Prevaricate: avoid giving a direct answer or firm decision.

"Mack is doing great. She's in better shape than you are. So tell me the truth. What's the real reason you're holding back? Because I'm sure this is your decision and not Scott's."

They'd reached the car and Lauren stopped.

"I guess I'm scared."

"Scared of what?" For a moment Jenna couldn't breathe. This was her sister. Her sister who never used to be afraid of anything. "Scared you might lose him the way you lost Ed?"

"No. Well, maybe a little—" Lauren bit her lip. "It's more that I'm afraid to let myself fall in love with him again. Or maybe I've always been in love with him and I'm afraid that if I admit it, I won't be able to handle what happens next."

Jenna hesitated. "You're worried he might walk away like he did the first time?"

She saw the flash of anguish in her sister's eyes and wondered if she'd been wrong to encourage the relationship. What if Lauren became involved with Scott and he let her down again?

Lauren gave a wan smile. "I guess that's part of it. I've taken all the emotional battering I can take for a while. Oh—" She broke off as Jenna wrapped her arms around her. "What's that for?"

"For love. For protection. For courage." Jenna held her sister tightly. Love was all about risk, wasn't it? And some risks were worth taking. "Remember when you used to drag me on all those adventures when we were young? I was terrified! I always tried to stop you doing it, but when that didn't work, I went along anyway. And I did it because it was my job to look out for you, the same way you looked out for me. No matter what trouble you found yourself in, I was there for you and I still am. I don't know what's going to happen in the future. None of us does. But I'll be there for you the whole way. That hasn't changed. The only thing that has changed is that this time I'm the one urging you to take the risk. You're holding back from the one thing that's going to make you happy, Lauren." *And if Scott hurt Lauren again, she'd kill him with her bare hands.*

"I'll think about it."

"You'll do more than think about it." Jenna nudged her toward the car. "Go, before that serious-faced yoga instructor with the incredibly annoying voice comes and drags us back. Given my track record behind the wheel, you'd better be the getaway driver."

CHAPTER THIRTY-FIVE

Lauren

> *Evolution: a process of gradual development in a
> particular situation or thing over a period of time*

JUNE MELTED INTO JULY, bringing with it crowds of people.
The island attracted everyone from artists to presidents.
Some came to spend time in the cafés, restaurants and galleries of Edgartown, others came for the landscape and the
beaches.

Lauren slept with the windows open and drifted off to
sleep with the sound of the ocean in her head and the cool
salt breeze on her face.

The ache and the sadness came and went like the tide.

One minute she'd be fine, and the next hardly able to
breathe, but somehow she forced herself to keep going.

During the mornings she focused on Coastal Chic.
Thanks to the loan from Scott, she'd been able to take on a
couple of clients and so far it was going well.

She had enough to keep her going into the winter months.

Work was great. Her mother was happy, and Mack was doing well.

Lauren was the only one who seemed to be struggling.

She missed Ed. She missed Scott. Then she felt guilty for thinking about Scott when she was still sad about Ed.

Her brain felt like a roundabout and she had no idea how to stop it spinning.

"Mom?"

Lauren glanced up from her laptop as she heard Mack's voice. "I'm upstairs." As her mother no longer used it as a studio, Lauren was using it as an office. She still hoped that her mother might paint canvases again at some point, but right now she seemed to be pouring all her artistic, creative urges into painting houses and designing gardens.

Lauren glanced at the blue and purple hydrangeas stuffed into the pretty rustic jug she'd found at the Goodwill store when she'd been helping her mother clear out her life.

She heard Mack's feet on the stairs and a moment later she appeared in the doorway. Her hair was windblown and streaked from the sun, the pink streaks long gone.

"Are you busy?" She was out of breath. "Can you come?"

Lauren was on her feet in an instant. "Is something wrong?"

"Nothing's wrong. Scott wants to take us sailing. There is something important he wants to say to us both."

Her heart lurched like the deck of a ship in a storm. He was leaving. What else could he possibly want to say to them both? Ever since her mother had told her he no longer wanted to buy The Captain's House, she'd been waiting for this moment. If he wanted them on the boat to tell them something, then presumably he wanted to remind them both what a sea creature he was. How he needed the ocean to survive.

Could she be sympathetic to that a second time, especially now that Mack had started to build a relationship with him?

"He wants to talk to us right now?" He'd taken her at her word and given her space, although whenever they saw each other it was as if the rest of the world disappeared.

"Yes. We were going out anyway, but he said he wants you there. He drove me here. He's outside in the pickup."

Lauren reached for her keys and her phone, reminding herself that she'd handled everything life had thrown at her up to this point and she'd handle this, too. Whatever "this" was. *Please don't let Scott be leaving.* "I'll send a text to Grams to let her know we'll both be late tonight."

"Where is Grams?"

"With Alice."

"Again?" Mack raised her eyebrows. "How is that going?"

"She's seen her a few times. I think it's going okay. I haven't asked for the details. Grams will tell me if she wants to."

"So they're BFFs again?"

"I wouldn't go that far, but there's hope." And hope, Lauren thought, kept life moving. Hope that things would improve, that sadness would pass, that you'd live feeling you'd love and live. *Hope that the few fragile threads of this new life won't be snapped before they can strengthen.* She grabbed a sweater and sunscreen. "Let's go."

"What would you have done if you were Grams?"

"I don't know." Lauren locked the door of the Sail Loft. "I don't suppose any of us really knows what we'd do until we're actually in that position ourselves. It's pretty easy to judge from the outside, but not so easy when it's your life."

She knew many people would have judged Scott for not wanting to embrace fatherhood, but she'd understood. She'd understood *him*. It was one of the reasons she hadn't wanted to divulge the identity of her baby's father. She'd wanted to protect him from the judgment and speculation that would surely have followed.

But what if he walked away now? How would she react this time?

He'd won his daughter's heart. Would she be able to forgive him if he broke it?

Mack waited while Lauren dropped the keys into her purse. "I know she broke the girlfriend code, but I kind of like Alice."

"I do, too. And so does your grandmother. That's why it's hard."

They walked to the road together and Mack sprang into the pickup.

Lauren followed more slowly, noticing the way Scott tugged at Mack's hat, teasing her. They argued all the way to the marina, over whether she should be allowed to take the boat out without him, about whether he should get another dog to keep Captain company.

"A puppy would be good."

Scott raised an eyebrow. "Are you going to take responsibility for this puppy?"

Lauren found herself analyzing everything he said. Would he be making jokes like that if he was thinking of moving on? Mack had been spending plenty of time with him and had even slept over on the boat once or twice.

It had made Lauren feel a little strange and she hated

herself for feeling that way because she knew how much Mack loved the water. And it was obvious she loved Scott, too. And that was good, wasn't it? She couldn't blame her daughter for wanting to spend time with him, or Scott for wanting to spend time with his daughter. She was *pleased*. So why did she also feel slightly sick?

Was it because part of her was always a little worried Scott might decide he'd had enough and move on again? Or was she turning into one of those mothers who couldn't bear having their children leave them?

Scott parked and turned to look at her. "You're quiet. Is everything okay?"

"Everything is good." Except that she was tired of being sad. And anxious. Sad and anxious. It was a toxic combination.

Still watching her, Scott reached out and stroked Captain's head. "You've been busy lately. I've barely seen you. How's the business?"

"Good." She tried not to look at those fingers. She tried not to think about that night in the kitchen of the Sail Loft. "We have more work than we can handle right now, including a client who wants us to take a look at her apartment in Manhattan. It's all very exciting." Manhattan. She'd visit for the weekend. Mack was perfectly safe with Nancy, so she could probably visit for longer if necessary.

For some reason she didn't understand, the idea didn't thrill her.

Mack frowned. "Does Coastal Chic even work in Manhattan? I mean seashells and Central Park? I don't think so."

Lauren smiled. "I think we can broaden our look if we need to. Maybe Coastal Chic could become City Chic for a while."

Scott kept his hand on Captain's head. "So you're moving to New York? It's what you wanted when you were a teenager."

"Move?" Mack looked horrified. "Mom?"

"We wouldn't move anywhere," Lauren said. "If we take the business in New York then I'd find a way to travel and do it. No way are we moving. We're here now and we're staying." And she loved it. The island. The people. The sea. How could she have lived so long without it?

"Good." Mack opened the car door. "Because right now I am done with change. I want to stay here, have tea with Grams, eat too many of Aunt Jenna's cookies, update your website, program a robot, see my friends, sail with Scott." She whistled to Captain and jumped out of the car.

Lauren was about to follow when Scott caught her hand in a tight grip.

"What's wrong?"

"Nothing. I'm looking forward to our sail. Where are we going?"

He gave her a long, searching look and let go of her hand. "You'll find out."

Refusing to say more than that, he loaded the cooler onto the boat and they all clambered aboard, including the dog.

Mack moved around the boat with confidence, following Scott's instructions.

It was obvious from the way they worked together that they'd done this plenty of times.

"Hey, Mom, did you know you can sail right round Martha's Vineyard?" Mack secured the rope. "It's 54.7 nautical miles. Scott says we can do it next summer."

"That's great."

So he planned to be here next summer. But what about the long winter in between?

She tried not to think about it. Right now her daughter seemed happy and that was good.

Good for her, and good for Scott. He needed this. It would be good for him to feel a sense of responsibility for someone. It wasn't something he'd had before in his life.

Sailing round the island gave them views of cliffs, headlands, open water, lighthouses and beach houses, some the size of hotels. Normally Lauren would have loved it, but today her mind was busy with other things.

Scott guided the boat into an inlet and Lauren immediately recognized the beach.

Eyes wide, she glanced at him.

Scott smiled. "Remember this place?"

Of course she remembered this place. It was their beach. The beach they'd treated as their own.

The house had been uninhabited at the time and they'd sneaked onto the beach and talked, laughed and made love in the moonlight. Everything she'd learned about him, she'd learned right there on that strip of golden sand. And he'd learned everything about her.

If a place could keep secrets, then this beach knew all of hers.

She ached for those carefree nights. She ached to be that woman again. She ached for *him*.

"Great house." Mack craned her neck to get a better look. "There are balconies on the upstairs bedroom and it has its own staircase down to the beach. How cool is that? Is it a holiday place? Who owns it?"

"Right now, no one," Scott said. "It's for sale."

Lauren tried not to think about a bunch of strangers walking on their beach, trampling on the memories. "I always loved this place." She was looking at the house but she could feel Scott looking at her.

"I know."

She turned to look at him and saw all of her memories reflected in his eyes.

"Who wouldn't love it? It's a pretty house. Pretty perfect in fact." Mack gazed at it dreamily. "I wonder what sort of person is going to buy it."

Scott's gaze didn't shift from Lauren's face. "A guy who loves the ocean, but has decided that the time has come to live near it and not on it. A guy who needs space because although right now it's just him and his dog, they're both hoping that's going to change." He paused, taking in Lauren's shocked expression. "A guy who made a big mistake once in his life, but believes in second chances."

Lauren felt her heart miss a beat. "You've bought this house?"

"Not yet. I wanted your opinion first. It's important that you love it, too. That's why I brought you here today. To check if this place works for you. It's close to your sister and not far from the Sail Loft." He tucked a loose strand of hair behind her ear. "What do you think?"

What did she think?

"I thought—I thought—" She looked into his eyes, and then at his mouth. She wished she could see into his heart. "I thought you were going to tell me you couldn't do this anymore and were going sailing for the winter. I thought you were leaving again."

Her knees were shaking and she closed her hands around his biceps to steady herself.

Scott gave a rough exclamation and pulled her close, this time ignoring Mack.

"I'm not leaving you." He held her tightly, kissing first her head, then her cheek and finally her mouth. "Never again." He breathed the promise against her lips. "Never again. Not unless you send me away and probably not even then."

She felt herself come alive under his hands and mouth. The present and the past melted together and her anxiety fell away.

"Hello! Teenager present." Mack's voice cut through the clouds of excitement. "Embarrassing public displays of affection are discouraged. You're supposed to wait until I'm not around to kiss my mom."

Scott lifted his head slowly. "You're not the public." Keeping one arm round Lauren he held the other out to Mack. "You're my daughter. And I intend to kiss your mom a lot, so you might as well get used to it."

Mack muttered something about living permanently in the Sail Loft with her grandmother, but Lauren saw her eyes mist and after a moment's hesitation she slipped into the circle of security Scott was offering.

"So does this mean you're thinking of sticking around?"

Lauren detected the insecurity under the casual tone and it made her heart ache all over again. One day, perhaps, Mack would stop thinking she was going to lose everything she loved.

Scott obviously heard the same note of insecurity because he nodded.

"I'm sticking."

"Are you sure? I mean, you don't know how annoying I can be. You might change your mind when we've had our first fight."

Scott's eyes gleamed. "I think I can handle it."

"That's good to know because I might have told a few of my friends that you're my dad so it would be kind of awkward if you walked away now."

Scott tightened his grip and Mack flushed pink with pleasure.

They stood, the three of them, feeling the boat move gently with the water, looking at the shore.

Mack broke the silence first. "Are you asking us to live there with you?"

"One day I hope you will, but I know it's early days and you might rather wait a little while. The house will be here when you're ready. And I'll be here, too. Whether you take a week, a year or ten years, I'll be here."

Lauren felt the strength of his arm around her.

She hadn't asked for her marriage to end, but it had ended anyway and the fact that she had chosen to keep living didn't make her a bad person. Ed would have wanted her to be happy.

Scott was right that they needed time, but she didn't think she was going to need much time. Time, she'd discovered, was precious. It didn't do to waste a moment of it.

Mack nudged Scott. "Do I get to call you Dad or is that freaky?"

"You can call me what you like."

"Cool. And when we move in, do we get a puppy?"

"She never gives up, does she?" Scott looked at Lauren.

Her head was spinning and her emotions were so close to the surface she didn't know whether to cry or smile. "She never gives up. Welcome to parenthood. It's a type of erosion. Gradually, over time, you're worn down like the rocks on the beach."

Scott winced. "Sounds tough. You're going to have to share your secrets with me."

"The secret," Mack said helpfully, "is to say yes to everything. It makes life simpler. Yes, Mack, of course you can stay out late and drink and take drugs. Have fun. You'd like a car? Yes, Mack. Which make and model? A new laptop? Great idea. See? It's easy. If I ask you a question, the answer is yes."

"I think that's called cupboard love." Scott was smiling, and they watched as Mack walked across the boat to stop Captain from hurling himself into the water.

When Mack was out of earshot, he turned back to Lauren. "And how about you?" His voice was soft and for her alone. "Maybe it's the wrong time for you to hear this, but I love you, Laurie."

It was never the wrong time to hear those words.

"I love you, too." She felt his arms tighten around her.

"We'll take this at whatever pace you want, but one day, at some point in the future, I'm going to ask you a question. Do you think your answer will be yes?"

"You're going to ask me if I want a puppy?"

He laughed and she laughed, too, and leaned her head against his chest.

She was going to be fine. Maybe not right away, but gradually, over time she'd piece herself together.

Her old life had gone, but there was a new one waiting for her. All she had to do was take that step...

CHAPTER THIRTY-SIX

Sisters

> *Bond: a force or feeling that unites people*

"I CAN'T BELIEVE *we're doing this.*"

"*I thought you wanted me to be more adventurous. More like my old self.*" *She grabbed her sister's hand and pulled her to the railing.*

"*You want me to jump, too? No way. I'm the one who stays on shore ready to rescue you. I'm your lifeline.*"

"*Not this time. This time we jump together.*"

"*Who will rescue us if we both get into trouble?*"

"*We'll rescue each other.*" *She climbed over the rail and poised, ready to jump. It was an island tradition, but one she hadn't followed in years.*

She remembered all the times she'd leaped without even thinking about what might be underneath. With the naivety of youth, she hadn't once thought about all the things that could go wrong. When you were young you thought you were invincible.

Was she too old for this?

No. You were never too old to leap, especially when you had someone you trusted by your side.

Her sister climbed over the railing and clung tightly. "Jaws is just a movie, right?" She stared down into the water. "It never actually happened."

"If a shark appears, I promise to distract it."

"What are you going to do? Tempt it with salted caramel ice cream?"

"Who said anything about ice cream? If it's between you and salted caramel ice cream, the shark gets you."

"Great. Of all the sisters I could have had, I got you."

"It was your lucky day."

"That's not how I see it. I really can't believe I'm actually going to do this. Does this mean you're going to be dragging me into trouble at every available opportunity like you used to?"

"No, but it might happen occasionally." She felt a stab of guilt. "You don't have to jump if you don't want to." She felt her sister's hand tighten on hers.

"I'll go wherever you go. We're sisters. Sisters always stick together. I made a promise."

Most people wouldn't have made a promise like that, Lauren thought, which was why she was lucky to have a sister like hers.

"If I could have chosen my sister, I would have chosen you. We'll go on three. One, two—"

* * * * *

ACKNOWLEDGMENTS

This book was a departure for me. Bigger in scope, with more characters, breadth and depth. I probably wouldn't have written it were it not for the encouragement of my wonderful agent Susan Ginsburg and the support of Dianne Moggy, Susan Swinwood and Lisa Milton. I'm grateful for the faith they have shown in me throughout my career and for their insightful editorial comments as this book developed.

People often assume that a book, even a work of fiction, is autobiographical in some way, but one of the many great things about being a writer is that you can invent families and problems that are entirely unlike your own. Fortunately for me, my family is much less complicated than the ones I write about. They give me very little fodder for a juicy story, but they give me no end of loving support and I'm massively grateful for that.

Writing the book is only the beginning, and it's the collective effort of so many hardworking people on the publishing teams that help each book find an audience. To everyone at HQN in the US and HQ Stories in the UK, thank you for everything you do.

Particular thanks go to my wonderful editor Flo Nicoll for her insight and patience in reading multiple drafts. Without her exceptional skills, this book wouldn't exist. We have worked together for five years and I feel very lucky. No author could have a more brilliant editor.

To my nonwriter friends who listen while I talk about characters who don't exist, and who patiently reschedule lunches and coffee dates when I'm on a deadline, thank you.

To my writer friends, particularly Nicola Cornick, Jill Shalvis and RaeAnne Thayne, without your cheerleading, understanding and humour I doubt I'd write anything at all. With you in my life, writing never feels like a lonely profession.

Last but not least I thank my readers, many of whom have followed me through all the various stages of my writing career. So many of you take the time to message me and write reviews, and I'm eternally grateful for that. Without you I wouldn't be doing this job, so thank you for helping to make my dream come true. I hope you enjoy this book.

Turn the page for an excerpt of Sarah Morgan's
captivating new book

THE CHRISTMAS SISTERS

Coming soon!

CHAPTER ONE

Suzanne

There are good anniversaries, and bad anniversaries. This was a bad one and Suzanne chose to mark the moment with a nightmare.

As usual she was buried, her body immobile and trapped under a weight as heavy as concrete. There was snow in her mouth, in her nose, in her ears. The force and pressure of it crushed her. How deep was she? Which way up? Would anyone be looking for her?

She tried to scream but there was nothing, nothing....

'Suzanne—'

Someone was calling her name. She couldn't respond. Couldn't move. Couldn't breathe. Her chest was being squeezed.

'Suzanne!'

She heard the voice through darkness and panic.

'You're dreaming.'

She felt something touch her shoulder, and the movement catapulted her out of her frozen tomb and back to reality. She sat up, her hand to her throat, gulping in air.

'It's all right,' the voice said. 'Everything is all right.'

'I had – a dream. *The* dream.' And it was so real she expected to find herself surrounded by ice crystals, not crumpled bedding.

'I know.' The voice belonged to Stewart, and his hand was on her back, rubbing gently. 'You were screaming.'

And now she noticed that his face was white and lines of anxiety bracketed his mouth.

They had a routine for this, but hadn't had to use it in a while.

'It was so vivid. I was *there.*'

Stewart flicked on the light. A soft glow spread across the bedroom, illuminating dark corners and pushing aside the last wisps of the nightmare. 'You're safe. Look around you.'

Suzanne looked, her imagination still trapped under the weight of snow.

But there was no snow. No avalanche. Just her warm, cosy bedroom in Glensay Lodge where the remains of a fire danced in the hearth and the darkness of the endless winter night shone black through a gap in the curtains. She'd made the curtains herself from a sumptuous tartan fabric she'd found on her first visit to Scotland. Stewart's mother had claimed it was their clan tartan, but all Suzanne cared about was that those curtains kept the cold out on chilly nights and made the room cosy. She'd also made the quilt that was draped across the bottom of the bed. The comfortable familiarity calmed her.

On the table near the window was a bottle of single malt whisky from the local distillery, and next to it sat Stewart's empty glass.

There was her favourite chair, the cushions plumped and soft. Her book, a novel that hadn't really caught her attention, lay open next to her knitting. A new order of wool had arrived the day before and she'd been thrilled by the colours. Deep purples and blues lay against softer hues of heather and rich cream, ready to brighten the palette of white and grey that lay beyond her windows. The wool reminded her of the wild Scottish heather that grew in the glen in early and late summer. Thinking of it cheered her. When the weather warmed she liked to walk early in the morning and see the heather as the sun burned through the mist.

And there was Stewart. Stewart, with his kind eyes and infinite patience. Stewart who had been by her side for more than three decades.

She was in the Scottish Highlands, tens of thousands of miles from the icy flanks of Mount Rainier. Still, the dream hung over her like a chilling fog, infecting her thoughts.

'I haven't had that dream in over a year.' Her forehead was damp with sweat and her nightdress clung to her. She took the glass of water that Stewart offered.

Her throat was parched and the water soothed and cooled, but her hand was shaking so much she sloshed some of it over the duvet. 'How can a person still have nightmares after twenty-five years?' She wanted to forget, but her body wouldn't let her.

Stewart took the glass from her and put it on the nightstand. Then he took her in his arms. 'It's almost Christmas, and this is always a stressful time of year.'

She leaned her head on his shoulder, comforted by human warmth. Not snow and ice, but flesh and blood.

Alive.

'I love this time of year because the girls are home.' She slid her arm round his waist, wishing she could stop shaking. 'Last year I didn't have the dream once.'

'It was probably that call from Hannah that triggered it.'

'It was a good phone call. She's coming home for the holidays. That's the *best* news. Not something to trigger a nightmare.' But enough to trigger thoughts and memories.

She suspected poor Hannah would be having her own thoughts and memories.

Stewart was right that this time of year was never easy.

'It's been a couple of years since Hannah, Beth and Posy were here together.'

'And I'm excited.' Anticipation lifted her mood. 'It will be all the more special because Hannah couldn't make it last year.'

'Which increases the expectation.' Stewart sounded tired. 'Don't put pressure on her, Suzanne. It's tough on her, and you end up hurt.'

'I won't be hurt.' They both knew it was a lie. Every time Hannah distanced herself from her family, it hurt. 'I want her to be happy, that's all.'

'The only person who can make Hannah happy is Hannah.'

'That doesn't stop me wanting to help. I'm her mother.' She caught his eye. 'I *am* her mother.'

'I know.' He rubbed his fingers over his forehead. 'And if you want my opinion she's damned lucky to have you.'

How could he say that? There had been nothing lucky

about the girls' early life. At the beginning Suzanne had been terrified that Hannah's life would be ruined by the events of her childhood, but then she'd realised she had a responsibility not to let that happen.

She'd done everything she could to compensate and influence the future. She wanted nothing but good for her daughters and the burden of it was huge. It weighed her down, and there were days when it almost crushed her. And she'd made him carry the burden too.

Survivor's guilt.

'I worry I haven't done enough. Or that I haven't done it right.'

'I'm sure every parent thinks that from time to time.'

Suzanne slid her legs out of bed, relieved to be able to stand up. Walk. Breathe. Watch the sun rise. She rolled her shoulders and discovered they ached. She'd turned fifty-eight the summer before and right now she felt every one of her years. Was the pain real or a memory? 'The dream was bad. I was back there.'

Suffocating in an airless, snowy tomb.

Stewart stood up too. 'It will fade.' He reached for his robe. 'I'm not going to ask if you want to talk about it, because you never do.'

And this time was no different.

She couldn't stop the nightmares, but she could prevent the darkness from creeping into her waking hours. It was her way of taking back control. 'You should go back to sleep.'

'We both know there's no going back to sleep after you have one of your dreams. And we have to be up in an hour anyway.' His hair was standing on end and his eyes were rimmed with fatigue. 'We have a group of twenty arriving at the Adventure Academy this morning. It's going to be busy. I might as well make an early start.'

'Are they experienced?'

'No. School party on an outdoor adventure week.'

Anxiety washed over her. Her instinct was to beg him not to go, but that would have meant giving in to fear. It also would have meant asking Stewart to give up doing something he loved and she couldn't do that. 'Be careful.'

'I always am.' Stewart kissed her and walked to the door. 'Coffee?'

'Please.' The thought of staying in bed held no appeal. 'I'll take a quick shower and then start planning.'

'Planning what?'

'Only a man would ask that. You think Christmas happens by itself?' She belted her robe knowing from experience that activity was the best way to drive the shadows from her head. 'It's only a few weeks away. I want to do all the preparation beforehand so I can spend as much time as possible with our grandchildren. I thought I'd buy a few extra games in case the weather is bad. I don't want them to be bored. They have so much to do in Manhattan.'

'If they're bored, they can help with the animals. They can feed the chickens with Posy, or round up the sheep. They can ride Socks.'

Socks was Posy's pony. Now eighteen, she was enjoying a well-earned, hay-filled, retirement in the fields that surrounded the Lodge.

'Beth gets nervous when they ride.'

Stewart shook his head. 'A lot of things make Beth

nervous. She is too overprotective. Kids don't break that easily.'

'As if you weren't the most protective father ever. Particularly with her.'

He gave a sheepish grin. 'Posy was like a little ball. She bounced. Beth was a delicate little thing.'

'She's always been a daddy's girl. And if she is an overprotective mother, then we both know why.'

'I didn't say I didn't understand, but you've got to let kids have some fun. Explore. Make mistakes. Live life.'

'Easier said than done.' Suzanne knew she was overprotective, too. 'I'll talk to Beth. Try and persuade her to let the girls ride. If the weather is bad they can help in the kitchen. We can do some baking.'

'Here's a radical idea—' Stewart picked up his empty whisky glass from the night before. 'Instead of planning everything and driving yourself crazy with stress, why don't you keep it relaxed this year? Stop trying so hard.'

Suzanne's mouth dropped open. 'You think food magically appears? You think Santa really does deliver gifts ready wrapped?'

But his comment was so typical of him, it made her laugh. To an outsider they probably seemed ridiculously traditional, but her life was exactly the way she wanted it.

'I'll have you know that the key to relaxation is planning. I want it to be special.' The fact that it was the only time the three girls were together increased the pressure for it to be perfect. She walked to the window, pulled back the curtains and leaned her forehead against the cool glass. From the window of her bedroom she had a view right down the glen. The snow was luminous, reflecting the muted glow of the moon and sending flickers of light across the still surface of the loch. Framing the loch was snow dusted forest and behind that the mountains rose, dominating everything with their deadly beauty.

Even knowing the danger waiting in those snowy peaks, she was still drawn to them. 'Should we have lived in a city?'

'No. And you need to stop thinking like that.' His voice was rough. 'It's the dream, you know that.'

She did know that. She loved living here, in this land of mist and mountains, of lochs and legend.

'I worry about Hannah.' She turned. 'About what being here does to her.'

'I'm more worried about what her being here does to you.'

It was a theme that came up every time their eldest daughter came home. 'I love her and so do you. How can you say a thing like that that?'

'I don't know. Maybe I'm being haunted by the ghosts of Christmas past.' He put the empty glass down and rubbed his fingers across his forehead. 'Now you're the one being overprotective. You need to let her be, Suzy. Let her find her own way. You can't fix everything, although I know you'll never give up trying.' The light softened the hard angles of his face, making him seem younger.

His job kept him fit and lean and there were days when he barely looked fifty let alone sixty. The only clue as to his age was the touch of silver in his hair, the same silver that would have shown in hers if she hadn't chosen to avail herself of a little artificial help.

They'd fallen in love when they'd worked together as

mountain guides, when life had seemed like one big adventure. All they'd cared about back then was the next climb. The next summit. They'd been together ever since and, for the most part, their life had a comfortable rhythm. A rhythm that was rocked at this time of year.

The past never went away, she thought. It faded, and sometimes it was little more than a shadow, but it was always there.

'I'm going to make the Lodge as welcoming as possible. She works hard.'

'So do you. Your life isn't all about the kids, Suzanne. You run a successful business and this is one of your busiest times of the year in the cafe.'

The source of her anxiety shifted. 'And now you've reminded me that I still have forty stockings to knit to raise funds for the Mountain Rescue Team. Thank you for stressing me.'

Stewart grinned and scooped up his clothes from the chair where he'd left them the night before. 'Now *that's* something I'd like to see. The rest of the guys wearing stockings. I'll be taking a photo of that and posting it on the team Facebook page.'

Suzanne pulled a face. 'They're not for wearing, you idiot, they're for stuffing with presents. We sell them for a good profit. And before you mock, I should point out that the profit from last year's Christmas stockings bought the team a new avalanche transceiver and contributed to that fancy stretcher you use.'

'I know that.'

'Then why –'

'I like teasing you. I like the way you look when you're

mad. Your mouth pouts and you have these cute little frown lines and – ow—' he ducked as she crossed the room and flung a pillow at him. 'Did you really just do that? How old are you?'

'Old enough to have developed perfect aim.'

He threw the pillow back on the bed, tossed his clothes back on the chair and tumbled her underneath him.

She landed with a gasp on the mattress.

'Stewart!'

'What?'

'We have things to do.'

'We do indeed.' He lowered his head and the last thing she saw before he kissed her was a pair of blue eyes laughing into hers.

By the time they got out of bed for the second time, the first fingers of weak sunlight were poking through the curtains.

'And now I'm late.' Stewart dived into the bathroom. 'I blame you.'

'And it's my fault because—?'

But he was already in the shower, humming tunelessly as the water splashed around him.

Suzanne lay for a moment, her brain fuzzy and contented, the dream all but forgotten.

She knew she ought to make a start on those stockings.

Knitting was the perfect form of relaxation, although it had taken her years to discover it.

She hadn't knitted a thing until she was in her thirties.

To begin with it had been her way of showing her love for the girls. She'd clothe them and wrap them in warmth. When she'd picked up her needles and yarn she hadn't just been knitting a sweater, she'd been knitting together her fractured, damaged family, taking separate threads and turning them into something whole.

Stewart came out of the shower, rubbing his hair with a towel. 'Did you want me to sort out a Christmas tree on the way home?'

'Posy said she'd do it. I thought we'd wait a few more days. I don't want the needles falling off before Christmas. How many trees should we have this year? I thought one for the living room, one for the entryway, one in the TV room. Maybe one for Hannah's room.'

'Are you sure you don't want one for the boot room? How about the downstairs bathroom?'

'There are still plenty more pillows on this bed that I can fling.'

But he'd distracted her from her nightmare. She knew that had been his intention, and she loved him for it.

'All I'm saying is that maybe you should leave a few in the forest.' He threw the wet towel over the back of the chair and then caught her eye and put it in the bathroom instead. 'Every year you half kill yourself turning this place into a cross between a winter wonderland and Santa's workshop.' He dressed quickly, pulling on the layers that were necessary for his job. 'You have big expectations, Suzanne. Not easy to live up to that.'

'It's true that things can be a little stressful when the girls are together—'

'They're women, not girls, and 'a little stressful' is an understatement.'

'Maybe this year will be different,' Suzanne said. 'Beth and Jason are happy I can't wait to have the grandchildren here. I'm going to hang stockings above the fire and bake plenty of treats. And Hannah won't need to do a thing, because I plan on getting everything done before she arrives so I can spend time with her. I want to catch up on her news.' She breathed. 'If only she would meet someone special, she'd—'

'She'd what? Eat him for breakfast?' Stewart shook his head. 'I beg you do *not* mention that to her. Hannah's relationships are her business. And I don't think she's that interested.'

'Don't say that.' She refused to believe it might be true. Hannah needed a close relationship. She needed her own family. A protective circle. Everyone needed that.

Suzanne had craved it. At the age of six, she'd dreamed about it. Her early years had been spent with a mother too drunk to be aware of her existence. Later, when her mother's internal organs had given up fighting the relentless abuse, Suzanne had been placed in foster care. Every story she'd written at school involved her being part of a loving family. In her dreams she had parents and siblings. By ten, she was resigned to the fact that it was never going to happen for her.

Eventually she'd ended up in residential care, and that was where she'd met Cheryl. She'd become the sister Suzanne had longed for, and she'd poured all the surplus love she had into their friendship. They'd been so close, people had assumed they were related.

Cheryl's love filled all the gaps and holes in Suzanne's soul until she stopped feeling lost and alone. She no longer wished for someone to adopt her because then she'd have to leave the care home and that would mean leaving Cheryl.

They'd shared a bedroom. They'd shared clothes and laughter. They'd shared hopes and dreams.

The memory was vivid and the need to hear Cheryl's infectious laugh was so strong Suzanne almost reached for the phone.

It had been twenty-five years since they'd spoken, and yet the urge to talk to her had never gone away.

The part of her that missed her friend had never healed.

'Suzanne? What are you thinking?' Stewart's voice dragged her back to the present.

He'd thought Cheryl was a bad influence.

The irony was that Suzanne never would have met Stewart if it hadn't been for Cheryl.

'I was thinking about Hannah.'

'If you mention her love life I can guarantee she will be on the first flight out of here and we will *not* have a happy Christmas.'

'I won't say a word. I'll ask Beth for an update. I'm glad they're both living in New York. It's good for Hannah to have her sister close by. And Beth is settled and happy and loves being a mother. Maybe spending time with her will be an inspiration for Hannah.'

Soon, the three sisters would be together again and Suzanne knew that this year Christmas was going to be perfect.

She was sure of it.

ONE PLACE. MANY STORIES

Bold, innovative and
empowering publishing.

FOLLOW US ON:

@HQStories